Joshua M Fitton is the third of four brothers born to his parents in Bradford, West Yorkshire and raised in the small country town of Silsden. He is a bricklayer by trade and works with his father and eldest brother in the family business. An avid fan of all things fantasy and science fiction, he was raised in a household that revered such things as Star Trek, Star Wars, The Lord of the Rings and more. He now lives with his wife, two children and dog, all combining to make for a busy life.

This is simple. I wish to thank my family for being the inspiration from which I have drawn these characters and stories. The King and Queen, my mum and dad for raising me in a way that allowed my imagination to flourish. For always encouraging me to read and be creative. For having a household that always had something like Star Trek playing on the television. For getting me The Lord of the Rings as a Christmas present when I was only twelve. The list goes on.

I wish to thank my brothers. Many of the situations the characters find themselves in have been taken directly from our lives together. Though often dangerous, painful and ending in disaster they have none the less given me a great many fantastic memories to draw from.

My friends, for all the fun we had growing up that has again given me great characters and experiences from which I could mould my story.

Finally, my wife Jayne. Thank you for everything, especially our children that have given me a new sense of determination and will no doubt provide me with many more stories to be used in future writing.

Thank you to you all.

Joshua M Fitton

THE FOUR-BORN

AUSTIN MACAULEY PUBLISHERS™

LONDON * CAMBRIDGE * NEW YORK * SHARJAH

A CIP catalogue record for this title is available from the British Library.

ISBN 9781035825585 (Paperback)
ISBN 9781035825592 (ePub e-book)

www.austinmacauley.com

First Published 2024
Austin Macauley Publishers Ltd®
1 Canada Square
Canary Wharf
London
E14 5AA

I wish to acknowledge all the fantastic writers whose work has influenced me. Far too many to mention but without whose work and fantastic stories I may never have found the desire to write for myself.

Also, Austin Macauley Publishers. Getting work published is a difficult egg to crack and they give opportunity where others do not.

Table of Contents

The First-Born

"Ride!" called Michael at the head of the group. "Ride, damn you!"

There were moments in life where it seemed that all the forces of the universe conspire against us. Moments when, no matter how hard we try, what path we take, what choices we make, victory of any manner seemed impossible.

There were times where it seemed the words on the tattered pages of history had been written long before that day actually came to pass and not one word was kind. For the riders out in the night, it felt like one of those times.

"Ride!" called Michael again. It was all he could do.

The sky was a swirling vortex of black and deep purple, illuminated every so often by washes of blueish white as long streaks of lightning forked down from the heavens. The wind was fierce, and the thunder had a way of reaching deep into the soul of man and beast alike, twisting them with each new rumbling growl.

The rain fell from the sky in huge drops, each one like a stone thrown down with riotous anger by the gods above. Roads turned to treacherous mud and every step was a fresh danger. The torches carried by the riders had long since been extinguished, no flame could survive such a deluge. Such darkness should not be traversed but this was a night without choice.

The riders pressed on relentlessly. Ten knights that were once the head of a long column now felt the isolation of their journey. They were pushing hard and as fast as they dared against the elements, followed by two carts which veered dangerously with every turn of the wheels.

The rest of the column was far behind. The carts, cooks and tents, all had to be left. Those left behind were the lucky ones, offered the chance to make camp and see out the storm. These few riders never received such an opportunity.

"THERE!" cried Michael and all eyes looked ahead.

With one word, one flick of the eyes and one solemn light shining in the darkness, all fortunes seemed reversed and the despair that had crept into the hearts of the men was wiped away. Few sights had ever been so welcome, the small house that the group now rode towards seemed more a shining beacon than a small stone building far beyond its best years. Like the lighthouse to the lost sailor, it offered salvation.

There were moments in life when it seemed that all was lost, and any glimmer of hope had long since been abandoned. Then, in that moment, just as defeat was about to be conceded, the fates switch on us and the universe twists and from the very clutches of defeat we grasp a victory. But there was always the ever-looming prospect of the universe twisting again.

The old man sat on a chair with his head in his hands. They were still shaking as he reached out for the flask of wine, the contents spilling down his chin as he failed to bring himself under control. This night was dark, and it had brought dark tidings.

He took another mouthful of wine and only wished it were something stronger.

Eyes suddenly turned to the door. He heard it first, the thundering of hooves on the ground outside, the shouts of men. He moved to the shuttered window and stared out through a crack past the beating rain. There were horses, men in armour with swords at their hips, already dismounting.

He watched with wide eyes as they approached the door and before he could do anything, a foot crashed into the wood sending it swinging on its hinges to smash on the wall beside him. He scurried backwards in a panic until his back met the farthest wall. In seconds, the room was filled with wet and weary, grimacing faces.

"Are you the healer?"

"What?" It was all the old man could manage in his shock.

"Are you the healer?" demanded the man again, this time stepping closer, imposing himself.

"Yes," he answered, his voice saturated with fear. "But how did you know I was here? I wasn't meant to be—"

"Are you alone?"

"Yes."

The man frowned at him. "Do not play games with me, old man."

The men looked to the side to see one of their companions come from the only other room, dragging a woman with him who looked even more petrified than the old man.

"Please, she is my assistant. Please do not harm her."

"You are not the ones in danger here, Healer." His voice was low, and his words held fear within. The old man was suddenly more curious than scared. "This is the place," announced the knight to his fellows. "Fetch them."

Two men left, stepping back out into the unrelenting storm. The old man watched on in silence, trying desperately to regain some composure.

"Your tables?" asked the knight. The old man was silent, as though the question made no sense. "YOUR TABLES?"

"In here!" called the other who held the woman.

The old man was dragged into the other room and placed before his tables, one long and empty but for a few cloths and blankets. The other was smaller, filled with medical tools, vials and jars. There was blood. Too much blood.

"What is your name, Healer?"

The old man looked up at the knight again. A large man, his face covered in a thick black beard. Oddly, he had a kind face, but this was not a kind situation.

"F...F...Fredrick," he answered.

"Fredrick, I am Sir Michael of House Ken. This is my brother, Sir John." He put a hand on the shoulder of the man beside him. "Do you know these names?"

He swallowed again, a hard lump rising then falling in his throat, only now recognising the emblem beaten into the armour of the men before him. The shape of a cross. "I do."

"Good, then you can guess the company in which we ride. We come to you in our hour of need, Fredrick."

"I don't understand."

His state of unknowing was suddenly erased by the entering of four more men. The first two were returning from whatever errand Sir Michael sent them on with two new faces that were just as weary. All four carried a large cloth, one man at each corner. Upon the cloth was a woman, obviously in terrible pain and trying hard to hold it in.

Fredrick quickly noticed two things. Firstly, the woman was Debreace Fait, Queen of the Cross. Secondly and the far more pressing of the two, she was giving birth. Right there and then, the heir to the throne was about to be born.

The men placed the queen on the empty table with none of the formality usually afforded to one of her position. They then turned their eyes back to the doorway. Frederick felt the last ounce of strength left in his legs give way as King Branthony Fait stepped into the dimly lit room.

His clothes soaking, his light-coloured hair stuck down against his head. His eyes were alive but stricken with anguish.

"Your Majesty," said Fredrick, eyes wide and voice high pitched. He was sure of it now. The wine had been strong after all, and he'd fallen asleep. This was all a dream.

"You are the healer?" asked the king. He had a voice of hard steel, solid, unbending and sharp. No, this was no dream. Such a voice would have awoken him.

"I am." It took the greatest of efforts to utter the simplest of replies.

"My wife is in labour. My child is coming. You must deliver it now. The child must be born under a fixed roof."

Fredrick glanced back to the queen who grimaced against the pains within her body.

"Wait, I know of this pregnancy. The child is not due for another two turns of the moon."

"Yet here it comes," stated the king, trying to remain calm.

"Your Majesty, I beg you, not me, not here. I have already failed in my duties once tonight, doing the very task you now ask of me." He moved his eyes to the side of the room and the knights moved aside to reveal the shape of a woman's body laid upon another long table, a white cloth spread over it, but a pool of blood had soaked through.

To the side of her, another mound under a second white sheet, this one small enough to hold within a man's hands. "I lost them, my king. Mother and child both. The fault was not my own, but it is a bad omen. The very sky above us is bad. Look at this night, my king. The sky is black and filled with death and death lies within these walls. All things point to the worst."

There are some men in this world for which the air itself seems to shimmer, who have about them an aura that stretches out beyond the physical restraints of their body. King Branthony Fait was such a man. He carried with him an unquestionable might.

Fredrick almost buckled under the power of his stare alone. The king looked down at him with hard eyes. Not callus. Not cruel but unwavering, solid and firm.

"My friend, there is nowhere else, there is no one else. We are here now. Fail in this and I know you are not to blame but succeed and you shall want for nothing for all the days you have left. I place my hope in your hands, Healer. Will you not take it?"

Who could possibly refuse such a man? Who would not at the very least try?

Fredrick glanced about the room, every pair of eyes was upon him, his stomach twisted within his belly, and he now deeply regretted the wine. He looked to the queen and saw her pleading eyes as her hands stroked her swollen belly.

"Remove her from the room," he said, gesturing towards the body. The men moved to do so but suddenly stopped to look back as the queen released a shriek at a horrifying pitch.

"The baby comes now," said Fredrick, moving to her side. "May I?" he asked, a foolish question maybe but he had never touched a noble before, never mind a queen. She nodded permission.

Fredrick lifted her skirts to peer beneath.

Another scream sounded through the room.

"Give her the Silent Milk," said a voice.

"No!" declared Fredrick. "It will dull her. She needs to be fully aware. I need you to fight," he said to her. "I need you with me, good queen. Do you understand?" She nodded. "Then prepare yourself." They both drew a deep breath.

The world seemed a different place in those moments. Everyone seemed to hold their breath with each push. Every second and minute seemed to stretch and yet each was filled with electric tension. As Fredrick yelled for the queen to push and saw the new life arrive, he had hope, but delivery had proven many times to be the easier part of the equation.

The queen was ferocious. She pushed with all her might and the men around her, hardened men, looked on in awe. The baby was small and came into the world with relative ease. Fredrick's assistant stepped in with a knife and cut the life cord that bound mother to child. Fredrick placed the baby down, rubbing gently with a finger at the tiny chest.

"The child does not breathe." The announcement brought gasps.

Fredrick worked frantically, rubbing fingers gently but firmly across the baby's chest. He lifted it, repeating the process down its back. He felt that flicker of hope begin to fade again but when the child inhaled, everyone in the room seemed to do so as well. The breath that Fredrick took was the best of his life.

"You have a son," he said but the announcement was not one of joy. Tension still held the room and was unwilling to abate. "He is weak, very weak. Too soon has he come. He needed more time. I would not think it likely for him to make it through the night. It is up to him and the God now." He passed the child to the queen and the mother wept as she looked upon her new-born son.

The king stared on with those hard eyes. They were unwilling to concede. "He breaths freely now?" he asked.

"He does," answered Fredrick. "But weakly." He noticed the queen look up and saw fresh fear in her eyes.

The king turned to the door. "She comes."

"Branthony, is there no other way?" The pleading of the queen sounded strange to Fredrick's ears.

The king stepped closer to look down at his son, taking his wife's hand in his. Fredrick saw great tenderness in that touch and yet he was again reminded of steel. He didn't know what was happening, but he knew the king would not relent. The eyes had told him. This was a man who had no understanding of such concepts.

"There is no other way," he said firmly. "The boy must receive his Gift."

Fredrick suddenly felt a chill run down his spine. It was odd, he knew someone else had arrived at the doorway but for a reason he couldn't explain, he feared to turn around.

The chill that ran down his spine felt supernatural, and he would swear that a part of the Devil himself waited at the door. He saw the knights around him recoil; their faces grimaced in odd expressions of horror, disgust and most of all, fear.

Fredrick struggled for breath as a figure brushed past him, the ancient, crumbling form of a woman. Her back bent, her skin shrivelled tight over contorted bones. She was swathed in black rags, thin tufts of hair fell from a wrinkled head, the bald patches taken up by sores and boils.

Whatever it was, Fredrick had no name for. He could not help but think the knights were surprised to see her. Had she not been travelling with them?

"Crone," said the king in a low voice. "It has been many years, but the time has come."

Fredrick wasn't sure what was happening, he could tell by the faces on the men surrounding him that they were just as unsure, but he knew that he was a part of something momentous. He had thought the king's presence overbearing, he now realised there was a comfort to it. That being around him made Fredrick feel stronger.

But the aura around this thing was different. Fredrick felt as though he were eavesdropping on a moment of history to which he should not be privy. She felt like a god, like something beyond this world, ancient and all-knowing and Fredrick wanted nothing more than to be away from her.

He could not help but feel a sense of pride for his queen and the way she held herself before this creature.

"Please, he's so weak, can't it wait?"

Branthony's unblinking glare gave her the answer. Reluctantly, she held her son towards the Crone. The haggard thing smiled, revealing black and bleeding gums. She reached out to take the baby with a hand that was not a hand. It was skeletal. No skin, muscles or veins. Just bones.

The hand took the baby and with her other hand, which despite its grotesqueness was the far more normal of the two, she began nipping at his skin, spinning him over, twisting him around unceremoniously.

She held him upside down by one leg and the baby wailed but the Crone showed no concern. With a wave of her hand, he was silenced, eyes closing as he fell into a deep sleep despite the treatment.

"Stop this!" demanded Fredrick, horrified. He felt the king's firm arm across his chest. Such a touch would warn off a lion, never mind a fragile ageing man.

"Your job is done now, Healer. Let her work." The words were not threatening but Fredrick knew to push no further.

She put the child down on the table, flat upon his back and then reached out a hand. "Blade," she demanded in a croaky voice. Without question or hesitation, the king drew a knife and placed it within her palm, as though handing her a rattle to entertain with.

She took it and pressed steel against the baby's skin. Several knights stepped forward but were warded off by the king's glare. The room watched on in silence. What were they witnessing? The king was the only one who seemed to have any notion of what was taking place.

The blade pressed into the baby's hand until blood welled. The child didn't make a sound, still appearing peaceful in his induced slumber, his mother yearning to take him back into her arms but fighting the urge. The Crone put the child's hand to her mouth, sucking on the blood as though it were sweet nectar.

"Umm," she moaned in pleasure, the sagging torn skin of her cheeks contracting as she sucked. The bones of her skeletal hand clenching into a fist. It was the single most horrifying thing Fredrick had ever seen.

"Strange, very strange."

"What is it?" demanded the king.

"Hard to tell." She took another suck at the hand, taking more of the blood, her body shivering as she swallowed, her eyes rolling back into her head.

"What is his Gift?" This time the words came at a low growl. The Crone's eyes flashed towards the king, menacing in their assessment of him.

"Tonight is a fearful night." Her voice was strained. "Dark skies, open heavens. These are omens, signs sent from powers beyond this world."

"His Gift, Crone. What is it?"

"Old," she answered. "Very old. I've not seen this one for a very long time. Not for a thousand years has a child of the Fait held this."

"Please, name it?" The words came from the queen who could wait no longer to hold her son once more. What a torture it must have been to see him in the arms of such a foul thing.

The Crone shook her head in dismay. The action carried a weight through the room.

"Two turns of the moon early is the child, this is too early. If it were another child, he would not survive the night. His lungs are weak. Breath does not come easy."

The queen gasped but the king remained calm.

"But he is not another child," declared Branthony assuredly. "He is my child. He is of the *Fait*."

The Crone's mouth twisted into a malicious grin. "Don't be so confident of your bloodline, Your Majesty." She made the title a jest as she pulled at the black rags that covered her body and they fell to the ground, leaving her naked. A walking corpse held the new-born prince and heir to the throne. On her chest, two empty sacks hung down, sagging and wrinkled, the nipples nothing more than black spots.

"Remember, it is I who brings the Gift. It is my milk that makes you strong. Without me, you are nothing!" She lifted the child once more and placed his head to her chest. Several men stepped forward but were once again halted by the king.

"It must be done!" exclaimed the king.

"My king, this is not befitting of a prince."

"The prince is of the Fait, John. He needs his Gift. This is how it comes." The knights bristled at the announcement. Fredrick looked at John who seemed little more than a child himself. How could any man, young or old, be expected to understand this thing?

"So, you—?" The question was never finished. The king's eyes gave an answer.

"This is not an event to be witnessed but this night has brought surprises for us all. You will not speak of this again, to kin nor love or any who do breathe. Swear it!"

They all did, without pause or hesitation. Branthony turned his eyes back on the haggard Crone. "Do it now."

The child stirred as the Crone's skeletal hand pushed him towards her breast, the small lump seemed more likely to deliver dust than milk. "Drink," she urged. "Drink and receive your Gift."

All the room looked on expectantly with faces of shock and disgust. The baby's face was pushed against the sagging meat, his lips pressed against the black nipple. Then they pursed and took the hard lump within their grasp.

The milk came, falling from the child's mouth to drip on the floor. He gulped it down with a thirst that none expected until his head lulled back, and he was silenced in sleep yet again.

The child was offered back to his mother's grateful arms.

"You never answered my husband's question," she said, not taking her eyes from her son. "What is the Gift?"

The Crone looked at the queen and then to the king as she lifted the rags from the ground to cover her shrivelled body. All the while offering them both a smile of decay.

"The child was almost denied the gift of life, the chance to see out his years, so the God has seen fit to ensure he will never be denied the chance of seeing that which lies beyond. Your firstborn son shall have the Gift of Foresight. If he survives."

A moment of silence before the king broke it. "Foresight," he repeated at a whisper.

The word held ominous tidings. Fredrick had no ideas what it meant and yet he knew without doubt, it would change the world.

"So be it," declared the king. The Crone bowed her head and again the gesture seemed mocking. With a twisted smile, she skulked from the room laughing as the men stepped away from her, purposely shifting towards them and enjoying their discomfort.

"Until next time," she declared with a gloating cackle.

Debreace lifted her child back to her bosom, uncaring of the Crone now she was gone. Her thoughts were only for her son.

"And his name, sister?" asked Sir Michael.

"Yes," said Sir John. "Tell us the name of our nephew."

She looked from her son to her brothers, then to her husband with tears in her eyes but a smile upon her face. "Aron," she pronounced proudly. "Our firstborn is named Aron."

Fredrick smiled, of all the things he had seen, the sight of mother and baby would be the one that stayed with him.

The Second-Born

"Sir Bolevard of House Bront," the voice announced in an overly chirpy manner. Bolevard turned his eyes on the Scroll-Master and had to hide his distain. "The thirst for knowledge has truly captured you. This must be the fifth visit to the library this month."

The Scroll-Master had one of those faces you just loved to hate. Little beady eyes, a sharp nose and lips like the beak of a bird, a hideous bird at that. Most others around the castle seemed to like him despite the disagreeable features. Not Bolevard. Not at all.

One of these days, I'm going to snap your neck, you annoying tick and I will revel in the process. Of course, such thoughts would not find a voice. Bolevard offered what appeared to be a perfectly sincere smile.

"It truly has, my friend. It truly has. Today, I think I will learn more on the seventh dynasty of the Western Cren family. A remarkable time in history."

"Yes, yes," said the Scroll-Master, turning on his heel and guiding them through the library. Not just any library, this was the castle library at the Centre, the largest, most comprehensive vault of knowledge in the known world. "It really was a very brutal period," said the Scroll-Master as he led the way. "Did you know that many forms of torture originated from the era?"

"I've read a little on the matter, yes, though I am sure my knowledge is limited when compared to yourself."

The little man smiled quaintly, obviously impressed by himself and lapping up the praise. It amazed Bolevard how well he could tell convincing lies, all smiles and politeness whilst all the while imagining thoughts that would shock and disgust. How apt was it that the Scroll-Master mentioned torture.

"Ah, here we are, scrolls on the Cren family dynasties. I trust you can find what you need from here."

"Yes, thank you." *Now leave me be so I can do my work in peace.*

"If you need anything else, just call."

"I will," he said, already selecting a few scrolls. He looked over several, taking his time, allowing the Scroll-Master to get a good distance away. As soon as he was out of sight, Bolevard turned and moved several shelves to the left and had to step up on one of the ladders to reach the area he needed. He'd already marked the scrolls that would be today's true objective.

He pulled out several but was careful not to take too many. He didn't want to draw attention to the area. If the Scroll-Master or any of his disciples came by, they were likely to notice if a section was missing a large quantity of scrolls. The last thing he wanted was anyone finding out what he was looking for.

He found space and opened up the first selection, hiding the others beneath the ones he'd taken from the Cren Dynasty shelf. *Useless*, he thought after several wasted minutes scanning the words. The second one was ineligible with some kind of water damage. If he weren't trying to hide his search, he'd call the Scroll-Master over and beat him bloody for such a poor execution of his duties.

Third time lucky or so he hoped. He unrolled the scroll, running his finger across the densely packed lines of writing. His eyes widened as he began reading about that which he searched for.

Interesting, he thought with excitement. *Very interesting.*

For months now, he'd been coming to the library executing his secret searches. He was careful not to come too often as to raise suspicion and always hid the true subject matter that he sought out but here was another clue to his true questions.

Bolevard had been there. Nearly two years now though it was hard to believe, at the birth of the heir. Ever since that night in the healer's cabin Bolevard had been obsessed. He'd found whatever reason he could to get to the Centre and to the library.

What he saw that night was beyond his comprehension. Beyond everything he knew. The common people of the Cross had the notion the Gift of the royal bloodline came from the divine, delivered from the God himself to the children of the Fait to assist their rule.

Bolevard now knew that was a lie perpetrated by the Fait to hide the truth. Their Gifts came from black magic and their power did not come from the God to help them rule, it came from a witch, and they lied to keep their power. The creature had said it herself. She brought them the Gift.

Bolevard remembered the first time he saw the king use his Gift. It was marvellous to behold. What a sight it was, wondrous and terrifying at the same time, like seeing the very image of the God. Back then, Bolevard had sworn his loyalty and obedience to his king. He had done his best to uphold those vows. Right up until he found out the truth.

If only people knew. What would they say? What would they do? How could the kingdom be led by people who allied themselves with such creatures? It was worse than heresy. It was the greatest betrayal Bolevard could imagine, and he would not allow it to continue. He now hated the Fait, but he hated that thing more.

Not that Bolevard could ever say anything. Once they'd returned to the Centre, King Branthony had called his sister back from the north-west. Princess Susan had the Gift of Obedience. She had commanded all those who were there that night to never speak of it again.

Of course, they had all already sworn an oath never to talk of those events. So much for the king trusting his knights. So Bolevard was commanded, so he would do. What choice did he have? Susan's Gift, after all, was sewn with the seeds of witchcraft.

He'd tried to speak, to tell the story, but the words simply would not come. He'd tried again and again to force them from his mouth, tried until his head pounded and blood flowed from his nose. It could not be done. He'd tried to write it down, but the words were mere scribbles on the paper.

Not being able to talk of that night did not mean that Bolevard would forget, far from it. For Bolevard had seen it and he could not stop seeing. Every night he dreamt of the haggard old Crone, that horrible, shrivelled skin, the boils and scabs that covered it, all but the single hand of bone. He dreamt of the child. A new-born child forced to drink the foul milk.

So Bolevard's search began. A search for knowledge about this Crone and how to destroy her. He searched for anything on the Gift. Any clue that may point him in the right direction. Most of the scrolls regarding such things were kept in the royal family's personal vault. But not all of them. Bolevard's grin grew as he read the words.

It wasn't much, just a few lines about the Gift being a solitary trait of the Fait and how the Gift could manifest in a large number of ways. But it was also proof that the Fait hadn't taken everything. Proof that the library still held secrets and that he was looking in the right place.

To hell with the Scroll-Master, he didn't know a thing. Bolevard would search the entire library if he had to. He'd find what he was looking for, even if he didn't know what he was looking for. He would find it and when the time was right, he would use it.

The lies of the Fait could not be allowed to continue. Their time would come to an end. The Fait would fall, and he would revel in it.

Aron ran down the corridor of the castle, it's richly decorated walls passing by in a blur as his tiny feet carried him forward. He was only two years old, yet his uncle Michael had to hurry his step to keep up. Michael allowed his nephew his fun and why not?

Today was a momentous day. It amazed Michael and everybody else just how quick Aron was developing. Aron was walking and talking younger than any child Michael had ever seen. It was remarkable. Perhaps a trait of the Fait?

Aron turned a corner that led to his parent's bed chamber. He saw the solitary figure of his father sitting on a bench outside the door. The seat was normally used by servants waiting to attend on the king or queen. It seemed strange to see his father placed upon it.

Aron suddenly stopped. He couldn't help taking a step backwards only to find his uncle had quickly caught up to him. He turned to look up at Michael with a pleading in his eyes.

"Do not be worried, child. Go to your father."

"But he's angry."

Michael looked over to his king and brother-in-law who was now staring back at them both. Michael offered a smile then turned it down on Aron. Uncle Michael had the kindest smile. It always made Aron feel safe. Why didn't his father's smile make him feel safe? Father was always angry or so it seemed.

"Your father was away for a long time, Aron. He has been fighting a war. Fighting to protect you and me and your mother. He is not angry, just tired. He missed his family. He missed his son."

Aron had never thought of it like that but who would blame him, at little more than two years old, he was not supposed to. This was, as his mother always told him, his time of freedom. One day, he would wear the crown and he would belong to the Cross then, whatever that meant.

His father stood as they approached. Despite his uncle's words, Aron still felt nervous. He stood in silence between the two men.

"Aron," said Uncle Michael. "Have you nothing to say?"

"Good morning, Father."

"Good morning, Aron."

Aron was sure he'd been right. His father was angry. He could tell. He could hear it in the words his father spoke and as for those eyes. They never seemed to hold warmth. He was glad when they rose back to his uncle. "A word, Michael."

"Of course, Your Grace."

They walked back a way down the corridor so there was no chance of Aron overhearing their conversation. He set off to follow them but halted at the return of attention from his father's hard eyes.

"Stay there, Aron. These are not words for children."

He stayed where he was, leaning back against the chair his father had occupied moments ago and stared on at them, his bottom lip stuck firmly out. Why was his father always like this? Aron was glad that being king meant his father was often away.

The war his uncle spoke of was far to the south and it seemed to require his father's attention and he only returned to the Centre every few months. He would not have been back now if not for the situation. The absence did not often concern Aron, after all, Father never wanted to play, never wanted to have fun. Everything was always serious.

"He doesn't even like me," he whispered to himself.

"Those are dark thoughts for one so young."

Aron startled, nearly falling over as he stepped away from the chair. He turned around, wondering what nightmare stood before him. An old woman, shrivelled and small, smiling at him with a mouth of blackness. She licked her lips as she stared at him, as though he were a juicy freshly cooked chicken.

"Who are you? Where did you come from?"

"I am a friend of your father's. He requires me here today. Do you not remember me?"

He shook his head, wanting to run and scream at the top of his voice, only he found that he could not. He realised in that moment, even at such a young age, that what he thought was fear of his father was not fear at all, rather just a simple discomfort. Seeing this thing, this was fear and it had frozen him in place.

"You breathe easier," she said, touching a finger of pure bone to his chest. "But you are still afflicted. Maybe you'll just die any day now," she said with a smirk as though it were funny.

"How?" It was all he could manage. Even if his lips would obey his command he still wouldn't be sure what he was trying to say. *How did you get here? How do you know about my breathing? How can I get away from you? What do you mean I could just die?*

"I was there on the day of your birth," she told him with a sneer. "I am always there when those of the royal blood enter this world. I have seen generations of your family come and go. I shall be there at the birth of your children. I shall be there at your death.

"I am the bringer of the Gift. I am the one that allows your family to rule. I am the one that gives you everything you have, remember that as you grow older. Remember that when it is you who sits upon the throne."

Her words made no sense. He could barely even hear them. He wanted to cry. Just standing near her made him feel cold. He could not stop a tear falling from his eye and felt a wet warmth on his thighs. He had never been so scared. If only he could move, he would run to his father. Was it only a moment ago he didn't want to be near him? Now he wanted nothing more than to be in his father's arms.

Branthony and Michael had walked to the side. The king had no intention of burdening his son with worries beyond his comprehension. He was still so young, yet soon his Lessons would begin. Youth would be denied to him in so many ways. For now, Branthony would have his son be a child and only wished he could allow himself to enjoy these precious years with his firstborn.

Alas, time it seemed was always working against him.

"Has there been any word from the south?"

"We received a raven this morning. It was from my brother, Grey. He reports our forces have made great progress. The Sile have fallen back to the border, their numbers dwindling with each day."

Michael's smile was growing with every word. Branthony enjoyed seeing it. He and Michael had been friends since before he was betrothed to Debreace. It was good to see him happy.

"It's not the same without you down there with me," Branthony said to him with a hand on his shoulder. "I want you there when I return."

Michael dipped his head. "Of course, Your Grace. With any luck, it may be the last time we are required. If the Sile can be broken, then this war will be over, and you shall be the first king to bring peace to all four points of the Cross for years."

Branthony could only dare dream. To stay here at the Centre and watch his children grow seemed a luxury he would never attain. He looked back to his son with longing eyes that suddenly widened at the sight that met him.

"Aron, get away from her!"

Branthony stormed across the distance and the Crone took a quick step back. Aron lost his footing, the clumsiness of small legs taking him to the floor. The Crone held up a skeletal hand to ward off a strike.

"Never fear, good king." Her words were spoken from behind a grin. "Never fear. I simply talked to the boy. Nothing more."

"LIAR!" he snarled. "I know your mind, Crone. You came here to scare the wits out of him exactly like you did to me when I was his age."

He looked at his son and knew the damage was done. Aron wouldn't sleep right for a week, and he already didn't sleep well. The boy had fretful nights as though plagued by bad dreams. How could he be? A boy of that age?

"Come," he said through a snarl. "The time has arrived. Michael, stay with Aron." He leaned to his friend's side, whispering in his ear. "If you could think of any way to explain this to him, I would be grateful."

"I'll try, my king." They both knew it was impossible. Michael would not even look at the Crone, he never wanted to see that thing again. It was not her appearance that frightened Michael, more her aura. He could tell how much she'd enjoyed frightening the boy. She thought herself above normal men. They were simply objects for her amusement. Michael picked up his nephew and left in a hurry.

Branthony didn't have the luxury of looking away from the Crone, instead he stared her down. His eyes ablaze with anger. There was no doubt in his mind when it came to the Crone that she was a cruel creature and she had confronted his son for no other reason than to torment him.

He nodded his head aggressively towards the door. She laboured forward in what he knew to be an act of frailty. He had dreaded the days when he would have to confront her again. Ever since she had scared him as she scared Aron.

Branthony was now determined to try and save Aron that same confrontation. He knew the Crone's secret. She was not as irreplaceable as she implied. He pushed such thoughts from his mind unsure if the Crone could pick at such things. He had tasks to accomplish before he could begin to think of replacing her, but even they must wait, for now it was time to meet his Second-Born.

It seemed like an age before the doors opened and Aron was permitted entry. He stepped inside to see his mother lying on the bed, coddling a newborn child.

Father stood at the end of the bed and a number of servants were just leaving through the second door.

Fredrick, the Healing-Master stood against the back wall, the sunlight washing over him. He smiled down at Aron who continued to scan the room from behind Uncle Michael's leg.

No sign of the witch. Had she gone out the other door with the servants? He barely had the nerve to enter, fearing she was still nearby.

"Aron," beckoned his mother. "Come meet your brother."

One more check, this time he spared a glance towards his father who gave him the slightest of nods, a sign that it was all right and she was gone. Aron rushed forward, struggling to climb up onto the large bed and needing a hand from his uncle to finally make it.

He shuffled forward to look down at the baby in his mother's arms as the tiny shape snuggled into her, feeling a shred of unconscious safety in her embrace.

"What's his name, Mother?"

"This is Luke," she told him.

It seemed so strange. Was this really what had been in his mother's belly all this time?

"Are you well, my sister?" asked Michael.

"Yes," she answered, smiling up at him. "Thank you."

"Well then, what is it? What is the Gift?"

Michael looked from Aron's mother to his father and the boy followed in turn, waiting eagerly to learn more. Once again, his father held a stern expression. Why was that not surprising?

"Fortune," said his father. "My second-born has the Gift of Fortune."

Michael smiled. "Well, why the glum face?"

"It's her," Branthony answered, obviously trying not to say too much in front of Aron. "My father warned me about her. Something is changing. I can feel it. We need to win the war against the Sile. Then I can concentrate on other matters. There are not often more than two children born to a generation so we may have time. But." He shook his head, never finishing the sentence.

"What does the war against the Sile have to do with her?" asked Debreace.

"The key to replacing her lies beyond Sile territory. Defeat them and we may finally have a chance of ridding ourselves of her."

Aron didn't understand a word. He'd barely taken his eyes off his new little brother. Who cared for his father's boring problems?

Plans in the Making

She looked at herself in the mirror, a face as perfect as any had the right to be. A body that was sure to set men on the path to war. A seductive smile with a stronger pull than any rope and eyes that could capture a man's soul in an instant and never let it go.

Such beauty was not as rare in the world as perhaps it should be. Such beauty gave power that was often undeserved, and Celia knew this well. She was still young, but she'd used that beauty to her extreme advantage from the moment she understood it and unashamedly so.

It amazed her just what men would do for a little taste of a woman. By the God, all she had to do was smile a certain way, flutter her eyelids, swish her hair and the pathetic mongrels were practically falling over her. Fighting amongst themselves and scrambling over each other for the smallest scrap. High or low-born, it made no difference. They all shared the same weakness.

She had used her body to her advantage, yes but she had always taken great care to hide such efforts from her father. Such behaviour was unbecoming from the daughter of a Lord. The self-righteous old man had his head so far up his own behind, he could not even see all the things Celia had done for their family. He thought he was the only one making sacrifices.

Did he really think he would be under consideration for Warden of the Eastern-Point if she hadn't used her charms on Sir John of House Ken? She saw the way the young knight had looked at her and so she had offered him that smile that all the men loved.

She'd spent one night with him during which she mentioned her father's petition to be warden and how she'd appreciate a kind word in the king's ear, now he was on the cusp of being appointed. The act wasn't completely selfless, nothing of the sort.

If her father was made Warden of the Eastern-Point, it would be nothing but good for House Trone. What's more, as warden there would be need of a direct representative at the Centre. Who could possibly be right for the position? She knew she was a perfect fit and wanted the position badly. No woman had ever been a Point representative, Celia was determined to be the first.

It was, after all, an ever-growing necessity that Celia get away from her father. As Lord of the Five Fingers, it was expected that his daughter marry appropriately, never mind act as much. If he ever found out about the things she'd done, there would be serious consequences.

If he found out her latest secret, he may even go so far as to see her—how to say, disposed of. Nothing was more important to Lord Carter Trone than the reputation of himself and his house. Nothing!

As she looked into the mirror, it was hard to believe what would soon happen to that perfect body. By the God, how had she allowed this to happen? She was so careful, always so careful. But sometimes precautions weren't enough.

She rubbed her belly and could not imagine that it would soon swell. Yes, her father would kill her, especially if he asked who the father was because in all honesty, she didn't know. There had been many lovers; some for pleasure, some for other reasons. Which one had actually done the deed? Who could say?

Yes, she really did need her father to be made Warden and she needed even more to go to the capital. She could take care of things there in a discreet manner. She'd already started making preparations.

Is it really that bad? she asked herself again and again. She was a woman now and the queen herself was younger when she got pregnant with her first born, and she was nearly ready to give birth to her third child. Celia suddenly had dreams of her child playing with the royal's, running the halls of the castle, walking the streets of the Centre. Her child should be a prince or princess. But no, such dreams were dust.

She needed her father to be appointed Warden of the Eastern-Point. Her work with John of House Ken had set him on the path but she could not rely on it to be enough. She had to put a final nail in the coffin. Time to go to work, she thought as a knock on the door announced her guest had arrived. It was a quiet knock, a discreet knock.

She moved to the door, opening it just a little, peering through the crack into a dim corridor. She smiled seductively as she opened it full, and Sir Thomas of House Crestfall stepped through the door. He looked her up and down with a hunger in his eyes as she quickly closed the door again before turning back to him, throwing herself back against the door, biting at her lower lip. He came at her.

The whole thing was over with rather quickly, not that Celia didn't enjoy herself to a point. She didn't even have to do anything afterwards; a girl can't get pregnant if she's already pregnant. Sir Thomas lay on the bed, proudly displaying himself. The smile on his face was content. Celia would take great joy in removing it.

"So tell me, Sir Thomas, where is your wife?"

She watched in the mirror as his expression turned suddenly sour.

"What business is that of yours?"

"Oh none, really. I was just wondering what she would say if she were to ever hear of this."

He sat up on the bed, reaching for his britches. "What makes you think she'd believe you?"

"Oh, nothing really. I wonder how many other women know about that little mole just above your little friend." She almost giggled as he looked down at his suddenly shrivelled manhood at the same time as she did.

"Are you threatening me, girl?" He stood up and she had to admit he was impressive. Tall, thickly set, muscular. He would be, Celia imagined, quite intimidating in the right situation.

"Now, now, Thomas. You are a Knight of the Cross. Please display the chivalry that is expected from such."

"You weren't concerned with chivalry a moment ago you filthy whore!"

"Ha," she laughed as she pulled on a robe. "Why is it that the woman always becomes a whore when things turn sour? You were just as willing as I, more so, in fact. Not to mention the fact that you are married and just broke your vows. If anyone is a whore, Sir Thomas, it is you."

"Don't spin your words on me!"

"Careful, you wouldn't want me to scream. People would come running and if you were seen here then your wife would surely find out about this. Think of her disappointment. Better yet, think of the disappointment of her family. Her brothers are notoriously protective, are they not and prone to fits of rage?

"You did quite well for yourself claiming her as your wife. Her father believed she'd married down, did he not? But none of that should matter, there's no need for this to go any further."

He started to grasp the situation and his face really did hold disgust. Celia found that terribly amusing.

"Out with it then. What do you want?"

"Ah, so there is a brain to go with that body." She turned back to the mirror and began tending to herself, speaking to the reflection as she dragged a brush through the long length of her hair. "Tomorrow, you are returning to the Centre before continuing south to continue your fight against the Sile."

She turned back to him for a second. "Your bravery is commendable, by the way." Back to the mirror again. "Whilst at the capital you will offer an opinion to the king. You stayed at the Red House before here and so you have been the guest of Lord Hive as well as my father. Both are being considered for Warden of the Eastern-Point. Guess which one I want you to put your support behind."

He actually smiled at her. Not what she had expected. Then he continued to dress, and all his anger seemed to have disappeared. The smile remained on his face.

"Do I amuse you, Sir Thomas?"

"You most certainly do. Look at you, standing there basking in yourself. Believing yourself so clever and special. You think you are the first woman to use your body to make your way in life? You think your schemes are clever?" She could only offer a self-assured grin in response. Her answer was obvious. Yes. Yes, she very well did think she was clever.

"Your dedication to your House is commendable in ways. I will speak to the king. Not that my words will affect his judgement. The king is as assured of himself as any man could be. If your father is to be Warden, then he will be Warden. If that is to be so, then I am guessing you will find a way to make yourself his representative at the Centre. You will go there and try to work your schemes."

"And?" she said, actually quite interested in what he had to say.

"And in the end, they will do little. You think you're clever. You think you're viscous? Wait until you get to the Centre. The women there will tear you to pieces. Here at the Fingers, you are a big fish in a little pond; at the Centre, you will be a minnow in an ocean of sharks."

"We will see," she said with confidence.

"What's more," he was dressed now and almost ready to leave. "If you think for a second that you can manipulate the king, you will find yourself up against a man like no other. He will crush you if you cross him, little girl. Crush you beneath his boot.

"Most of us are just men, as you well know. But Branthony Fait is different. All the Fait are different. If you truly wish to go against them, I will even go as far as to wish you luck. I for one would not like to go up against them and their Gifts."

With that, he opened the door and left.

Celia found the smile had left her lips. Damn it, she got what she wanted so forget him and his words. Everyone would find she was a far greater opponent than they ever expected. Even the Fait, if needs be. She had heard stories of their Gifts but paid them little attention. She had gifts of her own and she could wield them as well as any.

The Third-Born

"Luke," whispered Aron into the darkness. The bedside candles were lit but did little to illuminate the room. Only when his little brother sat up in bed could Aron see him. He yawned, one tiny hand rising to the air in a stretch as the other covered his mouth. Luke was two now and Aron four. Their mother was pregnant with her third child and Aron knew what that meant.

"What?" asked Luke, the sound muffled through his yawn.

"Do you remember being born?"

Luke looked at him, his tongue sticking out a little, pointing up towards his ear as his eyes looked off in the opposite direction. It was hard to even understand the question let alone answer it.

"I don't think so," he said, face relaxing and eyes focusing back on Aron. "Why?"

"So, you don't remember the witch?"

"Witch?" said Luke, suddenly alarmed and sitting up straighter in his bed, pulling the covers up towards his chin.

Aron quickly raised hands in a calming gesture, aware of his poor choice of words.

"Sorry! Sorry. I didn't mean to scare you." His brother exhaled a breath through the nose, crossing his arms and offering him a stern expression that was his best effort at imitating their father. Aron had to stifle a giggle, his brother being so tiny, the gesture was more comical than anything else. "I just meant, well."

He couldn't think of the words. What could he say? So many nights he'd dreamt of the witch.

He had once plucked up the courage to ask his father about her. He received a strange response. "She comes to deliver the Gift to the children of the Fait, but she may not have the job for much longer."

Aron understood some of it but not much.

"Luke, you know mother is going to have a baby?" Luke nodded his head. "You know what that means?" He had to ask. Aron could not remember what he understood when he was Luke's age. In fact, the only thing he remembered for certain was the witch, but he thought his brother would understand. Everyone was always saying how the two of them seemed more like boys twice their age.

"It means we're going to have a brother or a sister. I hope it's not a sister. I don't want a girl in my room."

Yes, that was what it meant but it also meant the witch would be coming back. He couldn't remember her exact words, but he knew she'd said something about being there at the birth of all the Fait.

"Luke."

"What?" His little brother had already laid back down, pulling the cover tightly over him.

"What do you know about your Gift?"

Luke rolled over again at that but didn't bother to sit up.

"It's called Fortune," he said through a yawn.

"Do you know how to use it?"

"Nope, but I heard Father talking about the Gifts once. He was talking to Uncle Michael about Valfargs and the Brayfort."

The Brayfort was home to the Warden of the Northern-Point and first line of defence against the Valfargs. Not that a Valfarg had been seen in the Cross for over three hundred years. That didn't stop everyone being worried about seeing them again though.

"And? What did he say?"

"Something boring about learning to use them when we're older."

"Anything else?"

"No. I stopped listening because there was a big dog. It was a scary dog," he said, turning again, the conversation apparently over. Aron would swear Luke found every dog scary.

Aron lay back, his head sinking into the plush, feather pillow. He couldn't help but wonder how much longer he would share a room with his brother. Father had been saying more and more that full lessons must start soon. Lessons were the start of being a man. Aron did not look forward to that.

Father had told Aron the same as Luke, they would learn to use their Gifts when they were older, but Aron knew in some strange way that he wouldn't be waiting much longer. He could feel something inside of him waiting to get out and the feeling scared him.

It seemed like an age before sleep took him. The anxious feeling that twisted inside him seemed to be fighting the thought of rest. He wasn't sure why, but Aron knew with certainty that tomorrow was the day. The baby was overdue according to Healing-Master Fredrick and mother seemed to think it was never going to come out, but Aron knew that tomorrow the wait would be over.

He also knew that the witch would come again. Not that he would see her. Aron had already firmly come to the decision that he would stay well away. There was no desire whatsoever to see her again. He would also ensure his little brother didn't see her. There was no need for them both to have nightmares.

He also knew, with a strange certainty, that the baby was another boy. He fell asleep, his legs twitching with a dream as he whispered into the darkness.

"Joshua," he whispered, though no one was there to hear it.

Branthony looked down at this third-born child. His third son. How in the name of the God did this come from his wife? The boy was huge. Debreace had truly outdone herself with this one.

He looked to his wife. For obvious reasons, she was exhausted. "Have you decided on a name, my love?" He'd always wanted to pick a name himself, but tradition dictated that the mother chose. Besides, as he looked down at the child in his arms, so big and yet so small and so completely helpless, he had no idea what name he would pick.

Debreace looked at him through heavy eyes. "Joshua," she said proudly yet weary.

Branthony looked down at the child again. "Joshua." The name came at a whisper. "Why?" he asked.

"It means the God is deliverance. That was quite the delivery," she said with a smile. "It seemed as though it was always meant to be."

Branthony's eyes lifted to the door. For all the joy that these days brought, there was always the few moments of strange dread. "Come," he said and the Crone entered.

She came towards him with that same old walk, that same twisted smile, holding out that decrepit hand of bone. She could have used her other hand, but he was sure she chose to use the skeletal one, simply for the fear it instilled. She curled her bony finger in a 'give it to me' motion.

Branthony often wondered if he was simply paranoid around the Crone, after all, her very nature invited such feelings. But he knew by the way she smiled that she thought him a fool. It was right there on her black lips. She mocked him with every gesture and thought herself clever for doing so.

"Make it quick, Crone."

"You make demands of me?" she hissed as she took the child from him. "You forget yourself! It is you who need me here, remember that."

"You serve your own needs, Crone. Let us not pretend any different."

"I see no other who comes to deliver the Gift."

"How much of that is your doing? You would have me believe you are unique, but I know the truth." Ah, he could see the hesitation on her. Good. He would guess it had been far too long since the Crone felt any sense of humility. Her smile had faded now.

Branthony may not know exactly what she got from this bargain, but it was certainly something. He had hoped to begin the process of finding out more about the Crone but the war with the Sile had prevented it. Until the war was over and he could do what was needed, the Crone was right; no one else would be coming to deliver the Gift. Perhaps he should have held his tongue.

"No one would serve you as I do. The Gifts I give are the strongest. I can promise you that. Find another if you think you can. See what pathetic Gifts they bring."

"Then serve me now. My first-born has a Gift that is a mystery to me. My second-born has a Gift that can a ruin a man if not cared for properly. What of my third-born, Crone? The Fait rule the Cross and we do so with the use of our Gifts. Give me something I know, something I can use."

She repeated a process he had witnessed before. It was as disconcerting then as it was the first time. She took a knife, pierced the skin forcing a scream, sucked on the blood, licking her lips. Legs trembling as she sucked and swallowed the blood, moaning in pleasure as she did so. That disturbed him the most, that she somehow took pleasure from tasting the blood of his children.

When she pulled the baby's hand away, a small line of liquid dribbled down her chin and she mopped it up with a finger then sucked it whilst her eyes rolled.

The Crone glared at him suspiciously. Her narrowed eyes burrowing into him.

"You asked for a Gift you know, a Gift you can use. Today, you shall have it. Your third-born shall have the Gift of Guidance, I can taste it in the blood. All he needs now is the milk," she said the words with a grin as she proceeded with the awful ceremony of feeding him, but her eyes never left Branthony.

"It is quite the array of Gifts your children now bear. Foresight, Fortune and Guidance. Tell me, King," she said the word mockingly, as though the title were nothing to her. "You wouldn't be planning anything foolish, would you?"

A tense silence fell on the room as the King and the Crone stared at each other, all the while Debreace sat there. Exhausted as she was, she was almost ready to leap out of her bed to retrieve her son.

"The boy," said Branthony, coolly. He reached out his arms and for a moment thought the Crone meant to keep him. He felt relief as she handed him over. Still her eyes remained locked with his.

"Three children is quite a rare number for your family. Yours was the first generation in a long time to reach such numbers. Yet I got no hint in the blood that this will be your last. Another? Four children of the Fait. It is unheard of. This could mean great change is coming.

"Make sure it is change for the best. The tide can turn quickly for those on the wrong side of history." She snarled the words at him. Branthony looked to his wife, the shock of the news that they could yet have another child sinking in. When he looked back, the Crone was gone. Just like that.

"Another?" asked Debreace. Branthony could barely contemplate such things. As the Crone had said, three was rare but four had never been seen before. Not to his knowledge at least. What could four children of the Fait mean?

"Perhaps," was all he could say but he knew his wife would be delighted with more children.

"She's getting worse, Bran," she added. "Every time she's come, she's been worse. I can see a hunger in her eyes. It's as though she's never going to give the child back. Keep it for herself. She thinks of it, I can tell."

"You're right," he said, as he passed the baby over and Debreace whispered gently to it. "My father long suspected the Crone was growing mad. He thought to find a way to replace her but passed away before he could make any progress.

"He didn't leave me much to go on, but at least I have somewhere to start. The Blood River is where I need to go but I cannot do a thing until I have peace with the Sile. Speaking of which, I have a council meeting to attend. I'm expecting an update."

"Then go," she said lovingly. "We will see you soon."

When Branthony told the council that he had a third son, the announcement was met with cheers and applause.

"Tell us, Your Grace. What is his Gift?" asked John.

"Guidance," he answered and as well as smiles and nods of approval, he could not help but see the concern on some of the faces around the table that seated the council. What felt truly bad to him though was that he understood it. Such a Gift was powerful, the Gift of a leader, the Gift of a king. But Joshua would not be king.

A rivalry between his sons could turn ugly. A rivalry born of the Gift could turn deadly, history had taught them such. He couldn't help but wonder if the Crone could choose the Gift and had done so out of malice to create friction between his sons.

"As always this is to be kept within the council." Everyone nodded their acknowledgment. "So," he said, pushing his thoughts aside. "Let us get this over with. I call to order this meeting of the Cross Council. What is first on the agenda?"

"The Sile," answered Michael. "We received word from the Southern-Point. Morbius Duvec has agreed to the terms offered and will sign the treaty. He will maintain leadership of his clan, maintaining all lands and holds beyond our southern border, all the way down to the Ravens Hill.

"In return, he will command the Sile to end all hostilities against the Cross. I believe they will listen to him. Morbius is a hero to them. They have thrived under his command as never before, but they know they are losing this war."

"I agree," said Branthony. Morbius Duvec was a name that caused him conflicting emotions. On the one hand, it was him who had rallied the Sile together, uniting the clans for the first time and driving their war effort forward. He was cunning, intelligent and a great warrior, but he was not ruthless.

He was not without a sense of morality as many Sile warlords had proven to be over the hundreds of years they had been at conflict with the Cross. "If Morbius calls for peace, the clans will follow him."

"We should not allow them peace," said a member of the council. "They have plagued us for generations and now, just as we have their throats, we allow them peace. We should set an example and show the people of the world the cost of fighting the Cross."

Branthony drew a deep breath. It seemed no matter how long his people spent fighting, there were always those who would have more.

"They have paid a price. They paid with their lives, with the lives of their sons and daughters, their horses, their crops. We have dealt them a heavy hand for their breach upon our land. They will not soon be raising weapons again. Not against us. How many men did we lose in comparison?"

"One in seven at the very worst."

"Thank you, Hogan," said Branthony, glancing to his Weapons-Master who glowed with pride at the announcement as he had trained many of the men sent south to fight.

"That defeat will weigh heavy upon them. So, do we rub salt in wounds for years to come? Do we give them more and more cause for grievance? Starve them and take from them, breeding another generation filled with hate until they have no choice but to take up the sword again? Or do we show mercy and try to build a future in which we may call the Sile our ally?"

Branthony forced his eyes across all the members of the council with all the intensity he could manage. For some men, the concept of mercy was beyond comprehension.

"There are also rumblings from the north, my King."

The words came from the representative for the Warden of the Northern-Point. His words grabbed the room's attention. The north was home to the Brayfort, beyond that were the White Mountains, home to the Valfargs. The most feared enemy of the Cross in times gone by. An enemy not heard of in hundreds of years and yet still one that commanded attention at the mere mention of their name.

"What rumblings?"

"The Warden asked me to bring it to Your Majesty's attention that he has not spotted the eagles for some time."

"What relevance is that?" asked someone.

"Maybe none, but the eagles fly over the White Mountains. In times past, the main cause for them to stop flying over was Valfargs. They are wild beasts," said the representative. "Monsters. They do not think and act as we do. They are creatures of necessity, like wolves. They are predators. Hunters. If the eagles have stopped flying, it doesn't mean the Valfargs are on the move again, but it may mean they have moved across the mountains."

Branthony's eyes caught those of John and Michael who both seemed to agree. His brothers-in-law cared little for unrealistic notions, but the rest of the table broke out into ramblings.

"Silence!" The response was instant and utterly complete. "Does it only take the mention of a name to bring about panic? Valfargs have not been seen for hundreds of years and in case you have forgotten, they dwell in the mountains because we put them there. We defeated them." He didn't mention the cost of that victory. "I will have decorum."

"Thank you for bringing this to my attention. Inform my Warden that he is to send a scouting party into the White Mountains. See what they can find. If the Valfargs are on the move again I want to know about it, but I suspect strongly it will turn out to be nothing."

The representative offered an always respectful dip of the head. "Of course, Your Majesty."

"Now, what's next? I want to get this over with. I have a new son and a wife in need of me."

Unexpected Events

Luke looked down into the training yard from high upon the balcony. Usually, it was the view point of the instructors as they looked down at the men below with eagle eyes. Weapons-Master Hogan was often seen here surveying his men, shouting orders in his bellowing voice. Always ready and waiting to call out and reprimand each and every mistake with words that Luke's mother would strike him hard for using.

Today's lesson was riding. How Luke wished he could join in but father said that even at four years old, he was still too young. He was allowed to ride but not with this group. Not in the lessons. Lessons were taught to the select few.

Once they had been a resource solely of the rich and powerful but in recent years, they had been extended to those that were showing an advanced level of skill or intellect. It was their father who had created the scheme when he first took the crown after he discovered that the lessons were wasted on many who were there simply because they were born privileged whilst better talents were wasted, talents that could be used to better the kingdom.

There were some lessons though that not even the rich and powerful would receive, lessons that had a deeper meaning. Lessons that were only for the Fait.

Luke watched on intently, hoping to pick up something useful. He had already decided that he would excel in the lessons or those that interested him at least.

Aron walked away from the stable and instructor with the reins to his horse in hand. Aron was over six years old now and was doing well in his riding lessons though Luke had his suspicions the horse did most of the work and had no doubt he himself would be better.

Luke was beginning to wonder what his brother was doing just standing there, looking almost lost in a place he'd been a thousand times. Then he saw their father walking out from the stables. He held long reins in his hand, a few steps behind came the war horse, Corv.

The beast was magnificent. It seemed huge. So strong and powerful. The perfect horse for a king, and everyone was well aware how much the king cherished his horse. The name meant battle and the two of them had seen many together.

Luke viewed it all in amazement. Everyone else stood back from the magnificent creature, waiting on him as though he were a king himself. *The Horse King,* Luke thought to himself. Another thought came to him with absolute certainty, that one day he would have a horse like Corv and together, they would ride to every point of the Cross.

Both Aron and his father mounted and rode out together. A small number of other riders followed but stayed at a distance, so the king and the prince were at the lead. Luke had to fight down the jealousy. He knew they wouldn't be gone long, it was only exercises and Aron could still only go at a trot.

Father most likely simply wanted to allow Corv to stretch his legs. That didn't stop Luke getting angry again at his father's refusal to let him go with them. He was quite certain he would be the best warrior in all the land if only he were allowed to be.

It seemed to Luke he was often left behind. Aron's time was taken more and more with lessons and father was always talking about the weight of the crown. Luke was not included in such discussions. Instead, he was told to play with Joshua.

Where was the fun in that? He wanted to ride, practise sword work, shoot arrows, and do all the things that actually looked fun. Not play with his little brother. It seemed ridiculous that they would soon have another baby arriving.

He knew it wasn't Joshua's fault, he could barely walk, but that didn't stop the resentment building up. It had only gotten worse when Aron was moved to his own room and Joshua came to share with Luke. Aron was suffering from nightmares.

Luke still heard him screaming in the night despite having his own room. Still, it was better than Joshua's crying. Why did he have to share a room with him? There were plenty of spare rooms that sat empty. It was mother who insisted they share for a time. Luke didn't care much for Joshua who was just too young. Luke wanted to do the things that Aron was doing.

He found himself walking to the stables, maybe he couldn't ride but that didn't mean he couldn't play with the horses. There were plenty of them around and the castle stables were home to some of the best horses in the entire Cross.

The stable boys looked at him funny as he walked in, none of them quite sure how to act. One of them must have fetched the Stable-Master because Boxy, as he was known, suddenly stood at Luke's shoulder staring down at him.

"Can I help you, young prince?" Boxy was a damn brute with no time for children. Prince of the Cross or not, this was Boxy's house and in here he was king. Much the same as Hogan in the training yard.

"No, I just wanted to look."

"Well, look from the side if you will, young prince. My boys have work to do and I can't have you in the way."

Well, that was that. Everyone was given strict instructions that when it came to the horses and stables, they were to listen to Boxy and that meant everyone. Even father would not overrule him when it came to the horses. "I so wish I could ride," he said to himself, lost in the dreams of desire. "I bet I could do it," he said to himself.

"What was that?" asked Boxy.

Luke looked up at him from over his shoulder, the man towered above him, his ageing grizzled face with wide dimpled nose stared down. What was that look on Boxy's face? What was wrong with him? Luke had never seen Boxy's expression be anything but a stern scowl. Even when he was happy, the scowl remained. The best anyone seemed to get from the Stable-Master was a stern nod of approval. Now his eyes looked wide, glazed over, as though he were barely looking at Luke at all.

"I said I wish that I could ride and that I bet I'd be good." The words came with hesitation. He couldn't help but think he was in trouble, that this was some kind of trick or trap that he was walking blindly into.

"Well," said Boxy. "Today is your lucky day. I've been training this horse, trying to calm his temper. Might be a good way to see if it worked."

Luke's eyes grew wide. He had to curl his tongue back as it lagged out of his open mouth. Where did that come from? Well, perhaps this was his lucky day.

"Yes," he said, not quite sure what was happening. "I do want to."

"All right then."

Boxy stepped to one of the stalls, grabbing a bridle and saddle. As he opened the gate and pulled it forward, Luke had to swallow a gulp. This was not one of the mules he practised on. It wasn't even a pack horse. This was a large palfrey, far beyond his abilities. By the God, the mules were beyond him.

Before he could protest, Boxy lifted him from his feet sitting him on the saddle, leading the horse out into the yard. Luke could feel the power beneath him, the urge to run, to surge forward. Could that really be his heart that pounded so fiercely within his chest?

He looked down at Boxy from high upon the horse's back. The Stable-Master allowed them to pass and raised his hand, ready to strike at the rump and send the horse running. Luke thought he was going to be sick. *Why did I have to ask? Why? Why? Why?*

"STOP!"

The thundering of hooves roared into the yard. Luke's father was at the head of a column. Together, he and Corv dwarfed all those around them. They stopped and both rider and beast seemed to stare at him with thunder in their eyes.

"Baxter, what is the meaning of this?" It sounded strange to hear Boxy's real name. The Stable-Master looked on in confusion; when he turned to Luke upon the horse, he seemed almost surprised to see him there and quickly lifted him down. He glared at Luke as though he were a demon. "Why would you even think to let him ride a horse such as this?"

Boxy seemed to think about it for a moment. "Apologies, Your Grace, he asked and I—" He trailed off, apparently unable to give a sufficient answer.

Luke saw the anger disappear from his father's face. He couldn't put a name on the expression he saw replace it. His eyes remained firmly fixed on Luke as he dismounted. "It's all right," he said, much to the surprise of everyone. He put a hand on Boxy's shoulder, giving him a reassuring squeeze.

"The fault is not your own, my friend. Please, see to the horses. I'll take care of this." He looked to Luke with a smile that was almost sad. "So young," he said, shaking his head. "You should be years from using it. What is so different about you all?"

Was he expecting a response? Luke didn't have one. He didn't know what his father was talking about. He caught eyes with Aron at the back of the column. They didn't need words to ask each other a question.

What just happened?

When Bolevard considered just how much time he'd spent over the last years looking through countless scrolls, it actually sickened him a little. Prince Aron was now six years of age, where had the time gone? What was worse, all of his instructors reported him as having an intellect more in line with that of a ten-year-old.

The prince had started his lessons and was on the journey to being a man and now the queen was pregnant and the fourth child of Branthony and Debreace would soon be born.

It was the pregnancy that refreshed Bolevard's resolve.

A fourth royal baby was unheard of. Never did any generation of the Fait reach such numbers. His research had told him that it seemed to be one of the drawbacks of the Gift. For whatever reason, it was limited and so one or two babies at most were ever conceived to the direct line.

Bolevard knew the Gift was not infinite. Only the direct line seemed to carry it down through the generations. It may pass down one or even two children of the indirect lines, but after that it would cease. The king himself had not seemed shocked at the announcement of a fourth child despite knowing how rare it was.

Bolevard was well aware what else the arrival would mean. It was such knowledge that drove him onwards in his quest with renewed vigour. He had hoped that his visions and memories of that fateful night would diminish with time. Such a thing was not to be.

Now she would be coming again, the filthy Crone. That witch, coming to feed the new child with the dust from her breast. Come to work her black magic and somehow pass it on, allowing the Fait to continue their deceit. Even after all these years, the thought made Bolevard retch.

The joy he felt in what seemed like a millennia ago at finding the reference to the Gift in the scrolls had proved short-lived. He had over the years found more, much more, but none of it substantial. None of it of any real worth. Nothing that could be used. The Fait had taken all the real information for themselves. But, as luck would have it, his frequent visits to the library had born unexpected fruit.

As time went by, Bolevard's face became a more and more prominent feature of the library. In order to maintain his search, he made lists and tables of what was there, keeping the reason for them cleverly disguised, of course. Gradually, the entire library was being restructured around those lists.

Bolevard was proud of the work. However, that old weasel the Scroll-Master had begun to claim Bolevard's work for his own. Even going so far as claiming credit for the incredible detail with which the new lists were made. The sneaky rat had to seek out advice about what was where in his own library and had the audacity to claim Bolevard's work as his own!

Bolevard's work had at least earned him the title of Disciple and he had quickly risen high among their ranks. As such he had duties and tasks to carry out in the library. As one of the most trusted disciples, he had been given access to the vault.

A place where the most valuable and precious scrolls were stored. It was the Scroll-Master and his most trusted disciple's job to copy these scrolls every few years if the parchment was becoming old or damaged. This was by far one of the greatest benefits of the job to Bolevard's mind.

Oh, what he'd learnt. The well of information was incredible and stretched far beyond the Gift. As time passed, Bolevard had discovered the thirst for knowledge had captured him indeed. He found the greatest interest in the most benign of subjects.

And to think he used to enjoy fighting. How insignificant his skill with a sword now seemed after considering the greater wider world. So much knowledge on so many subjects. What did the trivial doings of one man and his sword matter in such a grand scheme?

For all the knowledge he'd gained, he still lacked for any in the subject he craved the most. He had learnt much about the Gifts and their different iterations but there was precious little about the source of the Gift. Most scrolls that mentioned it believed the Gift simply came from the God.

There was not a single mention of the Crone. Who she was or where she came from. None that he'd managed to find, at least, though he had suspicions there was yet more scrolls still hidden away.

He was searching for such now at the very top of a long ladder on one of the highest shelves. He'd stayed late to try and avoid any prying eyes. He'd heard the other late-night readers retire and waited for the candles to be extinguished before making his climb.

His irritation was palpable when he heard someone call his name. He almost screamed out loud when he looked down the near thirty feet to the floor only to see the Scroll-Master staring up at him.

"Bolevard! What are you doing up there? None of the disciples are allowed in that section without permission."

"Apologies Master, I was just—"

"No, no, no," he heard as he saw a ladder wheeled along and positioned next to his. He heard the creaks as the weasel Scroll-Master began to climb. "This won't do, Bolevard. What exactly are you looking for?"

Bolevard gripped the wood so hard, his knuckles turned white. It was nothing to do with the height at which he was perched but simply to contain his fury. If there was one person in all the world he hated almost as much as the witch, it was the Scroll-Master.

The man was an imbecile and complete fraud. How he'd ever gained the position was a mystery to Bolevard. When he'd first started searching for clues about the Crone, the library was in complete disarray. People avoided it for knowledge their searches would be near impossible.

Only because of Bolevard's intervention had things changed. Now the same man that had allowed the library to fall into the disarray, the same man who had claimed Bolevard's work as his own, was telling him where he could and could not go!

"What is that?" said the Scroll-Master as he finally reached an equal height. The scroll was clear. "The Gift of Foresight," he read aloud. "Why on earth would you be looking at that? What have I told you about—" He trailed off, his eyes suddenly locked with Bolevard's, for the first time noticing the menacing stare with which they now fixed him.

With all the force he could muster, Bolevard brought his elbow down onto the Scroll-Master's forearm and felt a satisfying crunch. It was fortunate that the scream that escaped him was more a guttural one than high pitched. The senses left the Scroll-Master as Bolevard delivered a second elbow to his face.

Then, with great ease he pulled the Scroll-Master from his ladder and watched with glee as he fell to the floor and landed with a delightful thud.

Bolevard made his way down and checked for a pulse. He waited for a moment in silence to see if anyone was about to come running to inspect the noise. Nothing. No one came. No one would come for hours. He climbed the ladder again.

Took the scrolls he was reading to finish later and just in case someone was to inspect the area. Then he casually climbed back down and moved one of the ladders off to the side.

It should look to any as though the clumsy fool had simply fallen to death. There may be an investigation, but no one knew Bolevard had been here. He didn't see any way in which this could come back to him. He felt no fear and no remorse as he looked down at the crumpled corpse.

In fact, he felt as though he would have the most peaceful sleep he'd had in a long time. He even smiled as he walked away with plans to go to bed.

The Fourth-Born

"Jacob," announced Debreace. Once again, she proved to have her own gift for picking fitting names. When Branthony looked upon his fourth-born, he knew the name was well suited.

Fourth-born. Fourth son. This was truly a historic event.

The murmurs of the people were already playing over in his mind. He could hear talk of prophecy, words of a golden age. Maybe such talk would be acceptable. This was special and when his sons were grown, the Fait could perhaps have one as warden in each point.

The Gifts could spread over the entire kingdom. They could do more good than ever before. Perhaps then true peace would reign. Dare he dream of such a thing, of a time of prosperity and peace beyond all previous? When even the different regions of his kingdom didn't secretly try to undermine each other for profit and power? Could his children bring about such an age?

Unfortunately, the opposite could also be true. The Gift is offered in response to the times at hand or what is to come. Could four Gifts be needed? What danger could be so great that it would require such a thing?

One thing that Branthony had learnt was that despite the name, the Gifts could be a great burden. For all the benefits they offered, there was an equal number of drawbacks. Left unchecked and un-mastered they could be dangerous, even deadly.

Branthony's own sister had once underestimated her own Gift with fatal consequences, and she had never been the same since. Even now, she distanced herself from him and the family. Choosing to only use her Gift when asked by Branthony himself.

Out of respect for her wishes, he tried to do so as little as possible. He had only asked for her help once in recent years. That was after the birth of his first-born.

So, the time had come again and despite knowing what would happen Branthony once more found himself ill-prepared as a long bone-fingered hand crept over his shoulder. The Crone suddenly stood behind him, though no door or window had been opened.

The shiver that went down his spine was chilling. He suddenly relived a memory from his youth of checking under the bed for the Crone believing that was where she dwelt.

Turning to see her looking up at him, he felt that familiar rush of cold air flowing over him. It seemed not to matter how many times he encountered the Crone. He would never get used to her.

"It is as you said, Crone. I have fathered four children. Unexpected though it may be, it is a great gift, and they must all have a Gift."

"Yes," she hissed as her eyes dropped on the new baby. There was hunger in those eyes, deep and insatiable.

The Crone took the baby, this time using a sharp fingernail to pierce the skin. Strangely, the child did not cry. She sucked at the blood, licking her lips. There was no ceremony, no drawing out the moment. She took another taste of blood. Branthony stood by impatiently.

It seemed an impossible thing to have patience with the Crone, an impossible thing indeed. When she took a third taste of blood, he felt his hands clench to fists.

"Crone!" he demanded. Her eyes opened from an odd state of pleasure, but she did not remove the child's hand from her mouth. Her eyes stayed fixed on Branthony and there was a strange challenge in them he had never seen before. He felt panic begin to rise within himself as it seemed she had no intention of relenting.

"Branthony!" called Debreace as she sensed it too.

He stepped forward and the Crone raised a hand. Branthony suddenly paused where he was, unable to move. He felt as though he were gripped by strong hands. He strained to move but found himself bound by an invisible force. His eyes bulged as he fought against it. He could see the colour draining from his new-born son and he felt fear like never before.

Casually, the Crone removed her rags and stood naked before them. Finally, she relinquished Jacob's hand and put the baby to her breast. Branthony felt such relief as he had never felt before but he continued to fight against the Crone's hold.

"This shall be your last child," she announced. "He shall bear the Gift of Truth. A powerful Gift indeed." Was that fear he saw in her? "Perhaps it is time for a little truth of our own. You are close to finally garnering peace against the Sile. You could be free to finally do the things you've been planning to do, and you have been making plans, haven't you, little king?"

He didn't reply, instead choosing to concentrate his effort on breaking her grip.

"Did you think I wouldn't find out?" the Crone groaned. "Did you think you could keep secrets from me? For generations, I have delivered the Gift to your mongrel, cross breed family. You've ruled the entire kingdom with the Gifts that I delivered! Now, you think yourself above me. You seek to replace me! What makes you so special?"

"I know the truth," he said through gritted teeth. "It is you who gains the most from this bargain." He pushed with all his might and saw the Crone's eyes widen as he took a sudden step towards her. The words that came from his lips were near growls, his whole body trembled as he fought to take another step. "We do not get our power from you. You get yours from us!"

He forced another step and the Crone retreated one.

"Look how strong you are. There are few indeed who could resist my power. That is from the Gift that 'I brought you'!" She roared the words at him. The fury in her eyes burned but it was only matched by his own. "You think you're the first to try and oppose me?

"Your dear old daddy once thought as you do. Brave king Branthony the First. What a pity. He was still so young when I had to dispose of him! Perhaps he left you something to give you such notions of grandeur."

He would not think it possible but in that moment, Branthony's fury doubled. He took a step forward. Then another. The Crone's back was now pressed against the wall and Branthony's hand stretched towards her, his fingers now so close to her neck. He would crush the life from her.

"You wish to make an enemy of me?" she snarled. "Fine. I have survived for thousands of years. I will survive you. There is more than one way to draw blood."

She raised the baby. His new-born son, so innocent, and she threw the boy towards him. Branthony felt the grip that held him disappear as he heard his wife's cry of despair. He fell forward and caught the baby in his hands, bringing the tiny shape down into a gentle embrace. When he looked back up, the Crone was gone.

The sound of his deep breaths filled the room, finally they were met by a whimper from his wife who looked at him from her bed, tears flowing from her eyes. Jacob remained silently peaceful, completely unaware of his presence in what could be one of the most significant events in the known world.

Branthony staggered a little as he stood, all too glad for the seat next to his wife on the bed. Together, they stared down at their son. He now had the complete list. Foresight, Fortune, Guidance and Truth. After what just happened, he had a feeling they would need them all.

Peace/No Peace

Bolevard sat in a somewhat peaceful state. He found it quite therapeutic to copy scrolls. Reading the text on one to rewrite it out on fresh parchment. This particular piece was nothing of interest. It chronicled some sailor who travelled out across the Winter Sea to find new lands. That wasn't to say that he hadn't found some very interesting pieces over the years, especially since he'd been made Scroll-Master.

Yes, the most unfortunate death of his predecessor had left an opening and seen as it was Bolevard's work that had begun transforming the library, he was the perfect candidate. There had been one or two others, but Bolevard had none too gently dissuaded them.

As the Scroll-Master, he'd been granted access to even more scrolls, many of which pertained to the Gift. He would now consider himself one of the foremost specialists on the subject, but he had to keep much of that knowledge secret.

It was strange though. His search for the Gift and the Crone was being simultaneously carried out by another. The king himself. Once Bolevard was Scroll-Master, the king had come to him in confidence and asked him to locate any scrolls that mentioned the Crone.

It was a difficult task because Bolevard himself was unable to discuss her. The king's own bitch sister had used her black magic on him. Besides, there was practically nothing to talk about.

Many scrolls talked about the Fait and their Gifts. The different manifestations and their different abilities. Their differing effectiveness depending on who was wielding them. It seemed not every generation had taken to their Gifts so strongly.

As far as the Crone herself went, there seemed to be nothing. Not just a little but practically nothing at all. As though every trace of her had been purposefully and systematically erased.

The day passed quickly for Bolevard and he decided to retire to his rooms. He nodded politely to those he passed in the corridors on his way. It was no difficulty admitting how much he enjoyed the extra respect now afforded to him since becoming a Castle-Master.

Back in his room, he poured himself some wine and sat at the desk in the corner. He reached underneath to the secret drawer and once opened, pulled out the scrolls for his evening read. He'd built a collection on each of the Gifts of the four princes.

After all, if he wanted to bring down the Fait, the Crone and the King were only the first step. He would eventually have to deal with the boys as well. He began reading, hoping to find some weaknesses. It seemed that Prince Aron could be the most susceptible. There was little information on the Gift of Foresight and it appeared the prince himself didn't possess control of it.

The piece didn't say much but Bolevard still made a note to keep it out of the library. He had no intention of supplying the king too much information. If only the fool knew that the one person he'd trusted to find him information was the one person who didn't want him to have it.

Bolevard had to admit the situation was a difficult one to traverse. His new role had made him all the closer to the king. He had one-to-one meetings with him regularly to discuss their findings. They had grown a personal relationship far beyond anything they had before.

However, Bolevard's mind was as clear now as it had ever been. The king and by and large, the entire Fait were liars and traitors who only held their position because of their use of black magic. It was unholy. It was disgusting and he would see them fall. He had little concern for who would follow them.

Someone would have to take the throne and despite his admiration for his new, higher status, he didn't see himself as a king. Let someone else deal with that problem. So long as the Fait fell, he would be happy. So long as the witch burnt. There could be no compromise. No peace. Nothing else would do.

Branthony sat at a desk set up inside his pavilion. A fire burned in the centre, offering some heat to the cool night. Outside, he could hear the noises of the camp. The men would be preparing for the morning when they would pack up and head home. The journey would take several weeks.

Large royal trains did not travel fast. His work here was at an end, and he looked forward to getting home and perhaps staying there for a while. His children were growing up quick and he was missing so much of it.

It seemed an almost impossible thing in so many ways, but he finally had the peace he had fought so long for. He thought fighting a war was hard, it seemed an easy and simple thing compared to trying to broker peace. It had taken years, almost completely falling apart at times but finally it seemed near.

He'd never had any desire or intention to completely destroy or subjugate the Sile. An occupation would never work and the Angosh plains were vast. The Sile themselves were nomad clans who moved about frequently and randomly. There was nothing to rule even if he'd wanted to. All he wanted was a guarantee they would stop hostilities towards his kingdom. That they would not simply fall back and regroup. Yet the Cross and the Sile had been in one kind of conflict or another for hundreds of years and there were people on both sides who found it hard to get past such things. But it seemed he had finally managed it. One last thing to do. He knew the time had arrived when the guard stepped inside.

"He is here, Your Grace."

Branthony nodded. "Send him in," he said, standing to meet his guest. He was the king here, but he was determined to show respect. "Good evening," he said, as Morbius Duvec entered.

Morbius stood at the entrance and dipped his head respectfully though he still held some hint of defiance. He wore minimal clothing in the style of his people. His long, dark hair hung to his shoulders where it sat on bare olive coloured skin.

Despite all the trouble that the man had brought upon the Cross, Morbius would still walk away from this meeting as Lord of the Sile. He would be forever remembered by them as the man who brought the clans together and unified them, all be it in a war against the Cross. A war the Sile were always destined to lose. Branthony knew Morbius was a man who would always carry a sense of that loss. It would always haunt him even when no one else considered it.

It was strange for them both to stand there in such a calm manner. Branthony had spent so many years wishing he could get his hands on this man. This one individual who was, in many ways, responsible for so many of the hardships that Branthony had faced.

The war with the Sile had been the reason he had not been able to make progress with his search to replace the Crone. He had to let his animosity towards Morbius go. Only then could he move forward.

"Please," said Branthony, gesturing for his guest to take a seat.

"If it is all the same to you, Your Grace, I will stand. I don't believe this will take long." He rolled his words with a hint of an accent but for the most part, he spoke the language of the Cross perfectly.

"No," said Branthony with a sense of acceptance. "Perhaps not. You will be eager to get underway, I suppose." He slouched forward, putting his hands on the desk before him. He felt tired and this was one of the rare occasions he allowed himself to show it. He wanted Morbius to see the man. Not the king or the warrior and certainly not an enemy. Just a man who wished to get home and raise his children. "I wanted this opportunity to speak in private. Just the two of us, as equals. You have signed the treaty and I believe you to be a man of your word. Which means I do not intend to see you for a very long time if ever again. But before we part, I wanted you to know," he struggled for words. Talking was certainly not his strong point. "I wanted to say. With you at their head, I believe the Sile can flourish. You have already performed miracles and I believe you will continue to do so. It is my sincere hope that one day our people will count each other as allies."

There was a long moment of silence in which Morbius looked at him with an expression that was somewhat shocked. "I." It was his turn to struggle for words. He settled for, "Thank you. War is not a pretty thing but I regret to say it is sometimes necessary. These past few years have unfortunately been one of those times. Nothing but war would have brought the clans together. I regret the cost but the end result was worth it."

Branthony was not sure he would agree with the statement. "You mean to say you have been fighting and killing my people simply to bring the clans together?" He tried to keep his tone calm. If Morbius felt any sense of threat, he did not show it.

"I think you will find it is your people who have done the majority of the killing." Branthony was about to retort but Morbius continued before he had the chance. "Have you any idea the difference in the clans of the Sile? There are hundreds of clans spread over every corner of the Angosh plains.

"Many do not even speak the same language, some of the southernmost clans barely speak at all. They have spent as much of the past few centuries fighting and killing each other as much as anyone else. By having a common enemy, they could unite and by fighting well, they could earn a sense of pride at that unity."

He pushed the fingers of his hands together to emphasise his point. "That pride and bond will not easily be lost. Some will fall back into separate clans, it is inevitable. But they will always remember what they can do when they work together. I will do all I can to keep them close and perhaps one day we will be allies. But—"

Morbius made sure their eyes were locked and Branthony stood straight once again. He had a feeling that this was the time to stand strong, as the man across from his was.

"The people of the Cross should also learn a lesson from this. They should learn what we are capable of if we put our minds to it. They should learn that we are not to be taken lightly. I have seen you perform your own miracles. Things I had heard stories about but never expected to witness with my own eyes.

"You are worthy of your throne, King Branthony of the Fait. We may never do the things that you can do but I want you and the people of your kingdom to know that we deserve our own place in the world."

Branthony nodded. These two men would likely never be friends. Morbius Duvec would always pose a threat to him but as for his terms, well, these were terms he could accept. There was one more thing he needed to ask.

"The time may soon come when I wish to travel the Angosh plains." He could see the surprise on Morbius' face. "Tell me, what is the best path to the Blood River?"

The Sile

Morbius looked out at the site before him and felt satisfied.

"You have done well, my lord. The blood of our people is in all that lies before us. It was not spilled in vain."

Morbius looked to his right. Farlik stood as stiffly as ever and hearing those words come from him seemed strange. Farlik would not normally talk unless addressed. He was one of those odd sorts that stuck to his duties and role like an obsession.

Morbius often tried to tell him that they were Sile, not men of the Cross. Morbius may be called Lord of the Sile, but he was no true lord. Farlik was Morbius' guard and there was no one who could do the job better or that Morbius would trust more, but he sometimes wished his friend was not so damn serious all the time. To hear him offer words freely seemed out of character.

"Thank you." He meant it sincerely. He looked forward again and knew his friend was right. A huge campsite was sprawled over the land before their eyes. Over fifteen clans were there and together, they were working the land. Planting seeds and irrigating crops. They would have a fine harvest and it would feed his people.

Other clans were doing the same or farming livestock. For the first time in who knew how long, the Sile would not face the threat of starvation. For the first time, they would not worry about being raided by other clans. The Sile liked to pretend that the people of the Cross were their greatest enemy but Morbius saw the truth.

They were their own worst enemy.

They were warriors, born to fight, but fighting was all many of them knew how to do and most of the time, there was no one else to fight but themselves. He had used the Cross as a common enemy to bring his people together. Now came the task of keeping them together.

He turned and began making his way through the camp to his own tent. Farlik fell silently into step behind him. "Some of the Clans have not reported in."

"Some have returned to the old ways. Many will find it hard to stay still. It is not our way."

"They don't have to stay still!" said Morbius with agitation. "This year the selected clans will sow the crops, do the work and next year they will move, free to roam the plains as our people always have. Others will take their place. All will share the food, the supplies. It is simple. Is it not, Farlik?"

"To some, my lord. Not to others."

Morbius growled his frustration, but he'd always known this would be the case. Some of the clans had come to fight the war from far away. The Angosh plains were vast and though the clans all considered themselves Sile the truth was that meant very little.

What was a Sile? The clans lived hundreds of miles apart, they spoke their own languages and had their own ways. There was very little to tie them together. That was why it was such a miracle he'd managed to unite them.

He knew not everyone would come around to his new way of life. What mattered was that most had. They had agreed to work together. With his new way they would all have more food than ever before, and they would not have to kill each other to get it. Clans would not steal the children of other clans.

They would have security. What was more, Morbius had the numbers to guarantee their safety. If one of the rogue clans decided to try and take what they were not contributing to, they would be vastly outnumbered. It was not perfect, but for now it would have to do.

"Have some food and wine sent to me," he commanded as he threw the flap to his tent open and stepped inside.

Farlik took up position at the entrance as the flap came back down and signalled for a nearby servant to fetch the supplies. He had no intention of leaving his lord. He would stay here. He did not flinch as the flap was suddenly raised again and he and Morbius were once more face to face.

"And Farlik."

"Yes, my lord?"

"Get yourself some food, go see your family," he said with a smile. "You can't guard me every hour of the day. Besides, who could reach me here?" He gestured out onto the mass sprawl of the camp site. *Who indeed?* Farlik thought.

The tent was dimly lit by braziers. The smell of incense made the air almost choking in its thickness. He sat upon his Throne of Bones, sweat glistening on his pale skinned body. He was oddly pale for a Sile and his flaming red hair had often made him stand out. He embraced such things.

At his side sat the Sword-of-Never, named so in mockery by those that once thought themselves better than its owner. The sword of a man who will never mean anything, they said. They had laughed but not so much when he cut them apart with it. The sword was always with him, as was the bear skin he wore on his shoulders.

The heat was almost unbearable, the others that shared the tent with him wore next to nothing, but he would not remove the bear skin. The skin was his. His symbol. He was the strongest of the clan. He had proven it, and he wore the skin so that others would know.

Forty men had entered that circle, he had walked out. Strongest of the clan was he. No one could dispute it, but he was not the strongest of all. He was leader of his Clan but not all Clans. He had tried to claim such a title but had been defeated. Morbius Duvec had beaten him, pummelling his face into the ground.

A tongue licked at the empty slots that used to hold teeth, teeth that Morbius had beaten from his mouth. His fingers touched the scars on his lips and nose, then moved to what was left of his ear. Yes, he had been beaten and beaten badly. Morbius made a show of him for daring to stand up against him but Morbius had not killed him as would have been his right.

He did not argue against the loss. Hands-of-Forty and his clan were from the south, where the plains met the sea. They had travelled north for the chance of glory. It was he who wanted more. He made the challenge, and he lost the challenge. It was fair. It was just.

Morbius answered it as a true warrior should. But that did not mean that Hands-of-Forty liked it. That did not mean he would sit in service forever. He was Hands-of-FortyForty, and he had ambition.

It was ambition that brought him here now. It was ambition that made him light the fires. If the people of his clan found out about this meeting, there would be consequences, but Hands-of-Forty liked to take risks. Great risks meant great rewards.

He had chosen only his most trusted servants to accompany him. To his left sat Silence-Of-Horror. A man with skin as black as night, whose face held a constant grimace and whose eyes spoke of blood. The two men were complete opposites in skin tone but completely similar in mind. They were brothers.

To his right, Cutter-Of-Men. She sat upon skins on the ground, her body covered in scars and ink. She looked at him, her tongue flicking outward. It was cut down the centre, forked like a snake. He had no doubt she was as venomous as a thousand. When this was done, he would have her. He could see in her eyes that she wanted him too.

"Where is she?" the grunting voice of Silence-Of-Horror. He had learnt the language of the Cross much better than Hands-of-Forty who struggled with the strange sounding words.

"No speak," he commanded. "She invites us, so we wait."

The message had been clear. It offered him power and strength. If he was interested, he need only come to this place at this time and light the fires. That is what he had done. The fires burned hot, and Hands-of-Forty sat waiting.

The tent flap opened and all three startled. Hands-of-Forty had fought many battles. Hands-of-Forty had bathed in the blood of men, women and children. Hands-of-Forty feared no one but he felt his chest tighten at the sight that stood before him.

The witch lumbered towards him. Hobbling, leaning heavily on a wooden staff, holding it with a hand that was not a hand. She was grotesque. A true horror worse than the stories the elders used to tell of such creatures. She came to stand before them and Hands-of-Forty stared down at her, the look of revulsion undisguised upon his face.

She looked up at him, his huge, muscular body shone in the firelight, sweat running down his pale skin in beads, his flaming red hair stuck firmly to his head and face.

"You send word to Hands-of-Forty," he said. "You promise you can make him strong. How do you do this?"

The Crone smiled. "How indeed," she said, her voice a grating sound that pained the ears. Her words, however, were easy for him to understand. She spoke his own language as though it were her own. "Strength, I can grant you. But before I do anything, a bargain must be struck."

"Bargain!" he spat, shuffling on the Throne of Bones. "What bargain?"

"Is it strength you want? Or is it the power to lead?"

He grunted. "Same thing."

"Maybe?" She smiled. "Maybe not?" The three Sile all grimaced at the horrible face. Cutter-Of-Men hissed through her forked tongue.

"Speak no riddles to Hands-of-Forty. Hands-of-Forty has no time for games."

"These are not games. This is creation of the future! I will make you leader of all the Sile. You will unite the clans once again and more. So much more. You will succeed where Morbius Duvec failed. You will conquer the Cross."

A grin spread across his scarred lips. Oh, he liked the sound of it. Yes, he did. That was glory beyond all measure. Men of his clan used to mock him, until he beat them and became leader. Then the other clans mocked him, until they saw him fight.

He had begun to rise high in Morbius' army. But then the northern king had crushed that army and sent it back to the plains. This was his chance to rise again.

"And you? What will you get from this bargain?"

"All in good time. All in good time." Her smile widened and black drool fell from crusted lips. "But before I can do anything for you, I need to know you are worthy. I need to know you can do what is necessary."

Hands-of-Forty shuffled in the throne again, sitting up straighter, pushing out his chest and heaving his shoulders.

"I can do anything," he proclaimed with confidence.

"Good," she whispered with a face of malice and snort of content. "Then prove it."

She removed her rags and all three Sile recoiled. Warriors as hard as stone, none of them could hold their eyes on her shrivelled body with cracked skin, warts and growths, old scars oozing with thick puss.

"Cover yourself, hag. I do not want to see this."

"You must take my milk," she said with a cackle, taking great delight in their discomfort.

Silence-Of-Horror stood, lifting an axe with him.

"I will cut those empty sacks from your chest before I let my chief near them, witch."

"You will sit down!" she screamed and the whole tent seemed as though it would lift from the ground. Frail and disgusting as she appeared, her voice carried power. Once it had died away, Silence-Of Horror was in his chair again, as though struck by an invisible hand. Her next words were back to low croak. "You will take my milk."

"Why?" asked Hands-of-Forty.

She grinned a grin of malice, of sordid pleasure. Her eyes slowly sunk to the Throne of Bones, and she snorted in contempt. "You sit upon a throne that no one else recognises. That chair has no power. You carry a sword with a name that no one knows, so the name holds no power. You call yourself Hands-of-Forty because you won a challenge that no one outside of your clan even heard about. That name holds no power!" She spat the words at him, and he flinched. He felt their bite, their bitterness, their truth.

"Take the milk and it will give you what you need." Her grin had now returned with far greater potency.

"What I need to get power?" he asked.

"Yes. All the power you could wish for. Enough to defeat Morbius Duvec," she answered. "Then the Sile will know your throne, they will know your sword, they will know your name!"

Hands-of-Forty had expected many things of this meeting. Many things indeed. This was not one of them.

"How can I be sure this will work?"

"You have seen the King of the Cross in battle. You have seen what the Fait can do. All of them got their abilities through me! I am the bringer of Gifts. They forget themselves and all I have done for them. I have seen their Gifts. They have many now. They will be able to challenge me. The time has come, so now I will give the Gift to another. One who will remember who he owes a debt to."

He had seen the King of the Cross. He had seen and felt and cursed the abilities of the Fait. The witch made a powerful promise indeed. Slowly and to the disgust of himself and his clansmen, especially Cutter-Of-Men who he now doubted he would be having, he stepped towards the Crone.

He fell to his knees, his huge hands falling over her tiny, bony shoulders. With a grimace of disgust, he took the milk. She laughed loudly as he sucked the milk from her skin.

To his surprise, it was sweet. It was oh-so-sweet.

Farlik stood watch. He was vigilant as always. The very best at what he did. No one better in all the clans of the Sile, of that he was sure. There were a lot of different clans, a lot of different people living in different ways. It amazed him how different some were to others. When they came together as one, it seemed a miracle.

But in all those clans, there was no man better at guarding than Farlik. He'd guarded his family tent when he was young, then he guarded his clan chief. When the clans were united, he knew there was only one man he should guard, and he'd been doing so ever since. Morbius Duvec was a man who lived up to the legend. He may not have defeated the men of the Cross, but he did unite the clans and he did bring glory to the Sile.

Farlik was one of the few people who knew and understood Morbius' greater plan. A plan to ensure a better future for all Sile. Guarding Morbius was the greatest honour in Farlik's life, and he took the job very, very seriously.

Farlik had watched his master fight many times. Morbius had proven himself over and over. Most of those fights had been duels, challenges from other clan leaders and chiefs or challenges to them to bring their clans under Morbius' command.

Watching those fights were the hardest moments of Farlik's life. When he had to stand aside and watch his master. When he had no choice but to wait helplessly outside the circle until the duel was done. There could be no champions to fight instead. That was not the Sile way. Morbius had to fight each and every duel himself and he had won each and every time.

Morbius was a great warrior. That was without doubt or dispute. The fact that he'd lost twice to the northern king of the Fait was, to Farlik's mind, inexplicable. He had not just lost but both times had been lucky to escape with his life.

Yes, guarding Morbius was a great honour indeed, and each and every time that Farlik was on duty, every single minute was spent with perfect diligence. He watched in that moment, staring out past the fires of the camp into the darkness. The clans of the Sile were always on the move. Their camp sites could stretch out for miles.

This camp site would not be moving for many months. Not until the crops were harvested. Though many of the clans had separated again after the war, many still remained together, forever forged in a new unity. All under the command of Morbius and all working to his designs.

As Farlik looked out into the darkness beyond the closest fires, he thought he heard something. His eyes narrowed. His head moved forward a few inches on a stretched neck. There it was again. A noise from the black but still his eyes could detect nothing.

On some occasions, he may have waited but something told him not to. He'd learnt to trust his gut. It was the reason he was so good at his job. His head now leaned back towards the tent.

"My Lord," he called inside but his eyes remained outward. The spear in his hand was suddenly gripped tighter. "My Lord!"

"What is it, Farlik?"

"A disturbance."

Whatever it was, it was coming closer now. He still couldn't see it, he could barely hear it, but he could feel it. His gut was starting to scream out. He spread his feet for better balance, lowering the point of his spear and taking it in two hands.

"Go," he nodded to the others on guard with him who still wondered what he was talking about. Cautiously, they moved outward. Further and further they went, right to the edge of the fire light. The nearest campfires were a hundred paces away. That made Farlik nervous. It was close enough so that he should be able to hear the voices of the people around those fires. He could hear no voices.

One of the guards looked back at him, shrugging his shoulders. That was when he was pulled into the darkness. Farlik heard voices then. He heard screams of pain that were quickly quelled. Then he heard the war cries, long howls rising from the dark.

The butt of his spear suddenly crashed against the gong at his side, sending out a warning. It didn't take long for the call to be answered. Men of the Sile were always ready for battle. He could hear fighting and see the silhouettes of men in battle as the fires began to grow and multiply. The camp itself now taking up the flame. He turned his back on it all, stepping calmly inside his master's tent.

Morbius was just pulling on his clothes, the women around him looked panicked. The Lord of the Sile simply looked angered.

"What in all the plains is happening?" Farlik didn't answer. He picked up a shirt and a pair of boots and threw them to Morbius who was now taking the situation seriously. "Farlik," he said. "I asked you a question." The look on his face said he already knew the answer.

"We are under attack, my lord. You must flee."

Rarely had a man looked so incredulous, so utterly shocked. It was not at the idea of being attacked. Morbius and Farlik had discussed the possibility of such a thing many times, it was inevitable that someone would come for him sooner or later. None of those conversations had Morbius fleeing without a fight.

"Flee?" he said, with mixture of amusement and anger. "I do not flee. If we are attacked by cowards who come in the night, then they shall find a challenge. Fetch me the Sword-of-Answers."

Farlik was stuffing a sack with food and flasks of wine and water. He stepped to his lord and pushed the sack into his grip. There he held the eye of the man he so admired.

"No fight, my lord. Not this time. There was no warning from the scouts. No noise from those in the camp. The enemy was not seen until it was almost within your tent." He could see that Morbius was starting to understand. He was never a fool, but Farlik said it out loud anyway.

"We are betrayed or we are outdone by something I cannot understand but for the enemy to get this close without even alerting us." He shook his head. "This battle is already lost, my lord."

"How?"

Farlik smiled at him. How he adored the man. This was a man who was worth fighting for, a man worth dying for.

"I cannot say. That is for you to find out, it is for you to bring these cowards to heel. But not now. Not tonight. Tonight, you survive. I will hold them off. Go now!"

He shoved Morbius through the back flap of the tent and when he came back determined to fight, Farlik pushed the Sword-of-Answers into his grip. "I beg you, Morbius." The name sounded strange on Farlik's lips. "I know you would die here tonight to fight alongside us. I know how much it pains you to run. But if you do not, then everything could be for nothing. You must survive. Find out what has happened and right this wrong." The sound of battle was getting closer. "Now go and let me do my job."

Farlik turned away from his lord and stepped back inside the tent just in time to see the front flap open and come face to face with the intruders. Farlik waited a moment, his body racked with tension. He actually relaxed when he knew Morbius must have listened. He knew how hard it would be for his lord to leave without a fight. For some men, a wound to pride is worse than any to the body.

"Where is he?" The words were spoken in a form of Sile. Farlik could understand the words but even for him it was difficult. The question came from a snarling mouth surrounded by blood. It belonged to a huge man with a bear skin spread over his shoulders.

His skin was paler than any Farlik had ever seen on a Sile and his red hair was a rarity. He carried a brutish sword, and his eyes were enraged. To his left was a man of dark skin who was even bigger than the first. To his right was a woman who carried a whip whose length was full of razors. They had all tasted blood.

Farlik recognised them, the one at the lead at least. Distinctive hair and skin made him stand out. Members of one of the smaller clans' maybe? Not anyone of any real note, not in the Sile ranks.

"Who are the cowards that come in the night?" He spoke the language of the Cross rather that matching the intruder's dialect. "Who are the weak souls that dare not even make a challenge?"

"I am Hand-Of-F—"

"Pah," Farlik spat on the floor, his face a grimace of disgust. "Save it for the worms. Your name, traitor, is beneath me. I will not hear it."

Farlik stood ready. The man was enraged. Good. Farlik meant what he said. The name didn't matter. How this traitor would die was all that mattered. He lowered his spear.

When the intruder came, it was hard and fast, with the power of a rhino but the finesse of an elephant. Farlik spun, sending the intruder falling past him. The spear in his hand darted forward, cutting at the tendons at the back of the knee. This brute would never walk properly again. Farlik was already impressed that he'd remained standing.

He spun the spear around and the crunch that sounded as the butt obliterated the intruders' nose would make stomachs turn. Still the beast remained upright. Farlik would say this for the man, he was a tough one but he'd dealt with tough ones before.

He stepped to the side, avoiding a swing that would have decapitated any man. Tough, yes. A good fighter, definitely not. Not with his blade at least. It was a hideous thing, all jagged edges and big enough to cleave a horse in half, the sword of a brute and nothing more.

Again, Farlik's spear struck out. Once, twice. Both times drawing blood.

Still the beast would not go down. There was tough and there was something beyond it. No one should still be standing after that. No one!

The intruder stepped towards him, that was when Farlik saw it, whatever it was. A swirling of darkness beneath the skin, as though his veins were filled with black ooze that began to surround the wounds. No. They healed the wounds.

The blackness flowed through his veins and could not have contrasted more with his pale white skin. The intruder stood before him without a scratch. That mouth was smiling again. Those eyes were thirsty.

Magic. Filthy black magic.

In his shock, Farlik had grown still. He barely avoided the sword as it came again; when the intruder followed through with a twist, Farlik stepped back but was caught by the tip. Blood was spilled and flowed through cloth. His wounds would not close. His wounds would not heal.

Farlik understood that he would not be escaping this place. But he'd known that since first noticing the disturbance. He'd always been prepared to die in service. He would not die disappointed. His charge had escaped. Morbius would be safe or so Farlik hoped.

All the more likely with each second of time he bought. But still, if he was to go, he would give this damned traitor hell before he did.

With blistering speed, he struck. His spear found its mark time and time again, the intruder barely bothering to evade. The wounds closed as fast as they opened. Fine, another tactic. Farlik threw his spear and drew his sword.

A slender thing compared to his opponent's, in the style the north men preferred. The men of the Cross certainly knew their blades and Farlik knew how to use his.

The intruder could heal. Farlik intended to find out just how much.

He stepped in, swords clashed. Spit and blood flew from mouths along with foul curses. He would never match the brute for strength, but skill would overcome it every time. How long passed? Like most sword fights, it was mere seconds that felt like hours.

In the end, Farlik found his mark. He wasn't the chosen guard for the Lord of the Sile for nothing. He bent at the knee, ducking low and swinging fast. His sword caught the intruder at the elbow and a forearm suddenly decorated the floor.

This time the intruder screamed.

That was when Farlik felt the bite of a whip and blades in his back. He writhed in agony, his sword released, his hands tried to reach to his back with no hope of getting there.

He turned to the other two intruders as the second man planted a boot into his face. He was on his back, blood and teeth filling his mouth. The man stood over him and raised his boot.

"STOP!"

All eyes turned back to the first intruder. Hands-Of-bloody something or other! In that moment, Farlik felt fear. Not for himself. His death was coming, and he did not shy from it. But fear for everyone else. This man was a monster. Anyone who would attack in the night and slaughter his own kind was monster but somehow this one had gained power.

Magical power which he did not understand. Farlik's fear was for all those still alive. He shuddered at the thought of a man like this left to wreak havoc on the world.

The intruder stepped closer. The black swirl had left his skin, stretching out at the elbow. Where seconds ago there was nothing, now there was a strange coil of blackness, growing quickly into a new hand.

"I cannot be stopped!" he declared with jubilation. "I will find your master and I will kill him. I will go north and do what he could not. I will kill that dog king of the Fait. I will kill his four mules. I am Lord of the Sile now. I am Hands-of-Forty, and I am done with—"

Farlik spat in his face. A thick mixture of saliva and blood.

"Get on with it, you coward!"

His face grew enraged.

Farlik saw the sword come down for him.

He saw nothing else.

Growing Up Quick

The stone floor felt like ice beneath their feet. The four princes scampered over the cold stone. The others had wanted to wear boots, but Joshua insisted on nothing but their stockings. The less noise the better. He'd planned the route, worked out the timing, and knew the routines of the kitchen servants. He'd spent weeks watching and planning.

Aron led the way, offering hand gestures to stop or move or get down, as well as other signals that the others had no hope of understanding. Joshua made a note to himself that they would have to create proper signals. Just making them up as they went would not do.

Behind Aron was Luke who scowled back every time Joshua made any kind of physical contact with him. They were huddling in dark corners hiding from people and Luke got angry at the brush of a finger. He was himself, Joshua noticed, brushing up against Aron whenever they came to a stop.

Besides, if contact was something to get mad about then Joshua should be screaming at Jacob, who practically crashed into him at every opportunity. At six years of age, it maybe wasn't the best choice to bring him along, but Joshua wanted him there. It had to be all of them, working together. That's what made it special.

Everyone kept telling the boys that it meant something important that there were four of them, that it was some kind of sign. Four children, four points of the Cross. It had never been seen before in their family, so it had to mean something. So, the plan had to include them all.

"I'll go first," said Aron. He was much bigger than the others but at twelve years of age, it was expected. Joshua hadn't been sure if Aron would want to come. He was so far apart from them now. His lessons were almost every day and he spent an increasing amount of time with their father or other boys his age.

Pages and squires, even knights now seemed to vie for his attention. Aron was, after all, the future king. It was perhaps, Joshua had considered, only because the plan was to be executed at night that Aron had agreed to take part. It was no secret that his elder brother did not sleep well.

Plagued by nightmares, it seemed a better option to be awake as much as possible. The whole castle seemed to know about Aron waking most nights screaming. Even from his room on the floor above, Joshua heard his brother's cries.

They waited for the right moment and Aron dashed across the floor, sliding into a crouch behind some casks.

"I'm next, don't mess this up!" Luke spat at Joshua with a scowl. He seemed to forget that this was Joshua's plan.

Luke was across quickly, sliding into cover beside Aron. They all paused at a murmur somewhere. Someone had heard something. Joshua imagined querying eyes peering in their direction. The seconds passed by. Nothing happened. The four children of the Fait breathed a sigh of relief.

"All right, Jacob. You're next."

"But I thought—"

"No, you're next. I'll go last. I'll make sure it's safe behind us." Of course it was safe behind them. They weren't being followed. But it seemed to do the trick as Jacob nodded enthusiastically. "Ready," whispered Joshua into his little brother's ear, "now."

Jacob scurried across the floor and joined the others, crashing into them without a word from Luke, Joshua noticed. Luke wasn't the most patient of boys, but he seemed to have even less when it came to Joshua.

Even at night, the kitchens were a busy place. Preparations for the morning meal would already be under way, not to mention the night guards frequently popping in to see what was available. The fires never cooled, not in the castle kitchens. The boys had to move carefully but preparation was key.

They waited for Agatha to make her rounds. The Kitchen-Master always did a night check. One time, when she missed her rounds and the oats got burnt, Agatha apparently beat several cooks around the head with a pan. All because of burnt oats!

Joshua had even heard that she killed one of the cooks and instead of burying her, Agatha cut her up and served her to the guards she didn't like. The Kitchen-Master was the last person they wanted to get caught by. Princes or not, they would all be in for a beating or worse.

The old cook wobbled through the kitchen, her fat rear barely seeming to fit between the rows of tables at which the other cooks prepared their dough. There were only a few up working at this hour but still, they were an obstacle.

The four boys pushed themselves through a narrow gap behind a stack of shelves. One false move and the shelves would go tumbling, spilling an unholy amount of all sorts everywhere and rendering them quite caught. It was dangerous, this whole thing was dangerous. But even at eight years old, Joshua had already learnt a valuable lesson in life. Sometimes, great risk could bring great reward.

With the maze traversed, the beast avoided, and the danger passed, the target was now close. Aron began making his way to a pantry when Jacob stopped him.

"Not that one," he said. "That's where she pretends to put them, so the night guards don't steal them all. One of the cooks told me the truth, she really puts them in that one." He pointed off to the side. They all looked at the new destination with dismay.

"It's got a latch," said Joshua. It was on the top of the door and well out of reach. This was not part of the plan. Time to improvise. "Luke, you're up."

Luke swaggered forward as though he'd just been called up to fight in the last duel at a tournament, but there were no crowds here and their mission depended on not being seen. He looked around and, in the end, reached for a fork on a nearby table. He threw it upward, it caught the latch, lifted it and wedged into the frame. The door creaked open an inch.

"Lucky shot," said Aron as he stepped passed him.

"Lucky is just another word for fortunate."

Aron stepped to the pantry door and opened it. Inside was like an Aladdin's cave of treats and goodies. Sweet pastries filled with cream and jam or even honey. Juicy fruits, cheese, bread. All stored neatly away ready to be devoured. The four princes planned to bring that moment forward.

Aron stepped forward first, helping himself. Luke and Jacob joined in, grabbing hungrily at the delights.

"Wait," said Joshua. "Not too much and take from the back otherwise, they'll tell. We can't let them know we've been here."

They didn't seem to like the thought of that.

"What's the point in all this if we only take a little?" The scowl on Luke's face was ferocious.

"Joshua is right," said Aron. "If we take too much now the game is up, then we can never come back again. Just take a little and take from the back."

Luke offered no objection this time, and Jacob didn't appear to have listened at all. His mouth was firmly filled with pastry and cream.

They spent a few moments indulging themselves and then took what they could carry, nothing in excess, as per the plan. Joshua stuffed two current scones into a sack he'd brought.

They exited the pantry, closing the door. A little force and the fork dislodged and fell to the floor. There was a moment of panic as they all thought it would clang and make a noise. Instead, it fell straight into the top of a bread roll Luke was holding. They all stared at it, amazed.

"All right," whispered Luke. "Now that was lucky."

Now the retreat. The route was planned, the operation well executed. Joshua was just about to congratulate himself on a job well done when Aron suddenly stopped dead at the front of the column, forcing them all to an abrupt halt. This was certainly not in the plan. Joshua looked around nervously. They were in the open, likely to be spotted at any moment.

"What's wrong?" he asked his brother.

Aron turned on them and Joshua didn't recognise the expression he wore. It was as though he were looking right through them all.

"Have we done this before?" he asked. The three others looked at him in confusion.

"What do you mean?" asked Luke.

"This. Have we done this before?" He looked around the kitchen with wide eyes. He was drawing quick breaths. The others could see the panic rising. "It's just. I've seen this before."

"You're talking nonsense," bit Luke. "Come on, before we get caught."

"But Jacob knocks the jar." Aron spoke the words with closed eyes, as though searching for a memory.

"What jar?" The question came from Joshua and Luke in perfect unison. They turned to their little brother who seemed panicked by the sudden attention. Joshua could see it in his little face that Jacob believed he was suddenly in trouble and began his retreat, edging away from his suddenly menacing brothers. He took a step backward, bumping the table behind him.

The crash that sounded through the kitchen seemed like the loudest thing any of them had ever heard. A jar hit the floor, shattering into a thousand pieces, some kind of liquid splashing out onto every surface within range.

All four boys drew a deep breath and held it, as though it could somehow hold off the inevitable consequences. It was Luke who broke the sudden silence.

"Damn it, we're done for!" he said.

"Go!" said Joshua, pushing Jacob into Aron's grasp. "All of you. Now."

"But," Aron tried to protest but they could already hear Agatha striding towards them, breathing hard like a dragon. Joshua pictured fire streaming from her open mouth.

"If we all go, she'll chase. There's no point us all getting caught. This way it wasn't for nothing."

"But father will—"

"Just go!"

They did, but Joshua could see the hesitation in them. Even Luke seemed to glance back with a look of worry and, he thought, some gratitude.

"You!" The hand that grabbed him felt as sharp as an eagle's claw. Joshua was hoisted off his feet as though he weighed no more than a feather. "Look what we have here," declared Agatha. "A bloody thief!"

Branthony had screamed, shouted and raged. Even throwing and smashing a vase at one point. All this in front of the other boys. They each winced at the sound of the crash. If he'd told them once, he'd told them a thousand times, princes or not they must live by the rules.

Interfering with the castle servants would not be tolerated, especially the Masters. He had to prove to them that he wasn't lying. Give them an inch and they'd take a mile. As they were growing older, they were becoming more and more daring, their exploits more and more adventurous. He had to make a point here and now, teach them that their actions had consequences. Even princes had rules to obey.

It wasn't lost on him how dangerous the boys could be. With all four of them together using their Gifts, there was no telling what damage they could do. Their Gifts shouldn't be manifesting at such a young an age, but his children seemed different to those that had come before, and he knew they were far more advanced than they should be.

Their Gifts seemed to be growing slowly but also having random bursts of extreme potency. It had made training them all the harder.

Yes, he'd screamed and shouted but the truth was he wasn't truly mad at all. He remembered himself and his siblings up to no good, running the halls of the castle with mischief on their minds, not that the boys would ever know that. As far as they were concerned, his fury was at new heights.

He'd sent Joshua away and the others had scurried after. He turned to Debreace with a small smile on his face. "The little buggers were in on it together. Was the vase a bit much?"

Debreace grinned back in response. It was obvious they'd all been in the kitchens, but Joshua insisted he was alone. "So he took the blame, saved the others from trouble. Perhaps allowed them to escape with a bounty. Very clever in a way and brave and yes, the vase was too much."

"Getting into the kitchen without being seen was a miracle in itself, perhaps I should be impressed."

"Perhaps it was Joshua's idea. Maybe that's why he took the blame."

"Maybe," he nodded. "But I think it's his Gift. They're all growing too quick. Children their age shouldn't have the use of their Gifts. Aron maybe should just be starting to show signs."

"They've all been the same," said Debreace, and Branthony could see the sadness in her eyes. "My babies are still babies and yet they're growing up so fast. Most children need their mothers for years, but I feel mine have already outgrown me in many ways. I can't keep up with them. The blood of the Fait runs too thickly through their veins."

The king took his queen in his arms and smiled at her. "Children always need their mother. It doesn't matter how old they get. Our children are just a little too clever for their own good at times. They're very likely stuffing their faces as we speak." They both found the notion amusing. "Should I be disappointed that the others didn't speak up?"

"Would you in their position?" They both knew the answer.

"Will you be here when I return?"

"I can't say," she answered with an over exaggerated expression of disappointment. "The women of the court demand my attention. It is such a tiresome life at times. So many of them try to sway my attention to this and that, compliments and scorns can be powerful things. I must be kept up to date with the latest gossip of court and castle."

"Ah, yes, and how is Lord Carter's daughter? Still trying to convince you to spend summer at the Five Fingers?" Lady Celia was quickly becoming quite the character around the Centre and was gaining a reputation as someone not to be trifled with. Debreace had found she had a scathing mouth that many ladies had learnt not to be on the wrong end of.

"Of course," she answered, moving away from him as they both finished dressing. "It's an offer I'm becoming more inclined to take her up on. It would be nice to spend a summer at the sea and her father is Warden of the Eastern-Point. It is only right that we visit him. It's been years. All the other points have had visits since then."

"All the other points have had danger," he countered. "The east has been at peace with its neighbours for decades. The trade between us and the nations of Golt and Mollak is some of the most profitable in the known world."

"Still," she said with a shrug. "It would be nice."

He had to admit the thought was inviting. It would give his children chance to see more of the kingdom. He hoped one of them would be warden of that point one day, after all. The words of acceptance were on his lips when a knock on the door stole their sound.

When he pulled it open, he did so with the intention of complaining at the interruption but when he saw the expression of the man outside, he knew the matter was serious.

"What's wrong?" he asked, his mind instantly going to the boys.

"A messenger, my king. From the Southern-Point. There's been an attack!"

The words were hard to hear but Branthony did so for the third time, slowly digesting the information. He looked around the table and saw the anxious faces of his council staring back.

Two of the members were his brothers-in-law. Of the three brothers of House Ken, two were common faces at the Centre, the third and middle brother not so much but the third was present now and it fell to him to try and explain the situation.

"How can this be, Grey? We spent years fighting the war and I've spent the last six bringing this peace treaty to fruition. How could things have grown out of hand so quickly?"

"I cannot say, my king. But the raven was clear. The words I have spoken are true."

Branthony looked to the floor. The war was over. Done with! Now this? Could it be coincidence? He'd spent the last years securing the peace between the Cross and Sile, but he'd also been preparing for another objective. One that would be made near impossible if the Sile were once again his enemy.

His first question was, "The Southern-Point Warden, did he survive?"

"Yes, my king," answered Grey and Branthony's relief was obvious.

His second. "Morbius Duvec was one of the greatest leaders I have ever encountered. With numbers that paled in comparison he fought, evaded and on some occasions beat my armies. He survived battle with me twice and not through luck. He was adored by the Sile. Revered! What changed?"

Grey took long, slow breaths. He knew all this and knew it well. All three brothers of House Ken had fought that war alongside Branthony. Grey had remained in the south when Michael and John had returned home, determined to see the peace hold.

"It appears we may have miscalculated their adulation, my king."

"So vastly? A few months ago, Morbius was Lord of the Sile. Now you tell me he is overthrown and the Sile are rallied behind a new leader. One hungry for war again. We dealt them such a hand that they should waver from war with us for the next thousand years. How is it they have come together so quickly and with enough strength to take Fallow Hold? All without Morbius at their head?"

It should not have been possible. Fallow Hold was the Cross' southernmost strong hold. The first line of defence against a Sile incursion into the Cross. It had been successfully held for hundreds of years.

"These are answers I cannot give, my king. I received the raven at Castle Wraith and rode at once to the Centre. I came personally, knowing the importance of the message."

"Castle Wraith is not so far north of Fallow Hold. Could they be going there next?"

"I have taken precautions, my king. We will be ready."

Branthony turned his glare to the representative of the Southern-Point. "Did you know nothing of this?"

The representative stared back with an open mouth that seemed so dry, you would think the man lost in a desert. "No," he answered. "I do not understand. Fallow Hold was strong. There has been no sign of any uprising. No word that Morbius had lost power. To rally the Sile this quick seems impossible. Many of the Clans had separated and spread back out across the plains, we confirmed it."

"Piss on impossible!" Branthony shouted, unable to contain his frustration. "Impossible has cost me Fallow Hold. Send word to the Southern-Point. Tell my Warden that once he had secured his people, he is to return to the Centre. I would speak with him myself."

"If I may be so bold, my king," said Grey. "The Warden will already be preparing our forces for a counter attack. Drawing him away now may not be prudent."

Branthony growled. There was something in all this that they were missing. He didn't say that he already had suspicions what it was. "No action will be taken until I know what has happened. I said I want my Southern-Point Warden here, so send the raven and get me my brother!"

The nightmares were getting worse. As the years of his childhood seemed to rush by, the more vivid and frequent they became. It seemed now that Aron woke every other night in a fit of terror. His howling screams waking half the castle.

An even worse occurrence than the nightmares was his inability to remember them. Whatever he saw, the images did not see fit to remain once he returned to the waking world. No matter how hard he reached, he could rarely grasp anything but blackness.

He was told he had a powerful Gift and now was the time he should be learning to use it. But how? No one seemed to know anything about it. His three younger brothers all seemed to have more use of their Gifts even though father said they shouldn't have any until they're older.

The dreams had to be a symptom of his Gift. If so that made him more fearful of them. What did he see every night that made him scream in terror?

As rare as it was, there were some occasions when he did remember something. Sometimes an image or a smell or a thought. Today when he woke, he could think of only one thing. It haunted his mind like a spectre in the wind reaching out to him. An image had remained, distant and cloudy but recognisable.

Corv. He had dreamt of riding Corv.

This was the one image he could remember. His father's horse staring down at him.

He told his brothers. All three of them came to the stable with him. Boxy was off attending to other duties; besides, the boys were a normal sight around the stables these days. Even Jacob had begun riding the mules now he was getting older and bigger.

All four of them stood before Corv's stall. The giant war horse peered down at them with eyes that seemed all knowing. The deep black orbs seemed as though they could see straight through a person, down to their very soul. He was magnificent. There was no other word for it.

"Are you satisfied now?" asked Luke. He hadn't wanted to come at first, saying Aron was just being stupid. In the end, the mention of Corv had piqued his curiosity too much. He'd had a strange anxiety around the stables ever since that day with Boxy.

He thought this was some kind of test or challenge and refused to back down. He'd been sure to walk into the stables first, hoping to meet whatever challenge was waiting head on.

"No," Aron answered him. He wasn't satisfied at all. He couldn't put a name on the feeling that held him. Something tugged at his guts, some kind of instinct that he just couldn't place.

He stretched out a hand and ran his fingertips down Corv's forehead down to his muzzle. Just touching the warhorse sent shivers down Aron's spine.

"I want to ride him," he said, not truly sure why. Whatever the feeling was, it seemed to demand the outcome. He hadn't come here to check on the horse, he'd come to ride him. Without another word, he began preparing a saddle. He'd have to stand on a foot ladder to get anywhere near high enough to mount. Next to the war horse, he felt like a baby again.

"This isn't a good idea," said Joshua, but Aron didn't even pause.

"I have to do this."

He opened the gate, stepping slowly into the stall. It felt almost as though he were intruding on a god at rest. He spent a moment in frozen silence, just him and the horse staring at each other. There was so much knowledge in those eyes. So much wisdom.

Any fool who would call a horse a beast like any other need only look into those eyes and they would see the truth. Corv could see into a man's soul and right then, he saw deep into Aron's, and he would swear he felt a connection.

There seemed to be an uneasy truce. Cautiously, he strapped on the saddle and bridle. He placed a foot in the stirrup and drew a deep breath. They all did.

He was on, mounted and holding the reins. Looking down at his brothers, Aron felt as though he were stood upon a mountain. He felt invincible. No wonder his father had won so many battles. No wonder he was so feared. How could anyone lose on such a stallion? A Destrier like this was made for a king.

He urged Corv forward and the horse obeyed. Each step felt like a shuddering volcano beneath him, ready to erupt. He could feel the muscles, the power and the raw force of one of Mother Nature's finest creatures.

"Father will kill you," said Jacob from the entrance. He'd stayed there staring out in case anyone came near.

"He's right," Joshua added. "You'll be knocking on Death's Door for this."

"Let me worry about father." *That was perhaps,* Aron thought, *the bravest thing he'd ever said.*

Joshua and Jacob stood together and watched him trot out towards the gate.

"How far is he going?" asked the younger of the two.

"I have no idea. But I don't think he's going alone."

Luke had saddled a pack horse who was still beyond his experience but controllable.

Aron glanced back at his brother who was following.

"You don't have to do this."

"Neither do you."

He looked forward again and drew a deep breath, eyes focused forward with determination set in mind and heart. *Yes, I do.*

The two older brothers rode out of sight and the two younger ones were left in the yard wondering what to do. It occurred to Joshua that someone should have been around to stop them. Surely the king's horse should be better protected.

It seemed they stood for an age. Jake began restlessly playing in the straw and stroking one of the stable dogs.

"Do you think they'll be all right?"

"No," said Joshua and looked at his brother with startled eyes. He hadn't meant to scare him. Normally, Joshua took care with his words, especially to Jacob but the answer came without choice.

Joshua felt tense, to say that riding Corv was a bad idea had been an understatement. He knew he should have done more to stop Aron but what could he do against his brother's determination?

He'd seen the look in Aron's eye, something there spoke of a challenge. There was something different about him this morning. Joshua had seen it the moment his brothers came to wake him.

It had not been a peaceful night. Very few of them were. Aron's screaming had woken Joshua twice, the sun could not have been far off rising when he finally got back to sleep only to be woken again when the others came for him.

Joshua was gradually growing fearful for his eldest brother. Whatever it was that plagued his dreams was something that no one seemed to understand. He'd heard father speaking to the Scroll-Master, a man whom Joshua already knew he hated and the Healing-Master, Fredrick. Neither had any clue what to do. An offering of the Pale Brew was all that Fredrick could come up with.

Suddenly Jacob looked over at him, Joshua could feel it too, the thumping of hooves on the ground. They both peered over to the gate to see Luke come thundering through. For a moment, Joshua was simply impressed by how well he rode, he didn't notice the panic in Luke's eyes.

It was only then that they realised he was alone.

"Get help!" Luke screamed. "Get help now!"

Joshua and Jacob could both see the blood.

The Crypts

Branthony sat at the desk, trying to keep his mind focused. It seemed an impossible task. "Urrgghh," he moaned as he pushed scrolls to aside to make room for the next batch. How could he concentrate? All his work was being undone, his people were being attacked, his kingdom was under threat. His Lords were demanding retribution whilst he felt the need for caution. He could feel it in his bones that this was far more than just another Sile uprising. On top of all that were his boys.

It had been weeks since Aron had taken Corv and fallen off. Branthony had barely spoken to any of his children since. His anger would not allow it. He knew he'd only end up shouting and making the situation worse.

He'd set the boys a strict new regime as punishment, but he knew it was like trying to stop a river with a pebble. The boys' Gifts were showing, and he was struggling to teach them. They were being overwhelmed by them, especially Aron. They were not to blame for this, he was. He just could not find the time.

He heard a knock at the door and stood from the desk as it opened. There were few people in the known world that could have made him feel slightly better right then, one of them was his younger brother.

Christopher entered and when the two of them approached each other, they embraced tightly. When finally they separated, Branthony kept his hands on his brother's shoulders. It felt good to lay eyes on him, even under these circumstances.

"It's good to see you, Christopher."

"It's good to see you too." They both meant it. Something about the world seemed easier when they were together. "Tell me, how are the boys?" It seemed as though he'd read Branthony's thoughts from the other side of the door.
Branthony shook his head gently from side to side, his joy at seeing his brother suddenly erased at the thought of his recent difficulties with his children.

"Trouble," he said, and it seemed an understatement. "They have no sense of responsibility. No notion of their position in the world. No idea what risks they pose to themselves or to others."

"Forgive me brother, but are they not children?"

"They are, and for normal children it may be acceptable. But they are royal children, and they have Gifts. Gifts which they are all using."

"Already," said Christopher, obviously surprised. "Even Jacob?"

He nodded. "My guess is they don't even know they're doing it most of the time. Worst of all, they can't control it and it's getting dangerous."

"Yes, I heard about Aron. How is he?"

Branthony shook his head again. "Physically, he'll be fine. But the whole experience has left him even more fearful of his Gift than before. But his whole attitude is wrong. It's not just what he did. He doesn't understand the reason he's in trouble."

"He thinks it's because he took Corv. He doesn't even understand how much worse it could have been. He could have been killed! His brother could have been killed.

"I can't describe the fear I had when they came and told me what had happened, yet all Aron sees is the anger. Now I feel further from him than ever before. He's becoming a man, and I just can't—" He held up his hand and clenched it into a fist, grasping for the word and for the missing link between himself and his son.

"I've set him to work in the stables to make up to Boxy. I keep going to check on him, but I can never find the words. He gets angrier every time because he thinks I'm just there to see my horse but every time I try to talk I just make it worse. He needs to be punished, but he also needs to learn. He will be king one day. How do I teach him what that means?"

"How were you taught?"

He shook his head. "Father tried but I always felt ill-prepared for the crown. I was hoping with Aron it would be different."

"I cannot help with that, brother. It's for a king and his heir and between a father and his son. But perhaps I can talk to them about their Gifts. That, at least, is an area I may be of some use."

"I was hoping you'd say that. Please. Any help would be more than welcome. But we must move onto the more pressing issue."

Branthony moved back towards the desk that was currently hidden under a small mountain of maps and scrolls, mostly of the Angosh Plains. Not that he didn't know most of them by heart. It seemed he'd spent half his life fighting wars on his southern border.

It still made little sense to him. The last war with the Sile was supposed to be just that, the last. Instead, he found himself under attack again. So, the question for his brother was how?

"How did this happen? How did the Sile manage to take Fallow Hold? Who is this new leader and where is Morbius Duvec?"

Christopher drew a deep breath. He was always so calm, so controlled. Qualities that Branthony admired mostly because he knew they were qualities he often lacked.

"I am sorry, Branthony. I truly am. You appointed me Warden of the Southern-Point and I have failed in my duty."

"But how? I appointed you because you're the best. The Southern-Point is our most dangerous border, which is why you were there. You've never been bested before. You're always one step ahead. You have the Gift of Knowledge, brother. The things you know, the way you see the world is unparalleled. So how were you defeated?"

Christopher stepped to the window and looked out at the city below. His expression said a lot. Branthony could tell his brother missed the Centre. He wished he could bring him back permanently, but it would seem he was needed in the south now more than ever.

"Fallow Hold is well protected," said Christopher as he turned back to his brother. "It was well protected."

"And yet it was taken. So, I will ask again, how?"

The expression his brother wore in that moment frightened Branthony. Nothing ever seemed to faze Christopher, but he was struggling now. Struggling to explain, worse even, struggling to understand.

"The enemy was different. We hit them with everything we had but they just kept coming. They took wounds that should have killed but didn't." He stepped closer to Branthony who had to fight the urge to step away. The look on his brother's face frightened him and he had no wish to be closer to it, but he held his ground.

"Then came their leader," said Christopher, his face pale and eyes wide. "I've never seen his like before."

"How do you mean?"

"He had the palest skin, but it was marked with a strange blackness. The others around him could take great injuries and carry on for a time but in the end, they fell. But not him. He could not be stopped. I only survived because I was knocked unconscious and carried out by my men. I tell you, brother, he could not be killed. If Morbius fought him, then Morbius is dead."

The king's anger boiled within him, threatening to spill out.

"I will find this man. You say he cannot be killed. I will put him to the test."

"Branthony, listen to me. This man, the things he did, the things I saw. I don't need my Gift to tell me it was magic!"

Now it was Branthony's turn to step away and look out of the window. He needed a moment to compose himself, to gather his thoughts. When he was ready, he asked a difficult question. "Use your Gift now, Christopher. Use everything it gives you. Use Knowledge and tell me how?"

Once again, his brother took a moment before answering. "I cannot say for sure. My Gift allows me to understand a lot of things but not all. The laws of magic elude me. There are few people in all the world that claim to have use of magic. It has always been thought to be lethally poisonous to all but our family. The only other we know of who can use it freely is the Crone."

Branthony bristled at the mention of her. "She has moved against us." He knew with certainty that this was the Crone's doing. "Just as I was ready to make my own move, she's beaten me to it. Years preparing, doing everything I can to allow myself the mere chance of replacing her and she has blocked my path again."

"The Blood River?"

Branthony nodded. "Come look at this." He began digging through some of the scrolls on his desk and pulled some from the bottom, spreading them out at the top of the pile.

"That's our father's handwriting," said Christopher, already beginning to read through. "This is what you told me about."

"Yes. Even back then, our father suspected the Crone was changing. He began looking for a way to replace her. There wasn't much to go on and of course he passed away but I think he found something. I told you what the Crone said. That she killed our father."

He watched his brother swallow down his anger as he continued to read. "Whatever he found, he must have been on the right path. Why else would she kill him? This is all he left me. He wrote that she was not always the bringer of the Gift and that she came from the Blood River."

Christopher turned his attention to one of the maps on the desk. "The river is far to the south. Deep into Sile territory."

"Exactly."

"And with a promise from Morbius for safe passage, you were ready to travel there and seek a replacement, but now he is gone, and we are at war with the Sile once more. Not a coincidence."

"Definitely not. I don't know how she found out, but she's been aware of my plans since Jacob's birth at least. Why has she chosen now to move against us? What's changed?"

Christopher tore his eyes from the scroll again and they had a fresh look of urgency.

"I know what changed. My wife, Karin," he said. "She's pregnant."

Nothing had been the same since Corv. For weeks now, the boys had been living to father's strict new rules. They had barely seen each other.

Jacob waited alone in one of the smaller courtyards that scattered the castle grounds between the different buildings. He was glum, to say the least. Jacob thought he'd seen Aron only three times since that day and that was just in passing.

Jacob felt bad for Aron. He'd lost control of the horse and fallen, breaking his arm in the process. That turned out to be the least of his troubles. Father's rage had been thunderous. Aron's lessons had now trebled and any spare time he had was taken with labour around the castle.

If the stable boys thought Boxy worked them hard, then that was nothing compared to how hard Aron was working. He cleaned the stables and horses and once done there, he went to the armoury to polish weapons and armour, then to the kitchen to help with any errands there under the watchful eye of Agatha who held a grudge against all four of the boys, despite only finding one of them at the scene. Then off to bed for it all to start again in the morning.

Even the lessons he was taking were part of the punishment. With a broken arm, he couldn't ride and practise archery and swordsmanship. No, it was all arithmetic and history of the Cross and all the other boring lessons.

Though Aron was being punished the most, the others had not escaped freely. Luke's lessons had increased dramatically, and he was sent to bed once they were finished. Joshua too had started lessons and seemed to have little free time.

Jacob was the only one left with a little freedom, but it was almost wasted on him. There seemed nothing to do without his brothers and besides, there was an odd tension around the castle that he didn't understand. Being around father felt like being around a volcano just waiting to explode. Jacob decided it was best to avoid his father whenever possible.

So now he waited in the courtyard. Every now and then, he'd have to hide behind a wagon carrying hay that had been brought in for the stables but hadn't been taken down yet. If someone saw a prince loitering, they were sure to ask questions.

The only entertainment he'd had was when a small troupe of City-Guard had marched through the nearby portcullis and out into the city beyond. Each emblazoned with this sign of the Cross. Besides that, there had been little to capture his attention, yet still he waited, bored and yet determined.

Hopefully, any minute now Aron would come past. That was when Jacob would make his move. He had a plan. It was usually Joshua coming up with the plans but not this time. This one was all his and he was proud of it. He'd had enough of being alone. He'd had enough of being bored. It was time to take action.

He turned at the sound of an opening door. This could be the chance he'd been waiting for.

He almost leapt for joy as he saw his eldest brother emerge into the courtyard. He let out a 'Psst', sound and Aron looked over to him. Aron walked towards the cart, staring down at his youngest brother with an amused if not bemused look upon his face.

"What do you want, Jacob? I've got lessons to get to. I don't exactly have time to be playing hide and seek."

"What if I had something more important than lessons?"

"Haven't you heard Father? There's nothing more important than lessons."

Jacob noticed his brother started absentmindedly rubbing his broken arm within its sling. It took a moment, but Jacob knew that curiosity would get the better of his brother and so waited patiently. Aron frowned at him.

"What is it then? What's so important it's worth missing lessons for?"

Jacob allowed the smile of victory to spread across his face. It was far too easy, his brothers far too predictable.

"A secret," he said, barely able to contain his excitement. "A big secret. A secret so big there's only a few people in the world that know it. Not even Father knows it yet. But he will soon. That's why we need to be fast."

He could already see the flare in his brothers' eyes, the curl at his lip as he tried to hide the grin that wanted to form. Jacob could virtually see the battle between Aron's common sense and his sense of adventure. If Jacob had tried this a few weeks back, there would be no debate, but Aron had been worn down. Father's punishment for acting out was the very thing driving him to act out. He was desperate for a break.

"Well," said Aron, one side clearly winning the battle. "What is it?"

"Not telling." Jacob's smile had turned to a smirk. "I'll only tell when we've got the others. I promise you'll want to know. Promise, promise, promise."

Aron drew a deep breath. He thought on it, and for a moment Jacob feared he would actually walk away and with the fear of their father looming over them all, who would blame him.

"What do we need to do?"

"First, we need to get the others and then I'll tell you all what I know."

Aron drew a deep breath then let it out, once again rubbing at his injured arm. "It's not worth it, Jacob. I have to be at the stables after my next lesson and father comes down there most days. Just to check on his damned horse. He cares more about Corv than he does me."

Jacob smiled again. "Father won't be going to the stables. Uncle Christopher is here. They'll be busy."

Aron's eyebrows rose at that. One more moment of deliberation then the smile on his face matched his younger brother's.

"All right, but this better be worth it, Jacob. I'm risking a lot for you."

"It is. I promise."

"Luke is doing archery. He'll be hard to get a hold of. Then again, he could always just ask to leave. He always seems to get what he wants. Come on, this way. One more time though, this better be worth it."

Aron set off across the courtyard and Jacob scurried after him. Oh it would be worth it, very much so.

Luke spotted them early. Aron peering over the back benches where the spectators normally sat. Jacob was with him about as incognito as a dog in a sheep pen. There were no spectators today, not apart from those two. That's what Luke thought at first, that they'd just come to spy.

Aron must have heard how good he was getting and come to check up on him. Well, why not give them a show. The thought was exciting. Luke's instructors were full of praise for him, and he was about to show his brothers precisely why.

He pulled back on the string. The target was ten paces out. He breathed slowly, aimed and released. *YES!* It was a good shot. He turned his grin towards the benches with his chest puffed out. When he finally caught eyes with Aron, his older brother waved him over. Luke scowled, he'd been hoping for looks of shock and surprise.

He put the bow back, gave the respectful bow that the instructors expected, revelled in their praises and when the time was right, he snuck over to the benches.

"What are you doing here?" he snapped. "Jealous because you have to spend your day staring at scrolls and parchment? I hope you saw that shot. I can hit the eye at twice the distance." That wasn't strictly true, it wasn't the aim but more that he couldn't get the arrow to go the distance, but they didn't need to know that.

"We've got a secret," said Jacob. The excitement on his face almost made Luke burst out laughing. He thought his youngest brother may actually wet his britches. Now that would make him laugh. The excitement, it turned out, was infectious. Luke suddenly found himself smiling.

"What secret?"

"He won't tell us," said Aron. "Not until we're all together. But he says it's big. Big enough that someone will be telling father about it at any moment. But Jacob found out first." Aron gave a sideways nod towards their brother.

There was a sudden flaw in the tale. "How did you find out?"

"Easy, I asked."

Aron and Luke looked at each other. The smiles faded quickly.

"Jacob, if this is a waste of time, you'll be knocking on Death's Door," Aron threatened.

"It's not. I was there when it came in. There were knights guarding it. Not just men-at-arms but knights and they were wearing the livery of the Brayfort. They said it was for the king. That Father had to see it straight away. It's only because he's with Uncle Christopher that they didn't take it straight to him. I used my Gift. I asked and they just started babbling the truth to me."

"You can use your Gift on purpose?"

"Well, not exactly." Jacob suddenly felt the pressure of the situation. "It just, I don't know, works sometimes. I can't control it."

"Did you ask them what they brought?" asked Luke.

Jacob stiffened up, folding his arms across his chest and shaking his head.

"I did, but I'm not telling, not until we get Joshua."

Luke scowled.

"Do we have to?" he asked, knowing the answer.

"I don't know," said Joshua. He had to admit the lure of a special secret was a large one. Jacob's excitement was intriguing. He also had to admit he missed what he referred to as 'the quests' with his brothers.

But he was usually the one to plan them. That was something he took great care doing. This was not planned at all. Still, how could he resist? "What is the secret, Jacob?"

Aron and Luke turned from Joshua and all three stared down at the youngest brother.

"Yes," said Luke. "What is it? We're all here now, so tell!"

"You promise we'll go look?"

"That depends on what it is, Jacob," said Aron, trying to take charge. "Tell us the secret. Tell us, and if it is as good as you say, then we will go look."

The smile Jacob offered them was delightful in its mischief. He waved them closer, not that they could get much closer. All four of them were crammed into a small servant's room.

"Knights came this morning from the Northern-Point with a cart. It had someone in it."

Luke scowled and scoffed, already sure that their little brother was playing a child's game. He went to barge past them and open the door, but Aron held him back with a hand and an expression that ushered patience.

"Why is that special?" he asked.

"Because that someone was dead!"

Dead, Joshua didn't like the sound of that. If the person was dead, then why would it be any fun to go see them? It seemed his older brothers were not of the same opinion. They both seemed a little excited, especially Luke. The castle had its own morgue, there were dead bodies in the castle all the time, this one must be special for it to be hidden.

"Where is it?" he asked.

"This is best part. They're keeping it in the lower crypts. They said it was to be kept secret from everyone until father has seen it."

Now that changed things for Joshua. Why, oh why would they take a body down to the lower crypts, especially a body that their father was supposed to look at? And why in the name of the God would a body come all the way from the Northern-Point escorted by knights?

"Is it someone important? Is that why they've been brought it to the Centre? Is it the Warden?"

"No," said Jacob, suddenly becoming frustrated. "It isn't anyone like that. It's just some man from the mountains."

"Did you ever think they were lying to you, Jacob?" said Luke.

"They can't lie to me, I told you. It's my Gift."

"How do you know you were using it?"

"I do know. I just know they weren't lying. There's a man from the mountains down in the crypts and he's dead. His body has been brought to the Centre so Father can inspect it."

"What's so special about this body?" asked Luke, seemingly still not convinced.

"I tried to ask but I couldn't make them. They figured out something was wrong and then it wouldn't work anymore. But Father will be going to see it soon. Right now, he's with Uncle Christopher so I say—"

"We get down there first," finished Joshua. "Find out what's so special about this body."

They all looked at each other, smiles slowly spreading across four young faces.

"All right then," announced Aron. "Follow me."

The Centre was one of the largest cities in the known world and the grandeur of the castle could not be understated. The grounds were huge and within them were endless secrets. The four children of the Fait had spent many hours endeavouring to discover those secrets; alas, they all feared it was an impossible task. However, today was to be a day that at least one more was revealed.

They'd travelled down past the stables and main courtyard, past the training grounds and servant housing, past the guard housing, past all the inhabited buildings and even the older uninhabited ones that were slowly turning to ruin. They left the higher crypts behind and moved further still.

Aron led the way with the others following unconsciously in age order. They had a tendency to do it but none of them had ever really noticed, though people around the castle had. None of the boys would be happy to hear how adorable everyone found it.

They were in the old graveyard now at the very limits of the castle grounds. Much further and they would hit the wall that ran around the grounds, the last line of defence if any enemy was ever to breach the city, not that it was ever likely to happen. Once upon a time, it had been the edge of the Centre until the city gradually grew around it.

The crypts and the graveyard were where those of special note were buried in times gone by, but not Fait. The Fait were burnt upon death, something to do with blood secrets. They weren't exactly sure what secrets. Even father had been trying to find out but apparently to no avail.

"Here's one," called Luke as he stood in front of an old gravestone. He beat at the long grass that had grown around it with a stick, gradually revealing the worn stone. The others all came to stand around him.

"Who is Master Grenoline?" asked Joshua. They all shook their heads.

"Whoever he was, he's been dead for over three hundred years. It's a miracle we can even still read the words," said Aron.

"Can't read many of the others," said Luke. "Which could mean they're even older. I wonder which one is the oldest."

They all looked around. The whole place was overgrown, most of the stones were broken and worn and many were toppled. Moss grew everywhere and the whole place had a smell of dampness. It was a strange jungle of intrigue, and it wasn't a stretch of the imagination to say they could spend the whole day here and not get bored.

They wondered why they'd never really come here before. They'd love to explore but today held higher priorities and they knew they were pushed for time.

"Come on," urged Joshua. "We need to go."

None of them argued. The lower crypts weren't far away. They all knew that however old the gravestones were, the lower crypts were older still. The first known generations of the Fait were buried there.

Not the blood Fait, but those who married into the family, many whose names and deeds had long since been forgotten. People who most likely deserved more than to be left to the dust and decay.

They were almost at the wall and were starting to wonder if they'd somehow missed the entrance. The four of them stood side by side, wearing matching expressions of confusion.

"Is that it?" asked Jacob with a voice awash with disappointment. "It just looks like a hole."

They all glanced over and saw a small hole in the side of a mound. It was barely visible through the overgrowth and looked more likely to be the entrance to an animal's den.

"I don't think so, Jacob." Aron said with a smile as he put an arm around his younger brother and ushered him on. "I think that's just a hole."

"Well, it might have been the entrance," he said, feeling a little foolish.

"This looks like an entrance," said Joshua and the others turned to him. He'd stepped away from them and found a more likely option. He tugged at some hanging vines, trying to hide how much effort it took to break them. They fell to the ground revealing an opening.

Stone jambs were built into the side of a small mound. They were covered in moss and the entire structure was overgrown but this was certainly it. They started to beat and pull the overgrowth away.

"Careful, we don't want to let anyone to know we were here."

There were words carved into the stone, but they seemed to make no sense. One word, however, was perfectly recognisable to all. "Fait."

Looking at the entrance sent a cold shiver creeping down their spines.

"This is it," said Aron as he rubbed his fingers down the stone and over the words etched into it. "It's in the old words. Something about 'laid to rest'. That's all I can make out."

"You can't read the old words." Luke made the statement with confidence; he seemed to be in the mood to argue today. Aron turned an almost sad smile on his brother.

"That's what you get from extra lessons with a broken arm with Father checking up on you." The other three all suddenly looked at his arm in the sling. All of them quickly remembered the fear of that day and father's anger. "Come on then," he urged, hoping to push the feeling aside and move on before they lost their nerve.

"Look," said Luke, pointing at three torches placed in sconces just past the threshold. Aron lifted one down and sniffed it.

"It's fresh," he announced. "Probably from whoever took the body down."

"I guess they left this as well," said Joshua as he spotted a flint.

"Come on then," said Aron. He wouldn't admit it, but he didn't welcome the idea of going into the darkness. They hadn't really thought about what to do once they reached the crypts but with flames lighting the way, he stepped forward.

In they went, down the old stone steps that were so rarely walked upon, down into the darkness, into the last resting place of their ancestors. They pushed past spider webs and felt the dust falling on their heads. The entire complex had an eeriness to it, as though the spirits of those so long dead were watching.

There were statues whose features had long since worn away. They had lost their faces, but it only made them all the more intimidating. If there was some kind of order or ceremony to them, then it was long lost.

Jacob reached forward and grabbed Joshua's shirt. Joshua hesitated at first but a few steps later, he grabbed onto Luke's. His brother made no move to discourage him. In fact, Luke grabbed Aron and Aron wrapped another hand around the solitary torch.

The stairs ended. They stood in a low corridor of kinds. Small alcoves stood at either side with what they guessed were once the tombs of their ancestors. The air was thin and carried a strange smell. The walls were close together and confined.

"I changed my mind," said Jacob. "I don't want to know. Let's go back up. There are ghosts down here. I'm sure of it." He suddenly twisted and startled at a scurrying sound.

"It's just rats, you idiot," Luke said, as though he wasn't in the least bit scared though his hand still clung tightly to his older brother's shirt.

"Maybe we should go explore above," Jacob offered, wondering what it was that made him set all this up in the first place. Had he really missed his brothers that much?

"Later!" spat Luke, apparently bored with the childish antics. "We came here to see something, so let's see it before the chance is gone. If Father needs to know about this, then I want to know why."

"He's right," said Aron whilst offering the younger ones a comforting wink of the eye. "Let's go."

They continued and nothing out of the ordinary happened. The further they went, the less they were scared. It was almost a disappointment when they came to end of the crypts. They had all expected them to be larger, reaching deep into the earth. Instead, it contained no more than five alcoves a side, stretching just a few metres.

"Where is it?" asked Aron.

"There," said Jacob, pointing into the last alcove. They could see it in the shadows. A bundle wrapped in cloth lay upon an old stone table as though the body was one of the old kings or queens.

They all approached slowly, Aron held the torch above, allowing the flames to carry their light over the body.

"Ready?" asked Aron. One by one, they all nodded. Aron reached forward, pulling at the cloth. It took a moment, but it came away revealing the body beneath. All four children recoiled at the terrible stench.

"Urgh, that's the worst thing I've ever smelt." Joshua pulled back to a safer distance but took a step closer again when he discovered he'd moved out of the light. They all looked down at the body, besides Jacob who had to strain to see it properly.

A man, dead for quite a while if the smell and colour of his skin were anything to go by. Then again, if Jacob was right, then the man had been brought all the way from the Northern-Point, so he had indeed been dead for quite some time.

"Look," said Luke as he pushed his finger into the skin, and it left an impression.

It felt strange to look upon the face of a stranger and know there was no soul behind it. That those eyes would never open again. Who had he been? What had he done in his life? What tales could he tell? Luke didn't say it, but he wished he'd never touched the man. He felt disrespectful.

"Why?" Aron locked eyes with each of his brothers in turn, even the youngest understood. Why was the body there? Why had it been brought all the way from the Northern-Point for inspection by their father? Why was it being hidden in the crypts?

If they had answers, then none was given the chance to voice them and if any of them thought the journey down into the crypts had been scary, that fear paled in comparison to that felt at the sudden sound of approaching voices, especially when one of them belonged to their father.

She found it all terribly tedious, the monotony of everyday life and the menial, repetitive strains of simply being. She wondered if people actually lived their whole lives like this. Living from day to day with no real concept of the greater game, happy to play their part as a pawn or something even lesser?

The hardest part of it all was keeping up appearances. She'd barely eaten all day, all in a desire to remain thin. It seemed to be harder to keep weight off than it used to be but her reputation as a rare beauty meant a lot to her. The women around her talked in soft gentle voices, taking dainty little nibbles out of the food on offer.

Celia had no doubt that they were all as hungry as her and would like nothing more than to drop all pretence and stuff their mouths. That, of course, would be unladylike.

Between the talk, most of which was consistently boring and useless, there was some attempt at needle work. Celia was, of course, damn good at it. That did not stop it boring her almost to Death's Door

She found excuses to miss these little gatherings whenever possible, but she couldn't miss them all, appearances and what not. She was the representative of the Warden of the Eastern-Point, a person of power and responsibility. She was also the only woman to ever hold such a high position and every man in the damned Centre seemed intent on making her job harder, which only made it all the sweeter when she outshone them all.

Useless little boys. She considered herself an inspiration and if all else failed, at least she had succeeded in showing these pathetic men that they could be outsmarted by a woman. The Eastern-Point had flourished over the last few years since her father's appointment and though he may not admit it; that was in large part down to her influence.

The days spent with the women of the court, loathsome as they were, did on rare occasions bear fruit. The women around her were not to be dismissed. Some were powerful ladies, linked to powerful families. By the God, the women in this circle had links to lands that covered almost the entirety of the Cross.

Perhaps more importantly, some were close friends to the queen. Celia had made good headway in getting closer to Debreace Fait, but the Queen of the Cross was a difficult nut to crack. Not at all the dimwit that Celia once imagined. It seemed Sir Thomas Crestfall spoke some truth all those years ago. How far away that conversation now seemed. How much had changed since those days.

She joined the conversation, adding her own little input on the subject of the summer celebrations that were coming up. Not a topic that interested her but sitting in silence would not do. If the opportunity arose, she would turn the topic in a more interesting way.

Celia had found many times that there were few places to gain information as good as a group of gossiping women. If only some of the women around her knew that she had used many of the things said in this apparent privacy to bribe their husbands and loved ones. *Serves them right for gossiping*, she thought.

Celia had no qualms about abusing the so-called friendships she had with these women or any other person for that matter. Celia had goals, ambition. It was becoming quite a nuisance, in fact. The problem with ambition is that, for her at least, it could never be satisfied. She wanted more, much more.

She'd just taken a small nibble of the food, biting off a pathetic piece of sweet bread before indulging in the delicacy of a single grape. She was savouring the taste when she noticed him. A boy stood in the doorway desperately trying to gain her attention without being seen by the others.

One of her many little spies. Celia nearly choked on the grape. The little rat was going to pay dearly for this. How clear did she have to make herself? She was not to be approached in public. There was only one thing for it. An excuse had to be found to leave before the mindless oaf got himself caught.

Explaining why a damned stable boy was trying frantically to wave her down would be a nuisance she didn't need.

"Will you excuse me, ladies?" she said as she stood, placing her needlework down. "I feel a little lightheaded. I will return to my room to rest."

"Are you all right," asked Lady Donna, looking up with her tanned skin and those confident eyes. She was wife to Lord Richard of House Dawsel and just happened to be one of the queen's best friends.

An interfering bitch in Celia's eyes, more than once she'd prevented the queen from taking Celia's advice on certain matters and those decisions had cost Celia advancements, but the woman was far from foolish.

"Yes, of course. Nothing a little rest won't cure. If you'll excuse me." She walked away knowing the excuse was weak. As she left the room, she imagined they were already talking about her, wondering what could force her to leave so suddenly, not a single one of them was under any illusion that she was going to lie down.

She imagined talk of a man and could hear the giggles in her mind. Leaving like that could almost be as costly as the boy being seen. Rumours started quickly in the Centre and once they started spreading, they were near impossible to stop. She knew this more than most as she herself took great delight in starting them.

She walked to her room, went inside and waited for the inevitable knock. It wasn't at the main door to her room but a discreet servant's entrance. The knock was coded. It had taken a lot of time and effort but in the years she'd been at the centre, she'd built up a considerable little network.

Her spies were spread all over the Centre and even beyond. She had eyes and ears in most of the major families, allowing her to keep a close watch on all the goings on. Some were already in place, set up by her father and other trusted servants of the Trone family.

Others were hers and hers alone. She had more than a few secrets that she didn't want anyone else knowing, especially her father. She used all this information to her distinct advantage.

She opened the door and the boy clambered in. He stank! She was almost upset to have his dirty little feet on her floor. When he looked up at her, he was met with a slap that would knock the taste out of a lion's mouth. He staggered back and bumped into the bed.

"What the hell did you think you were doing? How many times do you have to be told? NOT IN PUBLIC!"

"But Lady Celia, it's urgent."

"Nothing is that urgent! I don't care if a man is at my back with a knife, you never, EVER, approach me like that again. Do you know how important I am? How do I explain to all the women of the court why a damned stable boy is waving at me like a drunken old friend? Why would a stable boy even be inside the castle? What were you thinking?"

"Yes, Milady. I don't know, Milady. I'm sorry, Milady."

"Now," she said, pulling at her dress, it had risen with the swing of her arm, and she was trying to hide how much her hand throbbed. "What do you have to tell me?"

The boy wiped away a mixture of tears, blood and dirt and tried hard not to sob. Good. Celia could not stand the sound of crying.

"A cart arrived this morning from the north. It was carrying cargo and was taken straight to Sir Michael of House Ken for the attention o' the king himself."

Interesting but not a good enough reason to come waving her down in the open. "So, what is it?"

"I don't know, Milady, but it was taken straight to the lower crypts. Hidden well away, all secret and that. The king will be on 'is way to inspect it any moment now with Sir Michael and Prince Christopher."

Christopher! Well, that wasn't good news. She learnt of his arrival at the Centre but thought she'd have more time before being faced with his interference. Prince, Lord, Warden, he was a lot of things including a great big nauseating pain. He had a way of thinking that Celia had to admire on one hand and detested on the other. He was very difficult to manipulate. She hated that.

She'd always found men so easy to control. She almost pitied them, the stupid, pathetic creatures, capable of thinking only with their groin or a sword. Not that they didn't have their uses. But there were some rare finds that managed to impress her.

The king was one in many ways, his brother another. What made it worse was that they always seemed so much more when they were together rather than apart.

"None of this explains why you thought it necessary to approach me."

"Whatever it is, it's important, and I heard Sir Michael say to burn the bugger as soon as the king's done with it. I was hiding in the stables ya' see, when they brought it in. Said no one was to know and no one was to see it. The men that brought it looked like they were from the Brayfort."

Ah, there it was. The old twisting knife of intrigue. Why would it be taken to the lower crypts? Why would it be of such importance to the king? Why was it to be burnt? She had to know and know she would, even at the risk of discovery.

She tossed a coin at the boy who looked at it with an open mouth.

"If this turns out to be something good, then there is more where that came from. If it turns out to be waste of my time, then I would use that coin to get yourself out of the Centre because I'll come looking for you and I will skin you alive."

The boy nodded as he swallowed a large lump down his throat. Celia opened her eyes a little wider at him, an expression that asked what in the name of the God he was still doing there.

The boy was gone within seconds.

Well then, it's off to the lower crypts.

"Hide!" commanded Aron and they moved without a moment's hesitation, all terrified of the prospect of being caught.

Luke ducked down into the one of the alcoves, hiding behind the old stone tomb. "Don't follow me!" he whispered through gritted teeth as Joshua crouched down beside him. "Get your own hiding place!"

"Too late," said Aron as he and Jacob knelt down beside them. He doused the flames of the torch and all four were suddenly plunged into silent darkness. It seemed typical to Luke that none of them could even hide without him.

Each of them could hear the others breathing. The voice of their father became clearer and now they could make out two others. Uncle Christopher and Uncle Michael. Two incredibly different men, both of which were loved by the four boys but not one of them believed either uncle would be able to stem their father's anger should they be found.

It barely seemed possible, but they slowed their breathing even more as the elders came to a stop over the body just metres away, the light of their torches reached into the alcove and the boys shrunk further into each other.

"So, tell me what this is about, Michael." Their father already sounded angry. There was a tension to his voice that all four could hear.

"You'll see."

Much to the dismay of the others, Luke dared to lean his head out around the old tomb. Christopher was standing over the body unwrapping it. He uncovered the head then began to remove the cloth from the torso. If he could tell it had already been unwrapped, he didn't say so.

Branthony stepped closer to inspect the body. "Claws?" he asked as a gloved hand inspected the wound.

"Yes," said Christopher. "From a creature with six digits."

The boys looked at each other. Darkness may have stopped them seeing anything but it did not stop them knowing the expression that they all wore. It was just like Christopher to spot it so quickly where none of them had. One word came to mind. It fell to their father to speak it aloud.

"Valfarg!"

When Luke peered over the stone again, the two Fait brothers stared back at Michael.

"He was a mountain farmer. His wife said he trekked a little higher up the White Mountains to check on some goats that hadn't been seen. He never came back. They found him like this a few days later, took him to the Brayfort where the Warden sent him down here with all haste."

"A hoax?" their father asked.

"Always a possibility," said Christopher. "But the wound, though grievous, does not look fatal. A Valfarg's claws carry poison. That could be what finished him off. And if it was a hoax, who would also know that the eagles have stopped flying over the mountain? And why would they go to such lengths as this? I suspect the Warden believes this to be genuine. That's why the body has been sent for inspection."

The boys waited anxiously to hear their father's thoughts. Surely this would be some great call to arms. A glorious marching of the men of the Cross to defeat the monstrous Valfargs. At least, that's what the children imagined. Their father, apparently, had different ideas.

"Dispose of the body. Send gold to his family. I want them taken care of, Michael. They deserve it after this." Michael nodded with the understanding expression he had.

"And then?" asked Christopher.

"When the eagles stopped flying, the Warden sent a scouting party to investigate the mountains. They found nothing." He stroked his chin thoughtfully before saying, "If the Valfargs are moving again, then they're hiding their movements. That's not like them. Send word to Lord David. As Warden of the Northern-Point, this is his responsibility. He is to try again. I'll leave him to investigate however he sees fit, but I want this matter taken seriously. He will know what to do. Tell him he has my full support."

"That's all?" asked Michael, a little surprised.

"For now. First the Sile, now Valfargs. It seems to me there is suddenly an awful lot that requires my attention. One enemy that blocks my path to the south, another that draws my attention away to the north."

"You think this is her?" asked Christopher.

"I can't be sure, but I have my suspicions. Anything to keep me away from the Blood River."

Branthony took one last look at the body. Luke could just make out his father's eyes in the dim light. They were the eyes of a troubled man. Even a child could see that. "Come," he said as he walked away. "We have other matters to attend."

The boys remained frozen as their father and Michael walked away. Christopher turned back to the body and started replacing the cloth. He stood for a moment staring down at it, his chest rising and falling with steady breaths. Then, in a low voice, he spoke.

"You should not be down here," he said, his eyes never lifting from the deceased. "Perhaps it is fortunate for you that my brother seems to have received some bad news lately. He is too distracted to notice the tiny footprints." He looked up now, his eyes scanning the darkness.

"I trust you understand the importance of all this. Keeping secrets can be a hard lesson to learn. Be sure to learn it quick. You'll leave immediately after us. Do not be seen. Someone may already be on their way here. Do not let them catch you. If anyone else is approaching, there is a hole to the side of the crypt entrance. Use it and hide."

He turned and left; only when the light from his torch faded, did any of the boys dare to draw a breath. It took a minute before Aron could draw the flint to make a spark and when the torch was lit, four pale faces became visible.

"That was too close," said Luke. "Let's get out of here."

No one had any objections. When they finally started the ascent the light of the outside world seemed like a shining beacon. Each of them drew an exaggerated breath as they stepped outside.

If they thought they may have a moment to rest, they were sadly mistaken. Their uncle Christopher had been right. Someone was approaching. The boys felt their hearts leap once again. It was like running away from someone and thinking you'd escaped only to see them still right behind you.

"The hole," said Aron.

"We don't know what's down there," said Joshua.

"We're about to find out. Go!"

They all ran, trying hard to stay low and out of sight. The hole looked all the darker, all the more menacing. "In!" shouted Luke as the younger two paused before the blackness.

They pressed in one at a time. Jacob first who passed easily enough. Then Joshua who pulled his way through. Luke followed but struggled against the sides. Aron pushed him from behind then leapt in. He felt himself wedge against the sides, but his brothers were there to pull him. They all landed in a pile as he finally passed through.

Aron quickly stood and gestured for the others to be quiet. He looked out of the hole which he'd just squeezed through.

"What do you see?" asked Joshua.

"They're still coming towards us. Stay quiet."

Luke was apparently unwilling to wait, pushing up next to Aron.

"Is that Lady Celia?" whispered Luke. It definitely looked like her, though she certainly wasn't dressed like a lady. Instead, she wore stockings and a shirt. She had two young boys with her.

"I think I recognise them. One's a page and the other's a squire to Sir Folik. I've seen them around the castle grounds. What are they doing here with Lady Celia?"

"How the hell should I know?" Luke's language seemed to be getting more colourful all the time.

"It doesn't matter. We wait until they go inside and then we go past them."

"Oh, really?" The sarcasm in Luke's voice made Aron grit his teeth. One of the boys, the younger of the two, waited at the entrance as the others went down into the crypts. "And how do we get past the lookout?"They dropped back from the hole. It seemed that waiting for Lady Celia to finish and leave was the only option. "Erm guys," came Joshua's voice. "I don't think this is an animal's den. There's a bend here." Apparently, he'd decided to try and explore a little. "Look. A sharp turn, like a tunnel. You could light the torch."

They edged towards the sound of his voice, a little impressed he'd dared to venture further down. Slow cautious steps forward, sliding their feet across the ground. Joshua was right. It was a sharp turn that led deeper in. The light wouldn't easily be seen from outside. Aron lit it and they all looked around. Rocky walls stared back at them. Definitely not an animal's den.

"Where does it go?" asked Jacob. "Are there ghosts?"

"No, there are no ghosts. But where it goes, well, that's the question."

"There could be anything down there," said Joshua, excited.

"Treasure," said Jacob.

"A monster," offered Luke, hoping to frighten the little ones.

"Anything," said Aron again. The eldest took another few steps down, carrying the light with him. The others followed instinctively not wanting to be left in the dark again. He turned to them with a grin. "There's only one thing for it. We explore and see where it leads."

The other three looked at each other, all nervous at first, waiting to see if anyone would protest. None of them wanted to be the one that said no.

"Well, what are we waiting for?" asked Luke, deciding to try and push them on. "Let's go."

Jacob stayed next to Aron to be closer to the light. He'd admit to being scared but this was everything he'd hoped for and more. He'd reunited his brothers after weeks apart and now they'd not only explored the crypts, but they also found this new delight. It had all far exceeded expectations. The deeper they went, the more exciting it got.

"Perhaps this is part of the crypts?" said Joshua.

"Maybe," replied Aron quickly looking back. "Or maybe this is how the crypts started. No point digging down if there's already a cave."

"Is it a cave or a tunnel?" said Luke, pointing ahead. They all saw it now. Small pools of dim sunlight pierced the ceiling above to fall upon the ground. When Aron held the torch up, they could see the roots of a tree dangling down but that wasn't all.

"Is that a rope?" asked Joshua.

Aron passed the torch to Luke. He leapt into the air, reaching out with his one good arm and managed to snag the rope. It came down to hang on the floor with a hoop in the end.

"What is this?" Luke picked up the hooped end and looked up to the ceiling where the rope hung from. He passed the torch to Joshua and then gave the rope a tug, half expecting it to fall down. It didn't. That was when he jumped up and put his full weight on. Still the rope held.

He released his grip, spat on his hands and jumped again. This time he shimmied up the rope until the roots were brushing against his head. "There's something here," he said. He reached one hand into the darkness. The others all expected him to fall but he didn't. Instead, he just hung there. The next moment, he scrambled even higher into the darkness and disappeared from view.

The remaining three boys looked to each other. The moment seemed to drag on and finally Aron called out for his brother. "Luke? Luke!" He was beginning to panic. Why did they have to come down here? What were they thinking? Father would kill them all if Luke wasn't already dead.

They all gasped with relief as Luke's face appeared above them. He stared down with almost frantic eyes that seemed all the crazier on a face covered in dirt, a smile spread across it reaching from ear to ear.

"You are not going to believe this!"

Preparations

For Branthony, the day had been stressful. It was a tedious but necessary part of ruling but as king of the Cross, Branthony had to pass judgements, meet with certain people, broker deals and a thousand other things that apparently demanded his attention.

An audience with him was hard to come by for most, those that obtained one had often been waiting an obscene amount of time to do so. He made a point of always trying to put his full effort and attention into the meetings, though he was ashamed to say he often failed.

Today was one of those days. It seemed almost insane to him that he should spend the day dealing with these things when so much else was happening.

When necessary, he would leave the judgements to his council but when available, he would always take part. He'd attended through the day, but his mind was even further away than normal, and he felt his stress and anger at what seemed trivial matters threatening to overcome him.

He thanked the God for his brother who had sat in on the meetings. His younger sibling always had a way of dealing with people. He had a patience and empathy that Branthony knew he sometimes lacked. Maybe it was Christopher's Gift, who knew.

Either way, it was him who had dealt with most of the decisions today. He sat to Branthony's left hand side and was a blessing. If only he could remain at the Centre and do this all the time.

The other reason he'd attended today was because of the figure that sat to his right. His first-born son and heir, Aron. This would be his job one day and Branthony had decided he had best start learning early. Since Corv, he'd insisted that Aron join him at these meeting whenever his lessons would allow it.

He wished dearly he could have had more time with his own father, learnt the lessons he had to teach but his father had passed away years before and the time with him was now a distant memory.

Branthony's relationship with Aron had been frosty to say the least. Branthony had yet to find a way to bridge the gap between them since Corv. He wanted his son to learn responsibility. He wanted to teach him, but his efforts were seen as nothing but punishment. He could see how much Aron resented being here.

Now and then, Branthony would talk quietly to Aron, most often whilst Christopher spoke to the current guest. He would ask Aron's view, try and gauge the extent of his insight. It was hard.

Several of today's visits had been farming disputes. There was an argument about some shipbuilding rights, something else about an armourer's unique style being plagiarised. When Aron's insight was vague, he thought himself in trouble. Each time Aron answered, it was as though he thought he'd disappointed Branthony somehow. Yes, it had been a trying day to say the least, yet these were necessary lessons.

Branthony shuffled in his chair; eyes fixed on the man before him, a man from Mollak, a nation to the east where the Winter Sea met the Spring Sea. A nation that did frequent and profitable business with the Cross. He'd come here to negotiate a new deal for certain items of trade, as well as trying to sell slave warriors. Not something that Branthony was interested in. He had no taste for slavery. Still, he allowed the man to say his piece. Christopher glanced back to see if Branthony wanted to pass judgement himself or allow him to do it.

He would deal with this himself.

"As far as your trade negotiation goes, I will allow the following. A five percent rise on all your wines and cloths. Nothing more, and I expect an extra delivery every quarter in compensation. As for paying less for the catapults that you have no chance of replicating with any efficiency, the answer is no."

He didn't like selling weapons in the first place, let alone for cheap prices. He knew they probably could replicate their design but the wood from the forests of the Cross was strong, it was the wood that made the catapults so unique, and it could not be replicated, neither could the unrivalled craftsmanship.

"As for your slaves, they have no part in any bargain. Not with the Cross and certainly not with me."

"I understand, Your Grace. I will tell my superiors in Mollak of your decision, and I would accept on their behalf the agreement of a price rise in return for the extra shipment. As for the slaves, I am sure we will find other buyers. I thank you for your time, Your Grace, and wish you good day and good fortune." He placed his hands together and dipped his head low, walking backwards towards the door before exiting.

Christopher turned to Aron. "Tell me, nephew. What did you learn from that man?"

Aron waited a moment and considered his answer. "He wore lots of jewellery, he's trying to show off. He thinks money makes him important."

"As do many others," said Branthony and suddenly noticed his son wilt a little at the response. He hadn't meant it to sound discouraging. "Go on," he said, hoping to pry something else.

"He wanted to buy weapons but sell slave soldiers. It doesn't make sense."

"Very good," said Christopher with a smile and a glance to Branthony, a hint to say something of praise.

"They know we do not partake in the slave trade," said Branthony, iterating Aron's point. "He never expected us to buy. He just wanted us to know that others are. Most likely someone close to us. War would disrupt trade which would cost Mollak money."

"It won't stop them selling slave soldier to our neighbours, but they'll at least let us know they're doing it. Whoever it is, it won't be anyone who could threaten Mollak. Most likely someone further south. Find out who is purchasing these slaves, Christopher."

"I shall have our Eastern representative talk to the Warden. I'm sure Lady Celia and her father will investigate thoroughly."

The door opened again, and the announcer stepped forward to introduce the latest guest.

"Introducing Sir Malf. Here at the king's request." The introduction was by far the shortest of the day, lacking in the pomp and exaggeration that so often accompanied such things. Despite that, it was by far the most important announcement of the day.

Branthony sat back in his chair, surveying the latest comer with amusement. The man swaggered forward with a grin on his face and a ridiculous amount of confidence. His hair was black but for a white streak running down the right-hand side. His face carried a number of scars, and his nose was so misshaped that it looked as though it had no bone at all.

"Aron, you may leave now."

His son had wanted nothing more than to leave since they started. Only now that Malf had entered the room, did he suddenly seem interested. Branthony felt the guilt of suddenly sending him away. He knew he should say something more or risk making the divide between them even larger, but it seemed that talking often had the same effect.

"Aron," he said and as his son looked to him, it was hard to tell who was more nervous. "You did well today. You're smart and your observations were impressive." He could see his son's surprise and happiness at the compliments. "I must speak in private now. So run along to your next lesson. I know you don't enjoy them but we don't always get to choose what we do. Sometimes being king means demands are placed upon us."

"I understand, Father."

"Good. Now go." He hoped he'd done enough to start building a bridge but without making him think all was forgiven. Aron seemed to have a spring in his step as he left and Branthony was optimistic. Finally, he sat back in his seat and looked to the guest.

"Finally," he said. "You're a hard man to find."

"Not if you search the whore houses and taverns."

"You frequent them often?"

"Oh, I never bloody leave em, unless of course some royal arse beckons me," he said with a grin that revealed a number of missing teeth. Branthony remembered him losing them. Malf and he went back a long way. They were friends from an age when Branthony didn't have the weight of the crown on his head. They'd been through a lot together over the years and Branthony trusted him as much as he trusted anyone.

He looked past Malf as the door opened again. Michael and John stepped through to stand beside Malf. "Apologies, Your Grace," said Michael. "He took some finding and then I had to buy several drinks before he'd agree to leave."

Branthony frowned at them. "The drinks were just for him?" The two brothers of House Ken shrugged their shoulders apologetically. "Obviously not then." Branthony decided he would let it go. He couldn't deny them a drink, not when he knew what he was about to ask of them.

"Thank you for coming," he said, and he meant it. He looked each of them in the eye and hoped he could portray at least some small amount of his gratitude. "Allow me to get straight to the point. I need a small team of good, strong, reliable men who know their business when it comes to swords, horses and secrets. Unfortunately, all I could find was you."

They all grinned and laughed, looking at each other with amusement. These men knew each other well. Laughs always came easy between them. Good, that would help in what was to come.

"So why would you need this band of men?" asked Malf.

Branthony drew himself up straighter and drew a deep breath. "You men here have been selected. You are all my Chosen Swords. We have a job to do and to do it, we are going south."

"Ah, back down south again, eh?" mumbled John. "Gonna deal the Sile another beating? Oh well, back to war it is."

"We're not going to fight the Sile. Not yet at least, not if we can help it."

Now that really did grab their attention.

"If not the Sile," said Michael, "then who?"

This would be the hard part to explain.

"Things have happened, things beyond my understanding, things that change everything. The Sile may not be the greatest threat to the Cross. I need to go south, through the Angosh plains. All the way to the Blood River."

That drew gasps of disbelief.

"Let me get this straight," said John, by far the youngest of the group. "We're at war with the Sile and you want to take a small group of men down through their homelands, through enemy territory, all the way to the Blood River?"

"Yes."

"Why?"

Branthony finally rose from the throne, walked down the dais and stood before his friends. "For years now, I have been trying to make peace with the Sile. I had to do more than simply defeat them. I needed peace. That way I could one day travel safely though their lands. Just beating them wouldn't give me that. The clans would split, and they would always be a threat."

"We're not at peace with the Sile," stated Malf.

Branthony tried to explain his plan. He told them how he was now surer than ever that the Blood River held the answers he needed.

"This isn't going to go down well, Branthony. People will be upset. They need you now," said Michael. It was just like him to think of others.

"Your sister, the Queen," he emphasised the word, "will sit on the throne in my absence and my brother, a prince of the Cross and a Fait will be by her side. I have also asked my Weapons-Master to play a role. He commands respect in the Centre as well as any man."

Branthony looked at his younger brother. Of all the people in the room, he looked the most worried. Perhaps he was the only one that understood. "They will govern," Branthony said assuredly. "There's no one I would trust more for such a task."

Christopher stroked his chin in thought, his eyes now turned to the floor. "If we are at war again, then none of the Points will be easily quelled. They already demand vengeance for the attack on Fallow Hold. May I suggest calling upon Lord Richard Dawsel and his wife Lady Donna.

"They are trusted friends and allies, and they control the region of Rodley and so have influence in the west. The north will always trust to the Centre. I hope the south will hold strong to the crown and to me. That leaves the east. Always the most difficult point. Lady Celia could be a powerful ally in this."

"As always brother, your advice is welcome. I will talk with them all before I leave."

"So, when do we leave?" asked Malf. He was leaning back against the wall, arms folded across his chest. Who would believe the man was in the company of a king.

"As soon as possible. But there's more. We must reach the Blood River and return to the Centre again within four months."

Now that really did draw exasperated gasps.

"Why four months?" asked John?

"Because my brother's wife is expecting a child. The Crone appears at the birth of the Fait, but if we can break the cycle she will no longer possess that power. The child must have a chance of the Gift and I must be the one to break the chain. This is my chance. If things are as I fear and the Crone is responsible for our current predicament, then I dare not give her more time."

"You're asking a lot," said Malf, who now wore a frown that looked all the worse with his scarred features. "It's not as though we can ride a straight line. The Sile are our enemy. They've declared war against us. We have to avoid them. That will slow us down." Malf's eyes were staring off, as though already plotting a route.

"And there could be no finer prize than the king of the Cross," said Michael bluntly.

"And the Sile? What if they come further north? What about this new leader?" asked Christopher.

Branthony once again looked to his brother. "Buy me some time brother, and I will deal with him myself."

When Branthony opened the doors to his personal rooms that night, he took a moment to enjoy the sight before him. His wife and his four children sat together near a warm fire. She was telling them a story and for once, all the boys seemed at peace with each other as they listened intently.

He savoured the moment. It made it all the harder to do what he knew he must. He coughed, suddenly alerting them all to his presence. Debreace caught his eye. She knew it was time.

She put the scrolls she was reading from aside and ushered the boys to move closer to her, making room for Branthony to sit down. They both knew the relationship between father and sons was not at its best. It hadn't been since Corv.

Branthony was determined to teach his boys a lesson for their mistakes, especially Aron, but he also knew that if he didn't act soon, the divide between them could grow to a size that was unassailable. He wanted to try and bridge that divide. He also had to tell them he was leaving yet again.

"Boys," he said, and as always, he had their undivided attention but this time it seemed different. It wasn't simply because he demanded it. It seemed they wanted to give it. Perhaps they too were ready to heal the wounds between them.

"I'm going to be leaving soon and I will be gone for some time. Whilst I am gone, I want you to do your best to help your mother and your uncle Christopher. These are troubled times and the people of the Cross look to us for guidance. I want you to set an example. Be good boys."

"Are you going to fight the Sile again?" asked Luke, excitedly. "We could come with you."

Branthony smiled at that. "No, I'm not going to fight. Not if I can help it. I'm going to ensure the future of our family."

"You're going to replace her," said Aron, swallowing down his sudden fear. His brothers all looked to him strangely like he'd been keeping a secret from them. Branthony nodded. He knew his eldest understood.

"She is called the Crone. At least, that is the only name by which I have ever known her. I am going to try my best to find another to do what she does but that is a secret I need you to keep." He could see how much it meant to all of them that he was trusting them with a secret.

"Other people do not understand the Gift. They won't be happy about me leaving, and perhaps they have good reason. But this is something I have to do. But before I go, I wanted to tell you all how much I love you. I wanted to say that although I don't always show it, you are the most important thing in the world to me.

"But I am the king of the Cross, and I must do what is best for the kingdom and our family and right now that means going away for a while. It will not be easy. Like I said, there will be many people who are unhappy that I have gone. Your mother will have a lot to deal with. I need you to make it easier for her."

"Don't go giving her even more trouble than she already has. When I get back, we're going to start spending some more time together. It's high time you started using your Gifts properly."

Three of the boys were obviously excited at that. One of them not so much. Branthony smiled and put his arm around his eldest son, a display of affection he'd not shown in some time. "Together we can learn to control them. *Together*," he emphasised, and for the first time since Corv he felt at peace with his children.

The next morning, Branthony and the Chosen Swords began their journey south.

Away from the Comforts of Home

They ran through long grass. The slowly decaying graves and memorial stones flashing past. The four children of the Fait laughed as they ran. They never took the same path. Joshua thought it would make it easier to follow, so they always went a different route though the destination was always the same.

They came to it. The hole. Now even more hidden than the day they'd found it. They'd laid long branches down from above to obscure the already hard to find opening. This was their secret and they planned to keep it that way.

Father had been gone for almost two weeks now. He'd told them not to make things hard for mother. Well, what could be easier than staying out of her way? This way, she was free to concentrate on other things.

It took a few moments to clear a way and squeeze through and then they were careful to cover their tracks. Finally, they were back inside the cave. Had this place once seemed scary? It was hard to imagine it now. Now it was the pathway to a level of freedom they never thought to achieve, the pathway to more fun than they'd ever had before.

They reached the end of the cave where the rope hung down. Luke climbed it once again but this time, the others didn't panic when he released the rope and disappeared. This time, they knew that he was unlocking a special latch and pushing a trap door open.

Soon, he offered a hand down and helped Aron make the climb. It wasn't easy with his arm still in a sling. Soon all four of the boys had made the climb. Luke closed the trap door, but it could only be locked from one side so once again they hid it beneath branches and leaves. Then, finally they stepped outside.

The boys turned to stare up at the huge tree. The size of it always amazed them. It was within the trunk of the tree that the entrance back down into the cave dwelt. When they turned from the tree, their eyes were filled with the sight of the city.

They were at the edge of the gardens, not far outside the castle grounds but still a protected area. The public gardens were open to all but protected by the city watch. The boys knew it was one of mother's favourite places to visit but they couldn't imagine her or any of the ladies of the court bending down and crawling into the dirty dark trunk of a tree.

"Come on," said Luke, already setting off away from the garden. The others followed, all dressed in clothes that would blend with the people of the city. They knew they couldn't exactly walk the streets of the Centre in their finest velvet doublets.

Besides, they all knew how much trouble they'd be in if they were to get those doublets dirty. "Our lavishness comes at the expense of the people," their mother was fond of saying and they were told often enough that lavishness was not to be flaunted or squandered. It seemed almost strange that so many nobles did exactly that.

Within minutes, they were in the streets of the Centre and moving amongst the crowd like any other people. No one had any idea that the four Fait princes were walking at their feet. They'd actually heard themselves mentioned several times since they began making their expeditions.

Apparently, some people thought of them as some kind of prophets or something along those lines. Their being born was of great meaningfulness. The first time there have been four children to one set of Fait parents. To them, it sounded nothing but silly.

"Where are we going?" asked Jacob. The others all turned frowning eyes on him. He'd shouted out again, he had a tendency to do that. The boys had agreed to try and stay quiet when out on the streets and they'd come up with the plan to disguise their voices and use different names. It had proven remarkably difficulty to do.

"James," said Luke to Aron.

"What, David?" he answered back a little too forcefully, as though he was proving there was no chance at all that he almost forgot to use his brother's false name.

"Where are we going?"

"Not the market again," said Jacob. So far, the market had been their only destination when venturing out.

"Yes and no, Christopher," said Aron who still found it a little amusing that two of his brothers had just picked their uncle's names as disguises. They lacked imagination. He had picked James after the great sea Captain James Temol Karkin.

Aron loved the stories of Captain Karkin. How he sailed his ship around all four of the known seas. He was a fearless explorer and that's what the four of them were doing now and he was the oldest, which made him the captain.

"So where are we going?" asked Joshua.

"Yeah, where are we going?" Luke prodded him from behind. "Or are you keeping secrets from us again?"

Aron shook his head. "I told you. I wasn't keeping secrets. I just didn't know what to say." He'd tried to explain about the Crone. He told them of the time he'd seen her at Luke's birth. None of them could really comprehend it. They didn't understand how scary she was.

Hopefully, their father would succeed in replacing her and they'd never have to understand. They'd never have to see her at all. Aron prayed that was the case, he knew he certainly didn't want to see her again. "Everything at the upper market is boring," he continued, happy to change the story. "Food and clothes, nothing new and nothing I want to see."

"That doesn't answer the question."

"We're going to the market, but I've heard rumours of another market. One that sells items that are a little more exciting."

"Where?" asked Joshua with a glare in his eye.

He has, Aron thought, *that all too common and annoying tone of superiority.* He wouldn't like taking the risk without making one of his plans. Where was the fun in that? Sometimes, it was better to jump in headfirst. Attack the situation. He didn't want to admit that this tactic hadn't exactly done him much good recently.

"I know where, just follow me. Today, we're finally going to see the real city."

Branthony walked through the eerie darkness and silence. His feet left prints in the ash on the floor. Fallow Hold. Once the great southern fortress to protect the Cross against invading enemies. Now it was a cold and stark reminder of its own failure.

Everywhere he looked, the fort was marked with signs of battle. Scorch marks and blood stains. Bodies rotted and left for the crows. The once great fortress now brought down, and a ghost of a shell left in its place.

It was hard to look at. The fate that met those who hadn't been lucky enough to escape did not bear thinking about. Everywhere he turned Branthony saw the horrors of a battle lost. He watched his breath plume in the cold, dark night air and felt as though there were ghosts looking down on him from high on the walls.

The Sile had stayed here for a time, plundering and pillaging and inflicting who knew what other horrors on their captives. They had sat and drank in the great hall making a mockery of all the lords that had held this fort over so many years.

But in the end, they'd left. They hadn't even caused as much damage as they could have. As though sending a message. Your holds and forts cannot stop us. Nothing can stop us.

He clenched his fists in anger.

"Don't let it get to you." Malf had come to stand beside him, laying a comforting hand on his shoulder. "Don't let anger cloud your judgement. We've got a job to do." His friend was right. In the end, he didn't believe this was even about the Sile. It was about the Crone.

"Thank you," he said. "For your words and for coming with me."

It was not often that he got to be around Malf in such a way. They'd fought several campaigns together but there was always a hundred nobles or others vying for Branthony's attention. Many of them couldn't hold a candle to Malf when it came to fighting, even fewer of them would admit it.

In Branthony's experience, these men with him were some of the most loyal, trustworthy and able men of the Cross. He knew some others who he could count as their equals in terms of honour and trust, and he'd left them in charge of his kingdom.

"You really think we can do it, Bran?" The question came from John. It was rare for someone to use his abbreviated name. "You really think we can find someone to replace her. You've told us about her before. It's always been this way. She's always brought the Gift."

"Not always," he replied. "My father found out where she came from. He believed she could be replaced. He started investigating it and she killed him for it."

"You think we'll find answers at the Blood River?" asked Malf. Branthony nodded. "But if the Crone has been delivering the Gift for as long as you say, then what makes you think there's anything still there?"

Malf made a good point and the others looked on expectantly.

119

"The scrolls say she is from an ancient tribe, perhaps they were part of the Sile in an age long past. The tribe is connected to the river somehow. They cannot or will not leave it. Her people will be there and so will my answers."

"What makes you think they'll help?" asked Michael.

"I have something they'll want. It's the reason the Crone keeps coming to my family. The giving of the Gift is not a one-way transaction." He turned and began making his way to the ruined portcullis.

"So?" asked Malf. "What is it? What do you have?"

"Isn't it obvious?" he asked. "Blood. She needs the blood of the Fait."

He left Fallow Hold behind him, filled with fresh determination.

The gulf in difference between the lower market and the castle grounds could hardly be greater. The four princes were used to busy and crowded areas, they'd been in the middle of parades whilst the people of the Centre filled the streets. They'd been to balls where the lords and ladies of the Cross attended in all their finery. This was different, very different.

They had to push their way forward through the congested crowd, fighting as hard to stay together as they did to move forward. This was not just busy; this was a battle, with genuine risks. No one seemed to have a single care for anyone else around them.

The four boys held hands, much to Luke's disgust but it worked. No one even seemed to notice they were even there as each person fought their own personal war. Aron was the tallest but even he didn't stand a chance of pushing through.

The children scrambled between legs and ducked beneath swinging arms. They were all too used to others moving out of the way to let them pass. The people in the market seemed reluctant to even let them breathe.

"Up here," said Aron, pulling them off to the side. They had to move across the run of traffic rather than with it and the action was a truly monumental task. Some of the adults almost tripped at the sudden obstacles in the path. Curses were called out and some of the words were ones Aron thought not even the soldiers would use.

One man kicked out, his boot driving hard into Aron's backside, but the boys kept on moving. It was the first time he'd ever been struck outside the training yard. Would this man ever know he'd just kicked the heir to the throne?

Finally, Aron pulled his brothers from the torrent and up onto a small flight of steps. They looked down at the moving horde and it was hard to believe they'd just assailed such a thing. It seemed like a stampede trampling all in its path.

"Where are they even going?" asked Luke as he brushed himself down. "I mean, none of them even look. We should have the guards come down here and restore some order. One of them kicked you, he should be flogged. We should go back, get the castle guard and come and find him."

"I don't think there are enough guards," said Joshua and the others silently agreed. It was a frightening concept. Luke thought of a card game the adults played called Fait's Gambit. One of the lesser value cards, known as the Peasant, was also a very powerful card. It could be used to bring down even some of the highest value cards, one of which was the King.

"I thought you said this would be fun," moaned Jacob, sitting down on a step then moving up one, fearing he was too close to the rush and could be pulled back in at any moment.

"This way," said Aron, pointing off down what appeared to be a much quieter section of the market. There was still a number of people milling around, selling, buying or merely browsing wares. But nothing compared to what they'd just been through. He had to admit this was not what he'd hoped for.

As they finally gained a measure of freedom, they began to make their way further from the castle grounds and upper market. The stalls and shops nearest the grounds were the best, the most upmarket, the prime sellers with the most exclusive wares. These were the ones most likely to be visited by those from the castle. The further away, the more common the vendors. This far from the grounds was known as the old market. This was a different story altogether.

If the castle was considered the height of human culture, this was surely on the other end of the scale. Every face looked deprived, every surface filthy with grime and the God knew what else. The stench stung at the nostrils like an angry wasp and the air itself seemed to carry a threat. Mother and Father had been doing a lot to change areas like this.

They said no one should have to live in such poverty but it was no secret that many of the people here were likely on the wrong side of the king's law. Aron was beginning to realise the depth of his mistake. This was not their world and the dangers of being here were beginning to mount up.

"Come on," he said moving off up the street, hoping they would see something that would at least make the trip worthwhile.

Most of the stalls, if that's what they were, contained little more than castoffs. Old weapons or pieces of armour barely still fit for use. Old food that the boys thought would most likely kill anyone foolish enough to eat it. Clothing that appeared more rags than anything else.

All four of the boys were a little more grateful for all that they had in that moment. They'd never really stopped to consider such things before but this drove such thoughts home like a hammer on the stake.

"My, my," came a shrieking voice. The boys turned as a woman approached. Her hair was thickly matted, hanging in clumps from a flaky scalp. The bags beneath her eyes were dark and those few teeth that remained to her were black. "What have we here?" she was picking at them, grabbing at their clothes, long fingers pushing through their hair and pulling at their ears.

"What do you think you're doing?" demanded Luke, as he slapped her hand away a little too imperiously.

She pulled her hand back and glared down at them with a snarl, obviously she hadn't expected such a tone from a small boy. For a moment, there was nothing but silence, the four children stared up at her as she in turn stared down at them. The tension was broken when she turned a grotesque smile on them. It was far more frightening than her glare.

"Tell me, children. Are you 'hungry? Thirsty? I've got fresh bread," she said, gesturing back over her shoulder. "Would ya like some? I'll swap it for some o' those clothes."

The boys looked at each other. Joshua had suggested they wear less noticeable clothes but apparently in the old market, the ones they'd chosen were still of some quality.

"We're fine, thank you," said Aron pulling at Luke's arm, who in turn sent the gesture off down the line. They managed two steps before the woman had moved and blocked their path.

"What about that hair? That's mighty nice hair. I'll give you four coppers if you let me shave your heads. That's a copper each. It'll grow back."

"No, thank you."

Aron tried again to resume their escape.

"Come now," she pleaded. "Where are your parents? Are they 'hungry? Wouldn't they be 'happy if you returned home with food or coin?"

"We don't need coin," said Jacob as they stepped past her. Other eyes around shot him a quick glare as he rubbed his hand through his own blond hair wondering why someone would ever want to buy it.

"Don't need coin, eh? Got some spare, have we? Well, could I interest you with royal teeth? From the princes of the Fait themselves, ya 'know."

This, despite all their better judgement, intrigued them. The woman must have caught the flicker of something on their faces because she leapt on the opportunity.

"That's right, baby teeth from the princes themselves. Surely you know the powers of the Fait, the things they can do. You're too young to have seen the king use his Gift but I'll wager you've heard the stories." They had actually, many times.

The soldiers, guards, men-at-arms, anyone who'd ever been in a fight seemed to know a story about their father. But she was right, they'd never actually seen him use his Gift. "Take the teeth, grind em to dust and drink it down and you too could do the same things."

The boys looked to each other, Jacob subconsciously licking his teeth, considering the fact that a few felt wobbly and wondering if someone was going to try and drink them when they came out.

"Come now," urged the woman. "You're all good clean boys. Obviously, your parents love ya very much. Why don't you surprise them?"

"We're fine, thank you." Aron chose to try and put some authority into his tone as he dragged them off. It seemed to work because the woman straightened up and stood still, hands on her hips and a scowl on her face.

Jacob smiled back at her as his brothers dragged him off. It was a smile that showed his teeth and though he meant no offence, he wondered if she'd found it insulting. It took a moment to recall that she had no idea who they really were. What would she have done if she did? Jacob quickly closed his mouth.

"Oh," he said to himself, suddenly feeling rather clever. He reached into his pocket, pulled something out and tossed it back to the woman just as he was pulled around a corner. There was just time to see her catch it, eyes widening as she examined to object. Then she was gone.

"I don't like this," said Joshua as they moved off further into the market. Luke was trying to divert their path towards a weapons stall whilst Aron seemed interested in a man calling out about magical powders. "Is anyone listening? This is a bad idea."

No, they weren't listening. That was the simple answer. His two older brothers were jostling for control of their little convoy whilst Jacob seemed oblivious to the dangers all around them.

In one swift moment, the attention of all four princes was captured.

Aron suddenly stopped dead, Luke as well and Joshua crashed into him from behind, earning a swift and painful punch to the arm before Luke returned his attention forward.

"What's he doing?" asked Jacob, though they were all thinking the same thing.

Ten paces up the road stood a boy. He looked of an age with Aron and had long, curly, dark hair. He was staring at them with hard eyes whilst making strange gestures with his hands.

"I think he's one of those crazy people Uncle Michael is always talking about," said Luke, with an amused tone. "Move, crazy boy! Get out of the way!"

He didn't. Instead came more gestures as the boy became even more animated.

"What do you want?" asked Aron, holding an arm out across his brother's chest. Making sure Luke didn't do anything rash.

No answer was forthcoming, but the boy's eyes were simply bulging now as he began pointing an accusing finger at them.

"Who's he pointing at?" asked Jacob, holding up his own finger aimed back at himself, innocently asking if he was the intended target.

"Why doesn't he speak?" asked Joshua. "Can you?" he asked loudly, standing on his tiptoes so he could see better over Aron's shoulder.

Still no words, but the boy was certainly becoming more exasperated.

"Of course," said Aron. "He's a mute."

"Actually, he's deaf," came a new voice. The four boys spun to face the newcomer. It was another young boy staring back at them. He had a similar look to the other and the Fait boys guessed they were brothers. "He's been trying to warn you."

"Warn us about what?" demanded Luke, taking a step closer to the newest arrival. Luke was clearly the elder and was trying to intimidate.

"About the thugs following you, sent by that old woman you met back there."

They all glanced back. The street behind them was busy. They could see a hundred faces, but none seemed to stand out.

"Why would they be following us?"

"To kidnap you, of course."

He said the words as though it was the most obvious answer in the world and perhaps it was. The boys looked to each other and wondered how they ever hoped to get away with sneaking out of the castle. How had they ever believed they could walk the streets and not be recognised? They were princes of the Cross!

"I'm sorry t' say it's the little one's fault." The rest turned eyes on Jacob, and he immediately looked as though he would burst into tears. "People round ere don't see gold very often ya see."

"Gold?" asked Joshua, wondering what the boy was talking about.

"Yeah, gold. He tossed the old hag a gold coin as you went past. Do you know how much that makes you stand out, four children walking around the old market handing out gold? A damned lot, that's how much. So now she's sent two, no, three men to snatch you n' see if you got more."

The first boy began gesturing again. This time the four princes realised he wasn't pointing at them but past them and this time, they followed the direction of his accusing finger and noticed a man, tall and bald, scars on his head, trying to act innocent and blend into the crowd but he noticed he'd been pointed out.

That, apparently, was enough to make him forget about stealth. He began a charge. Two other men joined him, suddenly aware that their cover was blown.

"I'd follow us if I were you," said the young boy. "Either that or go with those fellas. But I really wouldn't recommend it."

They all glanced back. The three men were closing fast. Whoever these boys were, they certainly seemed like the better option.

"Go," commanded Aron. The elder of the two boys turned on his heel and began to run. The younger boy was quickly behind him and the two of them led as the four princes followed. The chase was on and getting caught was not an option.

If they didn't know the risk they'd taken when they first left the safety of the castle grounds, they surely did now because now their lives were on the line.

Celia had done all she could to find the reason for the king's sudden departure. It made no sense for him to just take off in such a manner. It wasn't that she cared too much about where he'd gone. It was more wanting to know if she could use it to her advantage. Could it have something to do with the body from the north?

The most powerful lords in the country didn't know where the king had gone. She could pass on such information for a high price if only she could learn it for herself first.

When the queen came to Celia herself and asked for help in quelling the eastern lords, Celia had believed she was about to be brought into the inner circle and given the information she desired. It was not to be. For whatever reason, the royals were playing their cards very close to their chests. This only made Celia all the more determined to find out, by any means necessary.

To her disappointment and frustration, she had found out very little. She was accustomed to getting what she wanted, used to finding whatever she was looking for, but not this time. Not yet at least.

The only people who seemed to be in the know were the Queen and Prince Christopher. Perhaps Lord Richard Dawsel and his wife Donna? Celia knew better than to broach the subject with any of them. The little group was keeping their own council and the secret tightly locked between them and quite frankly, Celia found it revolting.

She had learnt long ago that secrets were an extremely valuable commodity. One good secret could buy more than gold. The trick was knowing when and how to spend them. Cash in a secret at the wrong moment and it could be drastically undervalued, wait too long and it could lose value altogether.

She also knew never to overplay a secret. Threaten a man with exposure once and he would very likely bend to your desire but use the same trick too often and many would decide that paying again was not worth the cost. Pride and anger could get in the way.

What foolish things they were and so often they were the telling features of men. Pride, she firmly believed, was many a man's worst enemy.

But use a secret at the optimal time and place and the yield from it could be enormous. This was a trick she prided herself on. It was with a secret in mind that Celia now made her way through the castle. It was time to cash one in, and here was another trick when it came to secrets. Most often, the best and most valuable thing to be done with one was exchange it for another.

Celia considered herself an intelligent woman. She had wits to outmatch most, that was for certain, but she was also highly educated. Her father had made sure of that. If nothing else, his daughter would help with words and numbers and all the things she found so tedious.

Alas, if only she had been born a boy and her father could have practised swords with her. How bitterly disappointing it must have been for him to have only a single child and of the wrong gender at that.

She could almost certainly say that if she had been born a boy, her father would not be Warden of the Eastern-Point. She'd liked to have seen a boy try and coerce Sir Crestfall the way she had.

Yes, Celia thought herself intelligent, but it seemed that although she may have acquired knowledge over the years, she did not carry a thirst for further education. She had, after all, rarely been into the castle library. Yet even she would admit stood among the thousands of scrolls that the place was impressive.

She walked the criss-crossed corridors made up of shelves. Each one filled with endless scrolls and leather-bound tombs, stretching on and on, up and up. All placed in sections, each one labelled. At the end of each intersection were mounted lists that displayed what was in each. She was quite impressed how well organised it all was.

It seemed to take an age to traverse and at one point she actually became a little lost in the damned maze, but in the end, she found what she was looking for. There, sat at a ridiculously oversized desk littered with scrolls and inks and quills sat the man she had come in search of.

"Sir Bolevard of House Bront," she said in her sweetest, most seductive voice. He looked up from his desk. His face held an expression she recognised. It was a mixture really, of part pride at hearing the sound of his own name, which told her quickly of this man's weakness but also disgust that anyone should dare to interrupt him. She knew immediately his temper was short.

"It's Master Bolevard, if you please," he said with a sneer.

"Of course," she replied with a respectful nod and short curtsy, best to show respect even if it was feigned. She knew this type of pompous, arrogant old man. She'd known it all her life. Besides, one didn't become Scroll-Master without being incredibly boring, ridiculously finicky and ludicrously content in his own company. She had not expected a warm welcome.

"What do you want? If you search for a scroll then ask one of the disciples or aids, they will assist you."

She smiled a smile that held something special in it. A smile that said, 'I know something, and you'll want to know it.' Bolevard Bront was apparently no fool. He recognised that smile instantly. He sat back in his chair, eyes narrowing as he studied her.

He put down his quill and folded his arms across his chest; still, Celia noticed, quite a large chest. Bolevard Bront had been a knight once and of quite the reputation. Though she could not remember the exact details, Celia recalled a story about him fighting off three men at once. He took a sword through the hip and still managed to finish off the last of them with his bare hands. Something along those lines at least.

She knew for certain that he was promoted into the king's own company afterwards. Perhaps it was the sword being pushed through him that made him see the life of a librarian as appealing.

"Out with it then," he said with the same half grin half snarl. "Say whatever it is you have come to say. You obviously haven't come for a scroll, and you certainly haven't come for the conversation."

She stood before his desk, walking along its considerable length, dragging a finger across the old leather top.

"How well do you know your library, Master Bolevard?"

She saw the flicker at the corner of his eye. She had to be careful. This one was easily angered. Pride, it seemed yet again, was a weakness to be exploited. But her choice of words was right. On the cusp of an insult but with more than enough intrigue.

"Like the back of my hand," he declared with the utmost confidence. "I have organised it myself. I've been Scroll-Master for several years and I have turned this place from a rabble of confusion into the near perfect source of information you see before you."

Oh yes, a great deal of pride.

"Put it this way then," she said with a seductive smile. "How well do you know the secrets this place contains? Are there perhaps scrolls that you do not know about?"

He smiled again, confident of himself. Overconfident.

"Let me take a guess at this. You believe you know of scrolls that I do not. Could you perhaps be talking about the king's vault?" The sarcasm in his voice was so overdone, she almost laughed.

"Oh, so you do know about it?"

"Of course. Now if this is all you've come here with then be gone! You're wasting my time."

"So, you must know about the scrolls the king removed from the vault? The ones he does not trust even to that place. The ones he keeps in his own personal chambers?"

Bolevard's eyes grew wide before narrowing to slits. Not only did he not know but he hungered for them. She saw a glint in his eye and knew her information was correct. The Scroll-Master had been looking for something, perhaps something that those scrolls could offer.

"And how would you come across information such as this?"

She took a few steps away from the desk, feigning interest in some of the other random scrolls, all a ploy to draw out the moment, to add to his hunger. Finally, when she felt he had suffered enough, she spoke, apparently absent minded.

"Oh, I come across these things from time to time."

"I'm sure you do." The patience had gone from his tone. Celia knew she was on the point of losing him. His arrogance would block all other senses if she were not careful. She decided on a different tack. A rare show of honesty, mixed with a little flattery.

"I can see you're not a man to be fooled with, so I'll tell you the truth. I make it my business to know the little things that people don't want others to know." Now she turned her eyes on him. Cold eyes every bit as intimidating as his own. "I know that you have spent much of your time looking for scrolls that mention the Gift. I know you've been secretly taking some and keeping them for yourself. I know that despite the king seeking your personal help in finding these scrolls, you betray his trust and keep them for yourself."

She could see the twitch of anger at the corner of his mouth. He even had the decency to show a hint of fear.

"Oh, come now, Scroll-Master." She couldn't keep the seductive grin from her lips. This was a game she thrived upon. "Surely you're not so naïve as to believe that people don't have eyes in your library? That all of your disciples and aids hold some complete sense of loyalty to you?"

"I would wager more of them report to others than report to you. How much are your apprentices paid? How much would it take to buy them? How many others may seek information from this great place of knowledge?" She held up a hand to ward off any response.

"I won't ask why you want to know about the Gift. Instead, I will tell you what I want to know. I want to know where the king has gone and why?"

Bolevard sat up a little straighter in his chair which was almost as oversized as the desk. He clasped hands together leaving his forefingers in a steeple, touching them to his nose whilst peering over the top of them, his eyes narrowed to a glare. He was assessing her. Trying to figure her out. Good luck.

"So, you're telling me about the king's secret scrolls in exchange for what?"

"I want to know why the king has left. Fallow Hold was taken by the Sile. The kingdom is in uproar. The Southern Warden has been called back to the Centre and the king himself has all but disappeared. What is happening that we are not being told about?"

She didn't even mention the fact that a dead body had been brought from the north apparently killed by a Valfarg. This was information she was saving.

"And you believe I know such things?"

"Perhaps. But if not then I believe the scrolls he keeps hidden even from you will tell us."

He drew a deep breath, standing from his oversized chair, walking around his oversized desk to stand between it and her. She had to admit he was still quite impressive despite his age.

"Why not simply take them for yourself?"

"I will, if necessary, but I thought we could work together on this one."

"You mean you want me to do the dirty work and you think you can use your knowledge about my activities as leverage."

She smiled at that. So, he did understand. "Yes. But I also see an opportunity to forge a new alliance. We both want to know what's on those scrolls, we both want to know where the king has gone and this way, we both get to wash away the façade of the loyal little helpers to the throne.

"If I know you and you know me, then perhaps in the future we can help each other. Something is going on and we're not being included, and I don't like it. I don't like anyone thinking they're better than me. Fait or otherwise."

She had made sacrifices to get where she was and saw no reason to stop now. It took a great deal to survive in the higher echelons of so-called civilised society. Celia knew. She knew all too well. It was a constant battle, clawing and scratching your way up a never-ending ladder whilst you could barely get a footing.

All the while looking out for all those others trying so desperately to climb for themselves, even if it meant climbing over you.

"And if the scrolls give no clue as to king's whereabouts?"

"The scrolls will still be yours and at the very least, we shall say you owe me one." She could tell he didn't like that, but he chose to swallow it down.

"Tell me of these scrolls and who has betrayed me," he said, after a moment of calming himself. "Then we will have a deal."

She didn't really like the cost of the deal. Giving up her spy was extra. Oh well. "Then we have a deal," she said with a grin.

They ran! Faster than any of them knew they could, through alleyways and across streets, dodging through crowds, jumping over walls and ducking beneath the stalls of the market. By the God, they even ran through someone's house. The four princes of the Fait followed the two street boys with the three men in pursuit and something had to give.

Jacob was losing pace. Luke suddenly came up behind him hoisting his younger brother into the air and practically carrying him. Aron stopped and let the others take over, so that he was at the rear of the group. If anyone was going to get caught, it should be him.

The street boys knew the city well and it was a good job, the pursuers were not giving up easily. Aron could feel his lungs burning. His legs had turned to jelly five minutes ago. He urged the others forward whilst wondering how long he could keep going.

They were hot on the heels of the two street boys, constantly looking back over their shoulder to see their pursuers. It was only the tight confines and small spaces that kept them at bay.

"This way," came a call. "Almost there."

They ran between two buildings, the alley between them narrow. The light dimmed as the sun was held back. The further they went, the tighter the gap grew until they were shimmying sideways. Luke dropped Jacob and pushed him on ahead, looking back to see the men struggling on, the stone walls closing them in.

Aron was the last in the line and felt the pressure begin to build, the rough stone cutting into his skin. He could go no further. The closest of the pursuers was right behind him stretching out an arm, clawing for him just inches away from grasping his shirt and yanking him back.

Aron stretched out his own arm, the others had passed through the other end, he stared out into the open air and felt dread. So close and yet so far.

Suddenly, a hand took his.

"Come on," shouted Luke. "Push."

Aron did so as his brother pulled at him. With a great heave, Aron fell through and out onto the dusty street. If he thought it was a tight fit into the secret hole that led to the cave, this had clarified what tight really meant. His skin was covered in scratches and cuts where he'd squeezed through. The others were all there waiting for him, cheering as he picked himself up.

The elder of the street boys went to the gap and looked back at the three men, all forced to a halt unable to make it through. The boy offered them some hand gestures and turned his rear on them, smacking at it mockingly whilst laughing.

"Come on," said the younger boy. "We best get moving."

The boys followed without argument, all savouring the respite from the chase but none quite yet ready to simply walk.

"Who are you?" demanded Luke as they jogged along, his tone showing little sign of appreciation.

"My friends call me Joe, that's my older brother, Ollie. Say hi, Ollie."

Ollie said nothing.

"Thank you," said Joshua, eyes on the back of Joe's head as he moved forward. "My name's Matthew," he said, hoping to remind the others of the plan to use fake names. So far, their grand plan to go unnoticed hadn't worked too well.

"Well Matthew, if you're grateful then maybe your little friend back there could throw one o' them gold coins our way."

"So that's your game!" snarled Luke. "You only helped because you thought you'd get paid for it."

"No," answered Joe without looking back. "We helped because you needed it and because those men back there would'a cut you open like fish if we hadn't. But if we were to get paid in the process, me and Ollie wouldn't complain, would we Ollie?" Ollie said nothing. "Besides," continued Joe. "You obviously ain't short of a penny or two. I don't think I've ever even seen gold, never mind tossed one away like it was nothing and I can see what you're going for with the clothes. They're old and a little worn but I'll tell you all now."

He stopped suddenly and spun on his heel to face them all with a sarcastic smile on his face. "Old or not, those boots you're all wearing are good leather and those stockings, those tunics? Well, you didn't get them in the old market, did ya?" He gave them a knowing look for a moment before spinning again and setting off.

Aron glanced back at his three brothers, they were all a little shocked to find their disguises and the thought behind them may not hold the genius they had thought.

"And your voices," Joe called back from over his shoulder. "You all speak proper, not like me and Ollie, right Ollie?"

The boys all looked backwards expectantly.

Ollie said nothing.

"Here," announced Joe as he began ascending a small flight of stone steps. He opened a door into a small house and beckoned them inside, checking the street outside one last time before closing the door.

"You live here?" asked Joshua.

"Yep. Me, Ollie and Mum. Just the three of us."

"You don't have a father?" asked Jacob as he jumped up onto a seat, making himself at home.

"Nope, haven't seen him in years and if I did, I probably wouldn't even recognise him. It's just us but we don't mind, do we Ollie?"

This time it came as no surprise when Ollie said nothing.

"So, what now?" demanded Luke, head peering out of the shutters on the only opening besides the door. "We're supposed to just sit here forever. We've got to get back at some point."

"Get back where?" asked Joe, earning a round of paranoid glances from the four boys.

"Nowhere," answered Luke sharply.

Joe shrugged it off. "What're ya names anyway? I got Matthew, what about the rest of ya?"

"I'm James," said Aron. "That's David and the little one is Christopher."

"Christopher, is it?" Joe replied with a smile as he walked off through a small opening. Apparently, it must have led to a pantry because he came back with two lumps of bread. He threw one to his brother and they both started eating.

Joe offered the boys an apologetic look along with a shrug of the shoulders. "We don't all have gold to throw around."

It seemed Jacob still had little idea of what he'd done wrong. All three of his brothers made a point to remember to say something when they got back. Where did he even get the gold from anyway?

"So, Christopher?" The name was stretched out with a hint of amusement. All eyes turned to the youngest in the room. He sat at the table playing with a small wooden horse that he'd found on the table top.

"Christopher," Joe called again, the smile on his lips growing. Still no reaction. The child was engrossed in his game. "Strange, how he doesn't answer to his own name."

"CHRISTOPHER!" bellowed Luke as he smashed his hand down on the tabletop. Jacob nearly fell out of his seat in shock.

"Erm, yes?"

"He was talking to you. Answer him."

"Oh, come on!" said Joe, arms flapping in the air then falling back down in exasperation.

"What?" asked Aron.

"First of all, he doesn't answer to his own name. Second, Christopher not Chris? David not Dave? Matthew not Mat? I ain't met a single kid who woulda said the names like that."

"So what?" said Luke stepping forward. "They're just names."

"Third, he's carrying gold. Gold! No one here has gold! Not even the landlords have gold in this part o' town."

"How do you know he didn't just find it?" said Joshua. "He found it and didn't know its worth."

"Well maybe he did, but as well as all that there's the fact there's four o' you. And you, James, you look about an age with Ollie. And I'd guess that you're of an age with me, Matt?"

"And why is that important?" asked Aron, feeling both nervous and oddly excited by Joe's impressive deductions.

Joe said, "Well," and was clearly enjoying himself as he took another bite of the bread and chewed on it for a while, dragging out the moment. "Our mother always likes to point out that Ollie's about the same age as Prince Aron and I'm about the same as Prince Joshua. She likes to say that in another life, we could have been friends and that me and Ollie could have grown up in a castle with everything we could ever want."

Ollie tugged on Joe's baggy shirt and made hand gestures to his younger brother whilst the other boys stared on, uncomprehending.

"That's right. We saw them once at one of the parades. They went past on horseback. The two younger ones rode with their parents. We weren't close, mind you. No chance of getting close with that crowd. But still, even from a distance I'd say you lot looked remarkably similar."

There was silence. Joe's eyes switched between each of the boys whilst they stared back at him. Three of them were wide eyed whilst the fourth had gone back to playing with a wooden horse.

The tension drew out until finally, Aron made a decision.

"All right," he said.

"Don't you dare!" shouted Luke. Aron spun on his heel, taking a threatening step closer and raising a fist so Luke stepped back.

"Don't command me! I'm the eldest. It's my decision." He turned back to Joe and Ollie. "You're right," he said, "I am Prince Aron of the Fait, heir to the throne of the Cross and these are my brothers!"

If it had seemed like Joe had been smiling before, the expression was eclipsed by what he wore now. He beamed, his mouth seeming to stretch from ear to ear. His eyes were wide with delight. Ollie clapped his hands together loudly, laughing with a mouth full of bread. Apparently having no trouble at all understanding what was being said.

"This is the best day ever!"

Luke and Joshua seemed to relax a little at that. Their two savours seemed delighted at their true identities. Aron suddenly took the middle of the room, placing one foot up on a chair. He puffed out his chest and put his fists on his hips, trying his best to look regal.

"As your prince and future king," he announced in a mockingly loud voice, "you are duty bound to obey me. I would make you my trusted aides." He looked at them with more serious eyes. "No one can know of this." These words were said with honesty and Joe nodded, Ollie too after a nudge from his brother.

"Oh, we won't say a thing, will we Ollie?"

Of course, Ollie said nothing.

Compassion

They were riding steadily south. Progress was better than any of them had dared hope for. The Angosh plains could be a tough journey at the best of times. Huge spans of open landscape, searing hot sun, mile upon mile with no source of water. Their journey was made all the more difficult whilst trying to remain out of sight. In an often-barren landscape, such a thing was all but impossible.

So far, Branthony and his Chosen Swords had barely run into trouble. They'd taken some brief detours and managed to avoid the areas where they'd be more likely to encounter a tribe but nothing that had cost a great deal of time.

Branthony knew it was good that they hadn't had an encounter yet, but he couldn't help wondering if the tribes of the Sile were not here, then where were they? The answer, he feared, was that they were in his kingdom wreaking havoc.

He didn't really know what he was expecting to find here. Then again, none of this was really expected. Debreace hadn't been sure when he told her his plan but, in the end, she came around. She was always supportive. He had no idea how he would cope without her.

Then again, he wondered if she did not have the harder task dealing with their four children alone. Yes, she was queen and would have all the help she needed but she was their mother. Raising four princes was never going to be an easy task, especially when they each had a Gift.

He could only imagine what mischief they were getting up to. He also felt absolutely rotten for his brother and the others he'd left the deal with the consequences of his departure.

He suddenly snapped out of whatever daydream he had fallen into, reigning in his horse and coming to a stop staring ahead at Malf who'd taken the lead and now held a fist in the air signalling to halt. Branthony looked past his friend. A long way in the distance, they could see the unmistakable site of a battle.

They approached slowly and cautiously, though they could all tell the threat had long passed.

"Was this a tribe?" asked John.

"Ya," answered Malf. "This was a tribe all right, but not anymore."

Bodies littered the floor. Not just men but women and children. The broken remains of tents and carts were scattered across the site. Dead animals rotted in the heat of the sun and everywhere, the foul stench of death and decay hung in the air.

"Are Sile killing Sile now?" asked String. It was common enough for tribes to fight but usually they would make challenges or the warriors would fight in duels or small-scale battles. Women and children were taken as prizes not slaughtered like animals.

There was animosity between the clans, it had always been so, and it was the reason it seemed such a miracle when Morbius Duvec united the clans but there was nothing like this.

This was a massacre, Branthony thought with horror as he inspected the site. The bodies, it seemed, were all of the same tribe. Their skin, those that could still be made out, carried markings which identified them as such. All tribes scarred or tattooed themselves in some specific way. He could only make out the markings of one tribe on the dead. It would seem this battle had been very much one sided.

"This makes no sense." Michael poked at a body with his foot. His eyes scanned the scene, and he began pacing the remains of the camp site, pointing his hand in different directions. "Look at the markings, the tracks on the ground. The footprints. I can't be sure, wind could have obscured some of the markings but if I had to guess, I'd say these people were fighting no more than three, maybe four enemies."

"Impossible," spat Malf, speaking the thoughts of all four men.

Finding such a thing had put them all on edge and when a sound was heard from nearby, they each drew their weapons in quick motions, turning as though expecting to see the spectre of Death himself.

The four men stood with weapons in hand, but no one could see a target. John had notched an arrow to his bow and pointed it side to side searching for an enemy.

"There!" cried Malf. John was one finger twitch away from sinking an arrow into it, whatever it may be.

"Wait!" cried Branthony. They all paused, as still as the corpses that surrounded them. "Just wait." This time the words were nothing more than a whisper. He crept forward, one hand stretched out with an open palm. Slowly, ever so slowly, he reached out a hand grabbing at the remains of a tent canvas.

With a deep breath, he pulled it away and there she was. A girl. A small Sile girl. She looked at him with such fear, he almost felt ashamed. *Is that what we are? Are we monsters to haunt the dreams of children?* The sound he heard was her sobbing and the fear in her eyes made him want to weep.

How strange it was to see that fear turn to something more like relief as she took in the sight of him. He knew then that he was not the monster. Oh no, the monster was long gone, and all this was what it had left behind.

He picked the girl from the ground and cradled her in his arms. So small. So delicate. So scared. He could not help but think of his own children, so defenceless against the horrors of the world.

"And what exactly do you plan to do with that?" asked Malf as he stepped to Branthony's side. Branthony had no idea. No idea at all. But one thing was certain, he would not abandon her. As he thought on that something else became all the more certain. He would find these monsters.

There was little doubt in his mind it must be the doing of the same ones that attacked Fallow Hold. How else could so few destroy an entire camp unless they could do things beyond that of normal men. The Crone may be the one behind their new powers, but they were the ones who'd carried out this attack and who knew how many others. He would find them all and make them pay.

"Leave it." That's what Malf had said, not even acknowledging her as a person, just an 'it'. Branthony hadn't liked that. The Sile had been the enemy of his people for many years but they were still people themselves, and this one was just a little girl.

"Nothing but a burden. We've not the time or the resources. What are you gonna do, carry it all the way to the Blood River and back? You're a compassionate man, Bran. That's what makes you a good king, but too much can be a bad thing. Your compassion could get you killed. Worse, it could get me killed. What if someone comes looking for her?"

He'd not argued. He'd brought Malf and the others because they were good fighting men. Men who knew how to survive and though he didn't care to admit it, strategically the advice was sound if they wanted to survive, but he couldn't do it.

He couldn't just leave her. So yes, he'd carried her. He'd fed her, clothed her, cared for her and he'd watched her improve so much, it almost brought him hope.

In the end, the others had helped, even Malf, though reluctantly. She never spoke but when they rode on the horse, she clutched at him tightly. Every time they dismounted, she seemed reluctant to let go.

Branthony couldn't help thinking of Jacob who must be a similar age to her. Their time together had taught him some lessons, but it was almost done. Malf was right, she was slowing them down and time was not on their side.

As far as Branthony could see, there was only one option. Take a risk, and if Malf had complained before, then this time he practically ignited. He'd not spoken to Branthony for two days now but still he followed. He was loyal but loyal with a frown on his face.

They approached the camp site slowly, trying their best to show they were not a threat. It was not a large camp and as they approached, they saw mainly women and children. Still, Sile women could be as dangerous as their men. As small as the camp may be, the numbers were still far in favour of the Sile. It doesn't take a strong person to stick a blade between your ribs.

Malf walked at the lead with John next, then Branthony towards the middle. Michael took up the rear, just in case. Malf spread his empty hands out wide and called out in a clear voice.

"We come peacefully! We seek help!" He spoke the Sile language, one of the more common ones at least. It seemed almost every clan had its own version or dialect.

It was one of the females who stepped forward with a spear in her hand and it certainly did not appear a stranger in her grip.

"Who are you?" she called. Thankfully, she spoke the language of the Cross. It had the strong accent that always seemed to come with Sile, but she was easy enough to understand.

"We are simple travellers, heading south. We came across another camp a few days ago. It had been attacked."

The woman grimaced at him, curling her lip upwards. "What does this have to do with us?" She had several other women at her back, all with spears and some with bows with arrows notched. The situation did not look good.

"There was a survivor." He looked back and Branthony stepped forward, cradling the child in his arms. He pulled down the cloths that covered her and revealed a young face, eyes gleaming with fear and uncertainty.

With the caution of a wolf, the woman approached. Even the sight of the child, who obviously did not belong in the company of these men was not enough to make her trust. She snarled at the others, and they backed away. Malf cursing under his breath, leaving the woman with Branthony and the child.

She touched a hand to the child's face. Branthony had no doubt this woman was as deadly as any he'd ever met, but once she touched the child her snarl turned to a soft smile and though it was filled with sadness, there was also a hint of happiness.

"She is no safer with us than she was in that camp back there. She needs someone to raise her. She needs her own kind."

The woman took the child from Branthony's arms, hushing and calming her with gentle rocking. Though the child hesitated, she leaned into the embrace.

"And what are your kind?" she asked. "You are men of the Cross. Why do men of the Cross care for a Sile girl?"

He drew a deep breath and let it out again, a sad smile on his face. "Men of the Cross don't love the life of war as much as you may have been led to believe. We prefer peace. We wish to watch our own children grow. I do not think the Sile are the monsters many men of the Cross believe them to be, and I do not think we are the monsters you believe us to be."

She looked down at the child in her arms then back to Branthony, then past him to the others.

"There are true monsters enough in this world for us all to worry about, but I do not believe they are here today. Will you eat with us, in gratitude of saving the little one's life?"

All eyes looked to Malf as though the decision lay with him. This was the arranged plan. Either he thought the same as his king or he saw something in Branthony's eyes that gave him his answer.

"Aye," he said. "One night, then we're off. We've already fallen behind."

"Good," said the king of the Cross as he turned back to face the clan woman of the Sile. "It would be our pleasure."

She nodded, stepping back towards the waiting crowd of her own people but without taking her eyes from him.

"My name is Milun-of the-Sun, you may call me Milun," she said. "And for tonight, we are at peace."

The sun had set, and fires had been burning for several hours. A meal of fresh stew was served that tasted as good as any the men had ever had. Funny how a few weeks of rations and mostly dried bread could change things. The mood about the camp had been tense, not many words had been spoken between the Sile and the four strangers who shared their hospitality.

Most people had gone to bed. John took the watch. They all found it hard to place complete trust in the Sile. Branthony knew he should sleep. He knew how much he needed to rest. They were going to have to ride hard to make up for lost time, but sleep is often hard to come by for men with troubled minds and Branthony's was more troubled than ever.

He'd been raised with the weight of a kingdom on his shoulders. He'd always known pressure, expectation and most of all, fear of failure. He'd led his men to war, there was no greater test. But he'd rarely felt so troubled. Something about all this was different. The Gift had always been his ally. The tool of his bloodline to be used to rule. Now, for the first time it was being used against him. Seeing Fallow Hold for himself and then the Sile camp had proved to him how powerful this new threat was. He must find a way to stop them and most importantly, the one who empowered them.

It's funny how a man can become so lost in his own mind that he forgets the world around him. Branthony startled as Milun came to sit beside him and together they stared into the fire in silence for what could have been an age. He glanced to her in the firelight. She had the olive skin so common in Sile. Her head was shaved, and her shoulders were tattooed with the markings of her clan.

Finally, Milun spoke. "The girl will be safe with us," she said. "For now, at least."

He wished he could believe her but in times such as these, he knew promises like that were dust in the wind. Her carefully chosen words were not missed. Unless he could stop it, his own people would soon be marching down into these plains once again and his people were obviously not the only threat now. It was not men of the Cross that had wiped out the girl's clan.

"Do you know what happened to Morbius Duvec?"

"My guess is he met the same fate as the camp you came across. The same fate as all those who have defied the new leader."

"You saw him?"

"I did. Pray that you never do." She looked out past the fire to a young boy asleep beneath the stars. There was love in her eyes. "That is my son, Kelam-of-the-Beasts. He will be a clan leader one day. I am sure of it. I am lucky to have him. Those monsters took most of the men, but my son was too young.

"One day, they will be back for him. Morbius was his hero. They met once, on the day of the Ninth Sun, when all the clans came together. A glorious day. Now Morbius is dead, and all his work is undone. His camp was the first to fall. Those that did not die and could not escape were the first to be forced into the monster's new army."

Branthony could think of nothing to say. All he knew was he needed to end all this soon before it could cause more carnage.

"They say your king has magic," said Milun, her eyes now back on the fire. "They say all the Fait carry magic in their royal blood but the King of the Cross, my people tell stories of him. Great stories. He is revered amongst my people, perhaps as much as his own.

"They say he cannot be defeated in battle. That he is the greatest warrior ever seen. Morbius united the clans, he is the hero of the Sile but the King of the Cross is almost a legend to them. He defeated Morbius. Tell me, man of the Cross. Is your king's magic stronger than the monsters?"

Branthony drew a deep breath. He'd never really considered how he was viewed among the Sile. It was strange to hear her talk of him in such a way.

"I do not know," he answered truthfully. "But I have a feeling that we will soon find out."

A New World

They stood at the edge of the gardens. Not far away was the tree that contained the secret passage. It led into the old tunnel that would take the children back into the castle grounds. No one would ever know it was there. It would take, they all believed, a great deal of luck for someone to discover it. After all, isn't that what lead them to the discovery, a great deal of luck. All four boys felt assured the secret was theirs.

Soon they would lift the hidden trap door and descend the rope returning to their normal lives. They were, one and all, quite upset about it. They'd spent another day with Ollie and his younger brother Joe. There'd been as many as the boys could manage over the last weeks and it seemed that each was better than the last.

Ollie and Joe had supplied clothes, it was obvious to the Fait boys once they changed that the clothes they'd chosen for their earlier cunning disguises were not quite cunning enough. The clothes were old, yes but not like the clothing that would be worn by those who lived in the further reaches of the city.

Also, the boys took to using the abbreviated versions of their chosen fake names. Again, that was a part of their plan that they had perhaps not thought out entirely. In fact, it wasn't just the names they'd chosen but the way they talked in general that had been the problem.

They'd decided it was best to say as little as possible, let Joe do the talking for them since he seemed to be used to that. But when they did talk, they tried to imitate him. It was harder than they'd thought.

So with clothes that matched, names that didn't stand out and an attempt at talking that wouldn't draw attention, the boys had set out. They had, of course, avoided any areas where they might be pursued again. Joe led the way with Ollie always at the back, the four princes between them and they explored the city. They made jokes that Ollie and Joe were the royal guard.

The Centre had always been home but for the first time, the children realised they knew very little about it. This was not their world and it seemed that their titles made no difference to that.

They'd run for hours, laughing almost non-stop. Who knew it could be such fun to simply play. Other children joined in. It was the most fun any of the boys had had in a long time, especially since the accident with Corv.

The sun was on its way back down again and it was almost time to return to the castle. It turned out that when all four boys disappeared from the grounds altogether, people noticed. They'd adopted a plan of never being gone for more than a few hours and they spread their excursions out, never too many consecutive days.

It didn't exactly stop people noticing but no one had ever really been able to control them. It was obvious that mother knew they were up to something but as long as they were getting along with each other, she chose to let them have their fun. She had plenty to keep her occupied since father's departure.

The boys entered the gardens and made their way to the tree that would take them back to the castle, back to the world of princes.

Aron turned to Ollie and proclaimed, "Once I'm king, I'll fling open the gates and welcome you inside." Ollie smiled and the two clapped hands.

All of the boys had never been short of interaction with the common people of the city. Aron had spent the last months working in the stables with boys who may well live near Ollie and Joe. They had in fact talked about the possibility of being recognised. This though was different.

One day Aron would be king of the Cross, and he was playing out in one of the poorest areas of the city with boys he would truly call his friends. It was almost hard to say goodbye each time. They'd spent most of the day hidden away at some old, abandoned buildings, the city was crammed even more than usual so they'd decided to stay out of the way. Even so they'd had fun, and it was a shame it had to end.

They found the tree, climbed down into the tunnel locking the trap door behind them. They lit the torches they'd hidden there and made their way back to the small hole that led back out into the old garden. Even this was now even more concealed. Each of the boys paid a quick glance to the entrance of the crypts. They all hoped they'd never have to go down there again.

It seemed only sensible to adopt a policy of never returning using the same route. No one knew the castle better than them, all the servant passages, the so-

144

called secret passages, the gaps in the walls, the small holes no adult could squeeze through. They knew them all and used them well.

This time, they thought it best to go straight back to their rooms. Yes, someone would have checked them but they could think of plenty of excuses why they weren't found. 'Hide and seek' they would simply say.

They climbed up one of the small outer towers, shuffling inside through a broken section of roof, balanced their way across the rafters then used an old servants' passage to get deeper into the castle, from there it was a simple matter of making their way upstairs.

Each of their rooms had a secret exit for emergencies. None of the boys were supposed to know of them but what self-respecting young boy doesn't find a secret passageway in his own bedroom?

They split up and went to their own rooms, Joshua and Jacob shuffling off together as they still shared. They went inside and Joshua went to the door and peered out into the passageway. It was empty, strange but fortuitous.

"No one there," he said as he closed the door.

"They must be off looking for us," said Jacob, pushing himself up onto his bed.

"No doubt a nurse will come barging in any minute now and take us to Mother."

He climbed onto his own bed and lay down, feeling a little tired after the day's excursions. He wasn't sure if he fell asleep. When there was a knock on the door, he braced himself for the fury of the nurses but when the door opened he saw only Aron staring back at him.

"Why hasn't anyone come looking?" he asked.

Joshua and Jacob replied with a simultaneous shrug of the shoulders.

Aron's head disappeared again, and the two younger brothers were quickly off their beds and out into the corridor where they saw both their older brothers who were standing looking off in both directions as though expecting a stampede to emerge from either end.

"Someone should have come by now," said Luke with his familiar frown.

As if on cue, they heard footsteps and almost stood proudly waiting for the horde to arrive with worried faces and frantic questions. Instead, they saw one serving boy emerge around the corner carrying two large jugs and wearing a panicked expression. He barely seemed to notice them as he ran past.

"What in the name of the God is going on? You! You! Stop, I demand you stop!" Luke put every ounce of authority into his voice and it seemed to work as the boy stopped and stared back at them.

"Begging your pardon, Your Highnesses but I've to report back at once."

"Report back to who?" asked Aron. "Where is everyone?"

The boy looked confused, as though they were playing a trick on him.

"At the great hall, Your Highnesses. I thought you were already there yourselves. Shouldn't you already be there?"

"We will go where we damned well please," argued Luke. "But," he added in a more agreeable tone. "If we wanted to go to the great hall, what might we see there?"

"The new guests, Your Highnesses. Lords and Ladies and knights from all over the Cross. They've come to the Centre from every Point. Every maid, servant and messenger boy is attending them. The kitchens have gone mad. Agatha's going crazy. Screaming words I ain't even heard before.

"Throwing things, kicking things. I was glad to be sent for these. It's wine from her own rooms. Said she needs it before she kills someone, and I believe her."

The boys glanced to each other. Agatha killing someone would not at all be surprising.

"Why are they all here?" asked Joshua.

"All I know is there's talk of war. They're looking for 'ya father, the king."

"I should go," said Aron, taking a step forward. "As the future king, I should be there."

"Oh yeah," said Luke mockingly. "I'm sure they'll all just go back home and relax once they know future king Aron is there. Nothing else to worry about, eh?"

Aron turned back to his brother. His face snarled with anger.

"If I was any of you, Your Highnesses," said the servant boy, interrupting what may have been about to turn into a fight. "It's packed in worse down there than pigs in a pen and its far uglier. Not one of em is making sense and they all just seem to wanna scream at each other. I think I'd stay in my room tonight."

It was, they all agreed, very good advice.

The ensuing chaos that arrived with the visitors to the centre lasted through the night. The boys stayed together in Joshua and Jacob's room, it sat highest in the castle tower and so seemed the safest. They'd sat and talked about their adventures beyond the castle grounds, already planning their next excursion. Aron kept questioning whether he should go down and try and help. Each time, Luke mocked him but not with any viciousness.

The next morning, they woke early at the sound of Aron's screams. His nightmares interrupting sleep once again. It seemed almost normal to be woken in such a way, so after a moment of calming himself and an apologetic smile, they all rolled over again and went back to sleep.

Even Aron managed to fall away again, which was rare after his nightmares had woken him. It was well on its way to midday before they were woken again which was testament itself to how busy everyone must have been. There was a quick and harsh knock on the door before the nurses and servants came flooding in, all of them looking like they hadn't slept a wink.

"Come, children. Come now. Up. Up! Up! We're late. We're so late! No! No, Prince Jacob," called the nurse as Jacob began grabbing clean clothes. She wasn't one of the usual nurses that came to wake them. "Only Prince Aron is to dress in his finest today." Aron frowned whilst the others were relieved. "The rest of you clean yourselves up. Your uncle, Prince Christopher is awaiting you."

The maids weren't lying when they said they were late. The children were rushed like they'd never been rushed before; less than twenty minutes later, they were ushered into one of the minor halls where Uncle Christopher waited, standing over a table looking down at scrolls with a frown.

The Scroll-Master was with him and scowled at the sight of the children. He obviously took their arrival as his signal to leave, He rolled up several scrolls, tucking them under his arm and made for the door, giving the required respectful bow of the head as he passed the princes but saying nothing.

The Scroll-Master was one of those people living in the castle that the children actively avoided. He was almost as scary as Kitchen-Master Agatha. The difference was that Agatha always seemed angry. She didn't hate people, she was just in a constant bad mood, but the Scroll-Master seemed to despise everyone. The children always said that when he looked at them, it seemed as though he wanted to hurt them. They'd all agreed long ago that avoidance was the best course.

"Good morning, children," said Uncle Christopher, leaving the table and its contents behind him as he walked towards them. It was a shame as they all wanted to know what he was looking at. "I am afraid things are going to be quite hectic around here for the foreseeable future. Events dictate." He sighed with the words. "I wanted a moment with you all to explain so that you are aware of what is happening. A lot will be expected of you. You are princes of the Cross, after all."

"You don't have to explain," said Luke, shrugging his shoulders, always the self-assured one. "We know what's happening. We're at war again. The Lords have come looking for answers. They want to know where our father has gone."

Christopher looked down at them all with a grin. He was not used to dealing with children.

"You're right," he said. "They've come to demand answers. Some they will get. Some they will not."

"You won't tell them where Father has gone?"

"No Luke, I will not, and by I, I mean we." They all nodded, remembering their talk with Father before he left. "I wanted to reiterate how important these coming days will be. The lords and ladies who have come here are powerful people. They will question you. Demand answers from you but whatever you do you must not tell them where your father has gone."

"They would not understand. They think mainly of themselves and their own problems. They do not consider the larger game at play. Your father is doing what he must to protect us against more than the Si—" He didn't finish the word. Instead, he paused, his eyes focused on his eldest nephew. "Aron, are you alright?"

Aron had gone white. He reached out a hand to a nearby chair to steady himself. The others heard his breathing now. Quick, sharp breaths.

"Aron, what's wrong?" asked Christopher.

"I'm not sure," he said, his head whipping from side to side, eyes darting to every corner of the room as though searching for something. "I feel funny but I don't know—" he didn't finish the sentence. Instead his searching seemed to find a target as his eyes fixed on the door.

"Someone's coming," he said as all eyes in the room followed his, just as they all fixed on the door. Aron turned away from it once more to lock eyes with his uncle. "Aunty Karin is here," he said with a sudden smile. All the panic was gone. He now looked like a happy young boy once more. "And she's having a baby," he said merrily.

Christopher leaned down to one knee so he could better look Aron in the eye. He gently placed a hand on each shoulder, when he spoke it was with a soft voice.

"Aron, did someone tell you that?" Aron shook his head. Christopher continued. "First of all, you should know you are not in trouble. You have done nothing wrong. Do you understand?" This time, Aron nodded. "I want you to think about how you know that. Think about it and tell me anything else you can. Anything at all."

"I'm not sure," Aron answered honestly. "I remember her coming. She walked through the door." He gestured at the door behind them and once again, everyone glanced towards it. "She came through. She was wearing a green dress with a golden necklace, and she was holding her belly. She looked so happy."

At that moment, the door swung open and sure enough, there she was. Karin entered the room with a smile, saying hello before suddenly stopping. She looked at her husband and her four nephews as they all looked back at her with wide eyes. "Have I interrupted something?"

Sure enough, she was wearing a green dress with a golden necklace. "Not at all," said Christopher as he went to her, hugging her and kissing her cheek. "In fact, your timing was excellent."

"Oh? Why is that?"

"Because," he said, waving a hand towards the children. "Aron has just controlled his Gift."

The others all looked to him, finally understanding what had just happened. Aron, for some reason, looked at his hands as though they would show some sign of his new talent. All the others had used their Gifts before, even if it was mainly by accident. He'd never really been able to use his, but it all made sense now.

He'd seen his aunt enter the room before. It must have been in one of his dreams. For the first time in a long time, Aron felt a sense of excitement about his Gift. It was the first time he'd used it without causing some sort of trouble and it meant not everything he saw in his dreams was bad. For once, he felt good about it. Perhaps, Foresight might come in handy after all.

Suddenly, the thought of facing down the lords and ladies of the realm didn't seem as daunting.

Tell Me of the Gift

They came across the first trickling of water days ago, following it down the ravines it had spent centuries cutting through. Slowly but surely, those small flows of water joined together to form a river. At first, it had been calm and slow moving but it quickly became a raging torrent.

They followed its course and now finally, they had reached their destination. Branthony knew time was running short. He'd already cost them too much by delivering the young girl to a new clan. He did not regret his decision, he simply needed to make up for it.

"Why do they call it the Blood River?" asked Michael.

"Yeah," added John, "I half expected the water to be red."

"It bloody will be if you two don't keep it down," hissed Malf. "Look, there's smoke up ahead, a camp maybe?"

"It's a village," stated Branthony with certainty. "It's the one we've been looking for."

"How can you know that?" asked John, standing on tiptoes and stretching his neck upward searching for a better view. "We've never come this far south, not even with an army at our backs."

"I can feel it," came the answer. He'd not mentioned it to the men, knowing they would only question him and not understand, but he'd felt something inside himself over the last weeks, growing as they got close to the river. A strange feeling pulling him forward as though hooked into his very skin.

Right now, his chest pulsed, his fingers tingled, his tongue felt thick within his mouth. He knew without doubt this was his destination. The answers he was searching for were here.

"Look," said Malf pointing forward. Several figures were approaching, led by an ageing man. His skin was pale despite the ever-present sun and his beard as white as snow. He leaned heavily on a long staff and Malf almost had to laugh at the cliché image. "Is this the wise old leader come to greet us and offer his

150

wisdom?" Despite his sarcasm, Malf's hand went to his sword as John pulled his bow from his shoulder.

"No," commanded Branthony holding up a hand to stay his men. "These people are no threat to us. These are the ones we've been seeking."

"They look like Sile to me," said Malf.

"They are Sile, in a way."

"Then wouldn't that make them our enemies?" He didn't get a reply. The two groups now came face to face in a silent standoff. Malf took the lead, expecting the same charade as before, feigning his authority to protect the king but the old pale man looked past him, eyes locked with Branthony's.

"Welcome, children of the Cross and a special welcome to you, King Branthony of the Fait. We have been expecting you."

Charades would do them no good here, it seemed. Malf swallowed hard and wondered if his earlier words of a wise leader had just gone down his throat.

Even with their father absent the audiences continued, and Aron was still expected to attend some. He had promised he would do all he could to help whilst his father was away. Aron intended to keep that promise. He wanted to prove to father that he could be trusted. That he wasn't just some foolish child. He'd even used his Gift properly now and couldn't wait to tell his father all about it.

Aron sat in the small chair beside the empty throne whilst his uncle Christopher sat in the larger chair at the bottom of the Dias. His uncle handled most of the work, but Aron tried to listen and learn. As heir to the throne, it would one day be him making these judgements.

When his father had first disappeared, the meetings had been lively but consisted of just a few extra voices. Now, the hall was filled to bursting with stern faces. Everyone seemed to have something to say, and everyone thought they should be heard.

Normally, one person or one group would be admitted at a time for the king or his representative to pass judgement, but these were all lords and ladies or other people of power and reputation. Making any wait in favour of others could cause offence and tensions were already running high. In an attempt to placate them, Christopher had simply opened the doors.

It seemed to Aron that each and every occupant was determined to give it their best attempt to be heard, screaming at each other across the room. The jumble of raised voices as everyone tried to overpower the rest only ensured the opposite. Aron couldn't help but wonder if this is what it sounded like when he and his brothers argued.

He saw his uncle rubbing at his temples as the arguments in the room spilled into chaos. If there was meant to be some resemblance of order, it had long since disappeared. Aron knew his uncle was smart. The smartest man in the entire Cross or so his father would say, but Uncle Christopher was not a forceful man.

If his father were here now, Aron knew he could silence the entire room with little more than a stare and a growl. Alas, there was no king to calm the masses and so the different lords and ladies, knights and Masters, Warden Representatives and the God knew who else bickered amongst themselves.

Aron tried his best to listen, but it was hard to make any sense of it. One thing was easy to decipher though. The kingdom was under attack. The new leader of the Sile had struck again, this time even deeper into the Cross.

One question kept repeating itself and finding a clear voice even amongst the rabble. "Where is the king?"

It was Lord Richard Dawsel that seemed to be trying hardest to keep the crowd at bay. He was an ally in this crowded room and a well-respected figure in the kingdom.

"The king's whereabouts cannot be disclosed at this moment, but rest assured he is working to resolve this matter. He would never abandon his people. As king and as a Fait, he knows better than any what must be done."

"He should be here," cried a voice. Aron didn't even bother trying to pick out who it came from. He recognised few of the faces before him. Father always told him to watch, learn and to decipher as much as he could about each and every individual.

Aron had come to a similar conclusion about many of the people before him. They were opportunistic and greedy and despite their words about the kingdom and their people, most were here for themselves.

One person that Aron found particularly interesting was Lady Celia. The women in the room were few and far between and few of those had as much power and influence as her. As representative of a Point Warden, it made Celia Trone one of the most powerful women in the Cross.

The reason that Aron found her so interesting was because she had one of the quietest voices in the room, certainly one of the smallest frames but unlike most of her counterparts, she didn't constantly try to force herself on the conversation. When she did speak, she had a way of making everyone listen and although she spoke rarely and quietly, it was she, Aron noticed, that most often got what she wanted.

The other thing he noticed was that no one else seemed to notice. She waited. She watched. She listened. When she chose to speak, she seemed to twist the words of those around her, it was almost funny. He could see the confusion on people's faces as she spun their own words back at them.

He would swear she completely switched people's opinions in one sentence, forcing them to suddenly defend what they were moments ago attacking and then scratching their heads wondering how exactly it happened.

Aron saw her sit a little straighter in her chair. She was, of course, one of the only people still choosing to sit. The motion alone seemed to notify people that she was ready to speak and despite the complete lack of manners they showed to almost everyone else in the room, they quietened for her. It wasn't silence but it was enough.

"Why is it," she began, "that we are all here, in this hall, arguing amongst ourselves whilst our kingdom is attacked. Wasting time and effort when lives are at stake? Why is it that so many of you cower away from the threat of so-called magic when we are a kingdom governed by a family who have long since displayed abilities far beyond normal men? This new leader of the Sile is but one man, we have an entire family. Do none of you trust the Gift? Do none of you trust the Fait?"

Aron liked Lady Celia more and more, especially after that. He'd heard these so-called loyal lords and ladies say terrible things in his father's absence. It was no secret that the rule of Branthony Fait the Second had been one of the grandest ever.

He had brought peace to the Cross, brought about new alliances and trade negotiations and set the kingdom on a path of incomparable good fortune. Yet these people spoke about him as though he were a failure. Aron would even go so far as to say some spoke of him as a traitor, as though by bringing peace with the Sile, he had betrayed those that had died against them.

Lady Celia, it seemed, held faith.

"We would trust the Fait if the king were here!" The tone of Lord Basel, filled with authority, he was not a man to be trifled with and not an easy man to get along with. Aron had come across him before and decided he didn't much like him. "The king is not only the leader of the Cross, but he is also the leader of the Fait. A leader does not abandon his people in a time of crises. It is not right!"

"How many times must you be told he is acting in our best interests?" Lady Celia stood, and it seemed everyone else stepped back. She eased towards Lord Basel and held his eyes without a shred of doubt. "You and your banners belong to the Western-Point, Lord Basel. Your Warden has told you to hold faith. You would not listen to him and now you come here to the Centre and will not listen to anyone. I understand why. You are afraid."

He bristled and tensed with indignation but Celia quickly continued.

"Your fear, Lord Basel, comes from your lack of understanding. You do not understand this new enemy and that is why your legs shake when you speak of him." It was not hard to see Lord Basel's anger at the comment. "That same lack of understanding extends to the Gift and therefore, the Fait.

"You cannot understand them, so perhaps you should fear them and watch the words you speak against them. And if you cannot possibly comprehend the Gift then why should the king explain himself to you?"

"Because he has a responsibility. He cannot simply disappear. If he is not up to the task, then a new leader must be found. Appoint a general, someone to take charge in his absence at the least. If nothing more, we should assemble the armies."

"He left people in charge. Sir, I almost weep at your idiocy!" Celia circled him now and everyone else in the room listened. It was the quietest Aron had noticed the hall in weeks, let alone today. "There is no one better equipped to lead this kingdom or fight this enemy.

"I would be wary Lord Basel. Some could take your words as treason. As for the kings so called disappearance, it is no such thing. He has told those closest to him where he has gone and left what he believed to be sufficient leadership in his stead.

"I for one trust Prince Christopher. Does he not have the Gift of Knowledge? His is a superior mind. Or do you think you own intelligence greater than his?"

Lord Basel's eyes dashed to Christopher then around the room, instantly taking in the faces of those around him and gauging their reactions to Lady Celia's words. He knew he must choose his own very carefully.

"With all due respect to the prince, his Gift did not help him keep Fallow Hold. Now he is placed in charge of the entire kingdom, and you ask for faith."

Aron glanced at his uncle and saw him wince at the mention of Fallow Hold and he felt a pang of deep sympathy. His father always said that the deaths of men close to you, especially those under your command, weigh heavy on your heart. He knew the deaths in the south would weigh heavy on his uncle.

If not for that sudden guilt, he thought his uncle would shout out. Despite Lord Basel's high station, those were strong words and Aron felt an urge to speak up for his uncle. He stood from his chair.

"My uncle did a better job than anyone else could have done!" He shouted the words and felt almost shocked at how loudly they passed over the hall. All eyes seemed to turn on him and he felt his confidence waver. That was until he locked eyes with Lady Celia whose reassuring smile gave him new strength. "And my father will return soon to deal with the Sile and this new leader. Whoever he is, whatever he can do, it is nothing compared to my father."

He looked back to Lady Celia searching for approval. Her smile gave it and she took it as her cue to retake the attention of the room. Aron was glad for it.

"Prince Aron is right, once again proving why the Fait rule this kingdom and why he will one day make a great king."

Lord Basel swallowed a little of his pride, offering a respectful nod to Aron before saying in an altogether more agreeable tone. "Of course, His Highness trusts his own family, especially his father. But we need more than the words of a child. Prince Christopher lost Fallow Hold. Princess Susan has chosen to turn away from her Gift despite all it could do, and the king is not here! Surely you see how our faith could be swayed."

There were mumbles of agreement from all around the room.

"Then what of the children. Four children? Is it not said that this should be a great time, four children of the Fait born to one generation. Four boys. Four Gifts."

"Children is the optimal word, Lady Celia. Their Gifts are beyond their control. No use in a time of war. As lords of the land, it is our duty to ensure the safety of our people. We cannot simply take it on faith that the king will return on time."

The mumbles came again but this time sounded ever so slightly weaker.

"A duty to the people," Celia barked a laugh. "Lord Basel, since your arrival here I have seen you speak to no one but the other lords and ladies of the Cross. Meanwhile, there has been one person addressing the actual people and telling them they are safe despite all of you giving opinions to the contrary. Whilst we sit here and squabble, she has been out there in the real world reassuring the people of this city and this kingdom that they are safe."

In that moment, as though the whole thing was planned out and timed to perfection, the doors to the hall swung open. Aron watched as his mother entered the room. She had a steely firmness to her. She looked different. He knew that face. It was the face she wore when he and his brothers were in trouble. He had a feeling his mother was still far away. These people were not to deal with her today. Today, they would deal with the Queen of the Cross.

Branthony and his Chosen Swords entered the village. Though he'd spoken correctly, and these people were Sile in many ways, it became quickly evident that they were different. For a start, this was actually a village. These people were not nomads.

They remained here in this place beside the Blood River. This much was obvious by the dwellings. Different tents and canvases set up beside each other becoming a network of interlocking homes.

The old man who had greeted them seemed to be in charge and yet there was little chance that he was the strongest warrior. If this was any other clan, a younger warrior would have challenged him for control and no doubt won. In normal Sile clans, even the young walked the camp in streams of bluster and pride, each already trying to show themselves as the fiercest and strongest.

Even at a young age, those boys likely dreamt of one day becoming clan leader. Perhaps they dreamt of one day becoming another Morbius Duvec. There was no such bluster here. There were full grown men, boys of all ages, and yet none seemed to walk with the defining aggression of most Sile. None looked like fighters.

Malf and the others had an edge to them. If the old man expected them to lower their guard simply because he had somehow known they were coming, he was sadly mistaken; if anything it only made them warier. With the look of the men here, the Chosen Swords fancied themselves to cut through the entire village if the need so required and they would do so without a second thought if it meant protecting their king. That is why they were chosen.

Branthony could feel the tension. It wasn't like the first camp they'd entered. There they felt the understandable apprehension of being intruders, men of the hated enemy suddenly imposing themselves. This was different. There was something hard to explain, yet impossible to miss. It was as though something was expected of him but he had no idea what.

"Please," said the old man. "Sit. Rest. You must be tired. Allow your horses' some water. I am sure they have been pushed hard and you will no doubt wish to return to your home as soon as possible."

"Who are you?" spat Malf. "And how did you know we were coming?"

"I am Graf. I am the elder of this clan." His words carried a thick accent but it proved no difficulty to understand. "And I didn't know you were coming. I knew he was coming."

Graf nodded at Branthony, as the king knew he would. This wasn't premonition. He now understood the feeling that had been growing within him. Understood may be an overstatement, but at the least it made some kind of sense to him. He had sensed these people here and now realised that they must have sensed him in turn.

"I have come seeking answers." It seemed best to get straight to the point. The tension in his men did not seem to be decreasing.

"You have come to the right place. But you knew that already. We have felt your approach. We are connected, surely you feel it too."

"I do," he answered, earning another sharp stare from Malf, his friend wondering just when in the hell he would find it appropriate to mention this little fact.

"It has been far too long since the Fait came here, since they drank from the Holy River. We feared we may never see your line again."

Now Branthony was a little lost again, yet it felt that now wasn't the time to admit to such. If his family had been here before, he had little idea which member it was or even how long ago. What were Graf's words? "Far too long." It seemed there was little need for him to voice his lack of knowledge out loud. Graf frowned at him, his eyes sinking deep into his wrinkled forehead.

"You do not know of us?" It was a simultaneous question and statement full of sadness.

"I have come to learn."

"Good. There is much to teach."

Aron walked from the hall, aghast. He'd never seen anything of the like before. No, that was wrong. He had seen it before and that's what made it all the more amazing. He'd just watched his mother as she stared down the lords and ladies of the Cross as though, well, as though they were naughty children, and he knew exactly how that felt.

He'd just not seen grown men cower like scorned children. She didn't even pretend to listen to their bickering. She took control and commanded the room.

It had taken her less than an hour to bring the whole room to agreement. Aron heard his uncle say it wasn't an agreement that would last but right now, it would buy them some time and time is what they needed. Aron still couldn't believe that was his mother in there.

He would have to tell his brothers and was sure all of them would think twice the next time they crossed their mother thinking she was the easy touch compared to Father. Yes, Father would shout and scream and scare them but by the God, Mother nearly had those men curling up in balls after barely raising a decibel.

Sure, some had tried to speak up against her, but she shut them down quickly. "I am your queen," she'd said with total authority, and there were few arguments against that.

Aron quickened his step a little to get closer to his mother, she'd walked from the hall leaving the others to talk among themselves. He wondered if they were all as shocked as he was. She walked at the head of a small procession that followed her.

A small number of ladies had followed from the hall and vied for the queen's attention and wait they would, for at his mother's side was Lady Celia. Mother was thanking her for her words of support. Other ladies were trying to get their moment with the queen but none of them had spoken up in the hall.

Aron scrambled forward trying to keep up, stepping between the others, narrowly avoiding swinging arms and stomping feet. For a moment, he couldn't help but think of running through the old market. It seemed so scary at the time, being chased, fearing death, but now he couldn't help but smile at the memory. It seemed even a prince didn't matter so much when they were trying to get the attention of the queen.

He came up behind his mother and slowed his pace again. He arched his back and did his best attempts at imitating his father as he turned stern eyes on the following crowd, telling them he wouldn't be pushed back any longer. He fell in step alongside his mother, trying hard to listen in on her conversation.

"I told you." Lady Celia's voice was full of confidence. "They are nothing but snivelling, self-righteous buffoons. They would stand and argue among themselves for months, meanwhile our enemy moves as one. They need leadership and in your husband's absence, you are the rightful ruler until his return."

"You are too harsh on them, Celia. Most of them are good men, they are simply scared. As am I. But you are right. I am glad I came to you for help. We all have a duty to the Cross and arguing with ourselves only strengthens our enemy. I want to thank you, Celia, for your advice and for your confidence in me."

"I only spoke of that which I have always seen in you, Your Grace. Strength! You are mother to four boys, after all. Who could be stronger? I am sure those people in there were nothing compared to the princes."

His mother smiled at that. "Perhaps so, but children have their own rewards. Have you never considered children of your own? Your beauty is well known, your stature and position unrivalled amongst the women of the Cross, why no husband? No children?"

Lady Celia seemed to scowl at that, she looked away hiding the expression from his mother, but Aron saw it. If he didn't know her to be such a hard woman, he would think her the saddest person in the world in that one brief moment. It disappeared as quickly as it came and when she looked back at the queen, she simply wore a confident smile.

"I have yet to find a man to rival me, Your Grace. Perhaps one day. For now, I have far too much to do to worry about men. Besides, my father keeps trying to make these decisions for me. "

"I can imagine it would take quite the man to live up to you. Only a prince may be good enough," Debreace said the words as though jokingly but with a sense of seriousness. Celia's eyes flicked to Aron who stood beside her. She was technically old enough to be his mother, but the young prince was growing quick, and he seemed far older than his years, as did all the Fait children.

"Who knows if I will ever have time for such things?" She tried to make the question as lighthearted as possible, knowing full well she would make time for such a thing as a marriage to a prince of the Fait, let alone the heir to the throne.

"Well, if you are so busy, I won't keep you any longer. I thank you again, I won't forget this."

"I am here to serve, Your Grace, as is the Eastern-Point."

Celia bowed her head then stopped, the procession passing her by, her place quickly taken by one of the many followers vying for the queen's attention. She caught eyes with Aron again and grinned at him. Aron smiled back, even waving a goodbye as he followed his mother off down the corridor.

Branthony sat by the river's edge, looking out on the slowly flowing current. Not too far away where the water was knee deep men fished, casting out nets and lines. Further downstream a group of children played, splashing at each other inciting high pitched screams.

Graf was at his side, sitting on a large rock but still leaning on his wooden staff. Somewhere behind them, Branthony's Chosen Swords sat eating. Distrusting of these people they may be but not so much to turn down a fresh meal. Funny how the offer of good food can turn a man.

They'd been at the river for two days now and it was Graf who had asked most of the questions. He was desperate to know all he could about the Fait, about what they had grown into. What Gifts did they have? How powerful were they? How well could they use their Gifts?

He gasped when Branthony told him he had born four children and Graf had seemed awed when he recited their Gifts. He'd shook his head in dismay when told of Christopher's coming child and grimaced when told of the Crone. He'd asked so many questions and Branthony had tried his best to answer but now it was his turn.

"What do you want to know?" asked Graf as he looked Branthony straight in the eye.

"I want to know about the origin of the Gift and its link to this place."

"You have no knowledge of us whatsoever?"

"I am afraid that my family's knowledge of the Gift has faltered. We know little of it. There are scrolls and scriptures that tell us small things but we have been foolish and allowed our knowledge to lapse."

Graf looked back out onto the water, taking time for his own thoughts, breathing gently in through his nose. He was calm but Branthony could sense the dismay in him.

"It is not through mere foolishness that this happened. There have been forces at work for a long time now." It was hard to miss the emphasis on the word long. "Before we go any further, I must ask. After all this time, how did you come to know of us again? What led you back to the river?"

"My father," he answered simply. "I'm not sure what led him here, he passed away before he had the chance to make the journey." He didn't add that he now knows his father was murdered by the Crone. "He left me his notes and within them was the name of the Blood River."

Branthony watched as the saddest smile he had ever seen formed on the old man's face and Graf seemed as though he were fighting back tears.

"Then it seems that perhaps at least one of them finally made it through."

Branthony shifted his position on the ground to face Graf more head on. "One of who? What are you talking about?"

"The people of the Blood River and the Fait were once intrinsically linked. Over the years, we have sent messengers to try and find the Fait. To implore them to return to the river as they once did. None of the messengers have ever returned. We never knew whether to send another or not. Never knowing if the sacrifice was in vain. Now it appears as though it was not."

Branthony sat open mouthed. "How many?"

Graf shrugged his shoulders with a shake of his head. "Who knows," he answered. "Too many."

A silence fell between them as Branthony tried to contemplate this new information. He would discuss it later but there was little doubt in his mind why these messengers had not reached his family and even worse, not returned home. There was little doubt of the fate they'd met. There was only one person who benefitted from the messages never arriving. The Crone.

"Are you a man of faith?" asked Graf, breaking the silence.

"Which faith would that be? There are many faiths in this world. I have faith in my nation, my people. Faith in my family."

Graf drew in another long breath. "I do not believe in one religion or faith above another. I believe that once, long ago, this world was a very different place. The stories we tell and the gods we pray to, why do they have to be different? Could it be that the God could appear to people in different ways?"

"You're suggesting all the gods are actually the same one?"

"Hmph, I do not know such things. But what I do know is that there are great mysteries in this world. Things we cannot explain. Great powers we cannot hope to understand or comprehend. Once, these mysteries may not have been so far out of reach. I believe there was a time when the God or any version of him may have been closer to this world. You and your family are the last vestige of this time."

"Please," begged Branthony. "Do not speak in riddles. I am not the wisest man nor the most patient. I beg you, tell me what you know."

161

He prayed he hadn't come all this way to find a man who simply put everything in the hand of faith, who explained everything with mystic riddles of the God's great plan. The irony in the fact he prayed for this was not lost to him.

Graf looked off to his right, following the river's current. "Look there, tell me what you see."

He did as asked and smiled at the site of the men fishing, the same men he'd spotted earlier as they trekked out into the deeper water with their nets. He'd often wondered what his life would be like if he were not born to the crown. Would he be like these men? A fisherman, a craftsman, perhaps, a builder? Maybe in another life.

"I see fishermen," he answered.

"Look closer," urged Graf.

Branthony watched as the men lifted their bulging nets from the water. Each one was filled to bursting with fish, with some of the men even struggling with the excessive catches.

"I see damned good fishermen," he said with a smile.

"Really? Did they do something you have not seen before? Are their nets different from others you have seen?" Branthony shook his head. "Far be it from me to dispute their skills but they are not the only factors here. This is a special place. The river runs full all year round. The cattle are large and healthy. The horses fast. The people of this village thrive beyond normal men. Tell me, how old do you think I am?" Branthony shrugged his shoulders. "I have lived here in this village for over a ninety summers," he said with a smile. It grew when he saw Branthony's surprise.

"You lie," he said.

"Believe what you will but trust me when I say that is far from the strangest thing you will hear today. This place is special. The people who live here are special."

"Why?"

"You may not believe me."

"Tell me anyway."

Graf shuffled on his rock, adjusting himself.

"I asked you about faith. Almost all faiths believe in similar things. That there is a heaven and a hell, a place for the good souls and a place for the bad. I don't know which faith tells the closest stories to the truth, but I know there is truth in them."

"There is a story here among my people. Once, when the world was young, the angels of heaven waged war with the demons of hell for control of the mortal world. This war was on a scale we cannot imagine, spanning across a time we cannot fathom and in its final days, at its greatest battle, the mightiest of heaven's angels fought the deadliest of hell's demons.

"Each clash of their weapons sent out energies so vast they created the stars themselves. In the end, the two warriors summoned the last of their powers and thrust towards each other in one final assault. The demon fell back down to hell, forever dead, but the angel, the angel fell to the earth.

"He fell and he fell until he felt the rush of cold water over his skin. The battle with the demon had left the angel with great wounds. Blood ran from his body into the water."

"The Blood River," said Branthony, finally understanding where the old man was leading with his tale.

Graf sat silent again for a few moments, the wind blowing through his white hair, gently swaying the grass, the smell of the water sweet to his senses. "Imagine the power of such creatures, that their blood could hold such potency even now after thousands of years. The blood ran into the water, the water feeds the land and we feed from the animals and plants that flourish from both. The angel was injured," Graf continued without looking back at Branthony. "Near death, his blood flowed into the river as he looked up to the sky wondering if he would return home to heaven after his death. But he did not die. He was found by a woman who tended his wounds and brought him back from the brink of death. It took a long time and the angel and the woman grew close.

They fell in love and the angel decided to stay here in the land of mortals. He had children but they were different from normal men. It is said that his children decided to leave this place and explore the world beyond." Finally, Graf turned back to Branthony. "It is said they found a new home to the north, a place of great beauty. They made their home there and became rulers of a great kingdom."

Graf told the tale with wonder in his eyes and voice. It seemed almost mean when Branthony scoffed at him.

"You are telling me that my family is descended from an angel that fell from heaven."

"I am," he replied with the utmost confidence. "This is why your family and only your family carry the Gift. Your family name, Fait. Awfully close to faith, wouldn't you say?"

163

Branthony had no idea if he actually believed the story. Did it really matter? It was the future of his family and the Gift that concerned him, not the past. But one thing that Graf had said struck him.

"You say that only my family can carry the Gift, but what if someone else has it? What if magic is being used against us?"

As old as Graf was or said he was, he seemed to age further in that moment. Leaning heavily on his staff as though he may tumble at any moment and fall into the water.

"Then that would mean great danger for us all."

Always Learning

"I wonder if they're hot." Jacob stared up at the guards who stood perfectly still, the epitome of discipline. There were two, stood at either side of the doors that led to mother's chambers, her personal guards. As such, their armour was ornate to say the least, gold trim on white enamel.

Jacob's question was rather relevant. The weather had turned and they were now into the height of summer. The guards were in full armour and had to be sweating beneath the plates, though if they were uncomfortable they of course showed no sign.

The four princes all looked up at the two men whose eyes remained fixed straight forward. A nurse sat in one of the waiting chairs. She'd arrived at the crack of dawn and escorted the boys down from their rooms to be sure they attended the early morning appointment.

Apparently, people around the castle had become accustomed to the boys sneaking off and hiding somewhere, though no one was yet to find their hideaway. All four of them took immense pride in this.

"Leave them be, Prince Jacob. They are busy." The nurse sat with a straight back. Her hands clasped together on her lap.

"They don't look busy to me," he replied, pushing at a leg with his finger hoping to force some kind of movement. It was a futile effort. He could just make out the guard's eyes beneath his helm and they didn't even seem to blink.

"How long do we have to wait here?" demanded Luke, shuffling in his chair next to the nurse. He was already becoming agitated, and they'd only been waiting a few minutes. In truth, he was a little nervous. They'd been called by their uncle Christopher. Apparently, he had something to discuss with them, Luke didn't like the sound of it.

A call came from the inside and in perfect unison, the two guards shifted to the side, each pulling open one of the doors.

"Come now," said the nurse. "Inside, quickly, your mother and uncle await." She stood and ushered them in and suddenly, the wait did not seem long enough.

They went through to their mother's private rooms, the doors closed behind them, and they stood in a line, youngest to oldest as seemed so natural. Mother sat at a table, a small plate of food before her. She smiled at them, that warm comforting smile that she always had for them.

It seemed that with their mother, they were simply her children and not princes, at least most of the time. They all noticed however that she remained seated. Usually, she would greet each of them with a kiss. Not today, it seemed.

"Boys."

Eyes turned to their uncle.

He stepped forward and looked down at them. His posture was rigid, and he seemed a little uncomfortable. He opened his mouth to speak then closed it again, apparently rethinking his words. "I believe the time has come to begin active training of your Gifts."

Luke was about to say it's about time but decided against it. Aron would have hated the idea not so long ago but after the arrival of his aunt Karin, he felt a slightly renewed desire to know more about his Gift.

"So?" Uncle Christopher slowly paced a line across the boys who were stood before him. In that moment, he seemed very much like their father, although when he paraded in front of them in such a manner, it usually meant they were in trouble. This time, however, an air of excitement ran between the boys.

This was the moment they'd been waiting for. They all knew their Gifts and partially what they could do but not much more. Some of the teachers and instructors had tried on rare occasions to help but how could they when they knew nothing on the subject.

Finally, with Uncle Christopher who had experience in the Gift and even more, a Gift that should help him understand the others, they had a chance to really learn something.

"Only Aron should be showing any ability with his Gift. The rest of you should be too young. Your father and I didn't show any signs until we were in our mid-teens. But there is something different about you four. You are advancing at an unusual rate. I cannot help but think that whatever your Gifts are meant for is approaching us quickly."

The boys didn't really understand that. "Meant for." They just thought the Gift was something they were born with. Something almost everyone born into their family had. They didn't know there was something specific they were meant to do with them.

"Well then," said Christopher, clasping his hands together. "We come to it. I will address you all one by one, but you must all pay attention. There have never been four children born to one generation of the Fait. This is no accident. Your Gifts, although designed for each of you individually, are also meant to work together. This is where your greatest strength will lie. We start with Jacob."

The mention of his name made Jacob jump up and down on the spot, unable to contain his excitement. "But first a test."

Rarely could a person deflate so quickly and utterly. Jacob almost fell to the floor, his face scrunched up as he stared at his uncle. "A test!" he exclaimed in utter disappointment as though he expected parchment and a quill with written questions.

"Please Jacob, approach your mother."

Jacob sulked towards their mother with his back hunched and head held low, his bottom lip pushed purposefully out as far as he could manage. Their mother sat up straight in her chair. She smiled at her youngest son as she took his hands in hers and her face was a beam of sunshine, which forced Jacob to cheer up a little.

Their uncle suddenly stood a little straighter. He looked rigid now yet somehow more at ease. They guessed that this was the part he was actually prepared for.

"Jacob, you have been given the Gift of Truth. Each Gift has many uses. Some we know of and some we don't. The most obvious use for your Gift is that when used properly, people will not be able to lie to you. It will be impossible. So now the test. I want you to ask your mother what she had for breakfast."

"What?" he wailed. "I don't care what she had for breakfast."

"Jacob." Mother's voice was soft and delicate, so full of love that it drew her son's attention back to her and removed all the fight from him.

"All right. Mother, what did you have for breakfast this morning?"

There was a silence. Jacob stared at his mother as she stared back at him. After a long moment, she sat a little further back in her chair, keeping Jacob's hands in hers and said, "I had eggs this morning, Jacob." His face screwed up again in complete bewilderment. He turned to his brothers who all shared the look. None of them had the faintest clue what was happening.

"Anything?" Christopher asked, but the question was not aimed at Jacob but to his mother.

"Nothing much. Perhaps a flicker of a moment when I had to think. That's it. Nothing that was hard to overcome."

"What are you talking about?" moaned Jacob.

"Simple," answered his uncle. "I've asked your mother to lie to you. From now on, I want you to ask your mother the same question every day. She will always try and lie. I think you've used your Gift before but not consciously. You can't control it.

"It may have worked when you've caught people off guard, but your mother knows what to expect. She'll be trying to resist. It's up to you to beat that resistance. Do you understand?" Jacob nodded. "That's all for now. Remember, every day the same question."

"All right. Who's next? Luke, I think it's your turn. This one should be quick and easy."

Luke stepped forward with bluster, chest puffed out, head held high. "Let's do this," he announced loudly as though ready for anything. What he wasn't ready for was his uncle handing him two regular dice. Luke looked at him open-mouthed.

"Your Gift is named Fortune."

"I don't understand, they're just dice." He rolled them around in his hand, staring down at them. Two ordinary wooden, cubed dice numbered one to six.

"Yes. Now, I want to you think of a double six. Picture it in your mind and when you are ready, roll the dice."

"That's it?"

"That's it."

Luke closed his eyes, picturing the numbers. He bent to one knee and rolled the dice out across the floor. All eyes watched them expectantly. A three and a five.

"Damn it!" he shouted, earning him a hard stare from mother.

"Not to worry. Pick them up and try again. Picture the numbers. But this time, know this. If you roll a double six, then you and your brothers are excused from meetings and lessons today; if not, you will have to attend them all."

All four of the boys voiced their protests but were quickly hushed. Luke took up the dice, blowing on them as he'd seen others do to bring good luck. He really, really wanted the day off. "Come on," he whispered. "Come on!"

He rolled the dice. It seemed to take an age for them to stop and when they did, the boys' heads came together to look down on them.

"YES!" they all cried and when they moved away so their uncle could see, he stared down at two sixes. They looked to him, feeling victorious in the moment.

"All right, now go again. And this time, if you roll the same again, you all eat what you want tonight. If not, its gruel from the soldiers' barracks."

Luke looked to his brothers. They gave him thumbs up urging their encouragement. He once again blew into his hands and rolled, this time the result was met with full chorus of cheers and the boys danced around, arms locked around one another. Jacob even stood on his chair and danced in glee before sheepishly sitting back down after receiving a hard stare from Mother.

"I'm going to have cake," Luke declared, to which the others all seemed to like the sound of. Mother didn't seem quite so agreeable.

"All right," said their uncle in a serious voice, stealing their thunder right out from beneath them. "Last one. This time, if you win, you will get your own sword, made personally by the castle blacksmith. It will be all for you, Luke. Yours and yours alone."

Luke's eyes opened wide at the prospect as his brothers protested that the offer was not extended to them.

"Go on," urged Christopher.

Luke repeated his process of blowing on the dice and rolled them out. He half jumped into the air as one stopped on six then wailed in disappointment as the other came up two. "No!" he cried, falling to his knees. "Give me another chance," he begged, but the test was over.

"What does it mean?" asked Mother.

"I believe his Gift is showing but again, I don't think he can control it. It came when the prize was offered to all. I think this shows how much your Gifts are meant to be used together. That's when they're strongest. When the prize was for Luke alone, it didn't work. It responded to the needs of the many. This is a good thing."

He met Luke's eyes and talked directly to him. "We have records of your Gift before in past generations. The outcome has not always been favourable. You are already a prince of the Cross. What many people would call spoiled. Add to that the Gift of Fortune and it isn't hard to see it could create an unsavoury character."

"A spoilt brat, some might say. There have been wars between the Fait in years gone by. Wars brought on by the Gift. It's up to you, nephew, to ensure that doesn't happen."

Luke had never thought about it like that. He had so much. His time with Ollie and Joe in the outer city had shown him that. Thinking back on the way he'd acted on occasions didn't make him proud. He vowed to be better. Isn't that what Father was always trying to teach them? They must always try to rise higher.

"Joshua, you're next." The third-born stepped forward. "Your Gift is named Guidance." Joshua nodded at the already well-established fact even though he'd never really had a clue what 'Guidance' meant.

Joshua watched on as his uncle wheeled out a small table with a chess board upon its surface. Each piece upon the board was a work of art, crafted from gold and silver, flaked with black or white. Individually, they must have been worth a fortune and the full set seemed a treasure.

Joshua had to resist the temptation to reach out and touch them. Only when he stifled his movement towards them, did he notice that not all the pieces were there and the ones on the board were arranged as though halfway through a game.

"You know how to play chess, correct?"

"A little," he answered tentatively.

"Take a look at this. I am black, you are white. It is your go. I will have you in checkmate in three moves unless you protect against your king."

"But that's not fair. Start again. Why should we play when you've already nearly won?"

"This is the test, Joshua. Now, take a look and make your move."

"But all Luke had to do was roll some dice?"

"Different Gift, different test."

"And what's the reward if I do it."

"It depends if we ever get finished," said Christopher with a look of frustration that made Joshua think twice about continuing the argument.

He stared down at the board, trying desperately to decipher the threat. He'd played with his older brothers before and always lost, although he would swear they cheated. His hand drifted towards the single rook he had remaining, thinking to pull it back to protect his queen which in turn defended his bishop.

He looked up to his uncle, seeking a sign that this was the right move. He saw only a stern face looking back at him. No help there then. Tentatively, he moved the piece and dropped it to protect his queen. As quick as a flash, his uncle reached down, picked up his bishop, drifted it across the board and took Joshua's knight which he now realised had been protected by the rook.

"Your turn again. Look carefully this time. It is still possible to avoid defeat. But one more wrong move and I have you."

Joshua stared down at the board, trying to make sense of it. Looking at each piece and trying to map out all their possible moves in his head. It was too hard, too many moves to remember. His hand reached towards his other knight which was now in danger from the same bishop that took the first.

He thought to move it out of the way, at least preventing him from losing another piece. He picked it up, moved it away and then paused. Wait. There was another option. He didn't have to move the knight out of danger. He could protect it.

He put it back in its last position and instead reached for a pawn. It would not only protect the knight but also block the path towards his king from his uncle's queen. It wouldn't save him, but it would buy him time.

He looked up at his uncle and this time was met with a slight grin, it grew as he made his next move, pushing his queen across the board. Joshua immediately saw the dilemma. The enemy queen now threatened two of his pieces. Moving the pawn had opened up the path and left him in double jeopardy.

"Argh!" He threw his hands into the air, screaming his frustration. "This is impossible, you're cheating! You set me up to lose!"

It took a moment for his frustration to calm, only then did he realise his little tantrum may have gotten him in trouble. He certainly knew the price for behaving in such a petulant way in his father's presence. He tentatively looked up but was met only with the same stern stare. Apparently, Uncle Christopher had a different way of dealing with things, no less effective in this case, it seemed.

"Calm." Christopher's voice was a whisper, soothing. "Think. Don't just look at the board. Use your Gift. Let it tell you what to do."

Joshua stared down at the pieces. He couldn't see all the moves. There were too many, but he didn't have to. It came to him then. Not the move to make but the strategy. He'd been thinking about it all wrong. He moved his queen into the line of fire. Christopher swooped down and made his move, taking Joshua's queen.

"Well done." The simple words seemed the highest praise he'd ever had.

"I don't understand," said Luke. "You took his queen. You'll beat him in the next move."

"Joshua, do you care to explain?"

"You're right," he said to Luke. "He'd checkmate me in the next move but that wasn't the game. The game was survive for three moves. At first, I was trying to win but then something told me to stop. You can't always win," he said. "Sometimes, you just have to survive for long enough."

"That's right. You did well." Christopher pushed the table carrying the board over. "This is yours. I'm going to set you more challenges. I expect you to beat them."

Joshua nodded though he hadn't really listened. Instead, he stared at his new prise and knew he would cherish it. He pushed the table off to the side and joined his other brothers with their mother. That left only Aron still standing.

Uncle Christopher stepped forward and stared down at Aron who shuffled on the spot, suddenly feeling nervous.

"And so, we come to the first-born, heir to the throne and perhaps the most difficult of all to deal with because in truth, yours is a Gift we know almost nothing about. It is the rarest of them all. Your Gift is named Foresight, and I believe you have been using it for years now in some small way." The others may not have known what was coming next, but Aron did.

"Your dreams," said Mother with that warm smile of hers.

"Your dreams," Christopher repeated. "Your brothers have been tested here today. Not a test that they can pass or fail but a test to see if they are using their Gifts and if so to what extent. Can they control them, do they know even know how to use them? You are different. You're more advanced. In time, they may have the same problem as you."

"What problem?" he asked.

"The problem, Aron, is that you don't know how to turn it off. Or rather, in your sleep you can't turn it off. My problem is that I do not know how to test you. I know so little about your Gift and I've been unable to find anything that may offer any insight. In the most basic explanation I can think of, your Gift gives you an insight of things to come, but it is far more complicated than that."

"But I can never remember my dreams. All I know is they scare me." What could happen in the future to make him scream the way he did?

"As I said, the Gift is unknown to us. There is a lot to learn. We will have to try to figure out how to control it and to what extent it works. You will remember things even when you think you can't. Think back to when your aunt Karin arrived here at the Centre."

"You knew she was with child, but I hadn't told anyone but your father. This was your Gift speaking to you. From now on, every time you wake, I want you to write down what you remember from your dreams, anything and everything no matter how faint the memory or how inconsequential it seems. Even if it's sounds or smells or simply a feeling. Do you understand?"

Aron nodded but said nothing. Remembering his dreams did not sound appealing. In fact, he set about intently not thinking about all the times he'd woken screaming so loud that he thought half the castle would hear.

There was a knock at the door and Aron was all too glad for the distraction. Their mother called, "Enter," the door opened, and a guard stepped inside.

"Lady Celia for you, Your Grace."

The queen nodded and gestured for her to be admitted. The guard disappeared from view and was replaced a moment later with Lady Celia.

"Your Grace, Your Highness," she said with a dip of her head towards Mother and then Uncle Christopher. "Young princes, how good it is to see you all." She looked at them each in turn and offered Aron an extra wide smile which he reciprocated. "It's almost time, Your Grace. The lords have gathered and await your arrival."

Mother stood from her chair and smoothed her dress.

"We will continue this another time," said Christopher. "But for now, I want you all to remember what I have asked of you and think about the tests. See what you can deduct from them. Also, this is to remain a secret. Am I clear on that? You are not to discuss your Gifts with anyone but yourselves. In time, they may be known to the wider world but until you can control them, they may be dangerous." The boys nodded. "Promise me, each of you."

"I promise," said Aron.

"I promise," from Luke.

"Promise, Uncle," added Joshua. Christopher spun to look back at the fourth-born, even he wasn't going to escape without saying the words out loud.

"I promise, Uncle Christopher."

"Good, then off you go."

It took them less than an hour to sneak out of the castle grounds and find Ollie and Joe. Of course, the boys told them everything.

Branthony and Graf walked along the river's edge. It was early morning, and the sound of birds filled the air whilst many other creatures were just stirring.

The sun's rays shone brightly, and the day already whispered of the heat to come. The night, however, had sung a loud chorus of doubts and insecurities. The king of the Cross had found little sleep, instead stirring the cauldron of emotions inside him. It was an ill-conceived concoction. One he was unsure how to remedy.

Graf kept his head down as they walked, staring at his own feet stepping one in front of the other on the soft grass. Branthony had been trying to push him for more answers, but Graf had asked for time. It was the one thing Branthony had little of. Finally, the old man had come to him and perhaps now he would get the answers he so badly needed.

"So, your brother and his wife are expecting a child." Branthony nodded. He had told Graf about the expected baby and what he now needed, a new deliverer of the Gift. "I believe I can give you what you need."

Graf's words were like a salve on a burn and Branthony felt a rush of relief flow over him. This whole journey, everything he'd risked could have all so easily been for nothing. He never really knew if it could be done. Even when he'd found the village and felt the strange connection to the people here, he didn't know if it meant a new deliverer could be found.

"What do you know of how the Gift is delivered?" Graf's question made Branthony feel almost ashamed. He knew very little.

"I have read all the scrolls that contain any mention of the Gift as far back as any notable history of my family goes. They are few and far between and though much of the information regarding the Gift has been lost, one thing has been constant. The Crone."

Her name rumbled from his lips with unhidden distain. "She has always been the one to deliver the Gift. Her milk unleashes it and with a drop of blood, she can ascertain the specific type. She does not choose the Gift, only delivers it."

Graf listened on silently, but Branthony stole glances and watched as he became more solemn with each word. They continued for a short time with nothing said between them. Branthony was just becoming impatient when finally Graf spoke.

"It is all a strategy. A carefully thought out and executed strategy. So much of your knowledge has been lost and yet the stories of her remain, instilling your family with the belief that she is vital. It is her who has purposefully diminished your knowledge, all the while empowering her own position.

"Over generations, she has stolen your family's knowledge of the Gifts so that you would need her more and more. She has done all she can to keep you

174

from this place. Killing the messengers we sent, erasing all knowledge of us. Even your wars with the Sile are all by her design. An enemy between you and us, nearly impossible to get through. Have you never wondered why you have fought them for so long?"

Branthony could only growl his anger. That the Crone was responsible made perfect sense and she'd had generations to do her dirty work. How many lives had been lost because of her?

"You know her." It was not a question.

"Yes," Graf answered with a tone that spoke of an apology. "She is my relative. A great-great grandmother from somewhere far down my bloodline. She lived here, a long time ago, feeding and drinking from the river, drawing on its power."

"What is she?" Branthony growled.

"She was once like us. Now, I am not so sure."

"She must be stopped," he said through gritted teeth. "She has declared war against me and my people. She has given a Gift to a Sile warlord. He attacked my kingdom and killed good men. The stories say the warlord can heal from any wound."

Graf slowed his pace even more as the king talked, to the point where they were almost stood still. His head was dipped further to the floor as though it was suddenly a struggle to hold his own body weight. He sagged and Branthony stepped closer ready to catch him if he should indeed fall but Graf held out a hand to ward him off.

"I am fine," he said, appearing anything but. "I am shocked is all. Her powers have grown far beyond my knowledge."

"Tell me what you know about her. Anything that might help me."

Graf waited again before offering a reply, considering his words.

"I can tell you that her power comes from you. From the blood of the Fait and from this place, the Blood River. It is all tied together. Each and every time she has delivered the Gift, she has taken something in return."

It all made sense. Branthony had already suspected as much but this confirmed it.

"It is this blood that has nourished her for so long. It is blood that allows her to survive, and it is the blood that gives her strength. Every time she has come to your family to deliver the Gift, you have been extending her life and increasing her powers. Blood is the key and there is no blood as pure as that of a new-born child."

"The last time she came, at the birth of my youngest, she turned on me. She took far more than the usual small taste."

"She knew her time with you had come to an end. She decided to take what she could whilst she could."

"Why not take more? If the blood gives her power, why take such small amounts?"

"Because she has had a constant feed. For year after year, decade after decade, century after century, your family has fed her. But now the field of battle has changed. Now, she may decide to take more as she did with your youngest child. If she were to do this, if she were take more, who knows what power she may attain? But I suspect even now having too much at once would be dangerous even to her."

"It's not just her I have to worry about. It's her new Sile minions as well."

"The fools." Graf shook his head as he spoke. "The only reason it does not kill her is because she has taken the blood. This is what allows her to survive but even she is not immune. Using magic would kill her without the blood. Even with it, what has using magic cost her?"

Branthony suddenly pictured her in his mind and knew exactly what it had cost her. Is that why she always seemed to enjoy his discomfort at the sight of her. A small piece of revenge perhaps? Did she in some way blame his family for her appearance?

"Whatever it has cost her, it has also made her strong. The Sile she has empowered are not dying, they are killing."

"Perhaps she had found a way to prolong them but the more magic they use, the faster their end will come."

"She doesn't need them to live forever. She needs them to get her what she wants."

There was no response. There was no need for one. They both knew he was right. They continued to stroll along the river's edge and Branthony spotted a young woman who sat beneath a tree near the water. Graf gestured towards her.

"I know that time is short. You've showed great patience and I thank you. This." He re-emphasised the woman. "This is why I needed time."

As they approached the woman, she looked up at them warmly, a smile and the sun upon her face, but Branthony could see it straight away. It was unmistakable. There was sadness in her. Apprehension. Even fear maybe.

"This is Merleal, my daughter."

Branthony looked to the girl. She was pretty, with a soft face and innocent eyes. She looked young, but if what Graf had said about his own age was true, her appearance could be deceiving.

"It is nice to meet you, Merleal." He looked from her to Graf waiting for an explanation.

"You have come here seeking a new deliverer for the Gift." Suddenly Branthony understood. "Yes, this is why Merleal is here. This is rushed, I have not had time to prepare as I would have liked, yet time is against us."

"Merleal will travel north with you to the Cross. She will go with you to the Centre and when the time comes, she will deliver the Gift to the next child of the Fait. But she must go with you now and you must get back before—" he faltered, pausing and swallowing hard.

Branthony didn't need him to finish. They both knew what he meant. He must get back before the Crone came for the new-born child. Branthony merely nodded.

"I am trusting my daughter to you, Branthony, king of the Cross. We have waited so long for the Fait to come back to us but in truth, we were ill-prepared. I know she will serve you and your family well.

"I do not know what the future holds, but from what you have told me of your children and their Gifts, we can only assume there are trying times ahead. I hope Merleal can help you through these times. I think you will need all the help you can get."

Secrets, Bargains and Games

"You said there'd be no one there!"

First of all, Bolevard didn't like the tone in the young boy's voice. Not one bit. No one would ever know the amount of self-control it took not to reach out and slap the taste out of his mouth. Secondly, he didn't like that he'd been wrong. He'd sent the boy to retrieve the secret scrolls that Lady Celia had informed him about.

Quite how she came by the information, he still wasn't sure. Rest assured, Lady Celia was now under much greater scrutiny. But the boy was right, he should have been alone. If he'd been caught, Bolevard was of no doubt he would have squealed like a pig and given up the name of his employer in an instant.

Seen-as-though that employer was himself, it could have meant some very tough questions to answer. Very tough indeed. It was only because it was, in fact, himself that had supplied the wrong information that the boy wasn't picking himself up off the floor right now.

"So the queen was in her chambers?"

"Not just the queen, the bloody Warden of the Southern-Point as well who just so happens to be Prince bloody Christopher. One of the Fait! Who knows what the Gifts can do, I half thought they were gonna read my mind through the bloody wall or smell me or something weird like that!"

Bolevard had to suppress a snarl. It infuriated him to no end the ridiculous things that people thought the Fait could do. Lack of understanding of the Gift meant that people's imaginations ran wild, not that he had much of a better understanding despite his monumental efforts.

"So, the Queen and the Warden were together in the next room but obviously you avoided detection. Did you get what I asked for?"

"Not just the Queen and the Warden but the bloody children as well. All four of them. Who knows what those little buggers can do. You said it was a simple task. You didn't pay me enough for that lot. The Fait. Magic powers. That was way above a few silvers."

Bolevard angrily tossed a pouch of coins at the boy. A considerable sum, it better be worth it.

"Now tell me, did you get what I asked for?"

The boy smiled, confident, that was both a good and bad sign. On the one hand, it was another thing Bolevard didn't like, someone else thinking they were in charge. On the other, it must mean the boy had something.

"How many of those coins do you have?" the boy asked. That was a step too far and Bolevard was not a man to be pushed too far. He rushed forward, grabbing the boy by the shoulders and lifting him from the ground, slamming him into the wall.

The panic in the boy's face delighted Bolevard. People tended to forget he was once a knight, much to their detriment. Then again, the boy was a baby at best when Bolevard last fulfilled that role.

He spoke very slowly, being sure to put out his best menacing voice.

"Did. You. Get. What I asked for?"

The boy nodded frantically. Bolevard dropped him and he rubbed at his shoulders in pain. He looked up to see the snarl on his employer's face and set about delivering his news.

"The scrolls were hidden well but I found them. They're in the top drawer of your desk."

Bolevard glanced back at his desk, it was there in all its oversized glory, pristine and organised as ever. Turning back to the boy, he pushed down the frustration that someone had touched his property without permission.

"That drawer is locked."

The look the boy threw Bolevard's way threatened to bring the rage boiling back up. Bolevard clenched his fists suppressing the desires within him as the boy screwed up his face and shrugged his shoulders.

"You do know you hired me to steal for you, right? Picking locks is a pretty basic skill for any good thief. Anyway, the scrolls are in the drawer. I had a quick scan over them. They're what you were looking for. Let me know when you're finished, and I'll put them back. No one will ever know they were gone."

"You can read?" This sorry little excuse for life was actually becoming a little less worthless. Still, another shrug of the shoulders was wildly irritating.

"The more valuable skill I have is my ability to listen. Take earlier for example, when the Queen and Warden were talking to the princes. Now that was an interesting conversation. Very interesting." A silence stretched out. Apparently, the boy expected some kind of prompting to continue.

He would get nothing besides raised eyebrows. The boy smiled at that, still far too confident. "Remember when I asked you how many of those coins you've got?"

"You're testing me, boy!"

"I'm serious, old man." He really was pushing the limits of Bolevard's patience. "You want to know about the Gifts, right? Well trust me, you want to know what I know. You want to know what was said in that room today and you want to pay for it. I'll give you a teaser. Do you know what Prince Aron's Gift is?"

"Of course I do," he spat, internally raging that the boy actually dared to intone he was smarter than him.

"You may know its name but do you know what it does? How he can use it? I almost didn't believe my ears when I heard the Warden say it but Prince Christopher is one of the smartest men in the kingdom, everyone knows that. And, well, it's certainly something else, I'll tell you that."

"So," he urged, eyes bulging with impatience. "Tell me something, before I decide you're wasting my time."

"Foresight, that's what they call it. Well, you ever hear about Prince Aron waking up screaming all the time. Well apparently, he ain't just been having bad dreams. That's his Gift working. Showing him things from the future and from what I heard he's getting better at controlling it."

Well, well, well, this really was a turn up for the books. Yes, the little monster before him was proving to be a little less worthless than expected. Bolevard dug into the oversized pocket on his robes then tossed a second small purse across the room and the boy caught it with a deft left hand.

Bolevard walked around the oversized desk, sat in his oversized chair, quickly unlocked his drawer, glancing at the contents, once satisfied he sat back and folded his arms.

"So," he raised his eyebrows, somewhat surprised to discover he didn't even know the boy's name. He'd been hired after a recommendation and to be honest, Bolevard never expected to have a lengthy conversation with him.

"Res. You can call me Res."

Strange name for a strange boy.

"Well, Res. There's plenty more coin where that came from, so do tell, and pray I find it worth the cost."

Each of the boys occupied a different corner of the room, their backs to the walls staring out across the floor, eyeing each other with intent. Each had a weapon in hand. Some may look and see a pillow, soft and comforting and wonder exactly how dangerous such a thing could be.

But even a pillow, stuffed with the softest goose feathers could be a dangerous weapon, especially when compressed into the tightest ball possible at the bottom of the sack, with a twisted knot to prevent it uncurling; well, that was a dangerous weapon indeed.

Joshua and Jacob's room sat highest in the castle, so they chose it as their appointed battleground. Such activities as this were not seen as acceptable for young princes but to hell with that, it was fun, to an extent. They knew time was not on their side, someone would be coming to look for them soon.

They'd been seen out in the castle grounds earlier and had managed to give their minders the slip. The original intention was to go straight to the secret tunnel and out into the Centre with Joe and Ollie, but they had all agreed that they were pushing their luck, especially with so many added eyes around the castle at the moment and no small amount of them wishing to spend some time with the four princes of the Fait.

So instead, the boys came here for a quick game, knowing they would soon be found. They all agreed it was a good idea to get caught somewhere inside the castle grounds, it kept people away from the suspicion that they were sneaking away somehow.

"Are you going to try and use your Gifts to help you win?" asked Jacob to the room.

"No," said Luke with a grin. "Wait," he turned hard eyes on Jacob. "Did you just try and use your Gift on us?" He sounded incredulous.

"Well, if I did, it didn't work, but maybe I'm using it now because I know you're lying."

"Wait," said Joshua, "so you can be lied to but your Gift tells you it's a lie?"

Jacob shrugged his shoulders. The truth was he didn't really have a clue how Truth worked.

"If we all tried to use our Gifts at the same time, who's would win?"

Jacob's question was a good one. Since their lesson with Uncle Christopher, the boys had all been actively trying to use their Gifts at any opportunity. They had also it seemed, become rather suspicious of each other. Each now suspecting the others of having used their Gift to gain some advantage in any given situation. Jacob's question was excellent indeed and they all wondered at the answer. Joshua spoke his thoughts out loud.

"If Guidance tells me what to do but Aron has seen the future and knows what's coming, does my Gift know that he knows?"

"Yeah," said Luke suspiciously. "But does his Gift let him know that you know he knows. If he can see the future, how do we know he hasn't seen this already and knows how to beat us?"

"I'm confused," said Jacob.

"I'm gonna beat you because I'm better than you," declared Aron confidently. "And besides, how do I know your Gift won't just let you pull out some lucky shot?"

"It's not luck, its skill."

Aron shook his head. "Enough. We'll be here all day. None of us know how our Gifts work fully yet and none of us can control them. Let's just say no Gifts. Agreed?"

They all nodded agreement, yet they all still eyed each other with a look of distrust but for now, a compromise seemed reached.

Aron gave the signal to begin and each of the boys stepped from their corner to commence combat. Those same people who may see only a pillow would likely see this as just a game. This was not a game. This was war and Luke especially intended to win.

He quickly approached Jacob, swinging his case around with all his strength and bringing it down in an arc onto his youngest brother's head like a hammer. The fourth-born fell like a rock, a rock that squealed. He was out of the game and Luke smiled unscrupulously before turning his attention to the others, one opponent down meant one less complication.

Joshua stood frozen, staring first at his fallen brother and then to his older with fear in his eyes. Apparently, he had expected a softer approach; well, that was his mistake. Luke made to take him out next, but Aron saw his opportunity.

The eldest had the size and the strength advantage and intended to use it and seeing how the next in line had dispatched the youngest with the same method, he felt no qualms in delivering the first onslaught. The first and second-born came together in a whirlwind of blows.

When a shot got through and connected cleanly with the head, it was enough to knock more than a little sense out of the opponent and although Aron took a few shots, he started to get the better of the encounter.

Luke felt his head swimming. In fact, he felt it pounding. He found himself on the back foot but was determined not to go down. He could win this. He knew it. Intensifying his own attack seemed the only option, he placed his feet, taking the sack in both hands and swung with all his might.

He landed a solid blow, his older brother stumbling backward. Luke leapt forward. This was his chance. He landed again and a third time. Aron was crumbling, victory would be his.

Quite where the uppercut came from he didn't know, obviously from below but how his older brother pulled it off was a mystery and an uppercut in a pillow fight was not a common attack. Luke stumbled back, trying to adjust his feet and grip to try and defend, it was futile.

A side swing caught him clean and felt as though it nearly sent his head spinning the entire way around. When the return swing caught him just as cleanly, he was down on his knees.

Aron raised his hands in victory though he was clearly a little unstable. He smiled as Luke screamed at him in anger, the look on his brother's face would suggest he'd just lost a real duel and now his life would be forfeit. Aron turned his back on his downed opponent, adding insult to injury.

Aron now faced the last standing opponent. Joshua stood with his pillowcase gripped in two hands, Aron edged towards him, feigning a swing that made his brother flinch. Aron was much the taller and Joshua seemed to shrink further as he stepped back again.

The first-born raised his weapon, sure that he would smash through any defence. He was about to launch his attack when Joshua threw down his weapon in surrender.

Aron scowled down at his brother.

"You can't do that!"

"Why not? I give up."

"But. But!" He threw his pillow at Joshua, but the hit was taken easily enough. "You shouldn't just give up. You're a prince of the Fait. You should fight to the end."

"But I'd lose. Some fights aren't worth it."

"Never surrender."

"Never surrender," echoed Luke and they both left the room in anger. One at losing, the other feeling robbed of a victory.

When they'd gone, Joshua turned to his younger brother. "Some fights can't be won. Better to live and fight another day."

Jacob uncurled from the ball he'd been in on the floor and sat up straight rubbing his head.

"Wish I'd surrendered," he said.

"Sometimes, you've got to know when you're beat," said Joshua and they both agreed it was a good tactic. "Aron never does. It will get him in trouble one day. Which usually means it will get us all in trouble."

Bolevard sat behind his desk, arms aching as he continued to write, eyes glancing to the candles lighting his workspace. They'd burned down a considerable amount. It could only be an hour till dawn. He'd worked tirelessly through the night but was almost finished.

His task was to meticulously copy the secret scrolls brought to him by the boy, Res. The scrolls were exactly as promised by Lady Celia. They talked of the Gift in detail. What's more, they gave him the answer to not only the question of where the king had gone but the question of where the Gift comes from. The Blood River.

The writing was in the hand of King Branthony the First. Bolevard recognised it from other pieces written by the late king. It was, in his view, a clear admission of guilt. The Fait knew they were dealing with a witch. They knew she was evil and suspected her of insanity and yet they continued to align themselves with her. Now, in their desperation, they seek a new source for their black magic. A new witch who they can more easily control.

Some of the writing was in Branthony the Second's own hand and stated he now believed the Crone an enemy. Not only had he made an enemy of the witch, but he admitted he had no idea as to the depth of her powers.

Not only did the Fait have the audacity to dabble in witchcraft, but they also had the foolishness to not know the depths of such things. It was treachery of the worst kind in Bolevard's opinion, treachery without even understanding the consequences.

One of the more recently copied pages described in detail the Crone and how she delivered the Gift to each of the four princes at the times of their births. Even reading about it was more than Bolevard could stomach, and he found himself regurgitating what little food he'd eaten. Just the thought of that decrepit, rotting corpse was enough to make his insides turn.

So, he thought to himself. *The king has abandoned his people in their moment of need. Forsaking those he has sworn to protect for nothing more than ensuring the continued power of his own wretched family.*

It was all too much for Bolevard. Failure after failure. The Fait gained their power through most despicable and heinous of means, which in his mind meant they gained their power from the devil, not the God as they preached. If such an affront to the God were not enough to see them stripped down, then their failure to even understand their own power was surely the tipping point.

What kind of fool makes a deal with the devil without even knowing the terms? Even with such things aside, the fact that the king had sauntered off into enemy lands at a time of war showed that his own selfishness was all that drove him now.

There was only one thing for it and Bolevard became more and more certain of it with each passing day. The king must fall and not just him but all the Fait. The king may be gone for the moment, but his brother was here and acting like he was the king himself.

"Christopher!" He spat the name out loud. "The buffoon who lost Fallow Hold." The Fait would have people believe the Southern Warden an intelligent man. Well once again, Bolevard saw only failure of the gravest kind. Why was it that the Hold was lost and yet the prince escaped? No, he was worse than a failure, he was a coward.

His thoughts passed onto Princess Susan, the squanderer in Bolevard's eyes. Gift of Obedience and he well knew the power of that Gift. What she commands must be done, as she commanded him and the others in that room all those years ago. Those who saw that corpse walk and feed its dead milk to the new heir.

Bolevard had fought against that magic and was convinced it could not be broken. Such a powerful Gift and as far as he knew that was the only time she'd used it in years. Instead, she chose to hide away in the north-east, rarely to be seen.

Squander indeed, she made the deal and refused to try and do some good out of it. Bolevard thought of what he could do with such power, oh just imagine. Not that he would ever debase himself in such a way.

Then there were the children. The little horrors that they were, always running around the castle. Disappearing when they should have been carrying out their princely duties. It made him sick. It was not a pleasant thought, that he would have to dispose of children, but when it came to those four, he thought he could make an exception. They were poison, after all. Anyone with Fait blood running through their veins was poison to the world and he would find a cure.

So, as he diligently copied each word of the scroll, Bolevard became certain of one thing, the time to act was drawing closer. He knew where he would start. Firstly, he must hold up his end of the bargain made with Lady Celia. The woman thought she was so clever using him to do her dirty work, but he had plans of his own and he would find a way to use her in turn.

The Hunter and the Hunted

Malf offered over a wooden bowl filled with a decent stew with large chunks of fish floating in the creamy liquid with herbs for extra flavour, a gift from the people of the Blood River. Branthony took the bowl and despite the quality of the meal knew he would leave most of it. He couldn't eat. Not now. He simply stood staring out across the landscape looking north towards home.

"You're going to cross it, aren't you?" Malf asked the question, all eyes turned towards the recipient. Michael, John and Malf all waiting for an answer and all of them expected that they already knew it. Even Merleal sitting silently off to the side looked up at Branthony with wide, innocent eyes that seemed to say she shared their prediction.

"Yes."

There it was then, plain and simple.

"I know it's of little worth trying to convince you otherwise, but I'll try anyway. You think you're saving time. You think it's the better option and you think it's worth the risk, but you're wrong. If we travel that way, out in the open, nowhere to run, nowhere to hide, it will be the end of us."

"You want to get back, you want to help your brother, save his child, defeat the Crone and her Sile. I understand, but this is not the way to do it. You can't help anyone if you're dead. Going out there, across open land, making a target of yourself, it's foolish. Any Sile for miles around will see you and they will kill you and before you say anything, yes, there are still Sile out there."

Branthony listened but Malf was right in his first statement. He was wasting his time. Travelling the open plains could knock a week or more off their journey. They could travel at speed rather than the cautious trotting pace needed through the ravines.

What's more, they could travel in a straight line rather than the twisting paths of the hills. The other routes offered cover, but they cost time and that was the one thing he didn't have.

"We have to." Branthony turned his eyes from the direction of home and faced his friends. "There is more at stake here than any of us can imagine. It is no longer about me and my family. It is about the entire Cross. Maybe even more than that."

"We can't help if we're dead," said John, eyes to the floor, poking a stick into the dry ground.

Branthony had rarely seen his friends so despondent and that was saying something considering the situations they'd found themselves in over the years. He'd already asked them to put their lives at risk simply by coming with him and now he was asking them to edge the already unfavourable odds even further towards their own demise, but it had to be done.

He'd weighed the options and with added hope that the lands would be considerably more devoid of Sile than would be normal, he had reached his decision.

"We go," he said. The others knew the tone of his voice. They knew the decision was final and none of them would question it again. Though he allowed them the freedom of speaking freely to him when they kept their own company, he was still their king. He only hoped they would not all regret it but if they did, it would likely not be for long.

He turned away from the sweeping landscapes, an even mixture of grassy and rocky terrain and walked over to Merleal. He hesitated for a moment, searching for the words. Being sensitive had never been his strong point. Placing his back against the rocks, he slid down to sit on the ground beside her.

He couldn't help but notice her tuck her knees further into herself beneath her sleeping covers as though scared of his company. Her empty bowl was at her side, so he offered his in some small gesture. Almost reluctantly, she took it and offered him thanks.

"I want you to know, when we reach the Cross and our job is done, you will be taken care of, offered every luxury. Your efforts and sacrifice will be recognised."

For a moment, she simply stared back at him as though she hadn't understood a single word that had come from his lips. Finally, she replied in a voice so soft it seemed it would be carried off in the wind. Her words carried the same accent as her father. Not the thick almost brutish sound of many Sile but more than a hint of the unpractised words.

"I do not think you understand the sacrifice. I do not think you understand what will happen."

It was his turn to be silent for a moment. She was right, after all. He didn't understand. In fact, he understood little about any of this.

"Please, tell me."

"I am to deliver milk to the new-born. This I will do, instead of delivering to my own child who I have left behind."

Branthony opened his mouth to speak but couldn't think of the words. He had no idea.

"Once I have taken the blood of the Fait, I will grow stronger. The link between me and your family will be solidified. I will gain abilities beyond normal people. I will have the strength of the River and the Blood of the Fait."

"You will have a Gift?" The lack of understanding and scope of his own naivety were beginning to grate on him, and he had to fight to control his frustrations. "I am not used to being so lost. I feel like a child at my lessons again, listening to my teachers but understanding so little of what they say."

"It is understandable," she said and offered him a weak smile. "The truth is I am almost as lost in all this as you are. I will try and answer your questions but there is much I don't know. In a way, you are correct, I will have a Gift.

"I will have powers, but they will be linked to you and your family. For instance, I will know when I am needed. I will not have to travel again. I will come to you when the time comes, distance will not exist when the blood of the Fait calls to me. So long as the baby is born under a fixed roof, I shall find it."

Once again, it was not something he understood but it was at least something that made a little sense. The Crone had always appeared when needed. There was never a sign of her arrival, it didn't matter what guards were present or how many eyes watched for her, no one saw her come. She was simply there.

"Will your powers be able to help in the fight against the Crone?"

She shook her head.

"She has taken so much of the blood that no one knows the extent of her powers. The blood of the Fait is strong. She will not relinquish that power. The new-born will be her primary target but if she cannot have it, then she will seek another source."

Branthony considered this new information. He thought of his children, of his sister away from the rest of the family, his brother who normally resided in the south. He would have to make changes to protect them.

"My people are raised on tales of the Fait. We have longed for the day you returned to us. Taking the blood and delivering the Gift is a great honour and I consider myself blessed to be chosen, but it is not without its perils. The blood will change me and in time, I will crave it.

"Power is a hard thing to relinquish and the responsibilities that come with it are often a burden." He understood that perfectly. "I will deliver the Gift for a few generations at most but then I must stop, else the blood will corrupt me. The power of the river will protect me for a time but in the end, I will change. I will crave the blood and eventually turn into something I do not want to be."

"Like the Crone."

"Precisely."

"So, what will happen then?"

"Eventually another must be chosen. She will then bring the Gift."

"And you? If you stop taking the blood, what will happen to you?"

"The same thing that will happen to the Crone. I will die." Only her smile stopped him plunging into a pit of despair. "I hope when the time comes, I will be ready for it. The blood of the Fait will extend my life. My father and all those I know will be gone. The child of the child I have left behind will be old and withered."

Branthony grasped her hand in his. This was more than he'd expected. He had no right to ask this of anyone. To live and see all those you know and love grow old and die before your eyes. No parent should have to see their child pass. If he'd known the price she would pay, he would not have accepted the offer despite all that it would mean. That is why Graf didn't tell him. He began to wonder if there was another way.

"Do not fear for me," she said, placing a comforting hand on his. "The fact you feel such things at all proves to me you are a good man and a good king. Though the price is high in many ways, so is the reward. Besides, we must stop the Crone. Her powers have grown and if she has become so lost as to turn against you, then who knows what else she will do. She is madness embodied.

"Many years ago, my older brother volunteered to try and deliver a message to your family. He never returned. If I can help stop her, how could I refuse?"

Despite her words, Branthony felt no relief. His pain only deepened when he could think of no words to honour such a sacrifice. All he could do was look out into the night and hope he could honour her by succeeding in his mission. He must stop the Crone.

Merleal yawned and he was suddenly aware that she may have never ventured from her village before. "Get some rest," he told her. "We have a long journey. We will have plenty of time to talk."

Stealth was the key. They knew that. Stay hidden. Stay quiet. But sometimes even that is not enough. Sometimes there is no hiding. Sometimes getting caught is inevitable. This was looking more and more like one of those times.

"What do we do?" asked Joshua in the most cautious whisper.

Joe twisted his neck to look back at him and could only offer a simple shrug of the shoulders before returning his gaze back out around the corner. He leaned ever so slightly out, peering around the edge of the old stone wall. They both knelt in the shadow, unable to go back, unable even to stand from behind the short wall lest they give away their position. If they stood to make a dash, they'd be spotted but if they stayed too long, they would surely be found.

Joe's head suddenly retracted at great speed, and he pushed himself up even tighter against the wall. Joshua knew their time was almost up. He could feel the panic starting to grip him, the desire to run, to make a break for it even though he knew it would certainly fail. The mind has a way of convincing you it's the only way. Run! Run now or it's all over!

He resisted his instinct.

"Can't you think of anything?" asked Joe.

"Like what? We're trapped!"

"I don't know. Use your Gift! Strategy or whatever it's called."

"Guidance," he corrected, "and I don't know how. My uncle has me playing chess. How does that help?"

"Well think of this as a chessboard, what do ya see?"

That was easy. "Checkmate. He's trying to teach us but it's hard. He beats me every time we play. He asks Jacob silly questions, sends Luke on silly errands and as for Aron, well, I don't even know what he's doing with Aron. I'll tell you this, none of it seems to be working very well."

Joe sighed as he shook his head at the young prince; though the two were on complete opposite ends of the social spectrum, it was hard to tell when they were together. There was an ease between the two boys, a level of comfort that exceeded expectations.

"We definitely need to do more work on your talking. You still sound like you're fresh from an audience with the bloody queen."

Joshua looked bemused. "I am."

Joe sighed again. "Ya, but no one's meant to know that, are they?" He decided to take the risk of having another look, his head snapped back at twice the speed it did last time.

"You better think of something. He's coming!"

Joshua risked his own glance. A huge boy with dark hair and dirty face was moving slowly towards them, checking around every corner. He was known as Brutas and by the size of him, it was easy to see why. He was a giant compared to all the other boys. Simply put, he was a bully. It was terrifying when suddenly he glanced up and his eyes met dead with Joshua's. Brutas grinned.

Joshua looked around frantically, desperate for an option, for anything. He closed his eyes, willing his Gift to work, to give him a plan, to give him anything. In the end, there was only one thing for it.

He bolted.

He skidded on the pebbled ground as he came to his feet, launching himself into full sprint. His legs carried him forward with as much momentum as he'd ever mustered. Fear can push a person beyond their normal abilities. He surged forward not even thinking of looking back despite hearing Joe's cries of dismay.

An abandoned house sat within his path. If he could reach it, he'd stand a chance. It was getting closer. By the God, it was getting closer. He was going to make it. Run! Of course, it was always the best option. He should have just done it in the first place. Why did he bother to even try and fight the instinct? He was so close. Freedom. He could taste it.

He went down hard, face grinding into the dusty ground.

Did he black out? He certainly felt like he did. When finally he rolled over onto his back to stare up at the blue sky with its soft gentle white clouds, he was filled with despair as the tranquil scene was blotted out by the sneering triumphant face of Brutas.

"Got you!" The voice was loud and boastful, and he stood over Joshua like a hunter posing over his prey. From the look on his face, you'd think he'd taken down a lion.

As Joshua gently touched fingers to his wounded face, he couldn't help but think that the tag that had captured him had been harder than those suffered by the others; either way, he was captured and for him, the game was up. He tried to stand on wobbly feet, but Brutas pushed him back down. Joshua looked up at him, confused. That's when it happened.

From nowhere, Luke flew into view and swung a fist that crashed into Brutas' face.

"Get the hell off my brother, you fat lump!"

All went quiet. Some of the other boys that had still been playing crept out of their hiding places and stared wide eyes at the scene. Slowly, just as wobbly as Joshua had been a moment before, Brutas got to his feet. He rubbed at his cheek then turned angry eyes at Luke. "You little—"

"Shut your mouth." Brutas did, shocked at Luke's tone. "Who the hell do you think you are touching him? Nobody touches my brother!"

Joshua was still on the floor, looking up at Luke's back as he stared down the boy who was twice his size. Was this his brother? Luke had always seemed indignant towards Joshua at best. To see him now jumping to his aid seemed completely out of character. Joshua had never felt happier.

Brutas took a step forward, but Aron arrived at Luke's side just in time. Brutas still looked as though he may have a go but the added presence of Ollie who was bigger than Aron and Luke seemed to make him think again. He backed down, turning and walking away, shouting at some of the other boys as he went.

"Come on," said Luke, as he offered a hand down to Joshua. Was this the same brother that used to baulk at his touch? He pulled Joshua to his feet and said quietly in his ear. "Let's get out of here before he decides to come back."

They all left together and Joshua, despite his scratched and bleeding face, had never felt better.

Speed was the key. There was no need for stealth. How could one be stealthy in an open plain? Dry grasslands for miles around, barely a rock to intercede on the landscape. It all meant there was no place to hide. Speed was the key, but it could also be their downfall. Malf had succumbed to his king's desire to cross the open plains, what choice did he have?

But if he must do, he would do it his way. They took timed breaks; although short, they gave both horses and riders a chance to rest. He insisted the horses be watered and was sure to slow them to a canter and even a trot when needed. Speed was the key but too much speed would finish the horses before they'd even got halfway.

They were moving at a steady trot now with Branthony out in front. Usually, he would ride in the middle of the group but there was no reason for it, not here.

The one thing on their side was that if any enemy did approach, they would be seen long before they were close. The open landscape worked both ways.

"Here." Michael offered over a small loaf of bread and some strips of dried meat. Thanks to the resupply from Graf and the people of the Blood River, they should reach home long before they started running dangerously low on food. Water was another matter.

The chosen path was by far the more direct route home, but they were using water faster, especially on the horses. This land was the heart of Sile territory and if they were not off fighting in the Cross killing his own people, Branthony had little doubt they would have crossed paths with several clans by now.

"Thank you," said Branthony, taking the food. "For everything," he added.

"Oh, you can thank me when we get back, I expect a very large compensation for this added foolery," he said with a smile. Of all his Chosen Swords, Branthony thought Michael the most likely to actually come along even if he wasn't asked to.

He could have any number of knights or lords or men desperate to prove themselves or claim the glory and honour of accompanying the king but that was not what he needed. He needed the best and he needed people he could trust with more than his life.

"What's that?"

Branthony and Michael turned in unison to see Malf pointing off at the horizon. Branthony looked, shielding his eyes from the sun with a hand, still he could see nothing.

"Wait, I see it." John stood high in his stirrups. Whatever was out there, he'd spotted it as well.

"What do you see, John?"

"Riders," he answered with dread. "Heading straight for us."

"Distance?" Branthony demanded.

"It doesn't matter," came the unexpected answer. "They'll catch us long before we reach any hint of safety, and they outnumber us."

"Well, we still try!" exclaimed Malf. "Ride!"

"Breathe."

The instruction sounded simple, very simple indeed. It was just the intended result of the action that was proving so elusive. "Slow, steady breaths. In and out.

Eyes closed. Calm thoughts. Picture an ocean, the tide coming in and going out again, gentle waves splashing over golden sand. A scene of tranquillity."

All of this was supposed to make Aron see something. The exercise was supposed to make him unlock hidden corners of his mind. It didn't seem to be working. A headache was beginning to form from his efforts. Perhaps that was what scared him so much about his dreams. Perhaps they were visions of a future where he had to do this all the time. Now that truly was a frightening concept.

"You're not listening!"

Aron opened his eyes. The scene of the room washed over him. The decorated walls, the loungers with plush cushions, tapestries of old tales that Aron should know more about.

Joshua sat in the corner leaning over a chess board, desperately trying to figure out his next move whilst subconsciously picking at the scabs on his face. It was yet another exercise proving entirely futile. He'd never come close to beating Uncle Christopher.

By the God, he'd rarely beaten Aron. Luke was at a table rolling dice over and over, noting how many times he rolled double six. Jacob had asked their mother what she had for breakfast. He received the same answer he'd got every single morning for weeks. Eggs. Now, Mother was telling him different stories and he had to try and tell if she was lying or not.

Directly before Aron, sat on the floor with legs crossed and hands resting on his knees was Uncle Christopher. It was the same position Aron sat in. It was supposed to instil calm, make it easier to concentrate. The exact opposite occurred in Aron's mind. He couldn't take his mind from how uncomfortable he was. His uncle sighed.

"You need to be open to this, Aron. It won't work if you don't put your mind to it. Don't just picture a beach and an ocean, place yourself there. Think of yourself walking in the sand. Feel the heat of the sun, the water lapping around your feet. You need to be there in spirit as well as mind. I know this all sounds foolish and all you want to do is have fun with your brothers, but this is important."

Aron nodded as he always did, assured that he would try but almost just as assured that he would fail. He nodded his agreement then closed his eyes. He heard his uncle's voice, talking him through a story, laying out a scene before him. He pictured the beach and the water and the sun in the sky.

He breathed in and out, listening to the sound of his breaths. He sniffed, imagining the smell of the ocean air. That seemed to help. He had to put himself there, so he thought about that. If he was there, then so were his brothers. The four of them playing on the beach like they play when they're out in the city. It made the difference. He could picture the scene now.

In his mind, he turned from the sea and saw the long beach stretching out before him. Then he heard something, a voice and laughter. His brothers were running towards him, Luke at the back kicking at the water as the tide washed against his feet, sending splashes towards Joshua and Jacob who both laughed as they tried to make their escape. Aron smiled at them.

He could feel the sun on his back and the coolness of the water as it touched his skin. He felt comfort. Like the feeling of lying in bed just on the edge of sleep, knowing in a moment you will drift away. He closed his eyes, enjoying the feeling.

He opened his eyes again, but the beach was gone, replaced by grey stone walls. It didn't seem strange. The beach was already forgotten. This is where he was supposed to be.

"Where are you?"

It was his uncle Christopher talking to him, but he wasn't in the room. The voice seemed to come from the air. Aron looked around, finding nothing strange in the situation.

"I'm in a room, somewhere in the castle I think." As he looked around, he realised he was not alone.

"What do you see?" asked Christopher's voice.

"There's a man," he answered to the air. If the man could hear him, he showed no sign. "He's leaning on a table, there's maps laid out. He's wearing armour, a dirtied white surcoat with the emblem of the Cross on it. He has light coloured hair and blue eyes. He looks tired, so very tired. I think I know him," he added, almost as an afterthought.

"He seems familiar in some way." Recognition was there on the edge of his mind, but a name wouldn't come. Aron was looking at a young man, light coloured hair, an unshaved face. Aron knew those eyes, he would swear it, but they looked so weary, so beaten.

The man suddenly looked at him, those weary eyes staring out from a dirtied face. He wasn't just tired, he was sad. As though the weight of the world were on his shoulders.

"Who knew we had so many enemies?" he said with a dismayed shake of his head. The man leaned further over the table, resting his weight on fists, knuckles digging into the wood. *"We cannot defeat her. She is too powerful. How can we fight such a creature? We are besieged on all sides. Enemies from without, enemies from within. What chance do we stand? Did we once consider ourselves a great kingdom? How the mighty have fallen, brother."*

"We will find a way," came another voice. Aron knew the words come from him though he didn't speak. The words were his, but his voice was different. *"We will find a way, Joshua. We always do."*

"Joshua? Is that really Joshua?"

There was a noise then, a door opening and loud voices.

Aron looked around but saw no one. He turned back to the man, but he too was gone. There was just him in an empty room but even that seemed unreal now, less solid. The voices were growing louder, moving towards him. The walls were fading away, the room seemed to be filling with smoke or a thick fog. He began to gasp as though there was no air left to breathe.

Aron jerked forward as his eyes opened with alarm. He gasped in deep breaths and seemed almost shocked when the air filled his lungs. Uncle Christopher was glaring at him, as were his brothers who were now crowded around him. Chess, dice and whatever else all forgotten as they stared in silence.

"You did it," Luke said open mouthed in awe.

"You did well, Aron. Very well indeed."

"What was it?" he asked. "Was that really Joshua?" He looked to his brother. A child. Was that the man he would grow to be? He looked so sad. So beaten down?

"I do not know. I could not see what you saw. I only had your words. Your mind had travelled. To where and when I am unsure, but this is just the beginning, the first of many steps. But you have earned your reward. Go, the day is yours."

Christopher stood and moved towards Joshua who sat back in his chair, arms folded and smiling to himself, apparently confident in whatever move he had made. Uncle Christopher stared down at the board for a total of two seconds before moving his bishop and taking Joshua's knight. Joshua's eyes darted between his uncle and the board, dumbfounded. It seemed that Aron was the only one to make progress today.

The enemy riders came up alongside them, howling, screaming and snarling at Branthony and his men like rabid dogs. Many had tattoos, a common site amongst Sile warriors and these were most definitely Sile warriors. This meant the rumours of all the clans falling in line and following this mysterious new leader north were untrue. Some had remained defiant or perhaps just elusive.

The riders had blades drawn and the more skilled had arrows notched. Some advanced to close off all paths and force their prey to a stop. The men of the Cross drew into a defensive circle with Branthony and Merleal at its centre, all their horses struggling beneath them, sensing the danger.

Weapons were drawn, though this would not be a fight. There was no way to overcome the odds, yet the Sile seemed in no rush. No, they could have ended this a day ago, instead choosing to allow their prey to keep running, exhausting themselves. Even now they held back.

Perhaps they thought to take their prey alive for some reason. Did they have any idea of who they had actually captured? No, if they did, they would know that Branthony would die before being used a pawn against his own kingdom, even if dying meant failing his kingdom.

After seemingly growing tired of growling and snarling, the Sile quietened. A horse came a few steps closer. Its rider wore a grimacing face half hidden beneath a dark beard. The warrior carried a single edged axe with a short shaft. It was not hard to imagine the weapon had been thrown against many a man and not so many had lived to talk about it.

"My name is Shimmer-of the-Night. Clan leader! You are now my prisoners."

He spoke in the broken accent that many Sile have but his words were of the Cross. They might not know exactly who they had in their midst, but it was simple enough to see where they came from. The declaration was made as though it were absolute fact.

When Malf spat directly in his face, Shimmer almost seemed surprised. Not at the spitting, more that anyone would see any other alternative, even if that alternative was dying here in the sand.

In the end, the warrior simply grunted, not even wiping the spit away.

"Brave or stupid?" He shrugged his shoulders. "Can never tell with Cross men. Maybe a little both? Certainly foolish to be here in Sile lands."

"Sile lands?" said Malf with a cold grin. He snarled as good as any of the Sile and more than one looked at him with caution. It's obvious when looking at certain men that they're not quite sane. Some men hold within them a viciousness that always threatens to escape in the form of violence.

"We've been riding across these plains for weeks. Don't seem like Sile lands to me!" He spat the words at them making them every inch the grievous insult. Today, it seemed, these warriors would not take the bait.

"All run north to fight with their new leader," said John joining in. These words it seemed, had a little more effect.

Shimmer bristled in his saddle, eyes turning momentarily to the floor. He spoke to the sand.

"Not our leader. Nor anyone else's. Men do what they must to survive."

"So why aren't you with him now?" asked Branthony. "What makes you different?"

Shimmer stared down at the group; jaw clenched tight, eyes burning a hole through them. Yet, he seemed lost for words.

"It's simple," came a new voice. A rider trotted to the front, bringing his horse up next to Shimmers. He was a thick set man, muscular, heavily scarred. Again, a thick black beard covered a beaten face, a scarf was wrapped about his head obscuring much of it and when he spoke, he kept his eyes down towards the ground. "He killed our leader, killed the clan leaders and took the women, the children. He did what Sile do. He took rule through strength."

"You didn't answer his question," said Michael. "Why haven't you followed him?"

The warrior smiled, scarred lips rising beneath the beard of black, a knowing smile almost mocking in its regard. "Because we know the truth."

"Truth?" asked Branthony. "What truth?"

The smile only broadened and only now did he look up from the ground to look them in the eye.

"Is it so hard to see?" he said, beginning to unwrap the scarf from around his head, it fell to the floor releasing long, greasy hair. "After all, I can see through you. King Branthony of the Fait."

The Chosen Swords suddenly bristled, gripping their weapons tighter, moving closer in to protect their suddenly revealed king. Though the warrior seemed to know their secret, his companions apparently had not. They looked to each other, murmurs and whispers breaking out amongst them. Even Shimmer, sat atop his horse with axe in hand suddenly held a look of shock.

"Oh yes, I know every man that I have fought against, there are very few still alive. Fewer still who actually bested me. I will admit to some small insult that you do not see me."

Branthony stood staring, eyes narrowing as clarity came upon him. His next word came at a whisper, yet all heard it clearly.

"Morbius."

The bearded warrior dipped his head, an almost civil greeting in this most uncivil meeting.

"Alive and well, as you can see. I think it fate, King Fait of the Cross that our paths have crossed again. Fate has brought me the Fait and I cannot help but revel in the irony. A witch has given a Sile the powers of your family. Now, with you in my possession, I can regain all that I have lost."

Times of Change

Celia waited patiently for the knock at the door. Her guest would be arriving soon. She had left a discreet note asking him to visit her. Though this was a tactic she'd used many times, she'd never done so with this man and he would not be getting the treatment that many others got. When the knock inevitably came, Celia opened the door to see the ageing, stern face of Lord Basel staring at her. He was a short man whose temper was shorter still. Lord Basel was powerful. He was Lord of the Black Fort in the Western-Point but he was such a notoriously thrifty, cantankerous old git that most people had begun calling it the Bleak Fort.

What Celia knew about him for sure, he was greedy. He thought himself better than everyone and hated anyone being held above him and that included the king. His earlier outbursts at the meetings were simply a way to have a dig at the king. Celia had enjoyed shutting Lord Basel down in front of everyone. However, that was before she knew she needed him.

"Lady Celia," he said, his voice already displaying agitation. He didn't wait for an invitation into the room as he barged past her. He looked around as though expecting someone else as well as her.

"Only me," she assured him.

"What it is this about? Why did you summon me here? Your father may be the Warden of the Eastern-Point but that doesn't mean he or you can command me."

Well, actually it did but there was no point in pushing the fact. Usually when men came to answer her secret invitations, this is where the clothes would be coming off. She'd seduced men older than Lord Basel before but she was grateful this was an occasion where such a thing wasn't necessary.

"I have learnt," she began, closing the door that Lord Basel had left open, "some very valuable information. Information, I believe, you would be most interested in."

He eyed her and did not seem impressed.

"Go on," he said, sounding almost bored, as though he really couldn't care less. Celia found herself slightly thrown off balance, but she pressed on regardless.

"I have learnt the king's whereabouts. What's more, I have learnt his reason for leaving."

He narrowed his eyes at her now. The tables had turned. "What is your source?" he asked.

Celia smiled as she shook her head. "I cannot possibly say. But rest assured they are trustworthy, and I have every confidence in them." She knew Bolevard had learnt the information from the secret scrolls he'd acquired. She'd have to thank the boy Res for telling her about them.

The little sneak had even then managed to get paid twice by having Celia recommend him to Bolevard to steal the scrolls. They themselves had proved invaluable and if the thief was caught he had a name to offer instead of hers.

"Why tell me this?" Basel inquired as he eyed her suspiciously.

"Because after learning where he has gone and more importantly, why he has gone, I am of a mind to be more agreeable with you. His actions are not becoming of a king, and I believe many of our fellow lords and ladies would agree."

He considered this a moment and despite her offer, seemed reluctant.

"You have been a large supporter of the Fait over these last weeks. Why turn on them now? Wherever the king is and why ever he left surely isn't enough to risk your position."

She smiled back at him now. A venomous smile. She held the look of a predator in her eye. "My position is good but it could always be better. We must never stop climbing the ladder. Don't you agree?"

He returned that same smile. This was something he understood well. He practically started rubbing his hands together. "So, tell me what you know and tell me how we can use it to our advantage."

The expressions on their faces said it all and each of the four princes was suddenly a little more aware of all they took for granted. All these months, they had been journeying to the outer city, amazed by the sights and sounds, enthralled by all that surrounded them, enraptured by the world that was so close to them and yet so completely unknown. All this time and they had not thought to stop and think what the people of that outside world would think of theirs.

It had been an operation weeks in the planning. First, clothing. Aron had brought suitable attire for Ollie whilst Joshua brought some for Joe. Second was speech. Just as the boys had learnt to disguise their voices to not stand out, so too had their friends had to adapt. Well, one of them at least.

Third came the cover story. Just as the princes could not announce themselves as such out in the city, Ollie and Joe could hardly announce themselves as two boys who lived down near the old market. However, current circumstances had given them the perfect excuse.

Now they were pages, assigned to two knights from a border town at the far end of the Eastern-Point, come to the Centre with their lieges to address the recent problems regarding the king's absence. There were so many new faces around the castle that no one would question the story.

The two brothers turned to the four with open mouths.

"I've never seen anything like it," said Joe, now being called Joseph by the others. "It's amazing, isn't it Ollie erm Oliver?"

Oliver said nothing.

Joe turned and took another look at the gigantic iron gates of the portcullis. Never in his life had he expected to stand upon this side of those gates and inside the castle grounds. He could just see out onto the city beyond and recollected all the times he'd stood staring up at the castle from the outside.

"That's nothing, the rest of the grounds is even better," said Luke, taking the lead as he directed them through the courtyard and up to the castle itself. "And it doesn't always look like this. It's all banners and flags at the moment with all the people here, everyone wants their presence announced.

"They forget this is the Centre and this castle belongs to our family. It should only be the royal emblem of the Cross hanging from the walls if you ask me."

Things had certainly been different lately. More and more news was reaching them of enemy forces somewhere to the south making deeper and deeper incursions into the kingdom. So far no one had been able to stop the enemy and there was more pressure mounting with the continued absence of their father.

The princes knew what most others did not, their father had travelled south to try and find a way to stop this new enemy but to get home, he would have to pass them. He had been gone for months and now it seemed even Mother and Uncle Christopher were starting to doubt whether he would return in time.

"I'm sure he's ok," Aron had assured them all whenever they discussed the matter. "Nobody can stop Father." They'd all agreed that it seemed an impossible thing, though in truth they all feared for him. The longer that he was away, the harder it got to picture him coming back.

Aron told the others how Lord Richard Dawsel had brought his own forces from his lands to the Centre to bolster the defence, though it seemed now Mother was just as frightened of rebellion from the other lords as the approaching enemy. She had managed to stem the anger of the lords and ladies that day at court but that had been weeks ago and Aron had seen that reprise slowly fade away, now patience had run out.

Mother was organising and throwing a number of parties and celebrations in hope of lifting the mood and distracting from the problems, all an attempt to imply that everything was as usual. Strangely enough, it seemed to be working. Uncle Christopher said that people were willing to accept an excuse to carry on as normal. It was easier than facing the truth.

They entered the castle and the boys watched with smiles as their friends stared in open awe at all that surrounded them.

"Your Highnesses," said a young lady, dipping her head as she walked by.

"Your Highnesses," this time a knight that none of them could identify, dressed in the livery of one of the western lords. The princes recognised it but couldn't name it.

They all knew there would come a time when they would have to know such things, instantly able to call up the name and identity of each lord and the different liveries their men wore. No doubt, Uncle Christopher could reel them all off in a detailed list.

"I can't believe I'm 'bout to say this but I totally forgot," said Joe when they found a quiet moment.

"Forgot what?" asked Joshua.

"That you're princes. That you live here in the castle. That one day, Aron will be king!" He said it with a look of sadness. "I forget about it all when we're out there running in the streets, playing games. Then you come back through the tunnel to here and you live the rest of your lives in this place. What happens when you're all older? When you don't have time to come and play? Will you just forget about us? Leave us out there in the dirt. You're not going to want to come and see us, are you? Two little peasant boys?"

All four of the boys stopped and looked back at their friends. Dressed as they were in finer clothes and after a good wash, it would be hard to tell any difference between them all. It was the same when the boys visited them and dressed in their clothes with a little dirt on their faces. Why then, should there suddenly be a gulf between them?

"We're never forgetting you," said Aron. "Besides, you just said it yourself, I'll be king one day and you shall be my royal guard. You'll live here in the castle grounds with us."

"You might have to stay in the barracks," said Luke with a playful shove.

"No, we'll give them Hogan's room."

"Who's Hogan?" asked Joe.

"The Weapons-Master. Believe me, when you see him, you'll know."

"Aron's right." Joshua stopped and put his hands on Joe's shoulders, the way Father does to Uncle Christopher. "We're friends. Best friends, and we would never forget you."

"Well, I might forget you," said Luke with a smirk. He puffed his chest out and began sauntering around the corridor, chin held to the ceiling. "After all," he cried in a loud, blusterous voice. "I will be the greatest warrior the land has ever seen, the most renowned horseman, the most feared—"

"Of course you will," interrupted Aron. "You've just got to learn to beat me first."

"Oh, it's coming. Just a matter of time."

"Can it wait until later?" asked Jacob. "I'd rather show them around before you two start fighting."

Aron laughed. "Yes, I guess it can wait. So, what do you want to see first?"

Ollie's arm shot into the air, and they all watched him sign to his brother.

"What did he say?" asked Luke. Joe was about to answer but Aron beat him to it.

"He wants to see the throne."

"You understood?" asked Joe.

"Sure. We've been practising. Come on, I'll lead the way."

They all began to make their way under Aron's guidance to the throne room. If it was like most days recently, it would be packed with people shouting, much of it aimed at Uncle Christopher. The lords may be subjects of the royal family but they certainly felt confident enough in their own importance to make themselves heard.

Luke always said that they wouldn't sound so tough if it was Father who sat with them, but Father always said the Fait couldn't rule without the families of the kingdom supporting them.

As they neared the throne room, it was easy to see that it wouldn't be easy to get in, there was already a crowd of people gathered near the huge oak doors that led inside. As the princes approached with Joe and Ollie following behind who were doing their best not to look nervous, the crowd started to part at their arrival.

"Well, at least it's easy for you all to get around," whispered Joe in Joshua's ear.

The faces that looked at them as they passed looked stern. The closer they got to the throne room, the more they could feel it. A tension filled the air, and it was then they began to hear raised voices carrying out of the throne room.

"Follow me," said Aron, leading them all on as he noticed the guards holding back the crowd and trying to close the doors on them. When one stepped forward to block their path, Aron raised a hand and did his best to imitate their father. "I am your prince and future king. You will stand aside and allow me and my company past."

With a glance to each other, the guards ushered them forward. Luke looked at his older brother with raised eyebrows and a nod of acknowledgement, impressed by the attempt. As they passed the threshold, he gestured back to Ollie and Joe. "They're with us," he said in an overly deep voice, keen to try his own hand at brandishing authority. He picked up a little extra swagger as all six of them were let in just as the doors closed.

Inside, the room was densely packed. The boys saw their mother on the throne with Uncle Christopher in the smaller chair beside her. Both wore matching expressions. A look of worry but with a not so small hint of anger. Despite their attempts to remain inconspicuous, their mother spotted them instantly, giving them the slightest glance that no one else seemed to notice.

There was a heat in the room as raised voices shouted out in anger. It was easy to see they'd walked right into the middle of something vicious. One man seemed to have the attention of the room. He wore green livery with a large black circle. The emblem of the Black Fort.

That would make the speaker Lord Basel. He turned as he spoke and eyed the occupants of the room. His face was contorted in anger, and he continuously pointed an accusing finger back at their mother and uncle.

"They would have us believe their Gifts come from the God to help them rule but I have it on good authority that they are not so benevolent. In our darkest hour, the king has abandoned us and why? To travel south, through enemy lands. To what end?"

"To find a new source for the Gift. Not only does it not come from the God but whoever supplies it has turned away from him, so he has run off to find someone else. Who knows what kind of witch he will turn to?" Aron and Luke glanced to each other at the mention of a witch.

"His greed knows no limits. He puts himself and his family above the rest of the kingdom! His deception knows no limits. Who is to say anyone could not go and attain a Gift? How has the new Sile warlord attained such a thing? His cowardice knows—"

All four of the boys had begun pushing forward. No one talked about their father like that. They had almost reached the centre of the room but before any of them could do anything, their mother had risen from her seat and stared Lord Basel down with fury.

"You speak of my husband, your king, in such a way! Lord Basel, your insolence pushes me!"

He looked back at her, and the boys thought they saw a touch of fear. Did he worry he'd said too much? Mother wasn't finished yet. "You speak of things you have no knowledge about. Things you cannot possibly comprehend. I do not know how you have come by this information, but I assure you that you are mistaken in your understanding of it."

"Am I? Tell me then, tell us all. Do I lie? Or has the king gone to fine a new source of the Gift?"

The crowd grew quiet, awaiting the answer of their queen. She stepped towards him and took a breath to speak again. That is when the doors flung open.

As packed as the room was, the crowd somehow found the space to part as a small troupe of armoured men entered. They stormed through the centre and approached the dais, bowing before the queen.

Luke leaned to Aron's shoulder and whispered in his ear. "Purple livery with a green shield and swords, they're from the Crossed Hills."

"That's only just south of the Centre," he whispered back. "What are they doing here?"

"Your Majesty, we have ridden with all speed. I bring dire news from Lord Hughes of the Crossed Hills. The enemy, Your Majesty. They have been spotted and approach South Crave Castle."

The entire room burst into uproar with a hundred voices rising as one in a clamour of angry shouts. Struggling to see through waving arms and jostling men, the boys looked to their mother and could see the worry in her expression though she quickly masked it. She gestured to the guards beside her who began smashing the butts of their spears against the floor to calm the crowd.

"My lords and ladies, I assure you we have taken steps to protect the people of this kingdom. Castle Wraith and South Crave Castle have been reinforced and we have outposts up and down the country, patrols on every road."

"And yet the enemy has passed them all," said Lord Basel, even now refusing to give up his fight.

"The enemy has been hiding. They cannot hide forever. I had hoped my husband would return before this came to pass but he has not, and the situation is pressed upon us. The Sile have come north for a reason. They wish to fight, well sooner or later they will have to crawl out from beneath the rocks from which they hide."

"You have all come here to show strength. Strength we shall show. Gather our army. We will march to meet the enemy. Lord Basel," she said, turning hard eyes on him. "You called for action. You shall have it. You claim to be such a great leader and have all the answers, we shall see. I shall place you in charge of our troops. You take our hopes with you."

Lord Basel looked suddenly shocked but had no time to voice his opinion as once again, the room exploded into action, shouts and cries from all sides. The boys could just see their uncle speaking to their mother. Both looked suddenly tired.

"I think we should go," said Joshua and none had any argument.

Out for Blood

"Quickly!" called Aron. "Quickly!"

Aron willed himself to go faster though his legs burned with the effort. Upwards and upwards he went, forcing himself up the spiral stone staircase that led up the tower. His brothers along with Ollie and Joe followed behind. The muscles in his small legs throbbed as he took the steps two at a time.

He stumbled more than once but quickly got back up and carried on. He was near the top and could see the door. He pushed down the latch and put his shoulder into it, forcing the hinges open. Sunlight momentarily affected his vision, but it faded quickly, and he stood open-mouthed atop the tower, staring out onto a sight he'd never seen before. He was barged forward as Luke came through the door, quickly followed by Ollie.

"Wow!" said Luke, standing at his brother's side.

"It's amazing, isn't it?" Aron looked to Ollie, but Ollie said nothing. There was no need to. His wide eyes and open mouth were enough. A few moments later, the rest came barrelling through the doorway and they spread out across the circular wall of the tower. Jacob tried stretching up to see and, in the end, Aron had to pick him up to show him what the rest stared at.

It had been three days since the arrival of the men from the Crossed Hills. Three days since mother made her announcement. Those days had been filled with an organised chaos as preparations were made.

The castle grounds stretched out before them, beyond that the city sprawled over the land to the outer walls but it was what lay beyond even that which they had come to see. Lords from all over the Cross had come to the Centre to protest the king's absence and the decision not to retaliate against the Sile.

Each had only brought a portion of their strength to the Centre, more as a show piece than anything else, but now the Sile were close and the order had been given and those small portions formed up together in row after row as they prepared to march south.

Flags and banners of all kinds blew in the wind, line after line of men stood ready to march. Further out were the masses of cavalry and nobles ready to ride.

The boys knew they were just in time as even from such a distance, they heard the horns go up and the order to march was given. They stayed atop the tower for well over two hours, watching the slow and gradual disembarking of the army.

They played games trying to name the families and matching them to the flags that were carried off into the distance. Only when the last of the supply carts began to follow, did they finally retire back inside the castle.

As the children reached the bottom of the tower, Luke turned to them all with a grin on his face and said, "One day, it'll be me at the head of that army. I'll lead them all into battle and glorious victory. They'll tell stories and sing songs about it for years to come. Luke Fait, the greatest warrior the Cross, no, the world has ever seen."

"You'll be lucky," said Aron. "I'm next in line, remember. You won't go anywhere unless I tell you that you can."

Luke scowled at his older brother, but it was Joshua who spoke next. "What happens now?" he asked. "What happens when they meet the Sile?"

"They teach them a lesson," said Luke with bluster.

"What happens with Lord Basel? What about those things he was saying? Where's Father?"

There was a moment of silence as the boys all looked to each other. The truth was they'd all asked themselves the same questions. They were all worried about everything that was happening but none of them quite knew how to say it. Aron was about to give an answer but surprisingly, it was Luke who beat him to it by putting his hands on Joshua's shoulders and looking him straight in the eye.

"Wherever he is, he's fighting to get back to us. These Sile, Lord Basel and anyone else who tries messing with him will be sorry they did. We are the Fait. Always remember that."

They all seemed surprised by the display of tenderness from Luke and his eyes glanced to them all as he became aware of their scrutiny. "Now come on," he said, removing his hands and heading off. "The practise range awaits and I'm going to embarrass you all."

Debreace sat at the table looking across at her brother-in-law, Christopher. Besides him was a giant of a man with the thickest arms she had ever seen. She knew him well. His name was Hogan, the Weapons-Master. They stood together looking over the maps that were spread out across the table.

Scroll-Master Bolevard stood behind them at the back of the room, looking impatient. He delivered the maps stating that he had redrawn them all with his own hand and they were the most accurate in the library and indeed the entire Cross. He had retreated to the back after bowing to Debreace and remained silent from then on.

At the queen's request, Lady Celia had joined them and now stood at her side. Debreace had found Celia's input insightful, she had a bluntness about her and wasn't afraid to voice her opinion. With the army now marching south with many of the lords, the people in this room would be her immediate council.

"The army consists of two large divisions of infantry, one of heavy infantry, alongside one each of heavy and light cavalry. All supported by archers. A good distribution of knights and veterans," Hogan announced it all with confidence, this was his business. "There should be no way the Sile can match us."

"We don't know their numbers," said Celia, apparently a little more sceptical of the situation. "They've fought against larger odds in the past, have they not?"

"That was in their own lands when they were brought together under the command of Morbius Duvec."

"We don't know who their new leader is," said Celia. "Apart from a few skirmishes, we've had no reports of the Sile moving north since they took Fallow Hold. You've heard Prince Christopher's report. Whoever this new leader is, he is no normal Sile. How have they travelled north without being seen? Where have they been hiding?"

Celia posed excellent questions and Hogan had no answers for them. Debreace didn't say it, but she knew that the Crone had facilitated such things. Somehow, she had kept them hidden even as they travelled. North of Fallow Hold was Castle Wraith, not to mention all the other strongholds that spanned the kingdom. There was no other way she could imagine that the Sile could have passed them all without being detected.

Christopher pointed to an area of the map and drew his finger across it. "By tomorrow morning, our men should be as far south as Stetal, only half a day's march from the Crossed Hills. That means they should engage the enemy at any point in the next two days unless the Sile have retreated further south, which I would expect them to do. Drag out the march and tire the men."

"A few days won't make much difference, not with our supply lines in place. Not when we can be reinforced by any of the strongholds that come into range." Again, the positivity came from Hogan. It was once again Celia who had a more pessimistic view.

"They could keep retreating and draw it out, try to harry the supply lines, its typical Sile tactics, is it not?"

Debreace heard the confidence in Celia's voice and although she ended her sentence with a question, she was entirely sure of the answer. Debreace was impressed. Celia knew her stuff and she knew how to handle blusterous men.

"It is their usual tactics, but this is not their usual war. They've never attacked like this before. We've got scouts spreading out for leagues to either side of the army, there's no way they can get around us. We're going to smash them to pieces and send them scurrying back to the sand."

"We don't know what they can do. We thought they couldn't take Fallow and they did," said Celia.

At the bitter mention of Fallow Hold, Christopher took his cue to jump in.

"If we find them and meet them in open ground, it should be a quick and decisive victory. But the Lady is right, that is not normal Sile tactics. They're known for being evasive and elusive and thus far, we've had had little sightings of them. Somehow, they are avoiding detection." He glanced to Debreace and they both knew the truth. "The one thing I think we can expect is a surprise."

"It's not just the battle itself that concerns me," Debreace said, lifting her eyes from the map and looking at her makeshift council. "I want to know what the Sile want. If they simply wanted to fight, then why come all this way north? If they wanted to control, then why give up the strongholds? There is something we're missing. I can feel it and I fear it."

She looked to Hogan. "The people of the city will still need to be reassured there is no danger. Please double the patrols of the city guard."

Hogan dipped his head. "Of course, Your Majesty. I shall see to it immediately."

With that, she dismissed them. If only she could so easily dismiss the growing feeling of dread that filled her stomach.

The arrow made a 'thunk' as it hit the yellow circle that surrounded the bullseye. At ten yards back, Luke was reasonably happy with the shot.

"Wow," said Joshua. "That was good."

To the side, Aron was giving Joe and Ollie a brief lesson. Of course, neither of them had ever touched a bow and arrow before, so he was starting with the basics even though they were obvious. They both took up position in front of the target and took a shot each. Ollie's shot went wildly off to the left flying past the target whilst Joe's flopped to the ground just a few feet forward.

"Ha, well we've definitely got some real archers on our hands here," sneered Luke. "Guess the kingdom is safe after all." His earlier show of softness seemed to result in him doubling down on his obnoxiousness.

"They've never done before it," defended Aron. "You're down here every day practising."

"Yeah but I'm a natural."

"Because of your Gift, so stop showing off. You wouldn't be so confident if this was swords."

"What?" Luke looked incredulous. He was sure he could beat his brother, so sure that he immediately began stomping across the grass to the end of the target range where the practise swords were kept. The whole area was near deserted. Normally, there would be dozens of men running drills and practising but many of them had marched away and the rest were busy.

There were a few pages and squires polishing and preparing their master's armour and weapons and a few men preparing drills that would take place later. The city guard were always practising and were likely to be extra keen to show there was nothing to worry about in case the Sile somehow managed to reach the city. None of them seemed to notice when Luke picked up two wooden swords and stomped back towards the waiting group and tossed one to Aron.

The eldest brother caught the wooden weapon backhanded and turned it over, all the while keeping his eyes on his younger brother.

"You really want to do this?"

Luke didn't wait for a response, swinging his weapon wildly at Aron's head, it was only instinct that brought his own sword up to deflect the blow but it knocked him off balance. The swing was hard, there was no playing here. Stumbling to his right, there was no time to rest as Luke swung again, this time having gripped his own sword with two hands.

Aron's sword hadn't moved so again the attack came back off it but the impact rattled him. He fell a further three steps before catching his balance. As Luke charged at him, the space allowed a moment to think; it was only a second but as Luke's face was flushed with frustration, it was clear he wasn't thinking. There was only one thing on his mind. He swung again for Aron's head.

Aron remained completely calm. He felt odd. A strange sensation washed over him. He'd seen this before. He knew what was coming. He sidestepped Luke's swing and let his own weapon fly. It crashed into Luke's ribs, causing him to double over, his weapon tossed away in the process.

Aron raised his sword to bring it crashing down on his brother's back, but something was wrong. The weapon had snapped, he held only a handle in his hand. He looked down at Luke and muttered. "You're lucky."

Aron glanced to his side where Joshua, Jacob, Ollie and Joe all stood watching with open mouths, wondering where that had even come from. Luke had boiled over so quick that none of them had even had time to react. They'd just simply stood by and watched as the fight ensued.

Aron threw his broken sword down and stepped away.

"He started it, you all saw, right? He started it."

"Yeah, yeah, we saw," said Joe.

"Yes, we saw it," added Joshua.

Ollie said nothing, whilst Jacob nodded along.

Joshua opened his mouth to speak again but Aron didn't hear it as his head seemed to burst into fire. He fell to his knees clutching the back of his head. When he opened his eyes and pulled his hands away from his head, he saw blood on his fingers, then he saw the end of a wooden sword on the ground. The same one he'd just discarded into the ground and foolishly left within Luke's grasp.

"You didn't see that one coming, did you?" he heard Luke say.

Aron felt his own anger boiling over. He stepped towards his brother with a raised fist. "You'll need more than Fortune this time you little—" He felt himself hoisted into the air by strong arms.

"Master Hogan, I—"

"Save it! Of all the stupid things! Is this how princes act? You can explain yourselves to the queen."

Aron suddenly remembered his mother as she was in the throne room not too long ago. He was more afraid of her now than ever before.

Aron lay on his bed staring at the ceiling. He'd been there for what seemed like a lifetime although it had only been a few hours. Weapons-Master Hogan had marched them straight to their mother. Luckily, he had dismissed Ollie and Joe offhand after not recognising them.

They'd scurried away as quickly as possible. No one had any clue if they'd even managed to find their way back to the cave and out into the city. Their clothes were stashed in the tunnel so they could change and head home without looking completely out of place.

All four of the boys feared Father. Being sent to him when they were in trouble was one of the most terrifying prospects any of them could think of, but this time when they were sent to mother. It was somehow worse.

She didn't shout or scream. She simply seemed sad and tired. She reminded them of their promise to Father before he left. A promise to behave. It dawned on them all how much she was actually dealing with and how much she must be missing Father.

They'd all been sent to their rooms and Aron had been all too glad to go. He felt bad. They'd all been so busy having fun, they'd neglected to help. Aron was supposed to be king one day. Was this what Father was always talking about? Taking responsibility, stepping up to the task. Aron knew he'd missed an opportunity.

He'd looked at the small desk in the corner of his room and thought about trying to make amends a little by doing some reading for his lessons. Instead, he'd simply lain down on his bed. His head was splitting from Luke's attack and despite his mother cleaning the wound none too gently, it had started to bleed again. A small blob of crusted blood stained his pillow. Despite the throbbing, he slowly started to drift to sleep.

Aron opened his eyes to darkness. The candles had burnt away, and the fire had died to embers. The faintest glow came from the ashes and Aron felt the coldness of the night, his breath lingering in the air. He grabbed at the cover and rolled it over himself, shivering against the freeze.

He thought of adding some logs to the fire but the thought of getting out of the covers and putting his bare feet on the cold floor seemed unbearable. He shivered; every part of his body seemed to tremble. It wasn't even winter, but Aron would swear he had never been so cold.

He closed his eyes, hoping he could fall asleep despite the shivers. That was when he heard it. He sat bolt upright in bed, the covers falling away from his torso but now the cold was momentarily forgotten. His eyes darted around, staring into the darkness but could see nothing.

Aron. The voice was a ghostly whisper, carried on the air with the slightest growl to it.

"Hello?" Again, he searched the room but to the same end. "Who's there?" He leaned back on his pillows, feeling the crusted blood on his hand.

Aron. He heard the voice again. This time he was certain. He felt his breathing speed up and could see the clouds of vapour filling the air. Despite the cold, he pulled off his covers and stood up. He stepped closer to the embers of the fire but felt no heat.

He scanned the room again and froze in terror as he stared into the far corner near the door. His blood seemed to run cold through his veins, and he clenched his small hands to fists to stop them trembling. It wasn't just the cold that froze his feet in place.

He tried to think of his father, how he always told him to be brave and strong. With a deep breath, he took a step forward, then another. His mind was racing, his eyes desperately tried to focus, wondering if he could actually see anything or not. His mind told him there was something there, a shape, small and huddled into the corner. Another step forward. Could he see a pair of eyes staring back at him out of the darkness?

The blood. The blood. The blood. The voice rang out in an echo.

Smell it. Smell it. Smell it.

Taste it. Taste it. Taste it.

Against his instinct, he took another step forward.

His spine tingled.

His skin crawled.

He reached out a hand, grasping at the air.

He leapt forward.

Nothing.

He stood panting, facing the wall and feeling foolish. He laughed to himself, blaming his nightmares for making him so jumpy. What was he even doing? It didn't even seem so cold now. He was just being silly. He turned to go back to bed.

The Crone stood waiting.

"THE BLOOD!" she screeched as she leapt at him.

Aron fell backwards screaming in terror, legs scrambling in desperation to push himself away. The stone wall was at his back, arms held protectively over his face.

Nothing happened. When he looked, there was no one there.

The room seemed a little brighter. The shadows seemed to have retreated. The fire burned in the hearth now, flames licking upward. Aron called for his mother.

Games and War

Debreace and her brother-in-law, Christopher stood together and watched as her eldest son tried to calm himself. Together, they were two of the most powerful figures in the kingdom, perhaps the world and yet both had rarely felt so completely helpless.

Debreace had felt the tears run freely down her face at the mere sight of her son's terror. She knew the Crone and the fear she could instil. Debreace's husband was the king of the Cross and one of the most renowned warriors in the known world, yet she saw it clearly on his face whenever the Crone was brought up that even he held a great fear of her.

"What in the name of the God was she doing here?" asked Debreace, her eyes moving from Aron to Christopher, but it was her son who answered.

"I don't think she was actually. Not really. It sounds strange, but I know she wasn't really there in the room. It was more like she was reaching out to me somehow. Or more like looking for me. I think the blood called to her. But she is close, I could feel it."

Christopher walked to a side table and poured himself a drink, gulping it one and wincing at the sting in his throat.

"I believe you," he said to his nephew. "I fear that whatever game she is playing is nearing its end. Fears that are increased by my brothers continued absence. He went to find a replacement for the Crone. I am sorry to say that we must begin to consider the possibility that he has failed. We must start to consider that he may not return."

He held Aron's eyes whilst he said this. There was no way to shield him from this. "It is our duty to protect the realm and to do so, we must prepare for the worst."

Aron nodded resiliently and Debreace felt great pride in her first-born. "You're right," she said. "It is our duty. We must be strong for those that depend on us."

They all turned to the door as a knock broke through the sombre mood.

"Come," Debreace shouted, unable to hide her frustrations. A sheepish looking messenger came through the door.

"Apologies, Your Highness," he said, addressing Christopher but offering a bow of the head to all. "A bird has arrived, Your Highness. You said you wished to be notified immediately on this particular matter."

Christopher ushered him forward and took the small note. Reading it seemed to drain what little vigour he had left.

"What is it?" asked Debreace.

"A message from Lord Basel and his forces."

He didn't offer anything further and Debreace's frustration grew until she finally had to push him.

"And? Have they engaged the enemy?"

When he looked up from the message, the look of alarm on his face had grown.

"Quite the opposite. The message states the army is heading north towards the Centre at all haste."

"North? Why?"

"They believe the enemy has somehow bypassed them."

"She's using her magic," Aron said confidently. "That's how she's remained hidden. It's the reason she's so desperate for the blood. She's coming for us."

There were days when it seemed all the forces of the universe were conspiring against you. As the horns blew out over the city and Debreace looked to her brother-in-law with panic in her eyes, that day certainly seemed such. When the second blast of the horns came, they knew this was as dark a day as either of them had ever seen. Two blasts meant one thing. Enemy at the gates.

Debreace, as any mother would, could think of only one thing. She looked to Aron.

"Where are your brothers?"

Ollie and Joe stood near one of the entrances to the public gardens. This particular entrance was rarely busy and poorly kept, mainly used for groups of young boys to loiter away from the eyes of the grown-ups of the city but to Ollie and Joe, it was the home of the greatest secret in the world, a secret that allowed them to live a life alongside the princes of the Cross.

A connection that no one from their side of life would ever hope to have but they did. They usually met the boys here a little after midday. It was a little past now, so they were beginning to think the boys weren't able to make it. That wasn't an uncommon occurrence. They were princes after all, and they had demands on them that Ollie and Joe could not relate to. This of course went both ways.

"Come on," said Joe. "They're not coming. Maybe they got in more trouble than we thought. We'll come back tomorrow if we can make it." He headed towards the old gate in the wall that surrounded the garden. Ollie said nothing but followed close behind.

Joe had only taken a few steps out of the gardens when he heard the horn blow out. He looked to the sky, bewildered. As the second blast of the horn rang out, his brother walked into him.

He turned to face his Ollie who could already tell something was wrong. All around them, there was sudden commotion. Ollie used his hands to sign.

"I don't know," answered Joe. "But I think it's bad."

Christopher stood on the tower looking south towards the enemy. Sure enough, as the warning had said, the Sile had reached the Centre. They had crossed half the kingdom and reached the capital and all without being seen, let alone stopped by the army sent south to do exactly that.

He had no doubt his nephew had the right of it. The Crone had used her power to hide them. Now here they were. The one thing that brought him hope was the numbers of the enemy. The castle guard alone would outnumber the Sile, once bolstered by the not so small number of knights that remained in the Centre, they should be more than enough.

Then there would be the thousands who could be called upon if needed and many in the city had conscripted before. The numbers did not look threatening in the least and yet Christopher felt no shortage of unease. The one unknown factor was the most dangerous. The Crone.

He'd given orders on how to deploy the defences but for the moment had told the men to hold, much to the anger of many of the lords and knights that remained. Despite their anger, Christopher had no intention of running into anything. He'd rushed to meet the enemy at Fallow Hold and paid a great price. This time, he would not be so easily fooled.

Aron had re-joined his brothers and the four of them were safe, high in the towers of the castle. The last thing Christopher needed now was for the boys to do one of their amazing disappearing acts. Those four little rascals had a gift for getting in trouble and even worse, they had a gift for being nowhere to be seen when they were most needed. They certainly reminded Christopher of himself and Branthony in their younger days.

He would not put the children in harm's way, but he was beginning to think that they would be needed. Something about the boys and their Gifts and the way they'd developed told him they were crucial to defeating the Crone. But did that mean defeating her here today or saving them for the wider, longer game?

He pinched the bridge of his nose and felt a pounding in his head made all the worse as he heard his name called out once again. He turned to see who was demanding his attention now.

"Your Highness." The nurse staring back at him was not who he'd expected. "We've been looking everywhere for you. I thought you should be made aware. Your wife is giving birth."

It all made sense now. The universe was most certainly against him today.

"Steady!"

Weapons-Master Hogan screamed at his men and was determined to maintain discipline. In truth, he was immensely proud of how his men had responded to the threat. The majority of them were castle and city guards. Lining up in formations to fight a pitched battle was not what they were trained to do.

However, they had responded with efficiency and without hesitation. Hogan was well aware how many of the knights and lords of the realm viewed his men, as little more than jumped up commoners. Today, they would prove their worth. Damn nobles always had a way of looking down at men.

Strangely, it seemed the highest man of all, the king, was the one who never looked down on anyone. Hogan was a king's man through and through and he would not let his king down. Hogan and the others had been left in charge of the city and kingdom in the king's absence and Hogan would not fail. Not on this day, nor on any other.

"What are they waiting for?"

The question came from Austin, the second in command and in truth, Hogan was wondering the same. The enemy was lined up as though ready to charge but they were holding their position, stood back out of range of archers or any of the city weapons.

"It doesn't concern us what they're waiting for. We wait until they attack or until we get the order to advance. Either one will come soon enough. Then there will be fighting in plenty."

"The stories, Sir? The stories from Fallow Hold said the Sile can use magic now. What if that's what they're waiting for? To prepare their magic to use against us."

The Weapons-Master turned to his second with a deep frown.

"We are men of the Cross. We have the Fait." His arm stretched over his subordinate's shoulder and his finger pointed back towards the city. "The Fait is the only magic I have ever seen, and it is the only magic I believe in. Remember such things."

They both stared back at the city now, taking confidence in the thought. That was when they saw the fires, not just in the city but from the castle grounds themselves.

"What in the name of the God!"

Fires meant the enemy was within. Hogan took one step back towards the city. One step, that was all he took before he was stopped in his tracks by the war cry of the Sile. A shiver ran down his spine as the enemy began its charge.

"There's no way we're just staying here, right?"

Luke turned from the closed door and stared at his brothers. They were all in Joshua and Jacob's room, the highest in the tower, apparently the safest. Not that Luke thought there was any hint of danger. They were in the Centre, in the castle grounds and in the castle itself.

No enemy in the known world could get all the way across the kingdom to the Centre and take the castle. Luke was incredibly confident that whatever this was, it was not a threat. His father's men would crush these fools.

"My head is spinning," said Aron, squeezing his eyes shut against a throbbing pain.

"Oh, give over, I didn't hit you that hard," said Luke, knowing full well he'd put all his strength into the swing that had wounded his brother.

"It's not that," he said, leaning against the bed for balance. "It's like there's flashing lights in my head. I think my Gift is trying to show me something. Like my dreams are trying to come back to me but there's too many. Images, sounds, smells. It's too much."

"You've never had that before, right?" asked Joshua, to which his brother shook his head side to side. "Then maybe this is what your Gift has been showing you. All the times you've woken up screaming, maybe you saw the castle being attacked. Maybe your Gift was trying to help you."

"How?" he asked.

"I don't know. If it showed you what was going to happen, then maybe we could try and stop it."

"Concentrate," encouraged Luke. "Remember Uncle Christopher's lessons. Try to pick out one thing at a time."

Aron tried but the more he did, the more his head pounded. It was all too much. He didn't know if he was sifting through memories or dreams of the future. Were they somehow both? Things he'd seen in the past that hadn't actually happened yet. Trying to think about it only made his head hurt worse.

"There's too much," he said, tears beginning to fill his eyes as the pain only seemed to grow. "Too much to see and on top of it all, there's that damned crying!"

"What crying?" asked Jacob.

"That baby. There's a baby crying! It's so loud. Won't somebody make it stop?"

As he said the words, the room seemed to fall silent. The images were gone, and Aron felt relief washing over him. He looked to his brothers. "It stopped," he said with relief taking deep breaths.

"But why?" asked Luke. "What changed?"

"The baby," said Joshua. "You could hear a baby crying, right?" This time Aron nodded. "And you said the Crone always comes at the birth of a new Fait." Another nod. "That's why she's here now. She timed her attack. I think the baby's being born and she's coming for it."

"Well, that settles it," said Luke moving towards the door. "We're supposed to help. It's what our Gifts are for."

He threw the door open, ready to tell the guards outside that they needed to see their uncle and mother. They'd want to know this new information. He pulled the door open. A small axe flew past him, inches from his nose. A man was running towards him, growling and grunting. He had a bare torso with tattoos across his chest. A Sile! Luke slammed the door shut, barred it and turned to his brothers. Who stared at him wide eyed.

"Best get through the escape door," he said, as the first crash against the door came.

Christopher took long steps, the floor of the corridor running quickly beneath his feet. Two guards followed close behind. It was obvious now that somehow the Sile had breached the castle, how and in what numbers, he could not say. He had also received word that the forces led by Weapons-Master Hogan had engaged the enemy outside the city walls.

The Sile out in the field had been waiting for their fellows to breach the castle. It appeared the Crone had timed everything to perfection. She could sense the child's arrival and everything she'd done had been leading to this moment.

His only chance was to deal with one problem at a time. He'd distributed his guards across the castle, reinforcing all key areas. Hogan and his men were fighting and proving their worth against the enemy in the field. A group of royal guards were making their way up the tower to the boys and he was nearly at his wife.

His thoughts were so taken that he barely saw the sword that swung for his head. Luckily, his guards were more alert than he was. One guard surged past Christopher's left-hand side, his sword coming up to meet the attacker's. The second guard came past on the right, stabbing forward, skewering the Sile.

"Back, my prince!" he shouted as he pushed the Sile back with his boot, pulling his sword free.

Christopher stepped back, pulling his sword as he did so, frantically looking around for any more. "By the God, where did he come from?" The two guards looked back at him and obviously had no answer, so his attention turned to the far end of the corridor where two more guards stood watching with open mouths. With nowhere to hide in the empty corridor, no one could explain how the man had appeared and gotten so close.

Christopher's Gift was helping him understand. The Crone could move them, and her power was greater at the birth of a child. He knew she must be close. He felt a panic grip him and broke into the fastest sprint he could manage in full armour, his two guards hot on his heels. "Open the doors," he called as they approached, and the two guards obliged without question.

Christopher burst into the room with his sword in his hand and his two royal guards followed suit quickly followed by the guards positioned at the door. All five men were met with the aghast stares of nurses' and the midwife's, not to mention Christopher's wife, Karin.

"Prince Christopher," exclaimed the midwife. "You're just in time."

"In time?" he said, more out of breath than he should be, the adrenaline coursing through him almost making him shake. "In time for what?"

The midwife stepped aside so he could see his wife more clearly. Not just his wife but also the baby she held to her chest.

"It's a boy, Christopher. We have a son."

He was silent. He stared at his wife and new-born son and for once, he was speechless. He felt a tear come to his eye and had never imagined such happiness, especially at a time of such distress. He was so distracted that for a moment, he forgot why he had come here in the first place.

If only he could have remained in such a blissful state. But a voice cut through the distraction, a shrill voice that sent the coldest of chills running down his spine.

"There you are!"

Almost as one, the prince and the guards turned to the source. Christopher's eyes opened wide in horror, everyone else shared looks of fear and disgust. Stood in the open doorway was the shrivelled form of a woman, wrapped in ragged black cloth, her skin a pallid green.

Blackened, cracked lips covered toothless gums. A few grey hairs fell from an almost bald scalp over menacing, sunken eyes. A skeletal hand pointed at the baby and even in a form of such horror, they could all see the desire within her.

"Crone." The word came as a whisper from Christopher's lips. He had not seen the Crone since the day of his birth and was thankful he could not remember that solitary meeting.

"A royal baby is born, and I come. As it has always been."

"You are no longer welcome."

"You have no choice!" she screamed. Her voice held a power that sent everyone in the room back a step. Some of the women put hands to their ears as though they were about to burst, more than one pulled their hands away to reveal blood on their palms.

In a quieter but no less menacing voice, the Crone spoke again. "A child of the Fait has been born. You have no king here to protect you. He has shown his foolishness once again. You all have. I am not the one that serves. You are! And you will serve me now, with your son."

One of the royal guards had heard and seen enough. He may not know this thing before him, but no one would threaten a new-born child in his presence. He stepped towards her, thrusting his sword down through the Crone's neck. The Crone gasped and her breath gargled as black blood poured from her mouth. The blood only added to the horror of her toothless smile.

With a wave of her hand, the guard was flung to the wall, crashing against it with a sickening crunch of metal, stone and bone. The Crone pulled the sword from her own body and dropped it to the floor with a smirk.

"I'll be taking that baby now." Her voice was little more than a growl, spoken through pursed lips that still dripped with dark blood.

Christopher's heart pounded in his chest as his legs felt as though they would give way beneath him. He had never been a warrior, never possessed the skills that his brother so easily acquired, but if the Crone thought he would simply stand by as she took his son, then she was mistaken.

She held out her arm towards him, demanding the baby as though he were a simple object. The skin hung from her bones as though it were little more than an extension of the black cloth that wrapped around her body. Christopher gritted his teeth and launched towards her.

Weapons-Master Hogan pushed forward through the field of battle. The Sile fought with savagery and aggression but they were wild, their skills lacking compared to that of trained men of the Cross. He dodged an axe aimed at his torso, dancing back a step before plunging his sword through his attacker's sternum.

It should have been a killing blow, but he had discovered that the tales of Fallow Hold seemed to be true to an extent. The Sile were surviving what should have been mortal wounds, fighting on without limbs or whilst impaled with sword and spear, but they were not, as some of the tales had said, invincible.

He turned his sword into a two-handed grip and removed the head from the Sile warrior. The body fell to the floor and did not so much as twitch, though a strange black mist formed around the wound, it had no effect.

This fight could be won but it was proving hard. Seeing the Sile survive devastating wounds had put a fear into his men. Still, with some harsh words from Hogan, they feared the repercussions of fleeing more than they did the enemy and found their nerve again, holding their lines. Again, Hogan felt pride in his men.

A battle cry came over the field grabbing the Weapons-Master's attention. He turned to the source and saw a man staring back at him. As tall as any man he'd ever seen with skin as black as night, with pure black eyes to match. A man of hard muscle and sinew. Saliva hung from his mouth as he made his cry.

"You!" he screamed, and the Weapon-Master made no mistake about who the word was intended for. "I will kill you and eat your flesh." *Charming,* he thought to himself. He'd heard such threats before, though he'd admit to not seeing many men who looked quite so capable of doing it. "I am Silence of Horror and I have come for you."

The giant of a man crossed the distance between them in mere seconds. Hogan was no small man himself, but it took all his strength just to stay on his feet when the Sile brought down a huge sword onto Hogan's own.

Hogan stepped back in retreat as another attack came, then another and another, each one forcing him backward. His hands throbbed with pain as the vibrations ran through them and it seemed a struggle to maintain a grip on his sword. He ducked a high swing and parried a low one.

The beast of man lunged at him again, his speed and momentum did not falter in the least. All the while he screamed obscenities in the Sile language, spit flying from his mouth. Other men backed away in fear of the monster. Hogan knew he had to defeat this man here and now if his men were to have a chance at victory.

It was not hard to see how this man would be considered a great warrior. It was hard to see many men standing against such an onslaught, but Hogan was a veteran of many wars, including those against the Sile, and he had not become the Weapons-Master by chance. As he had noted earlier, the Sile fought savagely but they lacked grace and precision. This one was a prime example.

He absorbed the blows, feeling each one down to his bones but patiently waited for his chance. Doubt began to creep into his mind whether such a moment would come but then he saw it. With a quick double step to the side, he parried his enemy's weapon whilst knocking him off balance. The huge man stumbled forward and cried out as Hogan buried his sword between shoulder blades.

Drawing his sword back, he waited for his opponent to turn. He did so and as expected brought his weapon around with him in a wild swing. The wound should have made it impossible yet the Sile swung with strength and speed that caught Hogan off guard. He danced back but still felt the cut of steel through plate and mail. He felt the warmth of blood within his armour.

Around the two warriors, the battle seemed to slow. Eyes turned to the two as they fought. Hogan knew his men would lose heart if he didn't stop the beast before him. Despite the pain, he went on the attack. His skill with a sword was far superior and he began making cuts at his enemy but the Sile would not fall.

Twice more, Hogan felt the bite of his enemy's blade, but he would not relinquish his attack. Cut after cut he made and finally the Sile fell to his knees. Hogan would not give him chance to rise again. With a swift swing of his sword, he removed head from body.

A huge cheer rose up around him and his men took this as their cue to push the attack, freshly invigorated by their commander's victory. The Sile, seeing their man fall began to retreat. Hogan watched as the tide of the battle turned once and for all. He stood and watched his men chase down the enemy and once more felt great pride.

He was careful to remain on his feet as long as he could. It was with a quiet sigh that he finally fell, barely noticed by those who moments ago paid so much attention. As he closed his eyes for the final time, it was with a sense of self-satisfaction. He had done well and so had his men.

The boys walked down one of a hundred secret tunnels that led around the entire castle grounds and even beyond. Many were used to keep the servants out of sight and allow them to traverse the castle quicker than those they served. Many of the passages were not for servants though, many were secret to most people.

The guards knew about some, the spies knew of others, some were reserved for the royal family alone. The children knew nearly all of them. It would not be a far stretch of the imagination to say that the princes knew the castle and its grounds better than anyone.

They were ducked low, their heads scraping on the ceiling. How adults managed to make it down here they did not know but it was the fastest route. Lit only by small pools of light that spilled through every few yards, Aron had to search the wall with his hands to find the lever that opened the secret exit.

There was a small click and Aron pushed forward. The four boys spilled out into a small room filled with medical equipment. Bandages and cloths, sharp knives and horrible looking tools the boys hoped they never had to know the use for.

"This is it," said Luke. "This is where they brought Aunt Karin. If she's here, then so is the baby."

They hadn't exactly thought out a plan. All they knew is that they had to help. The Crone would come for the baby. They couldn't let that happen.

Aron moved towards the door, looking back at his brothers with a finger to his mouth ushering quiet. He opened the door the slightest slither and stared out through the crack. A tense moment of silence dragged out as the others waited crouched behind him. He drew back, his face suddenly pale.

"What's wrong?" whispered Luke. "You look like you've seen a ghost."

"Worse," he said. "Much worse."

Jacob knew the truth. There was only one thing he could think of that was worse than a ghost. A witch.

The Crone walked the corridor, listening gleefully to the chaos outside. Within the grasp of her skeletal arm, she held the new-born Fait. Her little Sile minions were doing their job well. Her decoy pulled most of the men of the Cross away to the south.

Her army, small though it may be, had pulled the remaining men out of the city and with the arrival of a new child of the Fait, she finally had the means to enter the castle grounds, though the effort had cost her. Perfect planning mixed with perfect timing. In her arms, she held her prize.

The baby was perfectly still and calm, that was a much easier task to perform than getting her men inside the castle. She was drained, but the child had replenished her and now would supply her with all she needed to continue to live and her power to grow.

She would keep him, grow him and in time, breed him. Supplying her generations of Fait and all the blood she would ever need. Certain steps would have to be taken to ensure the boy's line carried the Gift. All the other Fait would have to be erased. She looked forward to it.

She had survived and grown for generations on the tiniest amount of the blood of the Fait and her powers already dwarfed theirs. Imagine what she could do now. Already she could feel her new strength after just a few drops. She dared not take more at once. Its effect on her could be disorientating at best. Still, she took one more drop and felt a shudder of power run through her.

When the doors before her opened, she grinned at the sight of several armed men. After expending energy in the birth room, she may not have welcomed such a challenge but now she had tasted the blood and she welcomed it.

She gently placed the child down, still wrapped in the cloth as it was when its mother held it. She looked around, there was no one else to be seen but with a loud and clear voice, she said, "Do not touch this child!" She felt the power spread out through the surrounding area.

She moved towards the waiting guards. They backed away in fear at the very sight of her and so they should.

As she stepped through the doors, she waved a hand towards them, and they slammed shut behind her. There would be no escape.

The boys watched the Crone disappear into the next room, the doors closing behind her. They couldn't believe their luck. She had left the baby there all by herself.

"Now's our chance," said Aron as they burst out of the supply room. They stepped towards the baby and looked down at him with awe.

"It's a boy," said Joshua.

"Well, quickly grab him and let's get out of here," said Luke.

None of them moved. Instead, they all remained still and stared at the baby. "Well, isn't someone going to grab him? Quickly, before she comes back."

"But we can't," said Aron. "She said you must not touch."

"Why are we listening to her?" asked Joshua.

They all tried to make a move, tried to grab the baby. They couldn't do it. Something was stopping them. Something inside them, some unknown need to obey.

"She's using a Gift." Joshua knew it. The idea forced its way into his head. "She's using Obedience."

"Like our aunt Susan?"

"I think so," he replied.

"So we can touch him," said Jacob.

"She lied?" Joshua nodded.

"So, if she lied." Jacob took a step forward. Closer than any of them had achieved so far. "Then that means." He reached out. It was hard. He could feel his own mind and body resisting. Desperate to listen to the command not to touch. His nose began to bleed as he pushed against the power. "The truth is." He grabbed the baby and felt all the resistance fall away. "We can touch him," he said with smile.

The others felt it too. Whatever power that held them was now gone. Aron took the baby and gently brushed a finger down his young cousin's face. It took only a short moment for clarity to return. "Well done, Jacob." The youngest almost blushed. "Come on. We need to get out of here."

They ran in the opposite direction to the door the Crone had passed through. "Where are we going?" asked Jacob.

"The cave," said Joshua. "Out into the city. It's our best chance to hide and escape."

It sounded as good a plan as any. They crashed into the door at the end of corridor, and it remained firmly closed. "Locked," cried Aron.

"Here." Joshua pulled a ring of keys from the body of a guard. He looked to Aron but could see something was wrong. He followed his brother's gaze, which was fixed firmly on the far end of the corridor. The others turned.

They saw her. For the first time, they all properly saw her. She was worse than they imagined. Worse, even, than Aron remembered. They all felt the panic swell inside them like a tide in a storm.

Joshua fumbled with the keys. There were too many. Which one was it? Which one would fit the door? He felt that same feeling in his head. His Gift was talking to him. "Luke," he said, holding the keys up to his older brother. "You choose. We need some good fortune."

It took the smallest moment for Luke to grasp Joshua's meaning. When finally it dawned on him, he grabbed the keys. Looking at them, there was no way to tell which one would work. It could be any. The sound of footsteps behind him forced his hand.

He didn't look back, instead he simply picked a key and pushed it into the lock and hoped against hope. He cried out as the key turned. The boys pushed through the door and slammed it shut behind them, locking it again. They could all hear the shriek of the Crone. They did not wait to hear more and ran to the outer door, which would lead to the rear courtyard and from there to the gardens.

They ran into the open air, moving as fast as their legs would take them. Outside was an explosion of chaos. Men were fighting all over the courtyard. From all around, the clash of steel rang through the air mixed with grunts and cries.

231

They made it halfway across the courtyard before almost everyone seemed to come to a sudden stop as a thunderous crash came from the outer doors as they shattered into a thousand fragments of wood and stone. Stood in the gaping hole that remained was the Crone.

Sir Bolevard sat up, gingerly touching a hand to his head. It came back red and sticky. He pushed himself so his back rested against the wall. He felt himself trembling. He'd been making his way outside to join the fight. Though he may not be as keen in the ways of fighting as he once was, he was by no means a coward and would do his part.

The courtyard seemed to be where to bulk of the fighting was taking place within the castle grounds so that was where he'd headed. He'd barely been in the fight when a huge explosion of some kind had knocked him from his feet.

That was when he saw her. The witch emerged from the new opening and stepped out into the daylight. Bolevard could not believe his eyes. All these years, all the attempts to tell others of what he had seen that day so long ago and now here she was, in broad daylight. Everyone could see her. Everyone would know.

Bolevard knew somewhere in the back of his mind that he should feel some small glimpse of happiness, that this was a small victory for him. Everyone would finally know the source of the Fait's power and how treacherous they really were.

That thought however was pushed far away. The truth was the only thing he could feel in that moment was fear. When the witch turned to him, he shrank back. She looked him straight in the eye and he knew she recognised him. When she smiled and licked her lips, he felt the last of his strength leave him.

Bolevard had never considered himself a coward but in that moment, all he could think to do was escape. He pushed himself to his feet and ran. Every step, every inch of distance between him and that abomination brought relief.

When he was far enough away, he stopped and bent over heaving for breath. He cried. He cried in fear and shame. How he hated her. How he hated the Fait for aligning themselves with her. He did not know how but he swore once again that he would see them all burn.

Aron stared in part intrigue and part frozen horror as men rushed towards the witch to attack. They didn't get far. One by one, they began to fall to the ground around her clutching at their necks or screaming in agony from wounds he couldn't see. He watched in awe and dismay as they selflessly tried to defend him and his brothers.

"We have to do something." Aron took a step back towards the Crone. He couldn't just run away whilst all those around him fought and died. He could never live with himself. Luke was at his side. He'd lifted a knife from a fallen guard, what exactly he planned to do with it when the trained men could not get close enough to use their swords was anyone's guess.

"No," said Joshua, stepping between his older brothers and the Crone who was slowly making her way across the courtyard. "It's the blood she wants, if not the baby's, then ours. We have to get to safety. The only way she wins today is if she gets the blood. Anything else means she loses."

"We can't just run away."

"Yes, we can," pleaded Joshua. "Please, believe me. It's my gift. It's screaming inside my head. This is what we need to do. It's like that first game of chess Uncle Christopher made me play. It was a test, remember. You can't always win, sometimes you just have to survive long enough. If she gets the baby or us, then all these deaths will be for nothing. Please brother, listen to me. We're not ready."

Aron's eyes flashed between his brother's pleading face and the Crone, laughing as she slaughtered. She was getting closer. It was hard, it felt wrong, completely wrong but Aron nodded agreement. "All right. Let's get the baby to safety."

The Crone shrieked at the small insignificant ants that thought themselves capable of stopping her. She shivered with anger at the sheer audacity of the small-minded short-lived creatures that dared to stand in her way. With each wave of her hand, she dispatched another.

One by one, the men of the Cross were flung to the side, each and every one of them landing in a crumpled mess on the ground. It was not often that the Crone felt a sense of joy. Satisfaction came often to her but joy, the feeling of actually having fun; that was something from a life lived a long time ago.

It was with a grin on her cracked lips that she had to admit she was enjoying disposing of these foul creatures.

She looked through the small crowd that still remained, searching for her prize. Not only was the new-born child of the Fait within her grasp but now the fated four-born were as well, all of them together, ungrateful little wretches.

Where was the gratitude and respect she deserved for delivering the Gift to them? All they could do, all they could learn to be was due to her. Where was the worship she so rightfully deserved?

She could see the four children of the Fait looking back at her. Oh, they had some nerve, she'd give them that. She would even think they looked ready to attack her, pathetic as that was.

Were these not children of royal blood? Were these boys not supposed to be special even amongst the Fait? Four born to one generation, foretold to bring about a new age. They would all die at her hands, and she would devour anything special about them and take it for herself.

Whatever nerve they had seemed to abandon them as they turned away and yet again began to run from her, carrying her prize with them. She would not allow it. She stepped forward, summoning her power, ready to strike them down once and for all. That was when the sword was thrust into her back.

She looked down at the blade as it came through her sternum dripping with dark blood. With slow steps, she walked forward, pulling herself from the weapon. She felt it as it slid from her back and released a growl of pain. She turned to see Christopher staring back at her. Battered and bloodied from their earlier encounter yet defiant. She should have made sure he was finished.

"You shall not have my child!"

She snarled at him, a bestial sound rising from her throat. With a wave of her hand, she sent him crashing into the wall. Turning again, she could see the boys escaping. Short lived as it was, the prince had done his job and given the boys a few extra seconds to make their escape.

The distance between the Crone and them was growing. She tried to follow but felt her power waning. Rare was the occasion that forced such expenditure. She felt the breaths coming heavy to her. She felt her moment escaping, her victory being stolen away.

She would not have it.

Through cracked lips and blackened teeth, she sucked in air. She sucked it in, filling her lungs, filling them beyond their capacity. Filling them until it seemed she would burst. Her chest heaved yet she continued to suck.

Ribs cracked and broke as her chest ballooned outward in a grotesque mutation yet still she continued. The men of the Cross paused in their attack, stepping back as the Crone's body continued to grow in its deformity and yet still the Crone drew in air.

234

There was a pause of horrified silence from all around.

Then she screamed.

The sound hit them like a hammer falling from the sky. It smashed into them all with the force of a tornado sending them to the ground. Ears began to bleed. Putting hands to them had no effect; the scream pierced the ears and more.

Brains rattled in skulls and heads seemed as though they would pop. Though every man in the courtyard cried out in pain, they could not be heard. Nothing could be heard but the scream of the Crone.

The boys fell as one into the grass, crying out in distress. Eyes squeezed shut in pain as ears and noses began to bleed.

Aron felt the wave of sound hit him, sending him to his knees. It took all his effort to place the baby down before pushing his hand to his ears in a vain attempt to block out the noise. It did nothing. The deafening scream made his very bones shake.

His brothers were with him, writhing on the floor just like he. There was nothing any of them could do. They'd failed. The Crone had won. Aron clenched his whole body tight against the pain and could only wait for the end to come.

Through the pain, he felt something. A hand, shaking him. Against his instincts, he opened his eyes. The face looking down at him was familiar. Ollie? Where had he come from? How was he still standing? What did it matter? The pain was all that mattered. Ollie tried to pick him up, but Aron couldn't move.

Someone else was there with them. It was Joshua, pointing at the baby who somehow slept perfectly peaceful despite all that was happening around it. Despite the scream that caused so much pain to everyone else. Everyone except Ollie.

"It's the only way!" shouted Joshua, but the words did not carry. Nevertheless, Aron understood his brother's plan. With a great effort, he pulled his hands from his ears and pushed the baby towards Ollie.

All of a sudden, his friend realised what they were trying to tell him. They could see from his face that he wasn't sure. "GO," Aron mouthed. He hoped, if this was the end that at least the baby may escape.

Hesitantly, Ollie picked up the baby. He didn't want to do it but, in the distance, he could see the Crone and he knew he must. With one last look to the boys, he turned in the opposite direction and started running.

The Crone watched with glee as all the men around fell to their knees, screaming and howling like dogs. They wailed as they clutched their heads, blood trickling from their ears and noses, yet still she did not relent. No one could withstand her power.

No one could stop her. In the distance, she saw the children fall like all the others. With crooked steps, she began to walk towards them.

The first-born fell, barely managing to place the baby to the ground. She watched with satisfaction as they writhed on the floor, their escape put to a quick end. The magic flowed through her and despite the fatigue, the smile on her cracked lips grew wider. With a finger of bone, she pointed at them. Her prize was so close.

That was when she saw him. The boy stared at her. He was the only other person besides herself who remained standing. He was with the princes, stood over them with a look of confusion etched upon his face. He looked up from them and the Crone's eyes locked with his. She could see his fear, his desperation to get away.

How? she wondered. *How is this boy still standing? Who is he? Why is he not crying on the floor like all the others?*

The questions disappeared from her mind, replaced with disbelieving shock as the boy's expression turned from panic to determination. She could only watch on in rage as he picked up the new baby born of the Fait, took one last glimpse towards her then the boys and then he turned and ran.

With a great pulse, the Crone's scream ended. She sagged to a knee as the splurging of energies caught up with her. Her skeletal hand fell to the floor, and she coughed black blood around it.

In her mind, she spoke.

Come to me, my champion. The time is now. I need you.

End of the Game

Hands-of-Forty appeared at the Crone's side in an instant. He looked at the pathetically small body of the Crone and wondered how such great power resided within it. He placed an arm around her, the other held the Sword-of-Never. He would protect her.

"Rise," he said, disgusted by her feebleness yet still wary of all he knew she could do.

"My prize has escaped me," she wheezed. "But the day will still be ours." With a finger of bone, she pointed. Hands-of-Forty followed it. He saw his new target. Four young boys surrounded by guards. Their faces were not familiar, but he knew who they were.

The four-born. Princes of the Fait. Their blood would feed the Crone for a hundred years and she in turn would feed him. Together, their power would grow and he would conquer all.

Celia had ignored the warning to stay away from the window. She had ignored the guards that commanded her to stay with them. The guards had ushered the queen away to the highest room in the tower. Celia would head there soon, after all, she wanted no part in the fighting, but she had to see.

She had watched from high in the tower, staring down into the courtyard with surprise as the strange old witch had chased the boys out into the courtyard. She had watched with horror as the witch sucked in air, puffing up, her chest more than tripling in size.

Celia had heard the scream and felt the blood rushing to her head but it had not felled her as it had the men below. From the way they had all fallen to the floor, she could only imagine the pain they were feeling. Now, she watched in amazement as the witch's champion appeared as though from fresh air to stand by her side. Celia had seen men of all shapes and sizes, but this was one hell of a specimen.

Over the years, she had heard many men talk about the horrors of war. She could see the ones it had truly affected. It was there in their eyes. Some could not even bring themselves to even talk of such things. She had always imagined them quite pathetic.

Now, her attitude had changed. She even felt a hint of guilt at her feelings towards them. Thinking them cowardly. Now she had seen for herself, and it was horrifying.

She felt the presence behind her before she heard or saw anything. She turned, expecting one of the guards to begin trying to usher her away. A yelp escaped her. She had not expected to see a tall, muscular woman looking back at her. Her body was a thing of beauty.

Dark skin was pulled tight over muscles Celia had never seen on a woman. She was quite jealous in a way. If not for the sudden fear swelling through her, she'd offer a compliment.

When the woman smiled, a forked tongue appeared to lick at her lips. She held a whip whose length was embedded with blades. She eyed Celia up and down with an almost lustful expression.

The moment drew out and as Celia's shock died down, her mind started to assess the situation. She swallowed down her fear and spoke.

"I am guessing by the fact I am still alive that you are not here to kill me."

At first, she did not think the Sile woman would offer a reply. She was starting to think of ways to escape when finally a voice spoke the language of the Cross in a brutish accent.

"You are the woman who seeks power?"

Well, that was an odd introduction.

"Don't we all?"

The Sile woman nodded, her smile growing.

"Some of us. You, me and another." Celia knew exactly who the woman was talking about. "I come with an offer from her."

Aron tried to stand, his brothers and some of the men in the courtyard were slowly rising with him. He breathed deep, desperately trying to compose himself and regain some equilibrium. The screaming had made the whole world lose focus but now it was returning. A hand was offered and when he looked up, he saw Joe. Aron took the hand and was pulled to his feet.

"Ollie," said Joe. "He couldn't hear it. He—"

"Saved our cousin," Aron said. That was all that was needed.

"From her." Joe pointed back over Aron's shoulder.

The Crone was down but she was not alone. A giant of a man was cradling her. She pointed a finger of bone directly at them and the man stood. His skin was pale but for veins of near black.

He stared at them with narrowed eyes that looked past flaming red hair, and he slowly stood. One step towards them seemed to eat so much of the distance that the boys flinched.

"We need to get out of here," said Joshua, but it seemed too little too late as the Crone's champion began his charge. Each step eating huge chunks out of the distance between them. The boys were just turning on their heel to run.

"Look!" shouted Luke.

A fresh wave of Sile warriors were flooding the courtyard, but they did not join the fight. Instead, they surrounded the other Sile and held them back. The champion paused in his run watching in surprise as he was surrounded by snarling faces. Warriors stared at each other in confusion until finally a voice called out loudly and grabbed everyone's attention.

"Warriors of the Sile!" A man shouted out the words as he walked to the centre of the courtyard, turning as he spoke, looking at all those that stared back at him. "This battle is over. Following this creature is not the path of our people."

He pointed at the Crone's champion who grinned maniacally in response. "We fight for the honour of the tribes, for the glory of the Sile. This man fights for himself, and so I have come to put an end to him."

A low, menacing chuckle sounded. The champion stepped away from the boys towards the newcomer and they were all happy for any extra distance between them.

"Morbius Duvec," he said with a growl. "I looked for you on the battlefield when I crushed your forces and took them for my own." He spoke the Sile language and smirked with every word.

The boys looked to each other, mouthing the name. Morbius Duvec, the leader of the Sile, the man who had united the clans and sent them to war against the Cross. A war it took their father years to win. Every man, woman and child of the Cross knew that name.

"Battlefield," said Morbius, stepping closer to the giant, hefting his sword. "You mean a sleeping camp you ambushed in the night. A camp with women and children. You didn't even have the honour or the bravery to face us under the sun."

"Why fight what you can merely slaughter."

"Because it is our way!" screamed Morbius, his fury palpable to all. "Sile fight. We fight for the right to lead. You had your chance once. Oh yes, I remember you. I smashed you into the ground like the mule you are. Now you ally yourself with a witch because you know you could not beat me."

"I am Hands-of-Forty!" he screamed back, spittle flying from his mouth in rage. "I am the leader of the Sile now! I came for you once and you ran like a squirming pig!"

"Well," replied Morbius with a grin, holding out his arms to his sides in challenge. "I am here now. I have the Sword-of-Answers and so you shall answer for your crimes."

Hands-of-Forty started the intimidating walk towards his enemy.

"No!" screamed the Crone, speaking words the boys could again understand. "The Fait. They are what matters. Leave this fool!"

Hands-of-Forty would not listen. He would not be denied his glory.

Morbius watched with tense anticipation as the traitor known as Hands-of-Forty casually moved towards him. The monster smiled for a brief moment then leapt forward.

A huge swing came from Morbius' right. He ducked it easily, stepping back to avoid the obvious down swing that followed. The speedy upswing almost caught him by surprise, Forty's ability to wield the grotesquely oversized sword speaking to his strength.

Fast as it was, Morbius was faster. He sidestepped and brought his own sword down. It cut through the leather and metal of a wrist guard, through skin, catching on bone. Black blood flowed from the wound and Morbius had to fight to pull his weapon back.

He watched with narrowed eyes as the wound healed. He'd seen this already and would not be taken by surprise.

Hands-of-Forty laughed as he stood straight again then launched forward once more.

The huge sword swung at Morbius who parried the attacks away but each time, he felt the vibrations run up his arms rattling his bones. With effort and skill, he managed to force his opponent onto the back foot and launched his fist into the giant's mouth. It had no effect.

Not the first time nor the second nor the third. Morbius spun and ducked, bringing his sword around, this time chopping into Forty's thigh. The result was the same as before but this time, he had no chance to withdraw.

Hands-of-Forty smashed a fist down into his head and the world rattled. Morbius fell to the ground, desperately trying to scramble backwards out of the way. He avoided the sword but could not avoid a boot that crashed up beneath his jaw. He sank backward, screaming out in pain as the same huge boot pinned his sword hand to the ground, snapping his wrist.

"Now you see, little man. You were right to run the first time and a fool to come and try me now. The Sile are mine and you will fade into nothing."

To Morbius, time seemed to move in slow motion as Forty pulled back his fist and slammed it down into an unprotected face. Morbuis spat out his own teeth, coughing on blood. He was ready for his end should he meet it. Even so, it was with a great sense of satisfaction that he watched a hand descend on Forty's head, grasping it like a melon.

The breath rushed back into his lungs as Forty's weight was lifted from him and the Goliath was thrown clean across the courtyard, smashing through stone like a boulder from a catapult. Morbius stood on shaking legs and never thought he'd feel such relief at the arrival of a Fait.

Christopher watched his brother, the king, make his triumphant return. With seemingly no effort at all, Branthony threw a man almost twice his size clean across the courtyard with one hand. The Crone's champion disappeared in a cloud of dust and rubble and Christopher locked eyes with his brother.

"The children," said Branthony.

There was no need to say more. Christopher reacted quickly. Running for the children and checking over them one by one. "Are you alright? Are you injured?"

"We're fine," said Aron. "Uncle. We're fine."

"That boy. Where did he go? Where did he take my son?"

"That boy is my brother," said Joe. "And he saved your son."

Christopher didn't recognise him, but Aron spoke up.

"The baby is safe. Our friend couldn't hear the witch's scream. He was the only one left standing. He took the baby and escaped. You can trust him, Uncle, I promise."

Christopher felt the relief rush over him. "Thank you." He looked at each of the boys. His four nephews and their friend. These children had saved his infant son from the Crone. Where he and so many men had failed, they had succeeded.

"Thank you all." He meant it from the bottom of his heart. "Come on, we need to get you out of here."

"No," said Luke. "We need to see this."

Christopher turned and could see his brother approaching the pile of stone that hid the Crone's champion.

"Can he win?" asked Joshua. "That man, he—" The words wouldn't come, how can you say that a man can't be killed when your father is about to fight him.

Christopher looked back at them with a strange mix of confidence and doubt. He'd never seen anyone like Hands-of-Forty before but then again, he'd never seen anyone like Branthony of the Fait.

"Boys, have you ever seen your father's Gift?" They looked to each before all shaking their heads. They had heard so many stories and tales and in truth hadn't believed most of them. "If there's anyone in the world that can win this fight, it's your father. His Gift is special. He has the Gift of Strength, and you are about to see what that can do in a fight."

Branthony approached the hole with caution, his sword at the ready. Not the sword he had travelled south with, but the sword of a king. He waited with patience, knowing the fight was far from done. Getting thrown straight through a thick stone wall would destroy most men, Branthony was of no delusions that this was an ordinary man.

From the still settling dust, a figure emerged and stepped out into the daylight. By the God, he really was a giant. The Crone had picked her champion well. The second the beast stepped beyond the rubble, Branthony leapt forward, the distance between them swallowed up in one inhuman jump.

In mid-air, he raised his sword and in unison with his feet touching the floor brought it down. Hands-of-Forty was quick enough to raise his sword but could only watch in horror as the monstrous blade shattered on impact and the king's weapon cut down through it then skin and bone, through shoulder and chest. The Sword-of-Never never stood a chance.

Branthony pulled his weapon out and watched the Sile warrior stumble backwards. A killing blow to anyone apart from the Crone's champion.

Black swirls flowed around Hands-of-Forty. What should have been the blood-filled gurgles of a dying man became a shout of anger and defiance. When the cloud of black mist faded, the beast stood tall and healed, still holding his broken weapon, even halved it was the length of most normal swords.

"Huh," he said, with a shrug of the shoulders. In the language of the Cross, he said, "My turn."

Hands-of-Forty swung and swung his sword. Each swing had the strength and power to cleave a horse in half, but Branthony fought each and every one off, matching each blow for speed and strength. In fact, he did more than match, he overpowered.

With a disbelief etched on his face, the Sile warrior was forced back and when Branthony attacked with an upswing that sent his enemy's weapon and defence high, he thrust his sword forward through his enemy's chest.

Then, not waiting for Hands-of-Forty to recover, Branthony reached back a fist and brought it forward with the power of a god. He felt bones shatter beneath the impact and watched as his enemy once again smashed into a wall.

The crowd of Sile and men of the Cross alike parted as the huge warrior was flung back, all watching with anticipation as King Branthony ran forward, grabbing his opponent by the head, bringing up a knee with a blow to crush rock never mind bone.

He wasn't finished yet. A weak hand came up to grab his wrist. With ease, Branthony pulled the hand away and then brought his blade down through the wrist and with a spin and a twist, he took a foot as well.

Finally, Branthony stepped away. With cold eyes but an otherwise unreadable expression, he watched the black clouds once again begin to swirl over Hands-of-Forty. This time the cloud seemed to swirl over his entire body and once again, a scream of fury and pain came from the cloud until it dissipated, leaving the Crone's champion standing tall and whole once again.

"Don't you see," he said in his rough pronunciation of the Cross language. "I cannot be beaten. Hands-of-Forty cannot die, foolish man!"

"Foolish? You call me foolish? This from a man who blindly takes Gifts from the Crone. Magic is poison to all but my family. You know this, and yet you use it anyway. Trusting to a thing you know nothing about. Do you think you mean anything to her? You are a means to an end and nothing more."

"Ha. Then perhaps we are more alike than you think." Branthony tried to hide the sting of those words. "What does it matter? Hands-of-Forty will crush you. Hands-of-Forty will rule the Sile. Hands-of-Forty will rule the Cross. Let the witch have her blood. I will conquer. The magic is mine now."

"We shall see."

The two of them came together again. A Valfarg could have walked into the courtyard at that very moment and not a single soul would have noticed. All attention was taken by the battle between two unique warriors. Swords clashed over and over, again and again.

Hands-of-Forty felt the bite of the king's blade like a swarm of ravished locust, eating away at him. Yet the darkness swirled around him in a storm and healed each and every wound.

Branthony screamed out as his enemy cut down at his calf, when the blood came from it the wound did not heal. It was warm and red and flowed like that of any other man. Another wound to the shoulder forced him to take his own weapon in one hand.

Even with one arm, he attacked with devastating effect. When the duel finally paused again, the cloud around Hands-of-Forty swirled and twisted. Long, tense moments drew out before the cloud finally sunk back. Branthony watched it all with the same cold eyes.

He heaved with heavy breaths, feeling his chest rise and fall. Warm blood ran down from his wounds dripping to the stone floor. He was tired, the ache in his muscles was a fire that begged to be doused. In all his years and battles, in all the wars he had fought, he had never felt such exhaustion.

It was time for a gamble. Forget swords. Forget stabbing and cutting. Branthony would crush his enemy once and for all.

Aron and his brothers watched the fight with awe. Who knew their father could do such things. They'd heard the stories and the praise and wonder that people spun into them, but the truth was they'd never really understood it. They thought it was simply because their father was the king, people had to be nice about him.

To them, he had always simply been Father. Now they knew the truth, they had seen it for themselves, with their own eyes and the stories did not do it justice.

Their Father was the strongest man in the world and yet he was losing this fight.

For all father's strength and skill, the Crone's champion continued to heal. His body was as fresh now as it was at the beginning of the fight. On the other hand, their father was injured and fatigued. They could all see it. Uncle Christopher tried to usher them away, but they refused. They would watch until the end no matter what.

"What's he doing?" asked Jacob.

Their father stepped towards the wreckage of the castle wall. As Forty watched on Branthony leaned down, wrapping his arms around the largest stone he could see. His body strained and tensed. Veins pulsed beneath skin that turned red with the rush of blood.

The boys thought their father may burst as he lifted it from the ground. An unimaginable feat, the king stood, lifting the stone above his head. Even for those few men who had witnessed the king's Gift before, it was an amazing sight. His legs trembled as he stepped towards Hands-of-Forty who raised his weapon with renewed grip.

"Arrogant man of the Cross. I will cut you down before you can—"

Hands-of-Forty disappeared as the stone hit him faster than an arrow from a crossbow. It hit the ground with a crash, the Sile warrior pinned beneath it.

Branthony fell to a knee, exhausted. Everyone in the courtyard could only watch in horror as the black mist formed around the base of the stone. They listened to the cries of Hands-of-Forty as the magic enveloped him. Screams of agony rang out and they could only imagine such a pain. What could possibly be left beneath the stone?

With a great cry of effort, the beast pressed his hands to the stone and began to somehow push himself out from beneath it. He wriggled backwards and his mangled body began to reform. His torso was now free, and he watched with what looked like surprise as the magic reformed him piece by piece.

A smile formed on his face as he neared escape. Then, the Sword-of-Answers came crashing through his neck and severed his head. The black mist swirled in a raging torrent, growing and growing in its ferocity only to fade away to nothing, leaving a headless corpse still half crushed beneath stone, with Morbius Duvec standing over it with a grin.

The Lord of the Sile looked across the courtyard to the King of the Cross. "You should have done that in the first place," he said. Branthony offered a weak smile back at him with a small nod of the head. It seemed to take all the strength he had left.

Aron had seen enough, he ran forward towards his father, his brothers hot on his heels. They reached him and all four took him in an embrace, only when he yelped in pain did they realise they were smothering him. For all his strength, it was their father who leaned on his children to help him stand.

Uncle Christopher approached, surveying them all for a moment before asking the question they were all thinking. "Is it over?"

"Perhaps for now," answered Branthony, though he seemed unsure. The Crone was nowhere to be seen.

"Well then, perhaps it's time we go and retrieve my son."

When a torch fell through the hole and illuminated the darkness, Ollie felt his heart leap into his mouth. He held the still sleeping baby tightly to his chest, wishing he had gone through the cave and out into the city on the other side.

It seemed a good idea to hide rather than taking a newly born prince of the Fait into the dangerous streets of the Centre during a panic. Plus, he wasn't sure he could make the climb whilst cradling a baby.

He cursed himself for being so scared but when he'd seen everyone fall to the ground in the courtyard, when he'd been forced to take the baby and run leaving everyone behind including his brother, he had felt fear like he'd never felt before. It almost felt good to just sit there in the pitch black and hide from everything and everyone.

Seconds after the torch was thrown down, a face appeared at the entrance. It was Joe. Ollie breathed a sigh of relief and stepped from the shadow to look up at the smiling face of his younger brother who ushered for him to come up. Joe reached down and took the baby from him, and Ollie followed him to the outside.

It took a moment for his eyes to adjust to the daylight and when they did, they opened wide with surprise. Ollie discovered he was staring up at the king of the Cross surrounded by his children not to mention a few other famous faces. Standing with wide eyes and a dumbfounded expression was all he could hope to achieve in that moment.

Prince Christopher stepped forward. His son finally held within his father's arms. "You saved my son's life," he said with a smile. Though Ollie couldn't hear the words, he grasped their meaning. "I owe you a great debt."

"Erm, with all due respect sir, he won't answer. He can't hear you, ya see. He's erm, well he's—"

"Deaf," Christopher finished for Joe, now understanding. He looked at Joe, deciding to speak through him. "What is your brother's name?"

"Erm, Ollie, Sir. His name is Ollie."

"Oliver," he said, using the full version of the name, "I like it." His eyes turned down to his son, so new to the world yet already a key role in a tale that would become a part of the nation's history. "I like the name." He looked back to Ollie knowing he could not hear but wanting to look him in the eye all the same.

"I know that usually the mother names the child but, in this instance, I am sure my wife will be content. In honour of you and your bravery today, I shall name my son Oliver." He looked up at his own brother now and Branthony nodded his agreement.

"A fine name," said Branthony. "Now, shall we get back to the castle? I hate to think how worried your mother will be."

They all turned to leave. Aron came to Ollie and hugged him, offering his thanks. The two friends joined the others and Branthony put an arm around his eldest son's shoulder. "So, you found the tunnel." He could only laugh at the look of shock on Aron's face.

"Your uncle and I discovered it when we were about your age. I knew you boys would find it eventually. Let's not tell your mother about this, eh? After all that's happened, you're going to find it hard enough to get some time to yourselves. Best she doesn't have something else to worry about."

Celia stood at the queen's side. The room was filled with the ladies of the court, and they had all been whimpering and moaning not so long ago as the battle took place. Now, they all declared proudly how certain they were that the forces of the Cross would prevail.

How Celia detested them. She had been impressed, however, by the queen's decorum. Her quiet confidence had rubbed off on others and Celia had to admit she found Debreace calming.

When the doors flung open and King Branthony made his grand return surrounded by his children and the queen's brothers, his own brother and new-born nephew, that was when Debreace finally cracked and showed her emotions.

She ran to them and hugged them all excessively. The whole room erupted in applause and cheers to which Celia politely joined in but found immediately tedious. The fools were clapping like this was some huge victory. Did none of them see what she saw? Did none of them understand the repercussions that would come from this day?

Celia already knew that nothing would be the same. The world had changed here today. The field of play had shifted, the game had changed. A new player was on the board. Or rather, a hidden player had been revealed. Celia was already making her plans, adjusting her tactics to these new dynamics.

The stories of this day would get out and the world would know that magic was now a component to be considered. The world would know that the Fait were not as special as some had believed.

Once the hugs had finished, Debreace set about tending to her husband and children. The boys, to their credit, were remarkably fine. Especially considering they had been in the thick of the action. Celia eyed them almost suspiciously. How had they fared so well?

She was well aware they had Gifts, but she had never placed too much faith in them. Parlour tricks and mind games. She placed her faith in more substantial things like wealth and power. That was what she saw when she looked at the royal family, not mystical magic. But after today, she saw things differently.

Celia watched from her peripherals as the queen cleaned and dressed her husband's wounds. Wiping the blood away onto cloths. She did the same to her children who had all bled from their ears and noses. No one seemed to notice as Celia cleaned the bloodied cloths away. No one saw her hide them on her person.

When the time was right, she slipped away. There was so much commotion no one would even realise she had gone for some time. She walked out into the courtyard where the clean-up had already begun. She walked past the battle site and into the garden and then further still.

Soon she was down in the wild lower gardens. A place she had not been since she went to see the body of a man apparently killed by a Valfarg. She hadn't figured out a way to use that particular piece of information just yet but all in good time.

Finally, when she was sure to be far from prying eyes, she took the bloodied cloths from her dress and placed them in the shadow of a tree. She looked about herself and spoke to the air.

"I received your message or should I say, your offer?" she said and waited in the responding silence feeling more foolish by the second. "Is this what you wanted? These rags carry the blood of the Fait. The king's blood and all four of his children. You know what I want in return?"

Again, she waited and was sure she was simply talking to herself. She growled in frustration and was just about to leave when she noticed the cloths were gone. Then, as if on the wind itself, a voice spoke.

"Power. You seek power."

Celia felt a shiver run down her spine and would swear the temperature had dropped. Her breath turned to vapour and drifted before her eyes.

"Yes. But I have no need of muscles and black clouds or special screams. I want true power."

"The power to rule," growled the voice. "Then perhaps we understand each other."

Celia grinned. She knew she was playing a dangerous game, but wasn't it all dangerous when the stakes were so high? When the ultimate prize was available. When the winner of the game would rule above all. People like Bolevard may see the Crone and her power as a threat.

In ways, he was right but in other ways, he was oh so wrong. Celia saw tools that she could use. Celia saw opportunity and she would grasp it with both hands.

Safe and Sound

The next few days were strange, not in the least because Sile warriors remained not only outside the city but within the castle grounds. In fact, they were even charged with helping with the repairs and clean up and not one of them seemed to have any complaints.

For all the stories, the Sile warriors were not as expected. When the fighting was taking place, they were terrifying, but afterwards they seemed subdued. Branthony had explained to the boys that most of them were ashamed of their actions, and they were not here fighting out of their own free will but because they were forced to by the Crone's champion.

The boys themselves had tried to stay out of the way of all the commotion around the castle, not that Debreace seemed in any way inclined to let them out of her sight. She'd been a constant presence since the attack, but after a few days she was beginning to relent, though they suspected this was mainly because of her other responsibilities.

The time was made easier by the presence of Ollie and Joe who were now allowed in the castle grounds without any false identities. In fact, they'd been given free rein and were enjoying what seemed to them like a touch of fame. The boys who saved the prince.

Ollie and Joe stood to the side of the throne room in new clothes supplied to them. Shining new boots, new tunics with the emblem of the Cross proudly displayed. Leather belts, small daggers at their hips. All tailor made.

No one would know they were simple boys from the streets of the Centre. They stood proudly and couldn't stop smiling at the princes who stood on the dais next to the thrones which their parents occupied.

The room was filled with various lords and ladies, knights and Castle-Masters. It was not without a strange sense of irony that they all moved aside for the newly re-established Lord of the Sile. Of all the men in the world that had grand reputations, Morbius Duvec was one who did not disappoint.

He sported a number of bruises from his fight with the Crone's champion, not to mention his arm was held against his chest in a sling and splint. Yet now he was washed and cleaned. His beard shaved, his hair cut.

He wore a Sile style of clothing leaving most of his torso bare, his olive skin almost shining with oil, tattoos on display. Many of the men of the Cross looked at him with barely hidden resentment and scoffed at some of the women who looked at him with desire.

For a Sile, he was incredibly regal. He was a man who demanded attention and seemed worthy of it.

Morbius walked through the crowd and came to a stop before the king. The crowd watched on as he and the king shared a strange look, both with a hint of a smile on their face. It was a look of mutual respect. It was with a hint of reluctant acceptance that Morbius took a knee.

Each of the boys noted the nods from the various lords and ladies at the gesture. Like him or not, they would know it took a lot for a proud man to bend the knee. This was as meaningful a moment as any so far. A sight that many never thought they'd see and enough to quench the anger of many of the lords who still vied for revenge.

When Morbius stood, it was Branthony who spoke first. "You held up your end of the bargain, my lord. You escorted me and my men safely across the plains, quicker than we could ever have hoped without your assistance and upon our arrival at the Centre, you convinced many of your countrymen to lay down their arms. You fought the Crone's champion, or at least you tried," he jested with a smile as he placed a hand on Morbius' shoulder. Morbius gave an amused grunt along with a shrug.

"As I recall, Your Majesty, it was me who killed the beast."

This time Branthony nodded with a grin. "So it was. As reward for your actions, you and your men shall be safely escorted back to your lands and the peace between our nations will be renewed with no retaliation from the Cross for these recent attacks. The old terms shall be set back in place and you shall once again be Lord of the Sile."

Morbius nodded. "Agreed. Without you, I could never have defeated her champion and who knows what he and that witch would have done next. My people and I owe you a great debt."

"You have made promises to me before, but I think we both knew those to be somewhat hollow words. Not this time. This time, they will hold meaning. If and when the time arrives, I withhold the right to call upon you and the men of the Sile to come to our aid if needed.

"I plan on travelling south again when I can and look forward to passing peacefully through your lands. I hope the people of the Cross and Sile can truly become allies."

The Lord of the Sile nodded his acceptance and that was all that was needed. Not another word was spoken. Morbius turned and left, and tension left the room with him.

With the exit of the Sile, the day at court seemed to be over and the lords and ladies began to leave the hall. The king and the queen remained and called their children to them. It was strange to look down at them. So young and yet so grown up. Branthony and Debreace were now surer than ever that their children would play a vital role in the world.

"I've been talking with your mother and uncle, and we've reached a decision. Your lessons are going to be increased." The boys couldn't stop their frowns and it appeared things were quickly back to normal. Same old Father, it seemed. "Lessons on your Gifts that is."

The expression on the boys' faces softened a little. After all, after seeing their father in action, they finally began to understand the true potential of their Gifts. "We will all train together and will get the most from these Gifts so that we may give the most from them. Now, I would like you to meet Merleal."

The boys turned to see a young woman enter the room, she looked nervous as she dipped a head to them.

"Merleal is from the Blood River. She will be staying here at the castle for some time. I want you to get to know her. Learn from her. She is the one that will be delivering the Gift to our family from now on. When you boys have grown and have children of your own, it is her who shall give them the Gift.

"She delivered young Oliver's Gift when we retrieved him. It seems the Crone had not found time to do it herself. We were lucky. Her thirst got the better of her. Oliver has the same Gift as his Father. He has the Gift of Knowledge. He will be a great help to you when he's older, as Christopher is to me."

They boys all nodded respectfully to Merleal who in turn nodded back, though all included looked a little lost at the interaction.

There was a moment of almost awkward silence before Branthony finally broke it. "I want you to know how proud I am of you all." The boys looked to each other with fresh smiles spread across their faces. "With everything that happened, you all handled yourselves amicably.

"I know it is hard to understand, but there are great changes coming. These will be dangerous and difficult times but as a family and with good friends." He looked to Ollie and Joe who beamed with delight. "We can and will make it through. Together, we are strong. Now go, have some fun. Lessons will begin again tomorrow. I look forward to seeing what progress you've made."

With nothing that any of them could think to say, the boys turned to leave. As they reached the door and filed out, it was Jacob who turned back to his parents. "Mother, what did you have for breakfast today?"

She smiled at him and seemed to take her time before answering, her lips twitching before she finally said, "I had fruit this morning, Jacob."

"Not eggs?"

"No, not eggs," she said with a smile and Jacob grinned knowingly back at her before winking and following his brothers out of the room.

"What was that?" asked Branthony.

"Part of his lessons," she answered. "He's been asking me what I had for breakfast every day. I always reply the same. Eggs."

"I don't understand. You said fruit."

She smiled at her husband. "I couldn't help it. I tried to say eggs, but I haven't had eggs for breakfast once since we started their training. I was lying to him."

"And this time you told the truth."

Debreace nodded. "The boys say Jacob could see through the Crone's lies. Their powers are even stronger than we thought."

King Branthony looked back to the now closed door. He was seeing his children in a new light. He was seeing the huge potential they held. Four children, born with four Gifts. He knew that whatever lay ahead would be hard, he only hoped their Gifts would be enough to see them through.

Epilogue

Aron surveyed the battle with disbelief. The plan and execution had seemed almost perfect and yet his forces were being overrun. He looked down at himself. His once splendid armour now covered in dirt and blood. He wiped some of the same from his face and felt the stubble of his beard against his fingers. He had lost his gauntlet. When did that happen?

"Aron," called a voice and he turned to see Joshua coming towards him, Joseph followed close behind as he always did as Joshua's personal guard. Aron thought his brother looked exhausted and yet that wasn't what scared him the most. Joshua also looked defeated.

"We must withdraw," he said with panting breaths. "Retreat is the only option. You can't always win, Aron. Sometimes you just need to survive. If we don't withdraw now, none of us will survive this day."

Retreat? No, they could not retreat. This had been Joshua's plan. He had used Guidance to tell him all the best moves to make, and this was where they had landed. How could it have gone so wrong? "We can't," he heard himself say in a whisper.

Suddenly, the world seemed to spin. Jacob and Luke had joined them. They all stared down at a prisoner.

"What's happening?" asked Aron. "Who is this?"

"Part of the enemy command team," said Luke. "I came across him on the battlefield. A stroke of fortune I'd say. Jacob, ask him again. They need to hear it for themselves."

Jacob knelt down in front of the man, so their eyes met. "How did you know we would be here? Tell me the truth."

"You have a traitor," he blurted out instantly. "We were told when and where to expect you, how large your force was and how it was dispersed. We knew everything. You never stood a chance."

"Who betrayed us?"

The man shook his head. "I don't know." His words were a whimper. "I don't know. I swear it's the truth."

"Oh, I know it is," said Jacob as he stood.

Betrayed. Who? Why?

The world spun again, Aron looked on helplessly as an arrow took Jacob in the neck and he fell to his knees, gurgling. Aron simply stared at him, almost wondering what he was doing fooling around at such a moment. He turned slowly as Joshua and Luke drew swords and the cries and men were suddenly all around them.

Aron watched in a daze as they were overrun in an instant. He saw Luke go down beneath a sword. He watched with horror as they hoisted Joshua's body in the air and portrayed it like a trophy, chanting and cheering. Aron thought of his father as his end came.

With a scream to raise the dead, Aron jerked awake in his bed. The hands of a boy just entering manhood touched a face of the same description. His entire body poured with sweat. It was a dream. It was all a dream, yet he could not stop trembling, he could not stop the tears and the fear.

He knew it was more. He knew it for what it really was, Foresight. He remembered it all perfectly. They called it a Gift, but Aron knew it was a curse.

Printed in Great Britain
by Amazon

42798537R00143